LUST QUEEN

Joey Baldwin's got it made. He's got a beautiful fiancée, Lisa, and now he's got the perfect writer's commission as well. All he has to do is pack up in New York and head for Los Angeles, where he will spend time with movie star Mona Thorne, who wants him to ghostwrite her life story. It's a sweet deal all right. Mona moves him right into her mansion, and after a few drinks and a dip in the pool, she puts the real moves on him. Mona knows just what she wants, and she sinks her hooks in deep, spitfire temper and all. Before long Joey doesn't know if he's living the fantasy or just studding himself out for hire. His life only gets more complicated when, after weeks of neglect, Lisa decides to visit....

LUST VICTIM

Dave Lamson has been married for ten years to Moira, a decade of sexual wedded bliss. Lamson is a lucky man and he knows it. Then one night a burglar breaks into their house, overpowers Lamson and drags him upstairs to their bedroom, where he ties him up and makes him watch him rape his wife. Later, after the police have left, Lamson realizes that though the rapist hasn't hurt either of them physically, Moira is still very fearful and nervous around him. As the week goes on, her fear turns to sexual frigidity, and Lamson finds that besides suffering a terrible guilt Moira may even have known the rapist. His desire for Moira soon turns to frustration, and Lamson begins to take notice of the women around the office in a way he never had before. Will Moira be able to overcome her fear, or is Lamson now doomed to a lustless marriage—and an adulterer's heart?

Lust Queen
Lust Victim

by Don Elliott

STARK HOUSE

Stark House Press • Eureka California

LUST QUEEN / LUST VICTIM

Published by Stark House Press
1315 H Street
Eureka, CA 95501, USA
griffinskye3@sbcglobal.net
www.starkhousepress.com

ISBN: 1-933586-68-0
ISBN-13: 978-1-933586-68-7

Cover design and layout by Mark Shepard, www.SHEPGRAPHICS.COM
Proofreading by Rick Ollerman

First Stark House Press Edition: July 2014

Contents

Lust Duo: Introduction
by Robert Silverberg

Out of the past come two more of the hard-boiled erotic novels I wrote half a century ago, when I was a young man with dark hair, boundless energy, and the ability to keep my fingers flying over the keyboard all day long with fantastic speed. I wrote a lot of those books then. In that far-off era they were deemed erotic indeed, to the point where the U.S. government went after their publisher—unsuccessfully—on charges of publishing and distributing obscene material. But they weren't obscene at all, and now, from the perspective of a later day, are actually pretty tame stuff.

This is how I might write one of these books if I were writing it today:

"Come on," she said, her green eyes wild with hunger for it. "Are you ready to fuck or aren't you?"

Her clothes dropped away and instantly, at the sight of her full, hard-nippled breasts and the dense, dark thatch of hair at the base of her belly, his cock sprang up into aching rigidity. She grinned and came toward him and knelt before him, slipping one hand under his balls and grasping his stiff shaft with the other.

"Go on," Holman said hoarsely. "Suck it! Oh, Jesus, suck it, babe!"

She tickled the tip of his dick with her tongue and rubbed it voluptuously for a moment or two between the heavy mounds of her tits, and then her lips slid over him and she took him into her mouth. Deep. Amazingly deep. And moved slowly back and forth, back and forth, wringing moans from him, driving him wild with sensation.

Her mouth was as soft and as sweet as a velvet cunt. She squeezed his balls lightly as she sucked. He could feel the jism starting to pulse within him, on the verge of leaping forth into her throat. But then she pulled back and spread herself for him, and an instant later, to his amazement and delight, his hard cock was plunging into the hot, throbbing depths of her moist pussy, and—

The year was 1959, though, and the American government's ideas of what was permissible to print and sell through normal commercial channels was very different, so this is what I actually wrote:

She undid the garter-belt herself, and rolled down the stockings, and then she was nude, and he stood up, dropping his trousers, and she reached out and caught his arm and pulled him down again, and they rolled off the couch together, down onto the carpeted floor.

For what might have been an hour they lay there, side by side, lips glued, hands roaming up and down bodies, breath coming shorter and shorter. Holman opened his eyes and saw her staring at him, her eyes moist and the pupils that peculiar shade of green again. He smiled into her eyes and brought his fingers lightly down the small of her back, pausing at the dimples just above her firm, swelling buttocks.

It was like pulling a trigger. She began to gasp excitedly, and she dragged him over on top of her, her eyes going tight shut, her lips drooping open, moist and passionate.

"Now, darling! Take me now!"

She shuddered convulsively as the moment of union came. Her thighs tightened around him, and she began to writhe and moan—an animal moan, low and deep in her throat, coming from the same place that those deep, sad blues came from.

Holman clenched his teeth and gripped her shoulders tight, and she cried out three times, a whimper of excitement following, and then they were thundering away together on a tornado of passion, and she dug her fingernails into the skin of his back and gasped out breathlessly, "Oh oh oh *oh*," and Holman felt the explosion in his loins, and then they were lying quietly all of a sudden, limp and sweat-soaked, and he could feel the pounding of her heart when he touched her breasts, and the fireworks stopped.

It was over.

Hot stuff, yes? Well, actually it is, in its quaint fashion. No tits or cocks or cunts are mentioned, or any other nasty Anglo-Saxon words, no clits, no moist pussies, no vivid descriptions whatsoever of genital organs, erect or otherwise—not even of pubic hair; and an orgasm isn't a fountain of hot jism or anything else anatomically specific, it's a metaphorical "explosion in the loins." People don't fuck or screw, they experience "union." The tone is very antiseptic, almost prim, you would say. Even so, all the basic ingredients of the good old beast with two backs are there, the moans and groans, whimpers of excitement, and, yes, the explosion in the loins—everything you would want in a scene describing passionate sex, if you were living in 1959. But the difference between the hot stuff of 1959 and today's pornographic fiction is the difference between the lightning bug and the lightning.

The 1959 passage that begins with the undoing of the garter-belt was, in fact, the opening erotic scene in *Love Addict*, published by Nightstand Books of Chicago in October of that year—the first of about a hundred and fifty novels of what we now would regard as very innocent soft-core porn that I would write over the next five years for Nightstand under the pseudonym of "Don Elliott."

That's right. One hundred fifty full-length novels in five years. Thirty books a year, better than one every two weeks, month in and month out, between 1959 and 1964. Written on a manual typewriter, no less. (Writers didn't use computers then. The IBM Selectric typewriter, once considered a fast futuristic device, had not yet been invented, either.) Other writers who, as I did, went on to significant careers in other fields, were turning out similar soft-core books at almost the same sizzling pace. We were *fast*, in those days. But of course we were very young.

I was 24 years old when I stumbled, much to my surprise, into a career of writing sex novels. I was then, as I am now, primarily known as a science-fiction writer. But in 1958, as a result of a behind-the-scenes convulsion in the magazine-distribution business, the whole s-f publishing world went belly up. A dozen or so magazines for which I had been writing regularly ceased publication overnight; and as for the tiny market for s-f novels (two paperback houses and one hardcover) it suddenly became so tight that unless you were one of the first-magnitude stars like Robert Heinlein or Isaac Asimov you were out of luck.

I had been earning a very nice living writing science fiction since my graduation from college a few years earlier. I had a posh five-room apartment on Manhattan's exclusive West End Avenue ($150 a month rent— a fortune then!), I had fallen into the habit of spending my summer vacations in places like London and Paris, I ate at the best restaurants, I was learning something about fine wines. And suddenly two thirds of the magazines I wrote for were out of business, with a slew of older and better established writers competing for the few remaining slots. Most of the reliable writing income on which I had come to depend disappeared overnight.

But I was fast on my feet, and I had some good friends. One of them was Harlan Ellison, a science-fiction writer of my own age, who—seeing the handwriting on the wall in the s-f world—had left New York to accept a job in Chicago as editor of *Rogue*, an early men's magazine that was trying with some success to compete with its crosstown neighbor, *Playboy*.

The publisher of *Rogue* was William L. Hamling, a clean-cut young Chicago suburbanite whose first great love, like Harlan's and mine, had been science fiction. Bill Hamling had published an s-f magazine called *Imagination*, which bought one of my first stories in 1954. From 1956 on, he had paid me $500 a month to churn out fast-paced epics of the spaceways for him on a contract basis. Now, though, *Imagination* was gone, and Hamling's only remaining publishing endeavor was his bi-monthly girlie magazine.

Harlan, soon after going to work for him, convinced Bill that the future lay in paperback erotic novels. Hamling thought about it for about six minutes and agreed. And then Harlan called me.

"I have a deal for you, if you're interested," he said. "One sex novel a month, 50,000 words. $600 per book. We need the first one by the end of July." It was then the *beginning* of July. I didn't hesitate. $600 a month was big money in those days, especially when you were a young writer at your wits' end because all your regular markets had crashed and burned. One book would pay four months' rent. They were going to publish two paperbacks a month, and I was being offered a chance to write half the list myself. "You bet," I said. By the end of July Harlan had *Love Addict*— a searing novel of hopeless hungers, demanding bodies, girls trapped in a torment of their own making, et cetera, et cetera. (I'm quoting from the jacket copy.)

Bill Hamling loved *Love Addict*. By return mail came my six hundred bucks and a request for more books. I couldn't do a second one immediately because I was heading off to Canada for a holiday from New York City's summer heat, but when I returned after Labor Day I wrote *Gang Girl*, my second novel for Hamling, and I went on from there, month after month, year after year, until my published file of books for Hamling's various imprints (Nightstand Books, Midnight Reader, Idle Hour Books, Sundown Reader, etc., etc., etc.) filled shelf after shelf. I turned *Gang Girl* in in mid-September. In October I did *The Love Goddess* for Nightstand. Later that month I wrote *Summertime Affair* also. Two novels the same month? Why not? I was fast, I was hungry, I was good.

That same month of October saw the first two Nightstand Books going on sale—mine and one called *Lust Club*, by another young writer who also was making a quick adaptation to changes in his writing markets. His book, like mine, was really pretty tame stuff. What we were writing, basically, were straightforward novels of contemporary life, with very mild interludes of sexual activity every twenty or thirty pages. But the characters actually did go to bed with each other, and we did try to describe what they were doing and how they felt in as much detail as the government would allow.

At that time, fairly rigid censorship still prevailed in American publishing. It was illegal to publish or sell such classics of erotic literature as *Tropic of Cancer* or *Lady Chatterley's Lover*, and even the presence of words like "fuck" or "cunt" in a book could bring its publisher a call from the district attorney's office. To a reading public eager for vicarious sexual thrills, Bill Hamling's Nightstand Books, which were openly and widely distributed, offered a commodity that was in instant and enormous demand. Incredible quantities of the first two books were sold. It was impossible to reprint them fast enough.

Hamling sent me a bonus of $200 for each book I had written thus far, and raised my price to $800 from then on. And he decided to publish four titles a month instead of two. "Can you possibly write two books every month for us?" he asked.

A Nightstand Book, you understand, was a 212-page double-spaced manuscript. I was setting myself up for an unthinkable amount of typing—not to mention the problem of inventing plots, characters, setting, all that stuff. But I didn't hesitate to say yes. I could type quickly and I could think quickly. I had just demonstrated to myself that I could indeed do two Nightstand jobs a month, and, since they took only six working days apiece, I would still have time left over for other projects. And I had arrived at a perfect formula for these books. Apart from the kid-gang books, which were a subgenre of their own, most of them were stories about ordinary people who were in the grip of powerful sexual obsessions that got them into trouble.

What I did was take a sympathetic character (male or female, it made no difference) who has normal, healthy sexual desires that are somehow being frustrated—the hard-working husband who suddenly feels a powerful need to have an affair, the woman who unexpectedly discovers that drinking too much makes her want to let go of her sexual inhibitions. Removing the obstacles to the fulfillment of the desires leads to complications and then more complications, which create tensions that can best be satisfied by more sex, and so on and on, in and out of bed and in and out of trouble, until in the end everything is resolved and the protagonist's life shows signs of becoming calmer. (Or spirals into a disastrous crash.)

Any setting would do. I just had to pick my characters and set them in motion against a vivid background. I told tales of illicit goings-on at plush Caribbean resorts, of nice high school kids learning interesting things to do with their bodies, of suburban swap clubs. Where I could make use of my own experiences, such as they had been at the age of 25 or so, I did. The rest I spun out of whole cloth, or out of my own teeming, steamy fantasies. (I had grown up in the repressed Fifties, and had plenty to fantasize about.)

I wrote *Pawn of Lust* and *Nudist Camp* in November, 1959. I wrote *Warped Lusts* and *Suburban Wife* in December. January produced only *Sin on Wheels*, but in February came *Sin Ranch* and *Trap of Desire*. And so on and so on, month after month. Each book took me exactly six days: one stint of sixteen to eighteen pages before lunch, another of the same amount after lunch, fifteen or sixteen manuscript pages to a chapter, fourteen chapters and 212 pages in all. No book came out short and none, of course, ran long: I became adept in moving my characters around in such a way that the climax of the plot always arrived on schedule in Chapter Fourteen. The books sold well and more retroactive bonuses were paid me for the early titles. Now I was getting $1200 a book for the new ones. That was an income of better than a thousand dollars a week at a time when dinner for two at the finest restaurant in New York cost about $40, including a bottle of first-rate French wine. My new career in soft-core erotica was rapidly making me rich.

The two books reprinted here date from the midpoint of my career in the soft-core business. (I dislike the term "sleaze books." "Sleazy," to me, means "shoddy, badly done." I tried to be craftsmanlike about the books I did for the Hamling operation and I don't regard them as shoddy or badly done, of their kind.) I wrote *Lust Queen* in July of 1961, and it makes use of background details I had picked up on my earliest visits to California, a place that had long fascinated me, though at that point I didn't have the faintest notion that within another decade I would abandon New York City and go west to live there. You can see from the very first sentence of the book—"I was busy making the typewriter keys move"—that there is a certain autobiographical element to the book, the narrator being a young and vigorous and very prolific writer, but the autobiographical element very quickly gives way to sheer fantasy. As for *Lust Victim*, it was written seven months later, February, 1962, a time of high productivity even for me, a rate of just about a book a week, since I had just moved into a big new house in a fancy suburban part of New York City and I was hard pressed to pay all the moving and redecorating bills, as I will describe a few pages farther on—but a book a week for Hamling helped no little bit. It takes place not in Hollywood or in Manhattan, two of the most frequent sites of my Nightstand books, but in East Coast suburbia, Cheever/Updike territory, another regular setting of mine. (And concerns home invasion and robbery, a topic that is still getting plenty of attention in the suburban neighborhood where I live these days, fifty years later.)

The Hamling operation published *Lust Queen* late in 1961 as Midnight Reader 401, the initial title in that series. *Lust Victim* followed in mid-1962 as Midnight Reader 429. It came out under the dumb title of *No Lust Tonight*, but for this reissue—the first time the book has been reprinted since its initial appearance—I have restored my original title.

I felt absolutely unabashed about what I was doing. Writing was my job, and I was working hard and telling crisp, exciting stories. What difference did it make, really, that they were stories about people caught in tense sexual situations instead of people exploring the slime-pits of Aldebaran IX? I experienced the joy—and there is one, believe me—of working hard and steadily, long hours sitting at a typing table under the summer sun, creating scenes of erotic tension as fast as my fingers could move. Of course, what I was writing was not "respectable," not even slightly, and so when people asked me what I did for a living I told them I was a science-fiction writer. (I was still writing some of that, too, as a sideline.) I could hardly tell my neighbors in my elegant suburban community that I was a professional pornographer.

But was what I was writing really pornography?

Not if your definition of pornography involves the use of "obscene" words or graphic physiological description. As the sample I quoted above should show, the stuff was really laughably chaste and demure. Everything was done by euphemism and metaphor. No explicit anatomical descriptions were allowed, no naughty words. About as far as you could go was a phrase like "they were lying together, and he felt the urgent thrust of her body against him, and his aroused maleness was penetrating her, and he felt the warm soft moist clasping and the tightening...."

Unmistakably these people are Doing It. But his "maleness" is what's penetrating her, not his cock or his prick or his dick, and *something* is clasping and tightening, presumably a vagina, but we aren't told that in so many syllables. Characters didn't "come"—they reached "the moment of ecstasy." Men had neither cocks nor balls; they had "loins." Foreplay was a matter of cupping breasts and letting a hand "slip lower on her body." Anal sex? No such concept. Dildos and other sex toys? Forget it. Oral sex was indicated by saying, "He kissed her here and he kissed her there, and then he kissed her there." And so forth. None of it was much spicier than Peter Rabbit.

I limited myself to words that were in the standard dictionary because I had been warned at the outset that the publisher would not tolerate what he termed "vulgarisms." One reason for this was that he genuinely didn't like them—he was basically a very earnest and straight type of guy, who would much rather have been publishing science fiction—but he also knew that he might very well go to jail if he started printing them. *Jail,* yes—no matter what the First Amendment might say. (And eventually he did, many years later—not for publishing sexy novels, but for violating the postal code by sending an advertisement for an illustrated history of erotic art and literature through the mails!)

The list of what was a "vulgarism," though, kept changing in line with various court actions and rulings affecting Nightstand's competitors in the rapidly expanding erotic-book business. All across the nation, bluenosed civic authorities were trying to stamp out this new plague of smut. Whenever a liberal-minded judge threw out a censor's case, the word came down to us that we could take a few more risks in what we wrote, although our prose remained exceedingly pure by later publishing standards. But whenever some unfortunate publisher was hit by a fine, the word was passed to the little crew of Nightstand regulars that we had to try to be more proper.

One day the word "it" became a vulgarism. "*It*" as in "'*Do it,' she cried,*" I mean. By this time Harlan Ellison had moved along to Hollywood, and my Nightstand editor in Chicago was Algis Budrys, another top science-fiction writer who had found it necessary after the s-f crash to switch from freelance writing to editing. Budrys phoned me to say that I must restrict my use of "it" from now on. I took a look at a recently published book of mine and saw that they had indeed changed all my 'it's' to 'that's', creating stuff like: "'*Do that,*' she cried. '*I want that! I want that!*'"

This sounded nuts to me, and I told Budrys I would refuse to abide by it. To prove it, I turned in a book in which "it" was just about every other word: "*Give it to me! I want it! It! It! I must have it!*" I was the star of the line, the first and most reliable and prolific writer they had, and I got my way. "It" was removed from the list of vulgarisms.

By this time—it was about 1962—I was turning out *three* Nightstand books a month. It was a fantastic amount of work to do, but I had no choice. Like many writers (Sir Walter Scott, for example, or Mark Twain) I had gone in for owning fancy real estate. I had bought myself that enormous mansion in the finest residential neighborhood of New York City, close to the Westchester County line, for the immense sum (then) of $80,000. The place had 20 rooms, all of which needed to be painted and furnished, and then too I had to think about the heating bill, property taxes, etc., etc. So I upped the output. The record for June, 1962, for example, shows *Un-*

natural, Illicit Joys, and *The Flesh is Willing*—a typically productive month. That month the plumbing in the house broke down and I remember a team of five plumbers digging around in the back yard, simply trying to locate the water main, while I sat upstairs trying to turn out words fast enough to earn more than their combined hourly rate. And did.

One way I managed to keep up this amazing level of output was to assemble a sheaf of what I called "modules"—prefabricated sex scenes that I could simply plug into any book. Plots and characters had to change from book to book, of course, but under the highly restrictive rules we were forced to use there were only so many ways to describe what my people were up to in bed, and so I extracted relevant scenes from my books—a basic seduction scene, a copulation scene, a voyeurism scene, a rape scene, a Lesbian scene, and so on—and recycled them into the new manuscripts in the appropriate places, as needed. Nobody ever objected. (If computers had existed then, I could have done it all with a single keystroke. Instead I had to type it all out, over and over.)

Where I could, I would expand something I had written before. I still had a considerable backlog of crime stories that I had done in the late 50s for *Trapped* and *Guilty*, and, since these all dealt with people in extreme situations, it was easy enough to build one up to book length. That was what I did in December, 1962 with a novelet called "Mobster on the Make," from the August, 1958 issue of *Trapped*, which I turned into a novel I called *Sex Hoodlum*, and which Earl Kemp, who by that time had replaced Budrys as my Nightstand editor, renamed *Sex Bum*. (Earl almost always changed my titles.) It came out in May, 1963 as Midnight Reader 489.

The Nightstand line now was running to eight or ten books a month, maybe more, and as the list grew, a lot of other clever young men joined the roster of writers. (Entry to the list was by invitation only—the publisher didn't want to deal with amateurs, only with crafty young pros.) In an insecure career like freelance writing, those guaranteed monthly checks were very tempting. You would probably be astonished at how many eventually-famous writers were among my colleagues at Nightstand. We were like a bunch of future major-leaguers getting a chance to sharpen our skills in Triple-A minor league baseball.

I won't name names, because it's not my place to do so. But I can tell you that two writers who became widely admired mystery novelists, enormously popular and successful, were Nightstand regulars under the names of "Andrew Shaw" and "Alan Marshall." Their work for Nightstand usually had a broadly comic touch, which mine never did. (Sex was always Serious Stuff to me.) Another, who wrote under the name of "J. X. Williams," became a major best-selling author of historical novels, and I mean *major*, specializing in American history. The author of the "Don Bellmore" books went on to a career as a Hollywood writer. "Clyde Allison" was the pseudonym used by a brilliant young mainstream novelist who died of alcoholism while still in his thirties. And, though I have no proof of this, I was told on good authority long ago that one of the Nightstand writers was a man who was *already* a best-selling author even then, and who was knocking out Nightstands on the side for the fun of it, without his wife's knowledge (or his regular publisher's) and having the payments sent to the mistress he was keeping.

We were all working hard, and having fun, and making plenty of money. (So was the publisher, who left Chicago for a Palm Springs estate.) Of course, all sorts of governmental units right up to the Federal level were trying to put us out of business, and there were indictments all over the place, and a nasty censorship trial in Houston. Since we writers worked under pseudonyms, and got our checks from a dummy corporation, we weren't involved in that.

But one day two F.B.I. agents came to talk to me. It was all very silly. I received them in the paneled library of my imposing mansion. We chatted about my writing—my *science fiction* writing. I showed them a few recent books on archaeology and science for young readers I had written—I was doing that too, in my spare time, and I just happened to have the books close at hand. The word "pornography" was never mentioned. They did ask me if I had ever done business with a company called Such-and-Such Enterprises. Evidently that was one of the dummy corporations that paid the writers for the Nightstand Lines; but it so happened that my checks came from This-and-That Enterprises instead, a *different* dummy corporation, and the nice F.B.I. men had gotten things mixed up. "No," I said, absolutely truthfully. "I've never done business with Such-and-Such. I've never even heard of them." And that was that. The F.B.I. men left, probably thinking there was some case of mistaken identity here, and no one ever bothered me again.

But I did stop writing for Nightstand a year or so later—not because I was afraid of more government harassment, but because after 150 erotic novels in five years I was getting pretty tired of marching my characters in and out of bedrooms. I wanted to get back to the intellectual challenge of science fiction, which was making a strong commercial recovery after its slump of the late Fifties. And my non-fiction books on archaeology and science were very successful too; I wanted time to do more of those. So in a final flurry—*E for Eros, One Night Stand, Sin Kitten*—I went out of the business of writing erotic novels.

But I have no regrets about those five years in the sex-book factory—none. I don't think any of us who wrote Nightstands do. It isn't just that I earned enough by writing them to pay for that big house and my trips to Europe. I developed and honed important professional skills, too, while I was pounding out all those books.

Working at fantastic speeds (I once did a complete novel in 3-1/2 days, just to see if I could) I mastered the knack of improvising plots from scratch and making everything work out neatly at the required 50,000-word length: a wonderful exercise in structural discipline that has stood me in good stead ever since. I think the experience was useful for my colleagues, too. There was no time to make mistakes: we had to get it right on the first draft, and we did, telling good stories in crisp, no-nonsense prose. And because we all worked under pen names, we were free to let our inhibitions drop away and push our characters to their limits, without worrying about what anyone else—friends, relatives, book reviewers—might say or think about our work. We had ourselves a ball, and got paid nicely while we were doing it.

And also we never forgot that we were doing the fundamental thing that writers are supposed to do: provide pleasure and entertainment for readers who genuinely loved our work. Huge numbers of the books were snapped up as fast as they came from the presses, which meant that they filled a need, that *somebody* appreciated them a whole lot. It meant something to me to know that my novels were brightening the lives of a vast host of people in those dim dark days of fifty-plus years ago when puritanism was riding high and sex was in chains.

One hundred fifty novels! *Passion Patsy*! *Flesh Flames*! *Sin Hellion*! *The Orgy Boys*! Writing those books was a terrific experience and I look back fondly on it without shame, without apologies.

—JULY 2013
OAKLAND, CALIFORNIA

Lust Queen
by Don Elliott

1

I was busy making the typewriter move. My fingers were writhing as though they had their own private case of St. Vitus dance, and every time they twitched, more nice black marks appeared on the white paper in the machine. I was 40,000 words into the new detective novel, and only forty pages to go and I could tap out those lovely words, "THE END."

And then it was off for a weekend of celebration with Lisa. Lisa of the lovely breasts, Lisa of the pneumatic hips, Lisa of the big baby-blue eyes. Lisa who could lie there in bed and drive a man into frenzy. Lisa with the hourglass curves, with the round pink hard nipples and the funny little gasp just before she hit the jackpot.

I had it all worked out on a neat little schedule. Today was Tuesday. If I averaged 3500 words a day, I'd be through with the book by Thursday. I'd turn it in to my agent, Jack Thomas, Thursday afternoon, and by Friday morning it would be at the publisher. We already had the book sold to Hammond and Bryce for a $2000 advance, of which I had already collected $500 on the strength of three chapters and an outline of the rest. The other $1500 was due on delivery of the finished book. And then, on top of that, Jack was positive we'd be able to sell a condensation to one of the big slicks. Chalk up another $3000 right there. Not bad for a couple of weeks' work, I figured. And Jack would be glad to give me an advance.

So I'd have enough cash to see me through a weekend with Lisa, and also to pay the lawyer who was handling my divorce from Laurette. All I had to do was get this damn book finished and I'd be in the chips again. I'd been going steady with my typewriter for almost a month now.

Jesus, it was going to be good to get Lisa into a hotel room, to get my arms around her, to squeeze those big tits of hers, to feel her thighs against me, to look down and see her eyes going smoky, her lips moist and shiny, her blonde hair tumbling all around her, while I burrowed deep into her and let all my troubles flood away on a riptide of love....

Sure. Just another forty pages to the finish line.

I completed the page I was working on, slipped it out of the typewriter, grabbed up a white sheet and two yellow ones, went through the mechanical motions of interleaving them with carbon paper, and slipped them into the typewriter. I paused to light a fresh cigarette.

I typed a neatly centered 161 at the top of the page and shut my eyes for a moment, trying to visualize the scene I was writing about.

The phone rang.

Lisa, I thought. It's Lisa.

"Hello?" I said, glad that she had called but hoping she'd make it quick.

"Hi there, Joey-babe," came the booming masculine voice. It wasn't Lisa. It was my agent.

"Morning, Jack. What's up? Any good news?"

"Maybe," he said. "How's that stinking mystery story of yours coming along?"

"Page 161 out of 200," I told him. "It's really picking up steam. It's a sure bet for *Playboy*, Jack."

"When you going to be finished?"

"Thursday afternoon."

"Okay," he said. "Friday a.m. you leave for Los Angeles, boy. I'll have Dolores book you on the morning flight."

"Like hell you will," I snapped. "You only own ten percent of me, Jack. I'm spending this weekend in Atlantic City with Lisa, and nobody's interfering with that schedule."

He was silent a long moment. Then he said, "I've got a new assignment for you, Joe."

"Assignment?"

"That's right," he said, as though spelling things out to a backward four-year-old. "An assignment to write a book. But you've got to go to L.A. to do the research. It's pretty good pay, incidentally. MacDougal is doing the hardcover edition and they'll pay a 3000 advance. We've already sold a paperback reprint for 10,000 more. We're working on a magazine condensation deal that should bring in about twenty grand. There's an excellent movie possibility. Plus foreign rights and other crap. You have to split the loot with someone else, but even after that I'd say you'd clear a minimum of 15,000 from this job, exclusive of movie rights. You think you're interested?"

I gaped. "Sure I'm interested, Jack."

"I figured you would be. That's why I'm booking you on that flight."

"What's the deal?" I asked.

"You ever hear of a gal name of Mona Thorne?"

"Movie star," I said. "Kind of a brunette Marilyn Monroe a few years back. Made a couple of flashy pictures, got a lot of crazy publicity, and dropped out of sight maybe five years ago. What about her?"

"You're going to write her autobiography," Jack said.

"Huh? Who the hell's going to pay good money for the autobiography of some big-boobed imitation actress that nobody remembers?"

"You want to back out?" he asked me.

"I want to know what kind of story there is."

"Plenty," he said. "First of all, this girl's a lot more remembered than you think. She made six movies between 1963 and 1966, and they were all big box-office stuff."

"But she hasn't made anything since '66? That's a generation ago by Hollywood standards!"

"Her last movie was in '68. A bit part. She's been busy," Jack said. "Her first husband was Teddy Burns. He was a fag. Killed himself in '67 when some gossip columnist threatened to smear him. Mona went on a big bender, lushed around for months. A real alcoholic. She was in a movie and got so drunk on the set that they tossed her the hell out. Okay. Next stop was a torrid love affair with Lee Crosswell, the director. A junkie. He spent all his time trying to get Mona hooked so they'd be soul-mates forever. He didn't succeed. Summer of '69 Crosswell was killed on the freeway. What he couldn't accomplish in life happened after he was gone. Mona turned herself on. She was on heroin for a year and a half. Drove down into Mexico twice a week to buy the stuff, turned on down there, came back high. Early '71 she fell in love with some doctor named Robinson, and he got her off the stuff. They were going to be married and she was going to make a movie comeback. Only the good Dr. Robinson was mixed up in an abortion ring for juveniles and got caught. They were going to try him when he killed himself."

"Jesus," I said, "this story gets gaudier and gaudier."

"Doesn't it though?" Jack said gleefully. "Wait. After Robinson checked out, Mona hit the skids again. This time the nympho bit. She'd slosh around Hollywood trying to pick up anyone who was interested. The way I get it, she was getting laid three and four times a night by different men for a while. That went on for a year or so. Then she got religion."

"Oh, no."

"Oh, yes. She's been received into some local church they've got out there, and she's holier than hell. No more drinking, no more screwing. The bit is that she's going to make a movie next year. Her first since she went under. It's going to be a spectacular job, and the studio thinks it's a good idea to get out a book about her, her sufferings and sins and repentance and all that shit. So they set up a deal with publishers, and then called me up and asked me to find a writer."

"And you found me," I said wonderingly.

"I found you, right. I hate to see you wasting yourself on those crappy detective stories when you could be cashing in on real money. You want the job, Joey?"

"You kidding?"

"Okay, then. Here's the deal. It's a straight fifty-fifty cut between you and Mona on everything. She'll supply all the info, you'll do all the writing. She'll give you five grand as a starter, with more as she gets it from the publishers. The chances are about five to one in favor of a movie sale that could bring you fifty or sixty grand. She'll pay your traveling expenses both ways, and she'll pay your rent for as long as you have to stay out there. Today's April tenth. The manuscript has to be turned in by July fifteenth, so they can have the book out in the fall. It's not much time, but I know you work pretty fast. And you can knock off for the rest of the year on what you'll make out of this one."

"Sounds great," I said. "Give me till Thursday to finish the detective thing, and then Lisa and I will take off for the Coast on Friday."

"Uh-uh. No Lisa."

"Why not?" I said. "I can't leave my fiancée alone for three months."

"You better manage it," Jack warned. "Mona specified a bachelor writer. I get the impression that you're in for a pretty hot time out there. You bring any girlfriends with you and it's likely to fuck up the whole pitch."

"But—but—"

"You can explain it to Lisa, boy. Tell her you'll be on the Coast maybe two months, and then you'll be practically independently wealthy. Tell her anything. You aren't going to let a broad stand in the way of all this bread, are you?"

"I suppose not," I said.

"Damn right," he chortled happily. "Okay, get with that detective job and finish it off. I'll be talking to you as more stuff breaks."

I put down the phone, stubbed out my cigarette, and stared perplexedly at the pale-green surface of the bare wall in front of me. Funny, I thought. This was the kind of break I'd been waiting for during all my ten years as a free-lance writer. I'd written everything, just about—crime stories, Westerns, science fiction, kiddie books, anything that I could get a reasonably honest dollar for. I worked hard, never made a hell of a lot of money but didn't do badly either, and kept hoping that someday I'd hit the jackpot that other writers hit, the really big sale, the multiple sale to the movies and the paperbacks and one of the big magazines, the kind of sale that brought you a five- or six-figure return for your work.

Well, now I had the deal. All I had to do was to spend a couple of months talking to a has-been movie actress with a history of alcoholism, drug addiction, and nymphomania, and I'd be set up. The story was a natural.

Every sin in the book. Love affairs with three dead men (two of them suicides, and one of those two an illegal abortionist and the other a homosexual), plus the glowing Hollywood finale of a comeback—the book couldn't miss.

So why did I feel so crappy?

Maybe because I thought it was an easy way of making a lot of money. Maybe because there was a worm of integrity still buried in me that said there was something wrong with making that kind of bread for a meaningless book about a meaningless, self-indulgent broad.

Or maybe I was just afraid of going west and sticking my nose into the slowly disintegrating but still high-powered world of Hollywood. I knew I didn't belong there. I'm an Easterner, and I don't think the way those people think out there. So maybe I was afraid, pure and simple.

I shrugged. To hell with it. I'd go, and I'd write the book, and I'd make a fortune. And cry all the way down to the bank, as they say.

I pushed my chair back, got up, walked around the room. A hell of a thing for a man thirty-five years old to be living in a stinking one-room hotel apartment with dirty windows. Well, it was only temporary, I told myself. As soon as the divorce from Laurette came through, I could go back to living like a human being. I'd marry Lisa, I'd buy a new house, and we'd live it up on the proceeds of Mona Thorne's sordid autobiography. Yeah.

I looked at the bourbon bottle on the dresser and shook my head. That was no way to get a book written. I walked back to the typewriter table.

It was one in the afternoon. With some sweat and maybe half a pack of cigarettes, I could get to page 175 by tonight. Then fifteen or twenty pages tomorrow, the rest Thursday morning, and then Thursday afternoon for tightening up and revising. And I'd be through. The book would be done and I could think about heading west.

I reread pages 158,159, and 160 to get me back into the swing of things. Then I started to type. The words began to flow with the greatest of ease. Almost before I knew it, I had knocked off six, seven, eight pages. There had been a time, back when I was drinking heavily, when eight pages was a full day's work for me. Now I had turned them out in not much more than an hour and a half. And they were good pages. The plot was tight and hard, the pace swift.

By four in the afternoon, I had hit page 180, and I decided to quit. There was one chapter to go. I could do it tomorrow, and spend Thursday polishing the book in a leisurely way. There wasn't any point in continuing any longer today. I was tired and drenched with sweat and my back hurt from hunching over the low typewriter table.

I poured myself a good stiff slug of the bourbon. It felt good going down, and all the better because I had earned it through a good day's work. Then I peeled off my sweat-sticky clothes, wrapped my frayed and discolored bathrobe around me, and went down the hall to take a shower in the bathroom I shared with seven other residents of this flea-bitten hotel.

I took a long, luxurious shower, and fuck anyone else who wanted to use the john. I let the hot water sizzle me, and then the cold water wake me up, and then lukewarm to wash by. When I came out I was in a tremendous mood. Ready to go run around the block if anyone suggested it.

I pushed open the door of my room and there was Lisa sitting on my bed, reading the manuscript.

"When did you get here?"

"Five minutes ago," she said. "When are you going to learn how to spell 'deceive'?"

"I was typing that in a hurry."

"You spelled it wrong six times. I before E except after C. Didn't you go to school?"

"Sure," I said. "It was a long time ago, honey. Back in log-cabin days."

I hung up my robe and turned around to face her in the altogether. She looked me over shamelessly and smirked.

"`Exhibitionist," she said.

"Why not? It's good to look at, isn't it?"

"And conceited too."

I nodded. "I can even spell that word." I did. "See? I before E except after C."

"Shut up and give me a kiss, Joey."

"Gladly."

I held out my arms and she came to me, pressing up tight against my naked body. Lisa was really built. At five foot eight, she was only three inches shorter than I am, and in heels there was no difference at all. She was a real blonde with real blue eyes, and a real forty-inch bust that right now was trying to explode out of a tight sweater. She wasn't wearing any bra underneath. I could feel her breasts pressing into me, the nipples like little hard points of fire. Her lips against mine, her body glued against me from breasts to thighs. I clung to her as though I wanted to ball her right through her skirt and undies and all.

She was twenty-four, and I'd known her for about a year. I had met her when she was working as a receptionist for my agent. Now she had a job paying approximately twice as much, with a public-relations firm. When I had first met her, my marriage was in the first stages of coming apart. By now it was totally shattered; and Lisa and I had been seriously talking of marriage as soon as I got the legal formalities taken care of. Naturally, we'd been sleeping together almost from the first. And enjoying it.

We broke out of the kiss, coming up for air, and Lisa said, "How's the book doing?"

"Be finished with it tomorrow, maybe."

"Is it okay?"

"It'll do," I said. I tugged her sweater free of her waist and pulled it up over her head. Blonde hair, soft and silken, tumbled in every direction as I drew the sweater off. There were her breasts, bare and tender. I put my hands on them. I have medium-sized hands, and Lisa's breasts fill them completely. I stood there, savoring the heaviness of them against my palms, appreciating the way the nipples had hardened. My fingertips dug gently into the firm, taut flesh of them, hefting the breasts, caressing them. Lisa smiled and began to wriggle out of her clothes while I held her.

Off came the skirt, off came the gauzy green panties. Her body was glorious, wide at the shoulders to support those big breasts, then tapering in a startling fashion toward that twenty-one-inch waist, then flaring out again in full hips and descending in superb white columns of thighs to matchless curved calves and trim ankles.

Her eyes glinted mischievously into mine. I put my mouth over hers, drinking in those soft full lips, and feeling her tongue slip between my teeth.

We collapsed onto the bed.

Gaily, gleefully, we wrestled for a few minutes, her strong body resisting mine. Then suddenly the fire was kindled in her, and the mischief went out of her eyes to be replaced by sheer smoky desire, and she drew me to her.

I nibbled at her earlobes and kissed the strong point of her chin, and she smiled and began to move rhythmically, and I felt passion taking full hold. She was warm and soft and skilled. She knew how to use her body. I lay tight against her, and we matched each other in the great game of pleasure, both of us mounting higher and higher with each second as the tempo picked up, and then I waited, so Lisa could catch up with me in the climb toward the top of the mountain.

She caught me and passed me, forging breathlessly onward. Up, up, she strained, arching her back, heightening the bond between us, then sinking toward the mattress again, pointing her toes toward the ceiling. I held back a moment, and then it came, that odd little gasping sound of hers, the prelude to the finale.

As always, it was like riding a cyclone. Lisa went wild, as together we thundered on to the end.

Then we lay still, breathing hard, our bodies temporarily drained of desire. Side by side, relaxing on the rumpled bed, silently reliving the moments of ecstasy, the oneness that had just been achieved. I had never had that oneness with my wife Laurette. There weren't many girls who could give themselves as fully as Lisa gave herself in the act of love.

I didn't speak for a long while. I didn't want to spoil it. It was only when the afterglow had begun to fade, when we had descended into the real world again, that I sprang the bad news.

"I've got to go away for a while, Lisa."

She looked startled. "Why? Where? How long?"

"I don't know, honey. Maybe a couple of weeks, maybe a couple of months. It depends on how long the job takes, how tough it turns out to be."

Quickly I sketched in the new assignment for her—the kind of money involved, the publishers, the size of the deal. "It means I've got to work practically around the clock," I said. "Get the story from her during the day, write it up at night. Three hundred manuscript pages that have to be handed in by July fifteenth. It's a big job."

"You can't take me?"

I shook my head. "It wouldn't work, Lisa. What they're buying is a writing machine—a man with a typewriter and a dictionary. They don't want me to come out equipped with a mistress. They want me to work full-time. They specifically nixed the idea of your coming along."

"Did you ask them?"

"I asked Jack. He said no." I felt like a bastard. "Look, baby, it'll only take me till the end of May, if I'm lucky. I can come back here to do the final draft, I guess. And once this hits the stands, I'm a rich man. I can knock off for the rest of the year. We can get married as soon as the divorce comes through, take a two-month honeymoon, then spend the whole winter setting up our new home."

"You can't possibly take me, Joey?"

"No. Not possibly."

"So it's either leave me for a couple of months, or pass up the assignment?"

"Afraid so."

She bit her lip. "I'm going to miss you, Joey."

"I'll write to you every day," I promised solemnly.

Then her breasts were tight against my hands again, and her warm thighs were against me, and for another hour she told me with her body how much she was going to miss me, and I knew how much I was going to miss her.

2

I got the book finished late Wednesday night. I shoved the manuscript into a typewriter-paper box, stuck it in a dresser drawer, and went over to Lisa's place to spend the night. Her apartment was a hell of a lot more attractive than my little dump of a hotel room, so we both preferred to spend our nights there. Lisa had wanted me to move in with her, but my lawyer said no to that. It would screw up the divorce case, he said, if I was openly cohabiting with another woman while trying to unload Laurette. After all, I was the one suing for the divorce.

Wednesday night was a ball. The alarm went off early Thursday morning, and Lisa put together breakfast for us, and then she headed for her office and I headed for my hotel. I spent all morning and half the afternoon reading through the detective novel. It read okay. I tightened up a few things here, changed a comma or two there, but otherwise I let it stand. It was so good that by page 150 *I* was wondering who the murderer was. At three that afternoon, I stacked it back into its box and walked across town to my agent's Madison Avenue office. I gave him the book, allowed him to take me downstairs for a couple of martinis, and picked up my ticket for the flight west. It was a one-way ticket, first class.

I spent Thursday night with Lisa, too. Christ, what a night! She came at me hungrily, as though sex were being prohibited by Congress the next day and she wanted to get all she could before the ban went into effect. We hurled ourselves at each other all night, twisting and turning in her bed like damned souls. But we weren't suffering at all. We were having the time of our lives. And it was going to be the last night we'd spend like that for a couple of months or more, so we made it really good.

I would have overslept Friday morning, but Lisa didn't let me. She got me out of her apartment by half-past seven in the morning, going over to my hotel and helping me pack. By nine o'clock I was in a taxi bound for Kennedy Airport. I was traveling light, just my portable typewriter and a single suitcase. Most of my clothing was in storage anyway; I didn't need it while I was living out of a one-room flat.

The trip took five and a half hours, which meant we got to Los Angeles at not quite one in the afternoon, local time. I got off the plane and stood blinking in the hot April sunshine, looking around for the fellow who was supposed to meet me—Fred Koren, the manager of the West Coast office of the J. L. Thomas Literary Agency.

I spotted him, finally, just on the other side of the barrier. He was a short, Ivy-Leaguish fellow of about my age, with a soft voice and a receding hairline and an infinitely dapper manner. Standing next to him was a standard Hollywood type, about six feet three with a deep tan, rose-tinted sunglasses, a wild floral-pattern shirt, and yellow bellbottoms with two-inch-wide cuffs. He was about forty and looked like a native.

Koren took my hand limply and said, "Glad to see you again, Joey. I know you're going to do a great job on this project."

"I hope so," I said.

"I want you to meet Miss Thorne's agent. He's the man who's responsible for this whole deal in the first place. Carl Martinson, Joey Baldwin."

We shook hands. Martinson had a big hand, and it practically engulfed mine. He said in a deep voice, "Pleased to meet you, Mr. Baldwin. I've read a great many of your books. You might almost say I've become a fan of yours."

"Always glad to meet an admirer," I said, lying in my teeth.

"I particularly liked *Murder in the Caribbean*," he went on greasily. "There's the potential of a great movie there. I had Fred here send a copy of it over to a pal of mine last week. Now that you're going to be a part of the Hollywood scene, you'll pick up a lot of little deals that way, Joey."

I liked the way he had slipped to the first name so fast. "Here's hoping," I said. "I'm getting married again in the fall. I can use the cash."

Koren steered us toward the baggage pickup. In his Princeton purr he told me, "We'll stop off at my office first to sign the contracts. Then we'll all go out to Mona Thorne's place for introductions."

My lonely suitcase arrived. I had hung onto my typewriter rather than trust it to the baggage handler. Martinson beat me to the grip and we headed for a cab.

I had been in Los Angeles only once before, in 1960, when I was still a part-time writer and a part-time newspaperman. The place had changed tremendously since then, I saw, as we drove into town in Martinson's shiny Mercedes-Benz. There were even more freeways, more cars, and, of course, there was more smog. The ride into town seemed endless.

But finally we pulled up in front of one of the new glass office buildings on Wilshire Boulevard, and went up to Koren's office. It put the East Coast office to shame. Jack managed to get along on a couple of small rooms in a none-too-new Madison Avenue building. But his L.A. representative, Koren, had an office of opulent splendor.

The papers were all ready. I glanced through them—they amounted to a thick sheaf—and saw that Koren had set up a pretty good deal for me.

A straight fifty percent of all monies received from the book, including every imaginable subsidiary right. Martinson was to get his commission out of Mona's half, Koren and Thomas out of mine. So at least I wouldn't be hung up for a double ten-percent bite. Mona contracted to pay my air fare, to supply me with living expenses up to $800 a month, to provide any necessary stenographic services, and to pay me an immediate $5000 advance out of the money she had already received.

"But she hasn't received ten grand yet," I said. "There's only three grand from the hardcover people, and a net of five grand from the paperback sale. That makes 8000 to split, not even figuring in commissions."

Koren nodded. "You get a straight five grand to begin with, Joey. She gets the next two grand that comes in, to even things up. After that it's fifty-fifty all the way. Mona's got plenty of cash, Joey. She's having this book done for the publicity, not the money."

"Suppose it doesn't earn more than the eight grand already received?" I asked.

Martinson laughed. "I don't think you'll need to worry about that, Joey. But you get to keep your five grand no matter what. It isn't refundable."

"Okay," I said. "Give me a pen."

I signed the thick contract with a flourish. The moment I had dotted the i in Baldwin, Fred Koren reached into his pocket and handed me an agency check for $4500. My net advance after commission.

"You aren't wasting any time," I said.

Koren chuckled. "You aren't writing for the pulp mags now. This is the big league. Money moves fast out here."

I was getting to like the setup more and more each moment. Martinson signed the contract on behalf of Mona Thorne, and took his copies; I left mine with Koren, to be filed in the agency safe. Then we headed downstairs and got back into that air-conditioned Mercedes.

"Where does Miss Thorne live?" I asked.

"Westwood," Martinson said, handling the car as though this were the final hour of Sebring. He looped around slower-moving cars as if they were so many dinosaurs lumbering through the streets.

We drove westward along Wilshire Boulevard for what seemed like a hundred years. The neighborhood changed from one of shiny office buildings and shiny banks to one of plush hotels as we approached Beverly Hills. We kept on going, coming now into a secluded residential district thick with date palms. The car turned off Wilshire, and began threading its way through quiet streets studded with palatial homes barely visible behind their protective shroud of well-tended shrubbery.

I said, "If Mona Thorne hasn't made any films in years, how come she's so well off?"

"She invested her money pretty wisely when she was making it," Martinson said. "She had it put away for her where she couldn't get at the principal. So later when she—ah—hit the skids, she couldn't squander it. And she inherited half a million from her first husband."

"That always helps."

"It does indeed," Martinson said. "All told she's worth a couple of million. She's got an income of about fifty thou a year from her investments. Not bad for a little lass of only thirty-one who hasn't earned a penny since '68 or so."

"Not bad at all," I said. "Why does she want to bother with a comeback?"

"Money's not everything," Martinson said in a suddenly harsh voice. "The girl is bored. She's getting older, and she's got talents that aren't being used. She wants to work in the movies. I had to move heaven and earth to get her this job, though. She's considered poison around the studios because of her past antics. I convinced them that she is a safe risk nowadays. But the book'll help. It'll make her a figure of curiosity that'll bring people out to see the film. Everyone's curious to see a comeback from complete disaster."

"Including me," I said.

"You'll see her soon enough," Martinson promised. "The house is on the next block."

We swung into the driveway. It was a stucco-and-glass affair, big and imposing, the usual Californian architectural mishmash. It was about thirty percent imitation Frank Lloyd Wright, forty percent Spanish Mission, ten percent Mediterranean Villa, and twenty percent Modern Southern California.

The three of us walked up a front porch only slightly smaller than the playing field at Yankee Stadium, and Martinson thumbed the door-chime. There was a long wait, and then the glass door slid back, treating us to a blast of frigid air-conditioned air.

A pretty maid, about one-sixteenth black, smiled at us. "Good afternoon, Mr. Martinson. Miss Thorne's taking a sunbath in back. I'll tell her you're here. Won't you come in?"

We stepped inside, Martinson sliding the door shut. The maid vanished. I looked around at the lavishness of it, the welter of paintings and Chinese scrolls and statuettes and whatnot strewn around everywhere. Music was flooding out of speakers all over the place. Good music, a Bach concerto. So Mona Thorne has pretensions to culture, I thought. It would make a nice touch for her autobiography. How she turned to Bach in her moments of darkest despair. How the delicate loveliness of a Chinese scroll kept her from committing suicide.

The maid reappeared and beckoned to us. We followed her out into a back yard enclosed on all sides by towering palms. Mona Thorne was lying stretched on an air mattress in the center of the yard, eyes closed, beating time to the rhythms of the Bach.

She was wearing the bottom of a white bikini, nothing else. The halter of the bikini, discarded, lay a few feet from her. She was on her stomach, but I could see the bulging curves of her breasts flattened against the air mattress. She was very tan, an even olive color all over. Her hair was incredibly black, and cut in a short shag. She had a supple, slender body, widening breathtakingly at the hips. Her legs were long and curved, her buttocks—limned through the skimpy fabric of the bikini—high and exciting.

She sat up casually, reaching for the bikini halter in such a way as to give me a momentary but vivid view, in profile, of her bare breasts. They reminded me of Lisa's. Not quite as opulent, perhaps, but certainly big enough, and high and firm and pointed, the nipples tipped sharply upward. An instant later she had the bikini straps tied, and she was uncoiling from the mattress like a sleepy panther awakening from a noonday nap.

The bikini was blindingly white against the tan of her skin as she came toward me. The ripe swells of her breasts all but spilled over the top, while the bottom half just about covered her.

She held out her hand to me. "Joey Baldwin?"

"That's right. How do you do, Miss Thorne."

"Make it Mona," she said lazily. "I hate formality. You like martinis, Joey?"

"Most certainly."

She waved indolently to the maid, who was hovering in the background. "Bring out some martinis, Kitty," she called.

Martinson pulled over three beach chairs and we sat down, Mona squatting between us on her air mattress. I looked at her in fascination. She didn't *seem* to have suffered. There were no needle-marks on her arms, no pouches of dissipation under her eyes, no signs of wear. Martinson had said she was thirty-one, and she probably was, maybe even a few years older than that, but she looked no more than twenty-five. Her skin was taut, her muscles toned. Her eyes were clear. The California sun, I thought, could do wonders. Especially when combined with financial security and a rigorous diet.

Or maybe it was all a hoax, I thought. Maybe this girl *hadn't* been through a dozen different kinds of hell. Maybe the stories about two suicides were apocryphal. The drug addiction, the alcoholism—all some press agent's dream.

Kitty arrived with a tray of ice-cold martinis, extra dry. We raised glasses gravely and drank. I noticed that one of my paperback mystery stories was lying in a corner of the sunbathing area. It looked as though it had been read.

"You tell an exciting story, Joey," Mona purred. "I've been reading some of your books. After all, if you're going to write my life story, I want to see what kind of a writer I'm getting."

"Are you satisfied?" I asked.

"So far," she said huskily. She looked suddenly at Martinson. "Do you have any special business with me today, Carl?"

"Why—no. I just wanted to bring Joey over, introduce him to you—"

"Okay. You've done that. How about finishing your martinis and leaving, now? You and your friend. Joey and I will have to start work right away. I mean, he'll have to start getting to know me. If he's going to write my autobiography, he'll have to know me very well."

Martinson looked flustered and disconcerted at being thrown out this way. Koren was merely bored. He was the type who didn't mind being spit on, if the price was right, so why should a blunt ejection bother him?

They gulped down their drinks and made a quick exit, Koren asking me to call him later in the day if I got the chance. I nodded and waved goodbye.

Then I was alone with Mona Thorne.

"I see you've brought your typewriter," she said. "All right. I was going to rent one for you. I've already got a tape recorder set up so you can take down our conversations. And there's plenty of typing paper and carbon paper and everything else you need. I've fixed a study up for you on the second floor where you can work in complete privacy."

"I'm going to work here?" I asked, surprised.

She was surprised at my surprise. "Why, where else? On a bench in Forest Lawn?"

"Well, I thought I'd do my working in my hotel room each night after I've left you."

"What hotel room? You're staying with me, aren't you? I thought they had made that clear."

"I'm afraid I couldn't do that."

"Why the hell not?" she demanded in a flat, blunt voice.

"Well—" I hesitated, not having any particular answer. "I just wasn't expecting to."

"You aren't married, are you?"

"There's a divorce on the way."

"So what's the objection? You'll have privacy here. I won't intrude on you. I simply thought it would be more convenient all around for you to stay here. There aren't any hotels nearby. You'd have a long trip over here every day, and I understand you don't know the city too well. And it'll save on phone calls, too. Whenever you hit a snag in your work, I'll be right here to answer your questions."

I sipped my second martini thoughtfully. Was this a gigolo deal? I wondered. Were my stud services being bought along with my typewriter? I had anticipated a little fun and games before this collaboration was over, but I hadn't ever dreamed she'd move me right into her house. What would Lisa say about it all?

Lisa was three thousand miles away. There was no sense hen-pecking myself in advance. I was still a free agent.

"Okay," I said. "I won't fight it."

"Smart boy." She stretched out on the air mattress again and unhooked her bikini halter. Inside, Bach came to an end and a Beethoven sonata began. Kitty evidently changed the records too. Mona looked up at me. "Do you like Mozart?" she asked.

"Very much."

"That's one of my favorite sonatas playing now."

"It's a Beethoven," I said.

"So it is," she said evenly. "Silly of me. I thought it was Mozart. Just a slip of the tongue." She propped herself up on one arm, so that three-quarters of one lovely breast was bared. She didn't seem to notice. "I start filming in July," she said. "So the book has to be finished by then. Did they make that clear to you?"

"Quite."

"Until then I'm at leisure. I spend one hour each morning and one hour each evening studying the script. The rest of the time, we can work on the book."

"Any way you like."

"Today's Friday. That's a lousy time to start a book," she said. "Suppose we spend the weekend just relaxing and getting to know each other. Then Monday at ten sharp we can get down to work. I'll tell you my whole sad story and you can turn it into a wonderful book that will make millions weep."

"Fine," I said. "I can use a weekend of rest."

"You could use some sun, too," she said. "You've got an indoor pallor. Anyone can tell you've spent the winter in the east. I hate pale men. Suppose I have Kitty show you to your room, and you can get into a bathing suit and come down here to sun with me. Then we can swim a little. Have you eaten lunch yet?"

"Aboard the plane."

"But it's almost dinner time in New York, isn't it? So you'll be getting hungry soon. Well, we can have an early dinner." Kitty appeared. "Run along, now. Don't waste much time upstairs. You'll enjoy the sun."

I followed the maid upstairs.

"This is your room," she said softly. There was a faint smirk on her lips, and I felt more than ever like a gigolo. "It connects with Miss Thorne's through that door over there," she went on. "Any time you want me, just press this button here."

She padded silently out.

I looked around. The room was big, about twice as big as the one I'd been living in in New York. A typewriter table had been fixed up in one corner, all ready with a big stack of blank paper and some newly sharpened pencils. The bed was king-sized. There was a bookcase full of unread books and a big window that opened onto a view of the back yard, the patio, and the swimming pool. I saw Mona down below, baking in the bright sun. She waved languidly to me.

I waved back and stepped away to open my suitcase. I unpacked quickly, got out of my clothes, found my one swimsuit and put it on. I was pretty pale, and there was just the hint of a roll of flab around my middle from too little exercise during the last six months. Well, life in California would take care of all that for me.

I thought of Lisa and my promise to write to her daily. What the hell was I going to tell her about where I was staying? The truth? I'd have to give her a return address. But, of course, she wouldn't necessarily know that was Mona's address—

This was going to be an interesting assignment, I thought. I wondered if Mona was looking forward to it as much as I was. I slung a towel over my shoulder and went downstairs.

3

The pool was big and deep and fashionably free-form. Mona was standing on the diving board as I approached, and when she saw me she executed a neat swan dive, bobbing up in mid-pool. She came up grinning and wet, her short black hair glistening with beads of water.

"Come on in! It's great!"

"Coming," I said.

I wrapped my towel around a stanchion, stepped out on the board, and dived. I could feel my winter-softened muscles protesting as I sprang outward into space. But it was a creditable dive all the same. I breast-stroked under water until I ran out of breath, coming up closer to the far end of the pool than I had expected.

We swam for a while and splashed around, and had a catch with a big gaudy beach ball. Mona's supple body was a delight to behold, dark tan against the white of the bikini, all but nude in the bright sunlight. She seemed delighted to have a playmate. We capered around the pool, in and out of it, like two children.

After perhaps an hour of hectic fun at the pool, we came out and stretched out in the sun on two air mattresses side by side. Kitty appeared with another tray of martinis. I lay blissfully sprawled out, warm and relaxed, thinking of all those poor bastards back in New York on what was probably a cold and drizzly April day. And here I was toasting in the California sun, with a glamorous bikini-clad movie star lying at my side, and a frigid martini in my hand. And palm trees waving overhead. And not a hint of smog in the air. Maybe they didn't permit smog in this part of Los Angeles, I thought. A local ordinance against it, or something.

The lazy afternoon lazied itself away. Mona seemed to be sleeping, so I drank my martini in silence, and soon was in a light doze myself. When I woke, I had a faintly sunburned feeling, and there was nothing on the mattress next to me except Mona's bikini.

I looked around, pulse quickening, and there she was swimming up and down the pool in the nude. I caught sight of smooth tanned buttocks just below the blue-green surface. I gaped like a schoolboy, I have to confess.

She came swimming over to the side of the pool and hauled herself up until her breasts were all but in sight. "Enjoy your nap?" she asked.

"It was just what I needed."

"You were asleep more than an hour. I felt like taking another swim, but

I didn't want to wake you."

"You coming out now?"

"Yes."

"I'll turn my back," I said gallantly.

"Why? Does the sight of a woman's body offend you?"

"Not exactly," I said. "I just thought it was the gentlemanly thing to do."

"I'm not inhibited," she said. "And you're a friend of mine already."

She grabbed the stanchions and hauled herself out of the pool. Her body was dazzling, the breasts high and firm and perfect in size, like two big apples, the nipples pointing upward. Her belly was flat, her hips flaring, her buttocks taut-fleshed and wonderful. She crossed the distance separating the pool from the mattresses with amazing naturalness and aplomb, picked up a towel, casually swabbed the glistening beads of water from her body. As she turned, I could have taken a bite out of her backside just by leaning forward six inches. I resisted the temptation somehow.

Instead of donning the bikini, she put on a lounging robe that came down no further than her hips and thus hardly hid her nakedness at all.

"It's half-past four," she said. "Half-past seven on the time you're accustomed to. I've asked to have dinner ready by six o'clock. Think you can hold out till then?"

"I suppose."

"All right, then. I'm going to go get washed up and dressed, and you can do the same. I'll have Kitty knock for you when cocktails are being served. We'll eat out here on the rear patio. Don't bother dressing up—just sports clothes are fine. We won't be going out tonight."

"Just stay here and relax, is that it?"

"I thought I'd show you one of my movies," she said. "I know you've probably seen them, but I'd like to show you the lot of them, so you can get really familiar with them. I've got my own screening room here."

We went into the house and upstairs. Mona waved to me and headed for a room at the far end of the second floor. I was puzzled at that—the maid had told me that Mona's room adjoined mine—but then it occurred to me that Mona's *bedroom* adjoined mine, but that she probably used a different room for dressing. When one person inhabits a fifteen- or twenty-room house, living habits tend to get decentralized.

I went into my room and put my ear to the connecting door. No sounds from within. Just for the hell of it, I tried the doorknob. The door was locked. Shrugging, I turned away and got out of my suit.

Selecting a book from the ones Mona had supplied—a collection of short stories by Chekhov—I settled down to read for a while. But the sun had left me drowsy and overrelaxed; I turned the pages for fifteen or twenty minutes without getting interested in what I was reading, until finally I decided that the fault was in my lack of attention rather than in old Chekhov's story-telling abilities, and I put the book away. A brisk cold shower left me feeling braced and alert again. I dressed, putting on fresh clothes, and picking up Chekhov again, went out on the little balcony sprouting from my side window and read for a while.

It was a quiet half-hour. No traffic noises, nothing. I could look off to the east and see sprawling downtown L.A., gray in the distance. The sun, big and reddish, was getting lower in the sky behind the palm trees.

At twenty to six, Kitty knocked on my door. "Would you like some cocktails now, Mr. Baldwin?"

"Coming," I said.

I went downstairs with her. The back patio had been turned into an outdoor dining room, complete with table and tablecloth.

"Miss Thorne will be down shortly," Kitty told me. "Can I bring you a daiquiri? Or perhaps another martini?"

"Daiquiri will be fine," I said.

I settled into a comfortable lounge chair, looked out at the palm trees and the swimming pool, and told myself that This Was The Life. Kitty brought me a flawless daiquiri. Why stick to the New York rat race? I asked myself. The Hollywood rat race was no tougher, and a damned sight more lucrative if you had the right contacts, and you could live more graciously in a land where winter never came.

New plans began forming in my head. With the fifty or sixty grand I'd gross from this book, I could buy myself a house out here. Nothing so magnificent as Mona's place, of course, but I could get a pretty good one. Lisa and I could settle down here. I'd be a hot property, as the author of Mona Thorne's best-selling autobiography. Maybe Koren could get me a job like this once a year; there are always plenty of stars looking for a talented and experienced ghost. Or else I could go into movie writing. Maybe ghost the stars' biogs, then do the screenplay of the movie version. Without sweating too much, I could clear ninety or a hundred grand a year, or roughly five times as much as I ever made in my best year of strenuous typewriter-pounding in New York.

It was a nice dream. I sat there letting the daiquiri file all the rough edges off it. By the time Kitty brought me a refill, I was sold on the idea.

Mona arrived midway through the second drink. She was a vision of loveliness in a white strapless sheath that molded to her body like a second skin, rising to the lovely swells of her bosom and supporting them in a stunning way. Smooth tanned shoulders and brown arms stood out in pleasant contrast to the white of the dress. She was wearing only one piece of jewelry, a simple gold necklace. No rings, no earrings, nothing flashy at all. And no makeup. She didn't need it. Her face had a kind of classic perfection that the use of mascara and lipstick would only have ruined.

"Sorry to keep you waiting," she said.

"That's all right. I've been admiring the view."

"This is a lovely time of day."

"If you're in the right frame of mind, every time of day is a lovely time of day," I said. I pulled out a chair for her. I felt like a character in one of my dreams, sitting here on this patio.

Kitty brought Mona a drink. Mona said, "We'll eat in fifteen minutes." Kitty nodded and glided silently away.

Mona looked at me. "Before you get to know me," she said, "I'd like to know something about you. Tell me about yourself, Joey."

"Starting where?"

"Anywhere," she said.

I tipped my glass back, drained it, put it down next to my lounge chair, and looked out across the sumptuous back yard to the gently swaying row of palms. I said, "Born in New York. Bronx, to be specific. Thirty-five years old. Graduated from Evander Childs High School. Went to CCNY, didn't graduate. Two years of college, then two years of the Army. That brings the story up to 1960."

"You move fast."

I shrugged. "I left out some incidental details. Along the way I lost my parents, my virginity, and my illusions. Also my appendix. So much for the color."

"All right."

"In 1960 I was working for a New York newspaper, somewhat on the left side."

She looked at me in alarm. "Were you a Commie?"

"Christ, no. I just needed a job, and there was this liberal newspaper that all the intellectuals read. So I worked for them. As a rewrite man.

"In 1961 the newspaper started hitting some troubles," I said. "They put me on part-time work, three days a week. I started to do some writing. Pulp stuff, to bring in an extra buck. The second story I wrote, I sold. To a science-fiction magazine. Five thousand words, and it took me two afternoons, and I got a hundred bucks for it. A great deal this was, you understand. So I pounded out ten more stories in the next couple of weeks and got them all back. Then I wrote a detective story and sold that. And then some of my rejected sci-fi stuff began to sell too. And pretty soon I was selling pulp as fast as I could grind it out."

"So you quit the newspaper job?"

"Not quite. The paper folded. I wrote full-time for three months and averaged about a hundred bucks a week. Then I got a job with one of the big news magazines. I stayed there three years, got an ulcer, made a lot of money, and tried to write on weekends. Finally I quit. That was ten years ago. I've been a full-time writer ever since."

"You find it lucrative?" she asked.

I shrugged. "I've never had a year that didn't hit well into five figures. On the other hand, I've never had five really high figures. Say I've averaged fifteen grand a year over the last ten years. But I've done a lot of traveling and a lot of loafing, too. It's been okay."

"So this is your first big-time big-money job?" she said.

"Just about," I admitted. "But not my last, I hope."

"It won't be. You'll be set up, after this. You'll be a big name, Joey. You'll be able to name your own price." She smiled torridly at me. "Dinner's ready."

We went to the table. Kitty, impeccable in starched uniform, served. It was a spectacular meal, of restaurant quality, and I mean good restaurant. We began with clams *oreganata*, washed down with a half-bottle of Chablis. Then onion soup, then baked pheasant in truffle sauce, accompanied by wild rice and artichoke hearts and another bottle of wine.

"Does Kitty do the cooking?" I asked.

Mona shook her head. "Only breakfast and lunch. I have a chef for the dinners. He's so good I hardly ever eat out."

"I don't blame you," I said, finishing off the wild rice with gusto.

"You didn't finish your life story," she said. "You mentioned you were married."

I nodded. "Six years ago. It wasn't a smart marriage. It was a marriage for sex, and that kind never works out worth a damn."

Her eyes narrowed. "You don't look like the kind of man who'd need to marry for sex."

"I didn't need to. I wanted to. Laurette and I had nothing else in common except a fondness for a good night's screwing. It took a year for us to discover that we didn't even like each other. After that it was downhill all the way. We've been separated a year and a half. The divorce ought to be coming through soon."

"Won't she want alimony?"

I shrugged. "Wouldn't matter. She's remarrying as soon as she's free. Some rich Wall Street fellow. So for once in her life she isn't being vindictive toward me. She isn't bothering to ask for alimony, or any crap like that."

Kitty unobtrusively cleared the dishes away. There was cognac with the coffee.

"How do you stay so slim on this kind of diet?" I asked.

"Exercise," she said. "And I never eat lunch. Or much of a breakfast." She leaned back, smiling contentedly. "You should have seen me a few years ago, though. When I was so mixed up I didn't know which end was up. My escape was eating. I weighed 175 before I got off that kick. I have a few photos of me in a bathing suit. You should see them. I look like somebody's grandmother."

"I can't visualize it."

"Don't try. It'll spoil a good dinner."

We adjourned to the screening room afterward. Kitty was already there, setting up. It was a small room with a pull-down screen and camera cubicle in the rear. Mona curled up on a big couch facing the screen, and I sat down next to her. She kicked her shoes off and dug her toes cozily under me without comment.

"This is my first starring role," she said, "*Song of Love*, 1963. You probably saw it back then."

I made a noncommittal sound. The truth was that I had never actually seen a Mona Thorne picture, though I didn't think it was healthy to tell her that.

She dropped her head back and puffed at a cigarette. "Vince Clissold directed it," she said. "He was a tyrant, Vince was. It shows in the film, though. Every touch is just right. One of the finest men ever to work in Hollywood. Absolutely incorruptible, he was. Except with sex, of course. He had me in the hay two hours after we were introduced. That was the way Vince was. A magnificent man, a magnificent director. It was an honor to work with him."

"He's making movies in Europe now, isn't he?"

"In France, yes." Her voice was suddenly reflective. "We were thinking of getting married, you know. I was thrilled. Here I was just a kid turned twenty, practically engaged to one of Hollywood's greatest directors. And then he decided to go to Europe where his talent would be appreciated. He asked me to come with him, but of course I couldn't. I had my career to consider." She sighed stagily. "If he had stayed here and I had married him, my whole life might have been different. More stable. I'd have had none of my tragedies. Be sure to put that in the book, Joey. What might have been."

Mona snapped her fingers and the projector hummed to life behind us. I settled down for the show.

The film was better than a decade old, and already it had become dated, something to put away in the archives with *Intolerance* and *Birth of a Nation.* It was a flossy Technicolor love story, complete with lush background music and all, set in San Francisco and the Bay Area. Mona played a bookstore clerk, and her leading man was a professional football player with secret intellectual yearnings. So Mona did her best to seem nonintellectual and one-of-the-gangish, while the football player tried to act bookish and introverted, and naturally each one was disgusted with the other, since what Mona wanted was an All-American he-man, and what the guy wanted was a Kierkegaard-spouting avant-gardenik. So there were the usual twists and turns before both of them got the message, settled down as their own sweet selves, and got married—with the impression left at the end that each would work on the other until they both approached the good old American conformist norm, Mona abandoning her horn-rims and the football player giving up beer, and both turning into a nice adjusted suburban couple.

The picture was pure cotton candy, but Mona was right about the director; Vince Clissold had worked wonders with his nothing of a screenplay. The actors performed as though they believed the silly thing. And there were wonderful little touches in the Frisco fog, camera angles that were artistic without being arty, color work that was delicate and evocative. A tremendous amount of technical proficiency had been expended on an utterly trite and trivial story. I began to see why Clissold had broken with the Hollywood gold mine and taken his talents off to a country where he'd be allowed to put them to some worthwhile use.

A minor surprise of the film was Mona. She could act. She had a fine comic flair, a good sense of timing. How much of that was innate ability, and how much had stemmed from Clissold's tyrannical direction, I wouldn't know until I had seen her later films. But I was impressed.

She hadn't changed much in ten years. In the film, she had a kind of wide-eyed innocence that she had certainly lost over the years, a spiritual rather than a physical innocence. (I was willing to bet she had lost the latter before she was fifteen.) But the body was the same supple instrument, the walk was the same pantherish graceful thing. She had been a little smaller in the bust back then, a little wider in the hips and rear. Even so, it was hard to believe that a decade had passed since that film had gone into the cans.

I wondered if Mona were fated to be the kind of Hollywood glamor queen who remained virtually unchanged from age twenty to age fifty—and then came apart overnight, crumbling into old age. It was a pitiful thing to contemplate.

The film, a long one, ground to its predictable end some two hours after the credits had flashed on the screen. I sat blinking as the lights went on.

"What did you think of it?" Mona asked immediately, too eagerly.

"A very fine job," I said. "Clissold really knew his stuff. He could shape a film beautifully. And I liked the acting, Mona."

"You don't need to butter me up."

"I'm not. I thought you had a really good light style there. Was this your first film?"

"The first one I had any decent part in. There were three walk-ons first. I think I was on the screen a grand total of eight minutes in the three films. This is the first one that counts." She rose, stretching and yawning with infinite grace. "Ten o'clock," she said. "One o'clock your time. I suggest we call it a day. You can sleep as late as you like tomorrow, and then you'll be adjusted to local time."

"What will we do tomorrow?"

"Oh, maybe go on a picnic," she said. "Or sightsee. Or go riding. We'll talk about it in the morning."

We went upstairs. I waved good night to her and we went into our respective bedrooms. I could hear her moving about behind the adjoining door.

I undressed. Kitty had already turned down the sheets. I took another shower—the room had its own private bathroom, of course—and slipped into bed, enjoying the feel of the expensive linens against my naked body. Moonlight streamed in. I turned on a nightlamp and read for about fifteen minutes without taking in very much. Then I switched off the light.

I never sleep well in strange places the first night. I lay awake, eyes open, looking at the moonlight. I wondered what Lisa was doing this evening, whether she was thinking of me. I wondered how this job was going to turn out. I thought of Mona, in the next room. I wondered just how things were going to go, with the two of us living in this big house. Was I supposed to make a pass at her? Or was I just one of her servants, to be treated with familiarity but not to be allowed intimacy? I remembered the way she had come naked out of the swimming pool. A woman has no inhibitions about showing her body to her dog or to her cat, and maybe not even to her butler. Had she displayed herself to me because she regarded me as sexually out of bounds?

I wondered.
Then I stopped wondering.
The doorknob of the connecting door was starting to turn.

4

Mona came into the room like a silent sleepwalker, only she was wide awake. By the moonlight I saw that she was wearing a shortie nightgown that was nothing more than a gauzy white cloud. The proud thrusts of her breasts were clearly visible under it, and as the moonlight struck her waist I could see that she hadn't bothered to put on the panties that usually accompany shortie nightgowns.

"Are you awake?" she asked softly.

"Yes."

"I can't get to sleep," she said. "I came to visit for a while. Mind?"

"Not at all."

She wasn't being subtle. She hadn't come for conversation, and I knew it. This wasn't the swimming-pool bit. She was all but naked, and if I lifted that nightgown of hers I'd see all she had, and this was a bedroom.

The bitch, I thought. I was indignant more than anything else. *She thinks she owns me.*

Every man has his pride. Only when his pride has been taken away can he let himself be bought by a woman. A gigolo is a man who has been psychologically castrated, whether he knows it or not.

Mona was trying to make a gigolo out of me.

She had hired me to do a job of literary hack work for her. But that wasn't where the deal ended. Obviously. Otherwise why had she moved me into her house? Why had she put me in an adjoining bedroom? Why had she come into my room?

She wanted stud service, that was why.

There was nothing personal about it. How could there have been? She hadn't ever laid eyes on me. But here she was, a wealthy actress between pictures and also probably between lovers, and I was elected to scratch her itch for her.

In my first irrational burst of masculine pride I nearly told her to get the hell out of there. The words were rattling around in the back of my mouth and I kept them imprisoned there, with an effort. I wanted to tell her that I didn't like to be seduced, that I wanted to be the pursuer or nothing, that sex didn't mean a damn to me unless I had achieved some sort of conquest. And what kind of conquest was this? I was being bought, and I wasn't being given anything to say in the matter.

Then I came to my senses.

I swallowed all the things I was going to say. It was a magical transformation. There I was, bursting with a kind of schoolboy pride, a priggish moralizing load of crap about the relationship of the sexes in making sexual advances, and a moment later she was standing in profile with the moonlight illuminating the tips of her breasts and the rounded glory of her ass, and I was forgetting all my Boy Scout stuff and simply silently thanking the universe that there was a woman like this in my bedroom waiting to be entertained.

I got out of bed. I was naked, and she looked at me and smiled, as though she liked what she saw.

I smiled back. I walked over to her, where she stood by the window, and I slipped the nightie easily up over her head. Moonlight bathed her nakedness. She moved toward me, and her body was warm and exciting against me, her breasts firm, the nipples hard. Her lips went to mine. I felt her tongue running around my lips, then plunging into my mouth.

My hands stroked the silken smoothness of her back, then slipped lower, down to her tanned satiny buttocks. They had a springy feel, resilient, exciting. Her eyes were wide open and looking into mine. She seemed to have an almost mocking look in them.

I could practically read her mind.

I could practically hear her thinking, *Here's this guy who wants to be independent and self-willed, but he's just so much clay, really, and I can shape him into anything I goddamn please, just the way I shape everybody else.*

I saw that smile in her eyes and I hated her. But my body didn't hate her. My body didn't worry about matters of pride. My body was simple and direct about its needs, and it wanted her whatever the price in ego.

She was running her hands down my body now, doing thrilling things, and her teeth were gently nibbling at my earlobes, and her breath was hot against my jawbone. I cupped her breasts, fondling them, feeling the tautness of them. She was breathing faster and her thighs were moving and her lips were parted and moving with no words coming out. I kissed her all over that beautiful pantherish body, kissed every square inch of her there in the moonlit darkness, and she literally throbbed with animal passion.

"That's it, lover," she moaned, as we stood entwined by the window. "That's what I like."

Then, body pressed against body, we advanced toward the bed. I lay down and she clambered up like a wildcat, and then we twisted over on our sides, staring into each other's eyes and smiling.

It was a contest of nerves.

It was a battle of bodies.

I compared her with Lisa, and with Laurette. Making love with Laurette had been a kind of contest too, a contest of conflicting personalities. Laurette was a kind of sexual vampire. She tried to consume you, to devour you. When you were entangled with her, you had to keep alert at all times, because what she was doing had nothing of love about it. She tried to draw the life force out of a man.

And Lisa? There was something childlike, something innocent about Lisa, for all her woman's body, for all her knowing ways. It was as though each time was the first time for her. She hadn't been any virgin when I met her, Lord knows, but yet it had seemed that way. And each time I had made it with Lisa, there had been that element of surprise, of wonder, the little gasp of amazement as the full power of the act swept over her. She always seemed to be taken unawares by the frenzy of it.

There was nothing virginal about Mona, though. She was probably the most experienced woman I had ever been to bed with, barring none. She knew everything and she displayed it right in the first five minutes of our embrace, throwing her arts at me as a challenge. She was defying me to stay with her. She was defying me to prove my manhood. She was saying with her body, *Here's what I can do. Can you take it?*

I took it.

I took it and I gave back some of my own. Our lovemaking seemed to go on forever. The neatly made bed became a rumpled ruin. Pillows and sheets went sliding to the floor as our bodies writhed and twisted. Damnably, her eyes stayed open, still wearing that ironic smile.

Was she frigid? Was that her grim secret?

Wasn't I stirring her in any way?

Damn you, get that knife out of my guts, I thought angrily. I knew that this was a test, that she was putting me through my paces right at the outset. She wanted to know what I could do. She wanted to find out right here and now whether I was going to be boss or lackey.

I was drenched with sweat and my back ached and my heart was pounding so hard I thought it would rip right through my ribs. But I stayed with her. I pressed her down with my weight, in a way that was almost as sadistic as it was loving. She was hurting me emotionally by her coldness, and I wanted to get back at her, to rip her apart, to split her in two if I could.

Suddenly I felt her entire body throb.

It was an incredible experience. What she was having wasn't just an orgasm, it was an eruption. Her eyes lost their ironic gleam, and a moment later they were tight shut, and her lovely face was distorted and twisted with the intensity of what was happening to her, and she made a gasping sound that was more a sound of pain than anything else, as though the intensity of it was searing her nerve ends and frying her brain. Her body heaved convulsively, her back arched, lifting me high off the mattress, and for one timeless moment I could hear nothing but the rush of blood in my ears, and then she dropped back to the bed as though she had grabbed a high-tension cord and suddenly had released it.

We were still.

I was stunned and awed by the performance. That was what it was, a performance, a demonstration of the sexual art. Mona had led me on almost contemptuously, withholding any sign that she was actively enjoying what I had been doing to her and then, at some chosen inner moment of capitulation, she had pulled out all the stops, given her pent-up energies full rein, and turned on an explosive display of physical pyrotechnics.

We were silent in the dark for perhaps ten or fifteen minutes. Then I slipped free of her, got up, walked to the window. A cool breeze blew in, drying the beads of sweat on my body. I leaned on my knee, staring at the big cat curled up on my bed.

"Get me a cigarette, will you?" she said in a throaty voice, breaking the silence that had prevailed for almost an hour.

"Here." I found a pack on the nightstand, put two in my mouth, lit them, gave one to her. She smoked wordlessly for a few moments.

I said, "You always make love like that?"

"I'd like to. There aren't enough men around who can do their share."

"Did I do my share?"

"Your share and plenty more," she said. She sat up, blew smoke toward the ceiling. "Do you hate me?"

"Why do you ask?"

"You ought to hate me."

"Why?"

"Because I'm a bitch. I was putting you through torture just now on that bed."

"I wouldn't mind that kind of torture every night," I said automatically.

She saw through me easily. "Sure you would. You'd run screaming out of here in a week. Any man would. I've seen it happen. I can burn a man out, do you know that? I've done it. You'll learn about it when you start writing my book. Nobody can take what I just handed out for long. Nobody."

I stubbed out my cigarette. "Do you want me to play the idiot and try to test myself?"

"No. It isn't necessary. Other men have suffered that way already." She grinned. "We can be a little more relaxed from now on. I'll confess something to you. I couldn't stand much of that either. What we did just now, it was a little superhuman. I never dreamed we'd get that far. You've got a very special talent. Has any woman ever told you that?"

"I don't want to be immodest," I said.

"You've had plenty in your day, haven't you?"

"More than one, yes."

"Any like me?"

"No," I said honestly. "Nobody even approaching you. And yes, I'm glad of it. One of you a lifetime is plenty."

She left the bed, came over, kissed my cheek in a sisterly way. "You're an honest man, Joey. I appreciate that. I haven't known many honest men. Don't change, will you? Don't go Hollywood on me."

"I'll try not to," I promised her.

She scooped up her nightie and headed for the door. I looked at the curve of her body, that lovely back swelling out into the twin mounds of her buttocks, and there was a new dryness in my throat.

"Leaving?" I said.

She nodded. "You need your sleep. If I stay here you won't get any. Good night, lover."

"Good night, Mona."

She tiptoed through the door, closing it behind her. I picked the pieces of my bed linens off the floor and got them into a semblance of order, then stretched out again. As soon as I closed my eyes, the burning image of Mona's nakedness blazed behind my lids.

She was a lustful one, all right. I could see how she could drive a man out of his mind.

She wasn't going to do that to me. But, I knew, I was never going to be the same again when Mona Thorne got finished with me.

Saturday was a restful day.

I didn't wake until noon, to begin with. When I came downstairs half an hour later, I found Mona on the patio, in a one-piece sports outfit, deep in a hardback book. I looked at it. *The Magic Mountain*, Thomas Mann. She was about halfway through with it.

"Morning, Joey," she said casually. "Kitty will give you breakfast inside."

Kitty gave me breakfast inside. I ate lightly. When I finished, Mona suggested that we go for a drive, and I had no objections.

She had a trim little Alfa-Romeo, a cool white like her slacks and like last night's gown. She liked white, it seemed. I settled in next to her and she hit the accelerator and off we went.

We drove up into the canyon country north of Los Angeles, and then we made a big loop and dropped down to the sea, past Pacific Palisades to where we could look down and see the blue Pacific rolling in hard against the rocky beach. She didn't say much, but drove at seventy miles an hour with a kind of grim-jawed efficiency. She frightened me a little, I have to admit.

On the way back I suggested that she let me drive. She looked at me sourly, as though she were a society matron and I had just suggested taking a trial run in bed with her debutante daughter. "I don't let anyone drive this car," she said. "Sorry. It's a quirk of mine."

"Okay," I said. "I wouldn't want to get you irritated."

"You can drive my other cars," she said, backing down a little. "Not this. Nobody's ever driven this car but me. Nobody ever will. I've had it tuned to my personal rhythms. You understand? I couldn't bear to think of someone else's foot on the accelerator."

She sounded oddly like a possessive roué proud of his ex-virgin mistress. I shrugged the subject away.

We got back to her place around four in the afternoon. We had a swim and some drinks, then some sunbathing until the sun dipped out of sight. Dinner was on the patio again, by candlelight. Filet mignon was the main course, washed down by a spectacular Chambertin. After dinner she took me down to see her wine cellar. I was flabbergasted by it—cases and cases and cases of wine, all of it the best. It looked more like the cellar of some three-star restaurant than a private accumulation. I picked up a dusty bottle, saw that it was Chateau Latour '29, saw that she had a whole case of it, and coughed in surprise.

"Where'd you get all this stuff?" I asked.

"My first husband started the collection. Teddy Burns. Teddy loved wine and he had the money to afford the best. He would spend hours poring over catalogs. The first year we were married, he spent 20,000 dollars on wine. He taught me how to appreciate it. After he died I retained his wine merchant and we keep the cellar replenished. We just laid in twenty cases this month."

"But there must be thousands of bottles down here," I said. "Even at two bottles a day, you couldn't possibly ever drink it all, Mona!"

"Wine's an investment," she said. "A better one than most stocks. Any time I need the cash, I can sell off some of the wines." She tapped a case. "It's as good as gold. Better, in some ways. You can't drink gold."

Mona had the same hard-headed attitude toward the paintings scattered in such profusion around the house. In fact, I never really did understand whether she bought paintings because she liked them or because she thought they would appreciate in value. One thing was certain: she was loaded. She was worth a couple of million at the very least. And probably a good deal more.

That night we saw her second movie. This was a foreign intrigue cloak-and-dagger thing called *An Affair in Marrakesh*, and she played a sultry Arab dancing girl who ran a thriving spy business on the side, double-crossing everyone in sight until she got her expected comeuppance in the last reel. It had 1964-style Hollywood eroticism, by which I mean that there was a plenitude of shots of Mona in revealing costumes, but yet nothing really sexy. The allegedly provocative scenes had a kind of slick-magazine wholesomeness about them despite an intendedly steamy atmosphere.

I mentioned this to her and she said, "Of course. Teddy directed it, and Teddy was queer. So naturally there was no vitality in the sex scenes. They were all cardboard pasteups of the real things."

"Were you married to him then?"

"No, we didn't get married till '65. But I was dating him while we made the film." She smiled. "I knew he was gay, of course. I tried to help him direct the sex scenes, but he insisted on doing them his way."

"You knew he was gay, and yet you married him?" I asked, puzzled. "Can I ask why?"

"All in good time," she said. "Let's not rush things, shall we?"

That night she came into my bedroom again. There was none of the frenzied sexual acrobatics of the night before, though. She simply slipped into my bed and surrounded me with her body and we made love in a direct and uncomplicated way, coming quickly to a tender and mutually satisfactory climax. Last night she had played the siren; tonight, she was playing the role of the loving wife. Let her have her fun, I thought. Certainly I was having mine.

She stayed with me half the night. We made love a second time, half-asleep, and then she left. The taste of her was on my lips, the smell of her breasts was in my nostrils, as I fell asleep.

It was more of the same on Sunday. Up around eleven, breakfast together in the dining alcove. Then we played tennis on a court that turned out to be hidden away on the far side of the house, and after we had both worked up a good sweat we swam and sunbathed away the afternoon. Another gourmet-style dinner, another session in the screening room afterward.

Her third picture was a Western—an adult Western. Mona was the town whore, and it ended up with her sacrificing herself on behalf of the clean-cut young hero whose virginity she had stolen. He was in a gunfight with the villain, an old wrangler who had incestuous designs on his step-daughter, who was the hero's virginal sweetheart. The two men clashed, and finally when it looked certain that the peach-fuzzed hero was going to get nailed, Mona stepped in the way of the gunfire, getting a shot be-tween her bountiful breasts. That had provided a chance for a censor-teas-ing shot of the hero ripping away Mona's blouse, baring her breasts in his hurry to look at the fatal wound.

It was also a Teddy Burns movie, but this time the sex had been handled sexily. I didn't discuss it with Mona. I wondered if this had been her do-ing—if she had worked some kind of magic spell over the effeminate di-rector she would soon take in marriage.

We had a couple of drinks after the screening, and then went up to bed. I felt strangely troubled by the weekend, and thought about it for a while until I saw why. I had been cooped up with Mona all weekend. We had-n't met a single other person aside from Kitty. Didn't she have any friends? Didn't the phone ever ring? Was she hiding me from Hollywood society?

I didn't like it. I was starting to feel like a prisoner. I didn't want to be the center of her attention this way. I felt almost as though this were a hon-eymoon.

That night Mona didn't come into my bedroom. I lay awake for perhaps half an hour, waiting for her, but she didn't show. Finally I went to the door and gently tried it.

It was locked.

Apparently Mona wasn't in the mood tonight.

Shrugging, I went back to bed and burrowed into the pillow. I didn't sleep well. Naked temptresses kept drifting through my subconscious all night.

5

The next morning, after breakfast, Mona said, "We'll start the book today, okay?"

"Sure. We'd better get to it."

"How do you want to work it?" she asked me. I didn't really know. I hadn't ever done this kind of thing before, and I hadn't given too much thought to the matter since getting the assignment. I said, "Suppose we just go over the general outline of your life, first, so I can put together a kind of scenario. After that I can question you on specific dramatic points."

"Okay."

"You just talk, and we'll take it all down on the tape recorder," I said. "Then we can have it transcribed. I'll use your own words wherever possible in the book."

We set up the recorder on the patio near the pool. The morning sun was bright and hot, and we were both in bathing suits, Mona in a bikini of her favorite white. I had a notepad and a pencil in case I wanted to make jottings.

I switched on the recorder. It didn't inhibit her at all, as I had feared it might. Of course. Someone accustomed to spending hours in front of the cameras wouldn't worry about a mere microphone.

"Where do you want to start?" she asked.

"Anywhere. Your childhood. Your early experiences in Hollywood. I can assemble it chronologically later."

"Might as well start at the beginning," she said. She crossed her legs, leaned back, and started to talk.

She had been born, she said, in Ohio, during the war. Mona Thorne was her real name, she insisted. Her father was a storekeeper. She had two brothers and a young sister. The family hadn't had much money.

She did a little acting in high school, was told by everybody that she was so beautiful she ought to be in the movies, and finally, at the age of eighteen, she packed up and went west to Hollywood.

There followed a year and a half of trying to get noticed, then three bit parts in swift succession, followed by her first starring role, in the Vince Clissold picture. Also an affair with Clissold and talk of marriage.

Then Clissold left for Europe. Mona, now an established star with a fat contract, turned next to balding, pansyish Teddy Burns, a veteran of twenty years in Hollywood and considered one of the best directors of swishy comedies. She met Burns at the end of 1964, made three movies with him between 1964 and 1966.

"You had an affair with him before you married him?" I asked.

Mona nodded. "He was terribly frightened of sex. He hadn't slept with a woman in ten years. I told him I was going to make him normal again."

"Did you?"

"Not quite. I tried. Jesus, did I try! I gave him all I had, and he liked it, but he liked the boys better. Or at least he liked them just as much."

"And then he killed himself in '67."

"That's right. He was having this affair with Billy Joe Hart, and Billy Joe ran short of cash and peddled the whole story to a gossip columnist. The columnist was going to print it, and he called up Teddy to try to get bought off. Teddy wouldn't buy him. Instead he went into his bedroom and shot himself. That's the room you're living in now. I found him right by the window."

"You were very upset?"

"Heartbroken. I loved him."

"Even though he was gay?"

"Because he was gay," she said. "Listen, that man came to me and begged me to marry him. He wanted me to save him from being a homosexual. He said everyone in Hollywood knew about him, and he'd prove that it wasn't so even if he had to ball me in front of Grauman's Chinese. And it was working. I was saving him."

"Even though he was sleeping with Billy Joe Hart at the time?"

She scowled at me. "So he lapsed a little. He slid back. And they drove him to death for it. But he was changing. I know he was."

"Okay," I said, watching the tape spools going around. "Let's move on."

After Burns' suicide, she said, she went alcoholic. She went on a binge that lasted almost a year. She had very little recollection of what went on during that time, although she did remember having had a lot of sex, including some with her late husband's old playmates. In Hollywood, I was learning fast, the distinction between gay and straight wasn't a very sharp one. Everyone was handsome, everyone was golden, and everybody—or at least plenty of people—played around on both sides of the line, depending on whim and opportunity.

Her lush phase reached its peak in 1968, when she began work on a big historical epic, only to get summarily booted from the job when she showed up stinking drunk five days in a row, disrupting the shooting and sending the production schedules to hell in a hand basket. After that it was back to the bottle harder than ever, until she was rescued from alcoholism by a knight in shining armor named Lee Crosswell.

Crosswell was another director, the third one Mona had been in love with. I had happened to meet him at a party in New York around 1967, and I remembered him as a man of about forty-five, with a lean, craggy face, all chin and cheekbones, and the deepest, saddest, most bloodshot eyes I had ever seen on anyone. He spoke in a mournful bass voice, and never looked you straight in the eye.

"Lee was a tormented man," Mona told the microphone, while I sat back and soaked it all in. "During the war he'd been given some kind of torture by the Japanese, and when he finally got out of prison his nerves were completely shot. He couldn't sleep, because he had the most terrible nightmares. He tried drinking at first, and then psychoanalysis, and neither of them worked. So then he went to some wild parties and a friend of his got him hooked on dope."

Crosswell became a second redemption project for Mona. She wanted to get him off the stuff, and he wanted to get her off the booze. Eventually Mona stopped drinking, and at the end of '68 Crosswell got her a small part in one of his pictures; he couldn't get her the lead because of studio opposition. The word went around that Mona Thorne was going to make a comeback. She was watched very carefully, because she could be a valuable property if she stayed sober on the set.

"I made the movie," she said, "and I stayed sober, and it was decided that I could be trusted with a bigger part. They lined up an important role for me for the fall of '69. I spent all spring studying for it."

But Crosswell, it seemed, spent all spring trying to lure Mona into sharing his addiction. He had reached that stage in his own private hell where he wanted the whole world down there suffering with him, and he decided to begin with Mona. She resisted. She didn't want any part of the stuff. Pretty soon it became a stalemate; she couldn't get him to go for a cure, and he couldn't get her to try a shot of H. But at least she had stopped drinking, and she deluded herself into believing that Crosswell was starting to come to grips with smack and might soon break its hold on him.

In June of '69, she and Crosswell were secretly married, after having lived together for almost a year. Two weeks after the wedding, Crosswell went for a drive late at night, blew a tire on a freeway, and got flipped into the opposite stream of traffic. He was killed instantly, mangled practically beyond recognition.

There was heroin in the house. Mona was alone and frightened and depressed. Somehow she made the transition and started putting needles in her arms.

Sixteen months of addiction followed. Naturally, there was no moviemaking now. She lived in seclusion, getting along comfortably on the income from her accumulated capital—after six major movies and two dead husbands she had piled up quite a bit—while the narcotics took hold of her life.

"Then I met Mark Robinson," she said. "He was a society doctor, around thirty-five, very handsome. A bachelor. I passed out in front of his office, that's how it started. He took me inside and saw the needle-marks and next thing I knew I was living with him and he was giving me the cure. Christ, I suffered through that cure. He knew all the tricks. It was cold turkey for a while, and then when the withdrawal symptoms got bad he had some kind of substitute drug for me, and when that didn't work he could get morphine, for medical purposes, and taper me off on that. We became engaged, of course. I got free of the addictions. And then it turned out that Mark was a high-priced abortionist, specializing in illegal abortions for underage girls."

The D.A. closed in on Robinson, who saw not only his lucrative practice but his entire cushy life collapsing. Without his license, he'd have to give up the yacht and the sports cars and the big parties and all the other nice things he'd become accustomed to. So while the indictment was being prepared, he chose a quick-acting poison from his medical supplies and finished himself off.

It was the third time in less than five years that Mona's beloved had met a premature end. Small wonder that she cracked up so quickly and so hard.

The first time it had been alcohol. The second time, narcotics. This time it was sex.

"I could be had," she said. "Easily. You've got to understand the difference between a woman who can be had, in Hollywood, and an ordinary girl out here. The ordinary girls can be had, too. But they do it for love, or they do it for money, or they do it to get themselves good roles. There isn't a woman under fifty in this whole goddamn town who won't spread for somebody if she has a good reason.

"But I didn't even bother with a reason. All I wanted was sex, the more of it the better. Delivery boys and handymen and young actors and anybody else who came near me. Hundreds of them. Sex was my drug. If I didn't get it three times a night, preferably from three different guys, I was miserable. Absolutely miserable. I was on fire, you know how it is?"

"I can guess," I said. The tape reel ended and I slipped a new one on.

"How long did this phase last, Mona?"

"Till the beginning of this year," she said. "Then one day I walked into a crazy church in downtown L.A. Just a store-front deal, you know. And there was this big-nosed preacher talking about sin, and some old dried-out broads from Iowa down on their knees repenting things they hadn't even done, and I got down there with them, and all of a sudden I started to talk. I told about just a few of the things I'd been doing. And the whole place became quiet and everyone began to look at me, and I went on and on and on. Finally the preacher called me aside and patted me on the head and said, 'How about a consultation this afternoon after the service, so I can help you save your soul?' And I was willing to try anything once, so I said okay, and I waited."

"And?"

"And after the old ladies from Iowa cleared out, I went into the preacher's office in back. And he sat me down and started to talk to me, and I told him some of my troubles, and he got sympathetic as hell. So sympathetic that he came over and put his hand up my dress and started feeling me. I was so hysterical by that point that I didn't know what was happening, and next thing I know he's got my dress up around my elbows, and he's climbing on me to give me some more spiritual consolation. So I pushed him off and got the hell out, and somehow since that day I've had my bearings again. I haven't been a nympho."

"I don't follow the conversion," I said.

"Neither do I," Mona answered with a grin. "Except perhaps that it taught me that nobody was righteous, that everybody was phony. I don't know. All I know is that from that day on I stopped chasing men. I was back on the beam again. I didn't feel desperate about sex. I can take it or leave it now. I proved that last night."

"Yes," I said. "That you did."

"Ever since January. Four months now."

I tapped my pencil against the notepad. "This somewhat spoils the climax of the book I had in mind," I said.

"Why?"

"The way I heard your story from my agent, you had experienced a real religious rebirth. You had joined some church and went to services regularly, and it was the staff and mainstay of your life."

"That's a lot of bullshit."

"Obviously. But this was the way I figured the book to end. Redeemed by God, you know. Practically make a nun out of you. The sinner returned to the fold. And instead it turns out you went into some quack church and got redeemed through sheer disgust for so-called righteous people."

She looked at me for a long moment. "Do you want to write it the other way?"

"I want the book to go over big," I said.

"We'll do it the way you lined it out," she told me with a faint grin. "Make up a lot of stuff about my spiritual adviser and how I take all my problems to him. It'll put the book over big in the Bible Belt. The more I think of it, the more I see that the ending is no good as it stands. It's got to be a religious ending. I've got to be transfigured by communion with the Lord. I've got to look like a second Mary Magdalene, Joey."

I began to get a little troubled. "But suppose somebody says it isn't true?"

"Who?" she demanded. "Nobody knows my personal life that well. For all anybody knows, I do have a spiritual adviser." She shook her head vigorously. "This is no time to start getting artistic qualms, Joey. Why did you take this assignment on, anyway?"

"To make money."

"Right. And the way to make money is to tell the people what they want to hear." Her eyes gleamed with excitement. "Now, look at my story the way it really happened. I got into mess after mess and finally got out of it through my own efforts. Nobody helped me. I just woke up one day and decided it was stupid to throw my life away in boozing and sex. And I had the strength and courage to redeem myself."

"Okay," I said. "Isn't that an inspirational story?"

"Crap," she said. "You can't go telling that to Americans. It's a good pulp story, sure. The hero of a pulp story is always supposed to solve things through his own efforts. But not this kind of story. Not real life. In real life you must get help. You turn to God, or to Freud, or to the power of love, or some such thing. Because the millions of people who are going to buy this book can't help themselves. They're a bunch of spineless jellyfish. That's all ninety percent of the American public is, Joey. And they're the ones who'll read this book. You think executives will read it? You think professional people will read it? Don't be silly. Those are people who know how to do things for themselves. And they're too busy doing them to read a trash book about an unimportant movie actress. But you take all the little idiots with their little houses and little jobs. They can't help themselves. They're stuck in the muck for good, and the one hope of their lives is that God will come along and work a miracle and maybe drop a million dollars down in the mud next to them. And the kind of story they want to read is of a girl who was in trouble and ground down by adversity and redeemed by some outside force. You get me, Joey? You see the truth of what

I'm telling you?"

"Yeah," I said. I stared at her in amazement. I hadn't heard anything so cynical since my last conversation with my agent. And she was practically ecstatic about her philosophy.

The funny thing was, she was right. People read books to identify with the lead characters. And when it's a real-life book, they identify even more. They sin vicariously with Mona, and then they share in her redemption. If I showed Mona as saving herself through will power and fortitude, the way she had actually done it, identification would be lost, because all the readers have no will power and fortitude. True enough.

She put down the microphone. "We'll work out a good story when we get to that end of the book. Let's knock off for now and take a swim. I've been talking an hour and a half, and I'm pretty hot and tired."

I shut off the recorder, and a moment later we were both splashing around in the pool.

It occurred to me that I really didn't need Mona any more for this assignment. I had the bones of the story down, and I could handle it from here on in like it was a novel I was writing. The whole thing could be purely synthetic. All I needed was some snapshots of the important characters, so I could take care of the physical descriptions, and it didn't matter otherwise how I handled it. I could make up dialog, situations, the works. Reality didn't enter into the project except superficially.

But no. No sense deliberately hoking it up. I would do a conscientious job. Day after day I would question Mona, until her story took shape in my mind as though I had actually lived it, and then I would set it down on paper. The truth, except where it was necessary to change the truth for reasons of popular taste.

That was the proper way to do things, I thought. It displayed integrity.

It also would keep me close to Mona for a longer time, I realized.

You aren't falling in love with her, are you, Joey? Falling in love with this cynical devil-bitch?

What about Lisa?

Lisa! I hadn't even written to her! It was Monday, and I'd been here since Friday, and I hadn't written. Or even thought of her much.

Mona swam up against me. Her legs wrapped themselves around mine in the water. Her hands were busy, doing things to me below the surface.

"Having fun?" I asked.

"I always have fun."

"Can I have some fun too?"

"Anything you like," she said.

I paddled over until she was against the side of the pool. Then I pushed her bikini halter up, baring her breasts. I put my hands on them.

I caressed them for a couple of moments. She grinned at me encouragingly. Then I saw a calculating expression creep into her eyes.

A lustful expression.

"Want to fuck me?" she asked.

"Of course."

"Right here? Right in the pool?"

"I want to see if it works under water," I said.

She laughed. "It does."

"How do you know?"

"I've tried it," she said with a brittle laugh. She broke away from me suddenly, swimming past me to the shallow end of the pool. She stood up, not bothering to pull the top of her bikini down over her breasts. She looked at me mockingly.

"Come get me," she said.

"Maybe I won't bother."

"It would be worth your while," she said. Cunningly, artfully, she pulled her halter off completely and tossed it out of the pool. Then she reached below the surface, fumbled for a moment, held her panties aloft, tossed them negligently behind her.

She was nude, now. And waiting for me.

Feeling vaguely like a bull following a red cape, I swam toward her until I reached my depth, then waded the rest of the way. Like the teaser she was, she waited until I was about ten feet from her, then turned and scrambled up to the patio. A nude sprite, she raced down to the end of the pool opposite me and ran out onto the diving board.

She stood there.

She was unutterably beautiful, her tawny naked body gleaming in the noontime sun. She balanced there, making the board quiver with her weight, and her breasts swayed gently. I got out of the pool, came down to her end of it, and walked out on the board. She waggled her buttocks at me, then turned to face me. She was standing at the very end of the board.

She stuck her tongue out at me like a ten-year-old. "You can't catch me, you can't catch me, you can't catch me!" she chanted raucously.

I stepped toward her. She did a backflip and went into the water in a graceful display of thighs and breasts and buttocks. I dove in after her. She was halfway to the other end of the pool, but I swam after her as though an Olympic gold medal were at stake.

I caught up with her. She kicked at me, but I got one arm around her waist, the other around her breasts, and pulled her down under the water. She writhed and struggled and hammered on my chest with her fists, but I held her there a couple of seconds, then a couple more. I let her up and she emerged choking and spluttering, her eyes streaming. For a moment she did nothing but gasp. Then she flung herself at me with a kind of demonic intensity, ripping my trunks down over my hips and straddling my body with hers, locking her ankles behind me.

I seized her breasts. She gasped as my body knifed at hers. We moved wildly in the water, some thrashing eight-limbed sea monster. Water was in my eyes, and I couldn't see a thing, but I could feel. Could feel the warmth of her breasts, the hardness of her nipples, the whiplash action of her body against mine.

With a clap of thunder, I reached fulfillment, and she got there in the same instant, and we drifted apart, both of us hauling in breath. She smiled at me, all the teasing gone, all the aggressiveness burned out of her.

"That was fun," she said.

"Yeah," I panted. "Strenuous, but fun."

"That's the best kind of fun."

Then, abruptly, Kitty appeared on the patio, running toward us. She didn't seem to notice the fact that Mona and I were both naked in the water.

"Miss Thorne!" she yelled. "Miss Thorne! Mr. Marshall's here! I couldn't keep him out! He wants to see you, Miss Thorne! He's inside, looking for you!"

6

I shot Mona a what-the-hell-is-this glance, and she scowled and said, "Put your suit back on. This is going to be a damned nuisance."

My bathing suit was around my ankles. I hauled it up. Mona clambered up out of the pool, put her halter back on, and was just pulling the panties up when a muscular-looking fellow came lumbering out onto the patio. Mona stared at him, her bare buttocks taut as she bent to pull the panties up over them.

"Get the hell out of here, Clint," she said in a flat, even voice. "You know you've got no goddamn business coming around here."

"Shut up," he told her. He looked at me. I was still in the pool, in shallow water. "Who's your fag boyfriend, Mona? Looks like somebody new."

I was getting annoyed. I climbed slowly out of the pool, shaking the water off.

I looked him over.

He was just a kid. He might have been no more than twenty. In Hollywood, people are considered adults at fifteen, mature at twenty, old at thirty. This kid looked like a native Angeleno. He was about six feet four, all muscles. He was deeply tanned, his skin having that look of having been exposed to the sun for many years.

He had a kind of phony Hollywood prettiness about him. He was so handsome that it was repelling. His nose was short and snubbed and redolent of plastic surgery; his lips were full and pursed into bows; his chin was firm; his cheekbones were strong and jutting. His neck was like a bull's, and his head had that squarish contour that is considered the acme of masculine perfection by the producers of the sort of films he no doubt appeared in.

He also looked strong as hell.

He ignored me and said to Mona, "I've been trying to reach you all week, honey."

"I told Kitty I didn't want to talk to you."

"I got the message," he said. His voice was a smooth liquid purr. He talked and held himself as though he were on a sound stage. Like everybody else in this crazy city, he lived in some kind of private self-dramatizing fantasy world on which reality impinged only now and then. "How come you don't want to see me any more, Mona? It was good between us, wasn't it? Every time. Right there in the pool. You've been fucking him in the pool, haven't you? I can tell. I can see the look on your face."

"Will you get out of here, Clint?" Mona repeated.

"When I feel like it." He looked flatly at me.

"Who the hell are you?"

"My name's Baldwin," I said. "I'm a writer."

"What studio?"

"No studio. I write books. Magazine articles. I'm doing a book with Miss Thorne right now."

Pretty-boy guffawed. "The story of her life, huh? Well, you can put in a damned big chapter about me! Come around some time next year and I'll dictate it to you. Meanwhile, suppose you get your clothes on and split. Me and Mona have some important things to talk about."

"Hold on, Clint," Mona said. "Just take your muscle-bound carcass out of here. I told you we were through, and I meant it."

He pouted. Just like a petulant teen-ager, which he wasn't very far re-moved from being. Then he moved toward her. He said in a soft, croon-ing voice, "Mona's being mean to me. Mona likes to be mean to me. But I forgive her. I forgive her because she's so cute. Come to Clint, Mona. Put your arms around me and give me a great big kiss."

"Keep away from me," she warned.

She backed up. He advanced on her like a hungry bear in Yellowstone. I looked at the two of them balefully. It was getting toward the point where I was probably expected to intervene in the situation.

He grabbed Mona and pulled her toward him. He drew her mouth up-ward to his too-pretty lips.

"I'll bite you," she whispered. "I'll bite your lips off. I'll fix you so you can't ever go in front of a camera again. Let go of me, Clint. I'm warning you. Let go. Joey, make him let go of me!"

It was my cue, and I couldn't duck it.

I moved forward. I'm five-eleven and I've got a hundred ninety pounds distributed without too much fat, but I've never enjoyed a fight just for the hell of it. And this was a kid fifteen years younger than I was, four inches taller, and maybe thirty pounds heavier.

I grabbed him by the shoulder and, feeling vaguely like a character in somebody's television drama, said, "Let go of her, buddy."

He let go of her, all right, just like I told him to.

He let go of her, turned around, and hit me.

The punch caught me on the shoulder and rocked me. It was just a play-ful sort of tap, designed to teach me that I shouldn't poke my nose into his business. I tried to ignore the surge of pain in my left shoulder. I put up my guard and lashed out at him, hitting him in the stomach with about as much effect as a fly landing on a gorilla.

He came at me.

It was strictly a massacre. He was big and he was young and he had a kind of cocky confidence about him, and he was going to show Mona that he could wipe up the floor with anyone and everyone who got in his way. He waded into me, fists flying, catching me in the pit of my stomach, then in the shoulder again, then in the middle of my chest. I got the definite impression that he was pulling his punches because he knew that if he hit me really hard he would kill me. As it was I was retching and gasping for breath all at once.

"Had enough?" he asked.

I couldn't back out of it now. I waved my fists around in what I hoped looked like self-defense. In the distant background I heard Mona yelling, and then out of the corner of my eye I saw her running into the house.

Muscle-boy hit me again. He caught me in the cheek and I imagined I heard my jaws crunching; he belted me in the stomach; he smacked me in the chest again. I thought I was going to fold up. He was dissecting me easily, smoothly, smilingly, like a product of some Hollywood studio's boxing school. It's easy to be complacent about your boxing ability when you're that big to start with.

I was staggering now. One roundhouse punch damn near knocked me into the pool, and if I had gone in I most likely wouldn't have had the strength to keep my head above water. He hit me three more times, and each punch was like an H-bomb going off two feet in front of me.

Then the whole complexion of the fight changed unexpectedly.

He was standing above me, and I was tottering and about to fall, and he was wearing a gloating kind of smile as though he were searching the dim recesses of what passed for his brain for some appropriate cliché to use as he applied the *coup de grâce*. To my utter amazement I saw that I had a clear shot at his face. He wasn't bothering about keeping his guard up. He was too busy trying to compose an appropriately sneering knockout line for me.

So I hit him.

Hard.

I put all my remaining strength into it, taking him completely by surprise, and bashed him in the mouth. I wasn't pulling any punches the way he was. I couldn't afford to. I rammed my knuckles into his mouth, feeling the fiery pain of white teeth slicing into my skin, and a peculiar sensation ran up my arm at the impact.

I was a little amazed at my own boldness. *Now he'll kill me for sure*, I thought, stepping back instead of following through with a second punch. I looked around for someplace to run to. In a moment he'd be after me like a maddened boar, and if I didn't clear out I'd end up in tomorrow's newspaper stories.

But no. He didn't come after me.

Instead he made a little whimpering sound and slowly crumpled to his knees, putting both hands to his mouth. I knew I hadn't hit him hard enough to knock him out, so I watched him in puzzlement. He sat there, rocking on his knees and moaning. After a moment I caught on.

He took his hands away from his mouth to spit out the fragments of a tooth. Blood dripped down to the white tiles of the patio. I peered at him and saw that two front teeth had been cracked on top and one of the bottom ones seemed to have been knocked out altogether. And his lower lip had been driven clear through by one of the stumps. I could see the deep, jagged cut in that fleshy lip, penetrating right through it.

He was crying like a baby.

At that moment Mona reappeared, and I noticed she had a gun in her hands. She was as surprised to see the big boy on his knees as I was to see the gun.

"What the hell happened?" she asked. "Don't tell me you knocked him out!"

"I hit him in the mouth," I said. "He just folded right up like that."

Gun dangling loosely from one hand, Mona walked around him for a better view. She whistled. "Jesus, you really messed him up. Broke his teeth, split his lips—you gave him the works, huh?"

The kid made a moaning sound.

Mona prodded him with the gun. "Come on, you bastard. On your feet. Get moving."

"No—no—he hurt my face—"

"Up," she said. "You want a bullet through your arm? We'll really ruin you here today." She jabbed the gun into his back. The safety was off. I wondered whether she really would shoot him if he didn't get up.

Unsteadily, he got to his feet, keeping one hand cupped over his mouth. Blood streamed from between his fingers. He shambled toward the exit, Mona following him with the gun just in case he got rambunctious again.

"Out," she said. "Get out. And don't ever come back here. You make me want to vomit! Clear out, Clint. Clear out and stay out!"

He paused at the doorway, turned, looked at me. "I'll get you," he mumbled without using his lips. "Don't you worry, mister, I'll get you. I'll make you wish you hadn't done that to me!"

Then he was gone. I heard the sound of a car door slamming angrily, then of a car pulling out of Mona's driveway at top speed.

I sank down limply in one of the deck chairs. "Get me a drink," I said. "And for Christ's sake put that cannon away, Mona!"

She waved to Kitty, who went toward the kitchen. Mona herself went inside with the gun. I prodded and probed myself experimentally and noted that nothing seemed to be broken. I reminded myself that Clint had shown a strange reluctance to hit me in the face. As though he were so sensitive to being hit there himself that he didn't even want to put the idea in my mind.

Mona returned. "You all right?"

"More or less, I suppose."

"You really ruined him, you know? Clint's morbid about his face. He's practically a monomaniac about it. And now he'll need his teeth capped. And he'll have to have stitches in his lip. It'll put him out of commission for months. And a kid like that can't afford to leave the limelight even for a few weeks. There are always too many more like him coming up out of the bushes."

I shrugged. "If he was worried about his face, he should have had enough sense to keep away from fighting. I hope he has to spend the rest of his life playing monster roles. What the hell did the dumb kid want, anyway?"

"Me," she said.

"I gathered that."

"I met him in the studio commissary in February, when I was negotiating the contract for my new film. I could see he had hot pants for me, and he looked interesting, so I dated him."

"Interesting? A heap of muscles with a pretty face."

"Well, so I found out. But it took a little while to find it. I dated him three times and I didn't let him make me till the third time." She giggled. "He was lousy. The musclemen almost always are. They build up those muscles to compensate for their lousiness in bed. Well, I could tolerate a jerk if he was good in bed, but he wasn't, so I told him to split. Since then he's been mooning around me like a lovesick kid."

"That's all he is."

"I guess so," she said. "He's also a damned nuisance. Maybe today I got rid of him for good."

Kitty appeared with tall, cooling drinks. I gulped mine down gratefully.

"Will you be having lunch soon?" Kitty asked.

"Fifteen minutes," I said.

We lounged around the pool awhile, trying to forget the recent hectic activities. A few minutes passed, and then the telephone rang, and Kitty called to Mona, who answered it.

Five minutes later Mona appeared. "Guess who that was."

"Mr. Muscles?"

"Wrong. It was Jack Kline. The producer of my film. It seems Clint showed up at the studio with his face all battered, and Jack's furious."

"Furious with who?"

"With Clint, of course. He called me up to ask what happened, and I said Clint came barging in here and a friend of mine beat him up. They're going to suspend Clint from the payroll. I guess he's just about finished with the studio. Maybe he'll be able to tie on somewhere else after his face heals."

"Wait a minute," I said, getting worried. I didn't want to be responsible for anybody's career going sour. "The kid's a boob, but he doesn't deserve all that to happen to him."

"He was beating the stuffings out of you. He could have killed you, Joey."

"Well, he didn't," I told her. "Suppose you call the studio and ask them to take it easy on the kid. Suspend him, maybe, but not fire him. He's just starting out. No sense crippling him like this."

"Nobody had any pity on me when I had my troubles," Mona said. "As far as I'm concerned, the kid got what he asked for. The nerve of him, pestering me for two solid months! Breaking into a private home! I ought to have him arrested in the bargain."

"Look, Mona—"

She cut me off imperiously. "The subject's closed. I don't want to talk about it, Joey. Let's go in for lunch now, shall we?"

We went in for lunch. There was little conversation. Mona had crackers and a glass of Metrecal, and I had a salad and some fish, and the silence was pretty stony. I had been treated to a demonstration of Mona Thorne in action once again, and I didn't like it.

I felt sorry for the kid. I hadn't really been thinking about his career when I smashed him in the face. Of course, to a kid like that his face is his only negotiable asset. And I had messed his face up, maybe permanently.

The situation still could have been saved with one phone call from Mona. But Mona wasn't having any mercy. Let the kid fry, she was saying. Only if Clint Marshall got canned because of the fracas, it wouldn't be Mona he'd come after for vengeance. He'd come after me. He'd already told me that in so many words. And the next time, he wouldn't be pulling his punches.

I felt chilled at the thought.

Mona didn't feel like working after lunch. She napped for a while, and then we played tennis. She slammed the ball around the court like a Wimbledon champ, and we split two sets evenly, 6-4, 4-6. Mona took the second set, winning the final game in a series of aces that left me waving feebly at each service, and then she pranced off the court fresh as a daisy, telling me she was going to study her script.

It was only three o'clock. I settled down on the patio with my notepad and worked out a rough outline for the book, blocking out chapter by chapter and deciding which episodes in her life would get the highlights and which would be skipped over rapidly. The three tragic loves, of course, would be the main theme, the subject being her three periods of dissipation and sin. I figured on an 80,000-word book, with about 15,000 words going for her early life, 50,000 covering the years from her meeting with Teddy Burns to the suicide of Mark Robinson, and the final 15,000 words wrapping up the story with her dramatic return to the screen in whatever the hell her forthcoming picture would be called.

I realized, as I looked over my outline, that she hadn't told me much about her pre-Teddy life. Had Vince Clissold been her first lover? Or had she, like most high-school girls of Mona's shape and temperament, lost her virginity a couple of years before she came out to Hollywood. I'd have to check on that point with her. I penciled in a little note on my pad about it.

I doodled around for nearly an hour, planning the book. I even blocked in the break-points in case some magazine wanted to serialize it instead of running it as a condensation. The story broke well for serialization, I had to admit. A three-part serial could break with her marriage to Teddy Burns and then again with Lee Crosswell's death. A four-part serial could break after meeting Burns, after Crosswell's death, and after meeting Dr. Robinson. A five-part serial—

I slammed the notepad shut with the annoyed realization that I was just wasting time. Let the agent worry about the serialization. My job was just to write the book, and do as good a job as I knew how to do. After that it was in the hands of the others, the sellers and the manufacturers. The book would become a commodity once it left my hands.

I jumped into the pool and swam around for a while, then lolled in the sun. This easy life was okay, I thought, but there was something vaguely dissatisfying about all this indolence. I was more accustomed to the tension of New York, to the pressure and noise and urgency.

At half-past four I went up to my room, showered, stretched out on the bed for a while. Lisa, I thought. I've got to write to Lisa.

I unhooded the typewriter for the first time since my arrival here three days earlier, and rolled a sheet of paper in. I dated it today and put Mona's address on it.

Then I stared at the page for perhaps fifteen minutes. I emerged from my stasis long enough to peck out, "Dear Lisa," and then I froze for another quarter hour. Finally, grimly, I forced myself to write the letter.

Every word was a struggle. I talked about the flight out, I talked about the weather, I talked about the plans for the book. I didn't exactly tell her where I was living, but I said, "I can be reached c/o Mona Thorne at the above address," which was God's own truth, and left the rest ambiguous. I said I was already at work on the book. That was true also. I told her I hoped to be back in New York before July. That much was likewise true. I told her I loved her.

I felt like six kinds of heel.

I remembered Friday night with Mona. I remembered Saturday night. I remembered this morning in the pool.

Only three times in four days, Lisa. That isn't too much, is it? I can still tell you that I love you, even if I've slept with her three times already.

It was a difficult letter, all right. I finished it, finally, and signed it, and put it in an envelope, and addressed the envelope and stuck an airmail stamp on it. Then I put the envelope on my dresser and wondered what the hell to do with it. There wasn't any mailbox on the corner. I was in the middle of a couple of acres of Mona's land, and I didn't know where to go to mail the letter. I felt more than ever like a prisoner.

There was a knock at the door.

"Come in."

Kitty entered. She said, "Miss Thorne says to tell you that you and she are invited to a party tonight. She says to tell you that you're to wear good clothes when you come down to dinner."

Her majesty had commanded.

"Who's giving the party, Kitty?"

"I don't know that, Mr. Baldwin. Must be someone important. That's the only kind of parties Miss Thorne goes to."

"Okay," I said. "I'll dress up. Will you mail this letter for me, Kitty?"

"Of course, Mr. Baldwin."

She took the letter without looking at the address, and slipped it into a pocket of her apron. I smiled at her and she tiptoed out.

Party tonight. At least my captivity was ending. I was going to be put on display at last.

Shrugging, I searched through my meager wardrobe for something appropriately festive.

7

Dinner was a simple one that evening, as though Mona was not in the mood for anything ornate before a party. She was dressed simply, too, though ravishingly. She had the knack of choosing colors that set off her black hair and deeply tanned skin perfectly.

"Whose party is this?" I asked her.

"Martha Vartan," she said. "A local celebrity-hunter. She gives a party once a month and invites all the important people she can get her hands on."

"Sounds dull."

"Martha's dull," Mona said. "But her parties aren't. She gets quite a mixture together. Movie people, of course. And artists, gurus, visiting mathematicians, political figures—anybody who's in town and worth knowing. It's always an interesting group."

"Do you go regularly?"

"Two or three times a year," Mona said. "It isn't good to go too often. Martha has regulars who go every month. But they become celebrity-watchers, you see. I'd rather be a celebrity."

"Am I supposed to be a celebrity?" I asked.

Mona grinned expansively. "Of course, darling! You're a New Yorker, aren't you? That automatically makes you a celebrity in Los Angeles. Or hadn't you heard about the famous L.A. inferiority complex? It's the soft underbelly of all the showmanship out here. And besides that, you're a writer. A writer who doesn't write for the movies. Oh, Martha will be fascinated with you!"

It was something to look forward to, I told myself bleakly. "Who is this Martha? She in the movies too?"

Mona laughed. "Oh, Lord, no. She's just a rich old bag who gives parties. Her husband was a big real-estate developer. He was responsible for about half the hideous projects in the suburbs. He built by far the ugliest houses in California, so of course he died a multimillionaire. Martha couldn't even begin to spend all his money."

The party sounded gorier and gorier, but I couldn't very well back out. Besides, I figured, it would be interesting in a sociological sort of way. I could always make use of it as material in anything I later wrote about L.A. I suspected it would be that sort of party.

We left the house around quarter-past eight. As we stepped down to the garage, Mona handed me a set of keys and said, "Here. You drive tonight."

"Which car?"

"The Bentley," she said. "I'm not in a sports-car mood tonight. I feel like arriving in style." She pressed the electronic button and the garage door folded upward. A light went on. There were three cars in there. One was the little Alfa-Romeo. The second was a Buick station wagon that Kitty probably used to get the groceries. The third was a majestic iron-gray Bentley, an utterly magnificent hunk of metal. For a moment, as I opened the door and held it for Mona, I felt like Baron de Rothschild stepping out for an evening.

Then I settled behind the wheel, and a more accurate simile came to mind. Not like Baron de Rothschild, but like somebody's chauffeur. Nobody who owned a car like this actually drove it himself. My real status was obvious to me all of a sudden. No fantasies of being a millionaire would hold water; what I was was nothing but an unpaid chauffeur.

I started the car and it purred into life. Everything about it was absolutely first-rate. I had never driven anything more expensive than a second-hand Lincoln, and it was a real novelty to handle the wheel of this beauty.

I turned down the driveway and, at Mona's command, made a left turn, heading for the main road.

"How come you don't keep a chauffeur on the payroll, Mona?" I asked her.

"No need for one," she said smoothly. "I do most of my own driving. When I'm not in the mood to drive, there's always someone around to do it for me. I hate to clutter up my household with servants, the way some people do. It makes life so complicated."

Damned democratic of her, I thought. I leaned back against the plush upholstery, holding the wheel lightly. The car practically drove itself. Mona would say, "Turn left here," or, "Take the next right," and I would nudge the wheel a little, and off we would go. Other cars tended to move to one side, giving the Bentley the elbowroom it deserved.

"Where's the party?" I asked.

"Pacific Palisades. It's a nice section."

"So I've heard," I said.

I drove along Sunset Boulevard, down to the ocean. We skirted UCLA, then headed on a winding westward path. As usual in this town, the neighborhood changed half a dozen times as we went along, now quiet and residential, now full of neon-lit night clubs, now shabby and thick with bars and all-night cafeterias. But as we approached the Pacific, the surroundings grew better and better, until finally we were in a plush vicinity that matched for elegance the street Mona herself lived on.

"It's the next block," she said. "Careful of this turn. It's tricky."

It was. The street wound at an impossible angle, and there was practically no visibility either way. But there was no traffic coming either, and I wormed around it and pulled the car up in front of an enormous mansion. A couple of dozen cars were already parked in the streets.

I opened the door for Mona, feeling more and more chauffeur-like as I did so. She must have sensed it, because as she stepped out she murmured to me, "Give me your arm, Joey."

I gave it to her, and together we strolled down the broad curving approach to the house. It was a big, sprawling place, sheltered by towering eucalyptus trees. The architecture was the usual California mishmash, but somehow the conglomeration of styles held together. Floodlights illuminated the building the way the French illuminated their national monuments at night. Through a long picture window I could see what looked like hundreds of people milling around.

We went in.

Almost immediately, something small and furry bounded out to meet us. It turned out to be Martha Vartan. She was just about five feet tall, with an enormous fluffy head of blue-white hair, a heavily rouged face, big eyes, and a tiny cupid's-bow mouth glistening with thick red lipstick. She was piled down with jewelry: a diamond tiara in the mound of hair, a massive necklace, clanking bracelets, and what looked like half a dozen rings. Quite a character, in other words. She looked to be about fifty-five, lively, exuberant, extroverted, eccentric, and pushy.

She threw her arms around Mona. "Darling! So glad you could come! You're looking more beautiful than ever, do you know that? You have a positively radiant look!"

"Thank you, dear," Mona said with an irony that was lost on our hostess, judging by the way she continued to beam.

A tall young man at Martha's side extended his hand to me. "How do you do," he said. "I'm Kit Warren. Very glad to meet you."

"Joey Baldwin," I said, taking his hand and simultaneously wondering who the hell he was. Martha's son? He acted as though he belonged here, and wasn't just another guest. He was about twenty-five, and had his share of that artificial-looking Greek god type of beauty that seemed so widespread out here. His eyebrows, I noted with some annoyance, had been meticulously plucked. He had a deep tan, of course, and shallow blue eyes, and the usual flawless teeth and manly chin. His hair was combed down over his forehead as though his hairline were beginning to recede. His handshake was warm and moist and unpleasant.

Martha gleamed up at me and said, "You're a writer from New York, I understand, Mr. Baldwin."

"Yes, I—"

"How fascinating your life must be! We have another literary man from New York here tonight. Perhaps you know him. Jonathan Stein. Come, I'll introduce you to him, and maybe we'll have an interesting literary discussion, eh?"

Martha swept me off in her orbit, Mona following. Kit Warren remained at the door like a well-oiled machine to greet further guests.

We tunneled our way through dozens of people, Martha going first like a pneumatic drill. I glanced at Mona as if to say, "What the hell have you gotten me into?" but she merely smiled as though terribly amused by the whole thing.

We emerged at the far end of the living room, where a short, intense-looking man of about forty, wearing a suit roughly eight seasons old, was holding court while leaning nonchalantly against a grand piano. From his pallor, I knew him to be newly arrived from the East Coast, just as I knew that the circle of tanned acolytes around him were culture-hungry Angelenos. His cadaverous face was deeply pocked with the ravages of decades-old acne.

Martha burst into the circle and said, "Mr. Stein! Mr. Stein! Here's another writer from New York, Mr. Joseph Baldwin. Perhaps you've met each other, and if not I'll have the pleasure of introducing two fine literary artists."

She stood there, bubbling over with middle-aged joy at the delight of having brought about this meeting of the minds. Stein looked at me without extending his hand and said, "I don't believe we've met, Mr. Baldwin."

"I don't think so." Nor had I heard of him, but I don't pretend to know everybody in New York who calls himself a writer. "What sort of work do you do?" I asked affably.

"I'm a playwright," he said. His voice was cold. He didn't elaborate. He was letting me carry the conversational ball.

I decided to bluff it, just for the hell of it. "Oh, yes," I said. "I seem to remember—you had a drama on Broadway two seasons ago, a murder mystery—"

A muscle throbbed in his hollow left cheek. "You seem to be confusing me with someone else. I've never submitted a work to Broadway. Possibly you saw my lyric tragedy *Parthenope* when it was done at The Little Theatre in 1957."

Oh, one of those, I thought. "What brings you to Los Angeles?" I asked politely.

"I'm lecturing here on The Role of Verse Drama in Modern Theater," he said. Then, as though deciding that he ought to show at least token interest in me, he said, "Do you write, Mr. Baldwin?"

"Yes," I said. "Detective stories, mostly. I've done some science fiction and Westerns, too." He looked at me as though I had just admitted seducing his pet dog, and turned back to his rapt audience, dismissing me from his mind with a mental click that was all but audible. Pursing his lips, he said, "To carry on, I'd like to elaborate on the attempt of such poets as W. H. Auden to supplant the *kitsch* prevalent in the legitimate theater twenty years ago—"

"Nice to have met you," I said, and walked away. Martha Vartan had already vanished upon realizing that the meeting of the minds wasn't quite turning out as she had hoped it would.

I poured myself a tall drink from a pitcher standing on a low table. I sipped it, and it turned out to be some weird kind of punch spiked with brandy and vodka. Oh, well, a drink was a drink.

Mona came up to me. "How was the meeting of the minds?"

"We didn't quite mesh."

She laughed. "Martha's always overenthusiastic. Who is this Stein, anyway."

"An *avant-garde* playwright," I told her. "The kind who'd rather sell his daughter into prostitution than take any money for something he's written. You should have seen him wince when I told him I wrote for the pulps."

Mona smiled and sipped my drink, and I poured one for her. She said, "Did you notice the creepy-looking kid greeting people at the door?"

"Kit Warren?"

"That's what he calls himself these days, yes. It was something long and Polish when I first met him. Know who he is, Joey?"

"Prime stockholder in Twentieth Century Fox?"

"No. He's Mr. Martha Vartan."

"What? You mean—he's married to—"

"For six months, now. Isn't he cute?"

"He's half her age!"

"That's the way it's done out here, my sweet. Wealthy widows in their fifties are always buying themselves nice young boys to play house with. Kit didn't make the grade as an actor, so he took up being a gigolo. And Martha married him last fall."

I gagged on my drink. "The thought of the two of them in the same bed—screwing—"

"Oh, I'm sure they don't do that," Mona said. "Kit's gay. I've got Billy Joe Hart's word for that."

"The fellow who had the affair with Teddy Burns?"

"That's right. I'm sure it's just a marriage for public show. Martha isn't interested in sex any more. She just wants a man around the house. The younger the better."

I felt faintly dizzy.

A dark-haired female in a white dress drifted up to me and said, "Won't you introduce us, Mona?"

"Joey Baldwin, meet Maureen Palmer," Mona said.

I blinked and damn near said something foolish like, "Well, well. I was a fan of yours in the fifties, Miss Palmer." But I cut myself short and simply mumbled a conventional greeting as she smiled at me. I realized I hadn't even thought of the name Maureen Palmer since about 1952 or so. In the forties, of course, she had been a big star. But that was a quarter of a century ago.

She asked me a few questions about what I wrote, and I told her, all the while staring in amazement at her dress. It was the most bluntly revealing thing I'd ever seen at any sort of cocktail party. There was a wide-open scoop neck, and her breasts were just about ninety-five percent visible. I could look right in and see them, everything but the nipple, and I was willing to bet that when she was looked at from over her shoulder the nipples were visible too. I was right, I found out a moment later, as she turned to smile at someone passing on the left and I got a full view of two full, heavy breasts sitting atop a little shelf in her dress.

She turned back to me. It was almost impossible to look at her face with that blinding display down below, and it was just as well, because time hadn't been kind to her face. The scars of one face-lifting too many showed. Her nose had sharpened into a beak over the years, her lips were thin and bloodless-looking, her cheeks were sunken. She looked at least fifty-five, and probably was. But the breasts were the breasts of a young woman, and she had them out on display as though to tell the whole world that even if her face had gone, the rest of her was still up to par.

"I'll be doing a film in November," she said negligently to Mona. "We'll be signing the contracts in a week or two. I've finally decided to end my retirement."

"I'm so glad for you, darling," Mona purred.

"You must know how it is, being away from the cameras so long," Maureen went on. "Though in your case it was tragic external circumstances that kept you from making films, while I was simply unable to find a script I thought worth doing. The writers nowadays are so incompetent—oh. I'm terribly sorry, Mr. Baldwin. Present company excepted naturally."

"That's all right," I said tightly. "I've never written any film scripts. I'm strictly a book and magazine man, so you can say all you like about Hollywood writers."

She beamed at me. "Of course. I can see immediately that you're much more talented than the hacks we have here." An idea struck her. "Do you think you might want to do an article about me?" she asked shamelessly. "Now that I'm returning to films, I think there's a definite story of great human interest—"

"Joey will be busy for the next few months on a big writing project," Mona said quickly. "Maybe he can get in touch with you after he's free. Come, Joey. There's someone I'd like to introduce you to." She smiled sweetly at the older actress. "Adorable to have seen you again, Maureen. You must drop over for lunch some time."

Mona swept me away, toward the far corner of the room. "The bitch," she muttered fiercely. "The dirty old bitch! Wants you to do an article about her, does she?"

"Jealous?" I said.

"Listen, Joey. That old harridan hasn't had a part in twenty-five years because she's ugly. She's ugly and can't act. She can show her tits around at these parties all she likes, but it doesn't get her anywhere. That movie she's talking about is a figment of her imagination. Nobody in Hollywood would hire her except in a character role, and she's too proud to take one of those."

"Okay," I said. "So she's a harmless old fibber who doesn't know how to grow old gracefully. Why get so worked up about her?"

"She tries to steal men. Didn't you see how she looked at you? How she showed off her boobs? Practically waved them in your face?"

"I was only interested sociologically," I told her. "There's as much chance of my making a play for her as there is of my flirting with Kit Warren."

It was the wrong thing to say. Mona turned away, glowering angrily at me from the side of her face, and refilled her drink. I grinned at her.

We continued to make the rounds of the party together. I met actors, producers, a couple of script writers, three electronics engineers, a pair of lesbian dancers, a couple of talent agents, an odd bird who said he acted as a special consultant on monster movies, a teen-age actress who was visibly on the make, two directors, a studio executive, a silent-movie star, and a sly-eyed young fellow who said he was doing a takeout on the Los Angeles scene for one of the sophisticated men's magazines back east. Quite a conglomeration.

Mona, of course, was the object of great interest, and she never lacked for admirers. I came in for my share. Mona told them all quite frankly that I was writing her autobiography for her, and everyone congratulated me on having gotten such a lucrative assignment.

News seemed to travel fast in Hollywood and environs. Midway through the evening, I was being introduced to a blank-faced young actor named Rack Byron, and he grinned at me and said, "Oh, sure, you're the fellow who busted up Clint Marshall's face this morning. If you ask me, he had it coming to him."

"Where'd you hear about it?" I asked.

"Oh, it's all over the lot. Clint's been suspended, you know. I think they're going to rip up his contract."

"That's a lousy break for the kid," I said. "I didn't mean to screw him up that way. But he was throwing his fists around, and I had to defend my-self."

"He had it coming," Rack assured me. "Don't you feel guilty. Lot of other guys in this town wished they'd done it to him."

"Nice fellow," I said to Mona after Byron had drifted away. "He's all bro-ken up about his fellow actor's misfortune, isn't he?"

"Why should he be?" Mona asked. "It didn't happen to him, did it?"

"That the way they think in this town?"

"Listen," she said, "Clint and Rack are cut from the same cookie-cutter. There are only so many dumb-young-hero parts to go around, and each classic profile that gets removed from the scene makes it easier for the rest to find work. Rack's probably overjoyed at the news. He likely wants to hug you and give you a great big kiss."

"He better not try."

"Just don't let him sneak up on you, that's all."

I didn't. I kept close to the punchbowl, lubricated my throat at regular intervals, and tried not to let each conversation last more than five min-utes. It was quite a group. As Mona had predicted, everybody was inter-esting. But they were interesting as types rather than as people, if you know what I mean. They weren't the sorts you'd want as friends or reg-ular companions, but it was fascinating to stand back and watch them in action.

Then about midnight or so I met my first real person of the night, the first one who struck me as genuine and not a figment of some script writer's imagination. Her name was Joan, and she was a good-looking, pe-tite redhead in her middle twenties with a level smile and a level-headed mind. We talked for a couple of minutes, the conversation quickly turning into a what-the-hell-are-two-sane-people-like-us-doing-in-this-looneybin? kind of thing, and with a grin of recognition we accepted each other as outsiders in the Los Angeles scene.

"It's awfully close in here," she said. "Why don't we go out and wander around the grounds a little? I'm tired of this whole peculiar crowd."

"Amen to that," I said. I looked around uneasily for Mona—I was already coming to have automatic prisoner reflexes—and saw her with her back to me, talking to three or four older men who looked like directors or producers. I nodded to Joan and we slipped out a side exit, into the garden that sloped down to the swimming pool.

Nobody saw us leave.

I felt the pressure lift the moment I got outdoors.

8

We stepped out into a fairyland kind of garden, with huge cactus trees looming up like Martian vegetation all around. A little brook, probably phony, bubbled down the hillside. We found a bench.

"Okay," I said. "Who are you and why didn't you turn into a pumpkin at midnight?"

"My name's Joan Harris, I'm an announcer on a local TV program, and I didn't make the transformation because I'm not a member of the pumpkins' union. Who are you?"

"Joey Baldwin. Free-lance writer from New York, here to do a ghosting job for Mona Thorne. And I thought all TV announcers were men."

"I'm on a kiddie program," she said. "We prefer the softer touch."

"Are you a soft touch?"

"Not very," she said. "What the hell are you doing at this party?"

"Mona brought me. She wanted me to see the local fauna in their native habitat. And you?"

She shrugged. "My producer brought me. He's busy making passes at an old-time movie star named Maureen Palmer, just now, so I figured I could slip away. Have you seen her? She's the one with the—"

"With the navel-deep neckline," I said. "Yes, I saw her. Not my type. You aren't married?"

"Not currently. It didn't work out." She laughed. "He wasn't compatible."

"Neither was mine," I said. "Too bad they didn't marry each other instead."

"Too bad," she said.

I liked her. She was real, no phoniness, no arty airs, no pretensions. And pretty, though not flashy. Her low-cut dress showed small but nicely formed breasts. Her green eyes were alert, alive. Her smile was a straightforward, honest one. I could see she liked me, too.

"Quite a collection in there," she said.

"Quite."

"How about our getting out of here?" she suggested. "Drive back to civilization, have a couple of drinks, get to know each other."

"That a pickup?" I asked.

I regretted it right away. She looked a little disappointed and said, "I like to think a girl can ask a guy for company if she feels like it. You want me to put on an act and play demure virgin while you go through the approved courtship rituals, Joey?"

"*Touché*. I'm sorry."

"You needn't be. I guess it's a conditioned reflex."

"I wasn't thinking," I told her. "But the fact of the matter is we can't get out of here. I've got to drive Mona home tonight. And you'd better not ditch your producer friend, if you want to keep your job."

"You're right," she said. She moved closer to me on the bench. "How long are you going to be out on the Coast, Joey?"

"Till I finish the book. End of June, I hope."

"You don't like it here much, do you?"

"Not much. A good place to visit. Lively. I'd go out of my mind if I stayed here six months."

"I often feel the same way," she said. "But I stay."

"Why?"

"I was born here. In Venice. It's the environment I know. I'm a little uneasy about pulling up stakes."

"There's TV in New York," I pointed out. "You could break in there without any trouble."

"Means starting from the bottom all over again, though. I think about it, Joey. But I don't make the break. I stay here."

We were silent for a moment. Then I said, "Perhaps we could get together for lunch some day. This week." As I said it, I felt a sinking sensation of despair as I wondered how I could ever escape from Mona's eagle eye long enough to drive into downtown L.A. for lunch with this girl.

It just wasn't feasible, however attractive the idea—and the girl.

"That's a fine idea," she said.

Then suddenly my arm was around her, and my lips were moving toward hers, and then we were kissing. She kissed me hungrily—the eager, tense kiss of a girl who has been living too long in a world of gaudy phantoms, and who is fighting to get back to reality. Her lips were soft and warm and tender, and her small breasts pressed yearningly against me as we kissed.

We parted and she looked at me strangely, as though surprised by herself.

"I don't even know you," she said gently.

"We could remedy that," I said. "If you wanted to, that is."

"I do. Yes. Very much."

Then we were kissing again, and this time my tongue slipped into her mouth, and my hand came to rest on the firm little mound of her right breast, and then it slipped down into her lap and I touched the flatness of her belly through her thin dress. She twisted and gasped a little as I touched her through her dress. After a long moment we came up for air. She looked flustered and a little wild-eyed.

"Where can we go?" she whispered. "Where there's some privacy?"

"Right now?"

"Right now," she said. "I want you, Joey. You can't understand why. I'm just so lonely—so tired of all these people—"

"You aren't the only one."

"Let's go, then. Back of the garage. No one will see us. I want you to hold me in your arms, Joey. Tight. And I want to make love to you. I want to feel that I'm part of you. Oh, I know this is crazy, but it's what I want!"

In an odd way, I understood what she meant. Just the bare words can't convey it. It might seem that she was just a girl with hot pants, nymphing it up with a reasonably presentable guy that she met at a party. But it wasn't that way at all. It was a lot cleaner, a lot less neurotic. It was simply that—that she had met somebody, and inside of five or ten minutes she knew she was *simpatico* with him, and she wanted to show it, she wanted to form a bond between us, the bond of love, right here and now and on the spot. As though we were each trapped in our particular prisons, and had this one chance to leave the bars behind for a few minutes.

She wanted to make the most of her opportunity.

Hand in hand, we ran down the garden path. We came to what she had thought was a garage, and it turned out to be some kind of tool shed.

There was a bench behind the shed. We settled down there. Joan sat on my lap facing me, and I unzipped the back of her dress and unhooked her bra, and there were her breasts, bare in front of me like sweet little love-apples. She had tiny nipples, beautiful pale breasts. She was smiling strangely, a Mona Lisa smile.

She wriggled out of her panties and fluffed her skirt out to cover us, and sat there above me on my lap and she was still smiling the Mona Lisa smile as we began to make love. It was an odd way of doing it. I was afraid someone would come along and spot us, and then remembered this was Los Angeles, where you could walk nude at high noon on Wilshire Boulevard without drawing a crowd.

Her eyes were gleaming with a kind of little-girl pleasure, and my hands were squeezing her breasts, and her mouth was tight against mine and her body seemed to be on fire. And all of a sudden it was happening, first for her and then for me.

I put my arms around her and held her tight until she came to the end. Her head lolled against my shoulder and her breathing was harsh and irregular. When I lifted her head, I saw her smiling, and there were tears in her eyes, and her nostrils were flaring as she tried to get enough air into her lungs.

"Oh, that was good, Joey."

"Yes. It was wonderful."

"At least we had it once. That's the important thing, Joey. The moment came along and we took it while it was here. We didn't miss the boat our one time."

"What the hell are you talking about?" I asked, with the feeling that she knew some secret that nobody had bothered to let me in on.

"You know it won't work out for us, Joey. Be realistic. You're tied to Mona. You can't escape from her. I know her, know how she keeps a man. And I'm tied down too. We're both caught. There's no sense even trying to fight it."

"Don't be silly, Joan. When I finish this book, I can take you back to New York and—"

"And what? Marry me?" She laughed. "You've got a girl in New York, Joey. Eight to one says you do, and you're planning to marry her. I don't fit in."

I felt a stab under the heart as her words hit me. She was a smart one. She knew the setup, knew all the ropes.

"There's no room for me in your town, Joey, and no room for you in mine. That's why I dragged you back here with me, don't you see? For one moment, our worlds joined, our paths crossed. And now we've both got memories that'll last."

I had never known a girl like this. She amazed me with everything she said, everything she did. The lousy thing was I knew I was being told the truth. There was no sense in our fooling ourselves.

She rose from my lap and fastened her bra again.

I helped her hook her dress in back. She pulled her panties back on, and for a moment I caught a glimpse of her mysterious world and then she was back together again as though nothing had happened. Only forty minutes had passed since we had come outdoors. It seemed like an entire lifetime had gone by.

Hand in hand, we walked slowly up the hill and back to the house. We didn't speak. The forty minutes now began to seem magical and unreal.

But they had happened. It hadn't just been a dream. It had all really happened.

Joan said softly, "Do you think I'm a slut, Joey?"

"Why should I?"

"Because—because I let you have me that way."

"I think you're a wonderful girl."

"Girls are supposed to let themselves be chased a while before they give in," she said. "They've got nasty names for girls who don't play according to the rules."

"The rules stink."

"I've never done anything like this before," she said. "Oh, I don't mean sex. I've had my share. I mean so quickly—so soon. But that's the mood I was in, and I gave in to it. Spontaneously."

"There are people who pay psychoanalysts fifty bucks an hour to help them be spontaneous," I said. "Don't ever let yourself become one of them, Joanie."

"I won't," she said. She gripped my hand tightly. "It was a great party tonight, Joey. I thought it would be a drag, but it turned out great, because I met you. Give me a kiss, Joey. Just one last one. For the memory book. We won't ever see each other again, I guess. But we'll remember."

I turned to her and kissed her, kissed her hard, thrust my tongue deep into her mouth and crushed her frail body against me, held her lips to mine for a long moment. Then I let go and caught my breath and there was Mona standing like an avenging angel on the back porch of the house, looking at us with her arms folded grimly.

"I wondered where you were," she said bleakly. "I haven't seen you for almost an hour."

"I took a walk," I said. Joan stared at Mona, then said, "Goodbye, Joey. Thanks for everything."

"Yeah," I said as she slipped away.

Mona came down the steps toward me. I could see the tension in her face, the wild anger just barely held in check.

"Where the hell were you?" she said in a rigidly controlled voice.

"I told you. I went for a walk."

"With her?"

"Sure, with her. I got tired of all the quacks and queers inside, and she wanted some fresh air. So did I. And you were busy talking with some guys I didn't know, so we went for a walk."

"A long walk. You made her, didn't you? Down in the bottom of the garden. You pulled her panties off and grabbed a quick one, that's what you ducked out for, isn't that it?"

"Now, look, Mona—"

"You fucked her, didn't you?" she demanded again.

"What the hell is this, the Inquisition? I'm a free agent."

"You've got no right to humiliate me. You can't bring me to a party and then slip off to make some girl you don't even know. They'll all find out about it. What do you want them to think? That Mona Thorne can't hold a man? That she can be edged out by some flat-chested little kid?"

"Hold on, Mona. I'm just your ghost-writer, not your fiancée!"

"You're living with me, aren't you?"

"That was your idea."

Her eyes blazed. I thought she was going to claw at my face. "Did you ball that girl just now, Joey?"

I took a deep breath. "Yes. If you have to know, yes. We went behind the tool shed and had a quickie. I'm sorry if that upsets you. I didn't know there was any oath of fidelity in my contract. They forgot to tell me I was supposed to be chaste while working on the book."

"You sarcastic son of a bitch," she hissed. Her face was so angry she looked uglier than any woman I'd ever seen. Strange cords popped out on her throat. At that moment she looked fifty or a hundred years old, a wicked witch with magical beauty and youthfulness. Her jaws worked silently for a moment. Then she said, "Let's get the hell out of here. I can't stay any longer."

We went inside and paid our farewells to the Vartans, Mr. and Mrs. They were gushily glad we had come, and hoped we'd visit them more often. "Perhaps the four of us can get together sometime," Martha said. I nodded. All I needed right now was a double date with Martha and her fag husband.

I got behind the wheel of the Bentley and we pulled out. For the first twenty minutes of the trip back to Mona's house, there was nothing but frosty silence emanating from her side of the car, broken only by an occasional monosyllabic driving instruction. I was surprised that she didn't do the job up fine by sitting in the back seat. It wasn't really good form to sit up front with your chauffeur, after all.

Then when we were about halfway back she said icily, "I hope you understand that you're fired."

"There's a contract," I reminded her.

"Contracts can be broken," she said. "If I decide I can't possibly work with you, the contract is automatically voided. You should know that."

"I've already received five thousand dollars," I said. "That isn't returnable."

"Keep it. It'll be worth five thousand just to be rid of you."

I didn't answer. I was as angry at her as she was at me, and right then and there I didn't give a damn about the alleged thousands of dollars this deal was going to bring me. I wanted out. Mona couldn't work with me, and I was damned if I was going to spend a couple of months working for her under circumstances that made me virtually a slave to her.

"You can pack tomorrow morning," she said. "I'll get you a ticket back to New York. That's part of the deal. I'm paying your transportation."

"Don't bother," I told her. "I can afford the air fare back."

"A deal's a deal."

I shrugged. Koren was going to be furious, and so would Thomas be, back in New York. To hell with them. I regretted losing the money this job would bring, but it wasn't worth taking months of this kind of treatment from Mona. I valued my independence more. And I had already made five grand for doing nothing more than coming out to the Coast and spending a few unusual days as Mona Thorne's house guest. Plenty of sex, plenty of good food, plenty of money, and now I could go home and get back to the job of writing cheap detective novels, and let somebody else worry about getting into the upper brackets. I had had it.

We reached the house. It was dark and silent. I let Mona out and pulled the car into the garage. She was gone when I emerged. Of course. Why wait around to say good night to the chauffeur?

I went upstairs.

I was in a black mood. The job had gone to hell, and now that my anger was receding I felt bad about it. Lisa and I had planned to get married on the money I was going to make on this book.

Lisa. She seemed so far away. I'd all but forgotten her again.

Out of sight, out of mind. It was true.

I thought about Joan, who had gotten me into all of this. Would I see her again? She had said no. But now that I was free of Mona, I'd be able to contact Joan, get to know her a little better—

I shook my head. For one thing, I wanted to clear out of L.A. as fast as possible. For another, I was already engaged to one girl, and it was complicated to start fooling with another, especially since I might very well find myself falling in love with this one, and where would that leave me with Lisa?

The third thing was that Joan herself had said nothing could work out between us, because she didn't feel she could leave L.A. and I knew I couldn't stay here.

The fourth thing was I didn't have her address. Joan Harris, Los Angeles—and how many Joan Harrises might there be in this sprawling conglomeration of towns that called itself a city? Fifty? A hundred? And was I supposed to phone them all? And maybe she didn't live in L.A. at all, but in one of the outlying towns, of which there were dozens. I'd be thumbing through telephone books all month.

I showered and got into bed. I lay there in the dark, wondering how things would have worked out if Mona hadn't tossed me out. Maybe the book would earn a hundred grand, two hundred, half a million. And I had forfeited my chance to collect my share. All I had was a check for $4500, after agent's commission, and some rather unusual memories.

I closed my eyes, but I was wide awake.

I thought of Lisa.

Of Joan.

Of Mona.

Of this whole damned crazy city.

And then the handle of the connecting door started to turn. I heard it rattle, and I looked at it strangely, and my flesh began to crawl. Mona had a gun, I knew. Maybe her pride was so badly hurt that she was coming in to shoot me. Anything could happen in this wacky town. Maybe—

The door opened.

She came into my room.

She didn't have a gun in her hand.

She was naked.

She stood there a moment, moonlight slanting in to illuminate the deep bowls of her breasts with their tip-tilted nipples, the sloping flat curve of her belly, the lush contours of her buttocks. She turned slowly, walked toward the bed.

"I take it all back," she whispered harshly, standing above me in the dark. "I didn't mean it, darling! I was tense, that's all. Edgy. I had a little too much to drink and I flew off the handle."

I gaped at her.

The next moment she was in my bed, swarming all over me.

9

She was like some animal in heat. For the first few moments, I wasn't able to respond. I had already screwed twice that day, after all, and I'm not as young as I once was. The noontime bout in the pool and the midnight session back of the tool shed had just about taken care of my quota for the day.

But there was no denying Mona's furious need. Her body ground against mine, her breasts hard and taut against my flesh, her mouth wide, her tongue a thing with a life of its own. My body's reluctance vanished swiftly under her frantic assault. Within minutes, I was responding to her. Our bodies tangled, meshed, merged.

It was Friday night all over again, so far as the intensity of it went. This was like mating with a tigress. Her breath was hot, her eyes gleamed demonically in the darkness of the room. I caught hold of her breasts, held them tight, felt the nipples rock-hard in my palms. Together, apart, together, apart, together—our frenzied bodies turned and twisted in a fever that was part ecstasy, part torment. I was reaching the breaking point, the point at which my mind could no longer endure my body's ecstasies. This was too much.

Much too much.

I reached the peak, went up over it, letting out my breath in gusty gasps. Mona stayed with me. She bit hard into my shoulder and dug her fingernails into the muscles of my back, and moved with almost panicky urgency until the flood tides of sensation swept over her as well.

Then it was over.

She sank back at my side, limp and drained of her passion for the moment, at least.

The only sound in the room was the purring of the air-conditioner. I sat up, leaning against the headboard, and looked down at her. Her breasts were rising and falling slowly as her body returned to normal after the exertions just concluded.

She turned toward me. "I don't want you to leave me, Joey. Please don't leave me."

"You fired me, remember?"

"I was angry. I wasn't thinking. I take it all back, Joey."

"You think you can just play with me like this?" I asked. "Hire me and fire me like a butler or a chauffeur? I didn't enjoy the way you carried on tonight at that party, Mona. It wasn't any fun at all to be marched out of there, virtually with you pinching my ear and telling me I had been a bad, bad boy, Mona."

"I'm sorry. I didn't think. What do you want me to do, crawl to you? Lick the soles of your feet? I blew up, and I'm sorry for it. I'm asking you to forgive me, Joey. Will you forgive me?"

"You really want me to write the book?"

"Yes."

"And you'll stop regarding me as your personal property from now on?"

"Yes, Joey!"

"I'll be free to come and go as I please around here? To see anybody I like, and if the fancy strikes me to sleep with anybody I like?"

"Anything you say, Joey. Anything. Just don't walk out. Don't leave me."

It was the fastest complete turnabout I had ever seen in a woman, and what made it all the more impressive was the fact that the woman was a proud, haughty bitch like Mona Thorne.

She wanted me to stay.

Okay. I needed the money. I would stay. I told her so, and she seemed almost pathetically grateful, almost hysterically glad that I wasn't walking out.

An act?

Maybe, I thought. It was hard to believe that Mona could do this much crawling so sincerely. I was skeptical of this new deal she was promising. I wondered just how much freedom I really would have.

Well, no matter. The important thing was that we had both retreated from the brink of a couple of hours before. And I realized that I had more in this to lose than Mona. She wouldn't have to look around too far to find another writer who could handle the assignment just as competently, but I'd have trouble finding another assignment that promised to be as lucrative as this one. My agent would certainly be sour on me if I let this deal fizzle, and it would be a long time before he handed me something similar again.

But why did Mona want me so badly, then?

My bed abilities? Well, I could flatter myself and say yes. But there were hundreds of men in Los Angeles who could keep her happy in bed, I was sure. Maybe I was pretty good, but I certainly wasn't unique.

She drew me to her. Her entire body expressed its gratitude. Breasts and thighs told me how happy she was that I wasn't packing up and clearing out in the morning.

I woke around eleven o'clock. Mona, who didn't seem to need much sleep, had apparently been up for hours, had breakfasted and had studied her script and had even done some swimming. She was waiting for me on the patio. The tape recorder was all plugged in, and a fresh tape was in the reel.

When I finished eating, I went out to her. She handed me a sheaf of papers.

"What's this?" I said.

"Transcript of yesterday's session," she explained. "I had it sent out yesterday afternoon to be typed."

I leafed through the dozen or so pages, impeccably typed. "So fast?" I said, thinking of times I had waited two and three weeks to get a typing job done in New York.

"That's the way we work out here," she said. "Where do you want to start today?"

"Let's try early sex experiences," I said. "You skipped straight from your childhood to Vince Clissold yesterday. Clissold wasn't your first lover, was he?"

"Christ, no," she said with a laugh. She stretched out in the sun, closing her eyes, and I could almost see her roving back through her memories, turning the pages, looking over hundreds of love affairs to find the very first. I waited, watching the spool turn. She seemed almost asleep, lying there in her bikini.

Finally she said, "The first one was named Marty. Marty Hennings."

"How old were you?"

"Twelve," she said.

I gasped despite myself. "Twelve? You're kidding!"

"I was precocious, sweetheart. They bought me my first bra when I was ten. By the time I was twelve I was getting wolf whistles every time walked down the street. I could pass for sixteen. I've got photos to show you, if you don't believe."

"But sex at twelve—"

"You doubt it?"

"The readers might, Mona."

She shrugged. "Hell of a thing, isn't it, when you can't print the truth in your own autobiography because you're afraid people won't believe it. You want me to make up something you think's plausible, or do you want the truth?"

"The truth."

"Okay," she said. "Here's how it happened."

She started to tell the story. It turned out to be not only her first sex experience, but practically the first and last time in her life that she had been reluctant about sex.

It happened the week after her twelfth birthday. She was in the eighth grade, and despite her precocious physical development she had never been out on a date with a boy, at least never out on a single date. This day she had to study for her social studies exam. One of the boys in her class, this Marty Hennings, asked if he could come over and study with her that afternoon.

She agreed. Marty was the oldest boy in the class, past thirteen, and he was as big as a fifteen-year-old. And he was smart, too. Mona was worried about the exam, and she knew Marty's coaching would help her pass it.

It was a rainy day. Her parents were at the store; her brothers had gone bowling; her kid sister was spending the afternoon at a friend's house. Mona and Marty had the place to themselves.

They studied for a while, half an hour or so. Then they began to get bored with social studies, and got playful. Mona started to tease him by running her fingertips up and down his back. Then she started running her hands down his chest, and by accident one time ran them a little too far down. Her face turned crimson and she hastily drew her hands back.

But Marty took it as his cue. Studying went by the boards completely. His hands caressed the firm flesh under her thin sweater. She liked the sensation, made no attempt to discourage him. New feelings flooded through her body, strange inner tinglings that she had never experienced before in her life.

Then he had one hand under her skirt, and she wasn't sure what he was doing but she liked it. It was an amusing game, she thought, the maturity of her body unmatched by her mind. Only a moment did the hand linger on her smooth calf; then it slid upward, resting for an instant on her knee, then gliding further up her thigh. She could feel his fingers touching the soft flesh on the inside of her thigh. He stroked her tenderly, gently.

She began to squirm on the couch, to make little panting noises. She had never felt pleasures like these before.

With a skill far beyond his thirteen years, Marty drew her sweater up, not taking it off but leaving it telescoped around her armpits. He reached around behind her, toying with the clasp of her brassiere, finally opening it.

The cups fell away. There were her breasts, her virgin breasts, bare to his eyes and his touch. One hand still rested on her legs, while the other caressed the soft young globes of her breasts.

She felt as though her body were on fire.

But for the first time she was afraid.

"What are you doing, Marty?" she asked in a husky, desire-thickened whisper. "We mustn't—"

"Don't worry, Mona. You'll enjoy it. Just relax. It's fun. It's the greatest fun in the world."

"No, we'd better not."

He didn't reply. He just kept stroking her breasts with one hand while the other wandered into her panties. She had a sudden burning desire to touch him, too.

Marty was starting to moan, now that she was touching him that way. He changed his position on the couch, getting his hands underneath her, pulling her panties down over her hips, then past her knees. His weight was pressing down on her now.

"Come on, Mona! Come on!"

"No, Marty!" she cried in panic. "Get off me! What are you doing? Don't! Don't—"

"I can't stop now. I've got to. Let me, Mona!"

"No!"

"I've got to!"

He was insistent and he was bigger than she was. He pressed his mouth over hers to keep her quiet and his arms gripped hers. She could feel him at the gateway to her body, pushing, trying to enter. She writhed and struggled, but the struggling only made it worse, it brought him closer to her, and then she realized that he was actually inside her, and there was a sudden unexpected terrible burst of pain, and then she could feel him within her. It was a strange and new feeling, this invasion of her body.

"No—please, go away—"

He didn't answer. She fought him silently, clawing at him and twisting, but the damage had been done, the entry had been achieved, and he was moving on top of her, his face buried in her bare breasts, and her anger and fright vanished abruptly as she felt a sharp throb of pleasure in her loins, and something was happening to her, and she gasped out in her excitement and a moment later Marty was gasping too, and then he was shaking in her arms and she felt the starburst of pleasure and it was all over.

She was confused and terrified afterward. There had been the pleasure, but there had been the pain, too, and she felt wet and soiled and messy.

"You raped me," she said to Marty.

"No. No, you let me do it."

"That isn't true. I told you no, and you just forced your way into me. Get out of here! Get out or I'll call a cop, Marty Hennings!"

Flustered and frightened, Marty made a hasty exit. Mona went to the bathroom, positive that she was going to have a baby or that her parents would be able to tell at a glance what she had been doing.

She didn't have a baby.

Her parents didn't find out—or, if they did, they kept their suspicions to themselves.

She even managed to pass the social studies exam.

And the next time she slept with Marty Hennings, it was no rape. They did it in his house, on the living-room couch, and this time Marty wore something that he had stolen from his father's dresser drawer, and they smiled and laughed their way all through it until the moment of ecstasy. Afterward, Marty told her that she was the third girl he had done it with, and by far the sexiest of the three. "The other girls, they never got so excited at the end," Marty said. "They just let me do it, but they didn't jump around and get out of breath the way you do. I don't think they did it right, or something."

For two and a half years, Marty had a monopoly over her. They slept together perhaps thirty times during those years. She didn't sleep with anyone else because the older boys in the town, knowing she was under fifteen, never even thought of approaching her, while the boys in her own age group were still too young and timid to think of sex, except for Marty. But Marty moved to another town when Mona was fourteen and a half. By then she had come to enjoy sex as much for its forbidden nature as for its direct physical pleasure. She dated a couple of sixteen-year-old boys, seduced one of them whose name she could not remember, and from then on never lacked for partners.

"I guess I slept with a dozen different boys altogether by the time I was eighteen," she said.

"Did you have a reputation in town as an easy girl?" I asked.

She laughed. "Oh, I guess some of the fellows must have whispered things about me. But I don't think any of the adults ever regarded me as particularly shameful. They probably didn't dream of what was going on. I wasn't the only high-school girl in town who put out, you know. I just got an earlier start than most."

"And what were your personal feelings about this? Did you think you were doing something sinful?"

"I thought I was having a lot of fun," she said. "That's all. The first time, with Marty, I was scared and had to be half raped, because I was only a kid. After that it was always a lark for me. Sure, I was afraid of getting knocked up, but other than that I had no worries."

"You didn't feel you were cheating your future husband by not being a virgin?"

She looked at me as though I had asked her a question in Sanskrit. "Cheating my future husband? But—hell, after the first time the damage was done. So why not live it up? I could only lose my innocence once, you know. I wasn't any more or any less a virgin for each time afterward."

"So you were a complete hedonist in your teens, then," I said. "You gave yourself up completely to sensual pleasure whenever you got the opportunity."

"Naturally. And not only in my teens, either. I've always gone out for a good time. I don't believe in saving it for when I grow old. I gather my rosebuds when I can, the way the poet said."

I shook my head. "You're missing my point, Mona. I want to give this book of yours some dramatic contrast as well as some moral tone."

"Huh?"

I jabbed my pencil through the air at her. "Here's the pitch. You were a sinner from the age of twelve on. You gave yourself up shamelessly to sin. You screwed everybody in sight. You had no qualms, no morals. You were a completely amoral kid. And so God punished you. When you grew up, he killed off the three men you loved."

"What kind of crap is this, Joey?"

"It's the kind of crap that's going to sell five million copies of your autobiography," I said. "Remember, we're building this story toward your redemption in God's eyes. So you start off as a shameless sinner. Then you suffer. You fall in love with four men. One leaves you, and three meet violent deaths. That's your punishment. You sink lower and lower. You even attempt suicide."

"I never—"

"You attempt suicide," I went on mercilessly. "With sleeping pills. It doesn't work. You're condemned to live, to expiate your sins. And then finally you're lifted out of the mire by God's grace. You've atoned for the sins of your teens. Your body has been purified through suffering, and now you can return to movie-making with a clear heart and a clear conscience. You're a saint now, Mona. Saint Mona."

She began to laugh. "I like that, Joey."

"You follow what I'm trying to do?"

"Sure. You're trying to make my biography into a kind of a novel. With a message. Don't screw around when you're a kid, or you'll grow up to be a junkie or a nympho or a drunk or maybe all three, if you aren't careful."

"It's the only way, Mona. You think I can advocate premarital intercourse in this book? You think I can show a girl of twelve getting laid, without also showing how she suffers as a direct result? We've got to make the book conform to the mass morality if we want to sell it to the book clubs and the slicks."

"But everybody screws around when she's a kid," Mona said. "Or practically everybody."

"Doesn't matter. Morality isn't what people do, it's what they say. It's what they tell their children they ought to do. And this book's got to be right down the slot. It's going to be a sexy book, you see, but a sexy book with a moral—it's a natural! It's the great American fraud, Mona. Sex it up any old way, add a bit of religion, and it sells. Leave out the sermon and it gets burned by the same good citizens who'd rush to buy it and slobber over it otherwise."

"I think you're making sense, Joey."

"Glad to hear you're with me."

She grinned. "I think they gave me a goddamn genius as a ghost writer. I think this book is going to sell millions of copies. You really have the slant. You have it all figured out. I've got to hand it to you."

"I've been a student of American morality for years," I told her. "I'm an expert on the kind of shit people will pay money to read."

"So I was a sinful little brat when I was twelve, and I repented when I was twenty-three. And afterward." She looked at me strangely. "You know something, Joey? You might just be right."

"About what?"

"About my getting punished for my sins."

"You see?" I said. "You're starting to believe it already. Good. Sincerity is the only commodity that is always in demand. Believe it, Mona. Believe it."

"And I thought I was cynical," she said. "Brother, you've got me beat hollow."

"It's contagious," I said. "Let's go on. You finished high school, now. You're thinking about Hollywood. Tell me how you made the break. Where you lived when you first came out here. How you met Vince Clissold. All those little details."

"Later," she said. "It's time for a swim, don't you think?"

"Half an hour, Mona. Just talk for half an hour more, now that we're moving along so smoothly."

"I'm tired of talking," she said.

"Mona—"

I should have known better than to try to argue with her. She smiled smugly at me, reached down, switched the tape recorder off. Rising, she skipped across the patio and sprinted out onto the diving board. Her body arched neatly as she cut into the pool. A moment later, both halves of her bikini came flying up over the edge. She grinned up at me and waved.

"Come on in! The water's great!"

Shrugging, I put down my notepad and headed for the pool.

10

The week went along, smoothly, serenely, without storm, without stress. We sank into a pleasant daily routine that soon became a habit.

In the morning we talked. I went through my notes and asked Mona specific questions about specific incidents in her life, and she told it all to the tape recorder. Color, detail, even some dialog. She was good at recalling things that happened to her and at bringing them to vivid life in her narratives. Many people have her sort of knack for oral narration, but can't get their stories down on paper for the life of them. Just as well, because there wouldn't be much market for ghost writers otherwise. I wondered how much of what Mona was telling me had actually happened and how much was the product of her no doubt highly developed imagination. Not that it really mattered. So long as Mona said it had happened, I was willing enough to believe that it really had.

After lunch, we sunned for a while each day, and then I went to work on the transcripts of our previous conversations. I had enough material to make a beginning, now, and so I began to write. I did ten pages a day of first-draft stuff, basing it on what I had already learned from Mona. I figured that if I could average about fifty pages a week, I'd have the complete 300-page draft finished by the end of May. Then we could go over it, insert material that had come to light during further conversations, strengthen the anecdotes that were already there, polish up the narration, and generally put the book in shape. Then I would feed the whole thing through the typewriter a second time from beginning to end and come out with 80,000 words of final draft by July tenth or so, right in time for the deadline.

Day by day, the little pile of manuscript grew. I didn't show it to Mona. I don't like people looking at unfinished work.

I would knock off each day around four, and take a swim with Mona. Then we'd loll around the patio having cocktails till seven or seven-thirty, followed by the usual superb-dinner.

In the evenings, we had various ways of amusing ourselves. Mona continued to show me all her old movies until I had seen the six of them. One night Carl Martinson and some of his friends came over. Another, we went to the premiere of a new movie. Another, we partied with some of Mona's friends. She wasn't trying to keep me cooped up any more. She introduced me openly as her ghost writer, didn't hide from anyone the fact that she was having an affair with me, and took me to a lot of fancy places. It became almost a routine affair to find myself shaking hands with some big star or important director. One big happy family, that's what Hollywood was; you could run into Oscar-winners everywhere, busily stealing each other's mates.

I ran into ex-lovers of Mona everywhere too. The standard gambit was, "So you're writing about Mona's life, are you? Well, I hope you don't say anything too scandalous about me!"

To which I would reply, "Oh? Were you and Mona good friends?"

"Good friends! Why, let me tell you—" and the voice became a confidential whisper—"Mona and I had one of the most sizzling affairs Hollywood ever knew. It was last year, February, I think, and—"

Everyone had had a torrid affair with Mona, it seemed. But I started correlating the data and realized that most of these affairs weren't affairs at all, in the usual sense of the word, but just one-night stands, quick lays. Most of them had happened during Mona's nympho period, after Mark Robinson's suicide. By me a decent affair lasts at least a few weeks steady, and if Mona had been having an affair with everyone who claimed to have had one with her during that year, it was a year at least two hundred months long.

Typical of Hollywood. A roll in the hay becomes an "affair." Everything gets blown up out of all proportion. Words lose their meanings.

Also typical of Hollywood. Men ready to kiss and tell, to spirit me aside and whisper some juicy morsels in hopes of getting mentioned in a star's autobiography. I was willing to believe that most, if not all of the whisperers had made Mona once or twice—by her own admission, just about everyone in the film colony had at some time or other—but I wasn't much impressed with their willingness to tell all. And some of them went into fantastic details. It was a brand-new experience for me when somebody I had met only ten minutes earlier, a beefy assistant producer, started to tell me in astonishing specifics about his affair with Mona, citing the positions they had used, the particular perverse practices he had persuaded Mona to employ, and a lot of other stuff that no gentleman would ever tell to anyone, let alone a stranger. Typical of Hollywood. One big happy goldfish bowl, and the idea of privacy or personal discretion was unknown.

Though there was a reverse side to the coin. These were the fellows who would sidle up to me and say, "Listen, I hear you're writing an autobiography for Mona. For Christ's sake keep my name out of it, will you? I'll make it worth your while, fella."

I didn't accept any payoffs, of course. Whenever such cases arose, I made a noncommittal answer and let it go. Naturally, we weren't going to name names in the case of Mona's quickie affairs. I even intended to get a clearance from Vince Clissold before saying in print that Mona had been having an affair with him. But Hollywood seemed full of panicky characters who were afraid that their wives or their ex-wives or their fan clubs or somebody would read Mona Thorne's book and learn that a little extracurricular screwing had been taking place.

And so it went. Typing by day, partying by night. And, of course, after the night's gaiety was done, there was always Mona in my arms.

She insisted on a certain formality, as though determined to keep me in my place. She never let me come into her bedroom, for example. It was more a matter of Her Majesty graciously condescending to partake of sexual intercourse when the mood was on her. When the mood was on her, she would come into my bedroom, partake, and sometimes leave immediately afterward. Other nights she would stay through till morning.

I will say that the mood came over her fairly often, like about three nights out of every four. Nevertheless, I resented the fact that I had no say in when we would make love and when we would not. When she didn't feel like it, I didn't stand a chance. When she did feel like it, she got it, even if I didn't happen to be in an amorous mood particularly. I was treated like a useful household appliance, not like a human being. But her sheer dazzling sexual virtuosity helped to make the bitter pill easier for me to swallow.

There were letters from Lisa, and letters to Lisa. I wrote regularly. Not every day, as I had promised that evening that seemed so many years ago, but I managed to get a letter off to her about every third day. She answered promptly each time. Kitty brought me the mail, always with a little grin on her face. Mona never once asked me who I was getting the letters from, or who I was writing to. I checked the envelopes a couple of times to see whether or not they had been steamed open and resealed after reading—Mona wasn't above a stunt like that—but they seemed okay.

Writing to Lisa was a tough chore. I couldn't begin to convey to her the truth of what I was doing out here in Los Angeles. And so my letters were hollow and insubstantial, skirting around the edges of things without ever coming out and being honest. When I read them back before mailing them, they struck me as being vague and phonied-up letters, which of course they were. After a while I stopped looking at them, just stuffing them into the envelopes after I signed my name to them.

Lisa's letters back had an increasingly hollow ring to them too. The early letters were full of love and passion and intimacy, but by the fourth or fifth letter she had caught my tone of vagueness. Was she having an affair too?

Was she starting to forget me?

I was depressed about the situation. I had to make a special effort to remember what Lisa had been to me before I had come out here. What we had been to each other. Out here in the land where dreams are manufactured, my entire past seemed as unreal as the latest Hollywood extravaganza. Lisa was slipping away, day by day.

And the worst part of it was that I hardly cared. I felt no anguish. Even the thought that she might be laying someone else back in New York failed to rouse me. I was getting mine, wasn't I? And she was a healthy girl with needs of her own. So what if she was getting it?

So what?

It was that kind of life. Plenty of food and sun and swimming and sex, and reality slipping away. By the third week, I had fallen almost completely into the Los Angeles way of life. I was rapidly becoming One Of Them. I didn't like it. But I couldn't help myself. There was something insidious in the climate.

Beginning of the fourth week.

More than one hundred pages of first-draft stuff done on The Book. The transcripts of Mona's conversations were running up toward several hundred pages, now. The tape had been turned on, and she talked endlessly, easily, repeating conversations that had taken place six and seven years ago while the tape recorder hummed.

"And then I said to Teddy, if I marry you, will you give up all your boyfriends? And he said, yes, I'll never sleep with a man again. I won't need to after I marry you, darling. And I said, how can I be sure? And he said, don't worry, Mona dearest. And then he came over to me. He put his hands on my breasts. Timidly. He wasn't sure of himself at all. He started to squeeze them and I kissed him and we got into bed, and he made love to me. It wasn't very good. He was so flustered he climaxed right away. But then we waited a while and tried again, and this time I made it, and the next day we announced our engagement...."

"Lee said, won't you try it once, Mona? Just for me. And I said, what the hell are you trying to do, make a junkie out of me? And he said, I love you Mona, and I said you've got some pretty goddamn funny ways of showing it. Then he fell on his knees and said, forgive me, forgive me, I'm a damned fool, I don't know what I'm doing. I've got no right to make you an addict like me. And I stroked his head and he looked up and began to kiss me, and I put his hands on my breasts, you know, to encourage him. And I thought we were going to have some sex, but all of a sudden he got up and ran out of the room and locked himself in the bathroom, and I banged on the door but he wouldn't come out, and then finally when he did come out his eyes were all glowing and I knew he had turned himself on...."

"I hadn't touched the stuff for weeks, not for weeks, and Mark hadn't slept with me for two weeks either. And one day he came into the room stark naked, and I could see he was excited and wanted to ball me, and I wanted to ball him too. I started getting undressed and he said, not so fast. Let's try a little test first. And he went out of the room and came back and he had a deck of heroin with him, and a spoon to cook it in, and he had the syringe that I hadn't seen for so long, and he held it all out to me. He said, here. Go ahead and turn yourself on, Mona. Which do you want? Do you want sex with me or do you want to turn yourself on? You can have one or the other but not both. And I hadn't had either one for so damn long, and I ached all over, and I took the syringe from him and he looked at me strangely and then I bent the needle and threw the syringe in the wastebasket and laughed, and I yanked my clothes off and pulled him down on top of me like a crazy woman, and he went into me and we made it fast, made it right over the top, and I knew from that afternoon on that I was cured, that I had kicked it, that I was off the stuff for good...."

Once Mona got into the mood, she could talk almost endlessly, regarding it as an intrusion when the hour and a half was up and the tape had to be turned over. All I had to do was edit her ramblings and give them some external form. Certainly the material was there. Scads of it. It came flowing out of her with boundless copiousness.

The fourth week, now. A stack of manuscript over an inch thick.

And letters from Lisa.

"Darling, please hurry up and finish that horrible book. New York is so dull without you. It's spring now, and the trees are turning green, and I'm all alone...."

So I answered her with empty words about how I was almost halfway through the first draft, how I hoped to be finished on time, how much I missed her. And all the rest. And I sealed the envelope and put a stamp on it, and then that night Mona and I made love with furious passionate abandon for more than an hour.

The fourth week came to its end. The manuscript grew.

Mona and I sat sipping cocktails on the edge of the pool. She had been sunbathing all afternoon while I worked on a typing table set up on the patio. Now all she wore was a towel draped negligently across her hips. Her tawny, golden breasts were bare to the afternoon warmth. Here on the patio we had absolute privacy, except for Kitty, who moved about like a ghost in the house, keeping her thoughts to herself.

I finished my daiquiri and poured a second one from the pitcher.

"Me too," Mona said.

I got up, took her glass, filled it. As I handed her the drink, I playfully caught one of her nipples between two of my fingers and gave it a little squeeze. She grinned. A kind of affection was developing between us since the blowup at Martha Vartan's party. We were getting used to one another, to living together. There were times when I almost started to forget that I was a hired hand, bought to do a job of literary hack work and to perform miscellaneous escort and stud services.

"Joey?" she said.

"Mmm?"

"Is this leap year?"

"No."

"When is leap year, then?"

I frowned, wondering vaguely what she was getting at. "Not till 1977," I said.

I sipped my drink. There was a long moment of silence. I looked toward her, noticing with pleasure the way her breasts held their shape when she leaned back, while another woman's breasts might flatten out into shapelessness at that kind of an angle.

"Joey?" she said.

"What is it, Mona?"

"How'd you like to marry me?"

I damned near dropped my drink. "What did you say, Mona?"

"You heard me. I said, how would you like to marry me. It isn't leap year, but I thought I'd ask you all the same, just to sound you out."

I felt a chill in the pit of my stomach. "Isn't this kind of sudden?"

"We've been living together a month. Out in Hollywood people get married on the spur of the moment, you know. A month is more time than a lot of people need to make up their minds."

"I'm not Hollywood people."

"You're getting to be."

I looked at her in horror. "Well, whatever I'm getting to be, I can't give you any answer to that question."

"The translation of that is that you don't want to say yes and you're afraid to say no."

"That isn't it, Mona."

"Then what is?"

"First of all, I'm still theoretically a married man. My divorce hasn't come through."

"That's only a technicality."

"The second thing is—is that I'm not sure I want to get married again. Not to you or to anyone else."

"What about this girl in New York?" she said slyly. "This Lisa that you write to and get all the letters from all the time?"

"She's—just a good friend," I said, hoping I sounded more convincing to her than I did to myself.

"Don't you want to marry me, Joey? We're good together in bed. You know that. I'm the best you ever had. You can't deny that. Can you? Can you?"

"Well—"

"Can you?"

"No," I said. "You're something unusual."

"And you're one of the best I ever had, Joey. That's saying a lot. But I mean it. I wouldn't have brought the whole idea up if I didn't mean it."

My flesh crawled at the idea of marrying Mona Thorne. But I sought for some tactful way to wriggle out of this. I didn't want to insult her. Not now, not with so much of the book done. This would be a hell of a time for her to bounce me from the assignment.

I said, "Let's just keep the idea on ice, shall we? See how things work out while I'm finishing the book, and then we can make up our minds about whether we want it on a permanent basis."

"You'd do well out here, Joey. I'd get you into my studio as a writer, and they'd give you the best assignments. You'd write the scripts for all my movies. You know what they'd pay you? You'd start off at a thousand a week, maybe, and you'd go to about five grand. A quarter million a year, if you wanted to work that hard. But you wouldn't have to work at all, if you didn't want to. I'd make one movie a year, say three months, and the rest of the time we could just travel around, a month in Mexico, six weeks on the Riviera, a month in the Caribbean, a month in Paris—"

"Mona—"

She ignored me. "And another thing you ought to consider, Joey. In California we have community property laws. That means if the marriage doesn't work out, you're entitled to half of what I own. You'd be a millionaire, Joey. You'd never have to look at a typewriter again in your life. How's that strike you? You'll have it made either way. If we get along, you've got me, and a soft life. If we can't keep it alive, well, you'll still have a pile of money."

I looked at her almost imploringly, trying to get her to shut up. Marry Mona? I'd sooner marry Medusa, I thought. For the past few weeks her sunny side had been showing, but I had also seen her darker nature in operation.

And who wanted to marry a girl who had been screwed by half of Hollywood?

And who wanted to be bought this way?

I searched frantically for some lighthearted way of getting out of this nightmarish conversation, and finally I found a gambit that I thought would work.

"Mona," I said, breaking into her monolog.

"Mmmm?"

"It isn't healthy for me to marry you."

"Huh?"

"No, it isn't safe at all. You're a jinx, you know. Teddy Burns—a suicide. Lee Crosswell—an automobile accident. Mark Robinson—another suicide. It's dangerous to love you, Mona. You're too risky. And I'm too young to die."

Her expression changed in a moment, back to the Mona of Martha Vartan's party.

"You lousy bastard," she said. "Of all the tasteless remarks. Is that supposed to be funny?"

"Well, look, Mona, I didn't mean—"

She cut my fumbling off. She rose to her feet, and her towel fell away, and there she was in all her magnificent nudity, breasts and thighs and nipples, buttocks and calves and ankles, Mona Thorne in the flesh, a sight that many men would give five years of their lives to behold, and she was nearly shaking with barely contained fury.

"You disgust me!" she snapped. "You lousy hack, I wouldn't marry you for anything in the world now. Not if everybody else in the world was a eunuch!"

"Mona, listen—"

She turned her back on me, and I saw those delectable buttocks of hers, and with a pang I remembered how her body had felt tight against mine the night before.

Here we go again, I thought.

Only maybe this time I had had it. I looked despairingly at the pile of manuscript on the typing table.

With regal rage, the nude Mona swept past me and into the house, her breasts heaving wildly and her eyes stormy with anger.

11

Somehow we got it patched up. Somehow. It wasn't easy, because Mona had really been serious about marrying me, and in her egocentric way she had never taken into consideration the possibility that I might not like the idea.

For a day and a half, she didn't speak to me. We ate in stony silence, she treated me as invisible at the pool, and she refused to use the tape recorder. I didn't let it bother me. There was enough material taped already to make three books out of, and if one or two incidents never got written down it would be small loss to the world of letters. I sat at my typewriter, resolutely pounding out first-draft copy. That day, uninterrupted by Mona, I got sixteen pages written, my best record since the start of the project.

That night, the night after our quarrel, Mona watched films in her screening room. I didn't go in to find out what films they were, but I was willing to bet that they were her own. Watching her old movies was Mona's panacea for any kind of emotional upheaval. She had prints of some other films around, but the only ones she ever seemed to watch were the six in which she had starred.

I went up to my room, wrote another one of my vague letters to Lisa, and read for a while. Around half-past ten the door opened and Mona walked in without bothering to knock.

I looked up. "Hello."

"Listen, Joey, I want to talk to you."

"As long as you keep the topic away from matrimony, Mona," I said.

Her eyes were steely. "Don't worry, I won't slip the ring around your finger."

"Then what's on your mind?"

"I came to apologize," she said, and I could see that it was an effort for her to get that word apologize past her lips. "I'm sorry I acted up again yesterday. I know you hate my guts, and I shouldn't have suggested anything about marrying me. I know that all you want to do is get this job finished up and get the hell back to New York. So that's why I apologize."

Good old Mona, I thought. Even when she was allegedly making an apology, she had a way of seeming belligerent about it. I wasn't exactly touched.

I said, "You don't have to put it so bluntly."

"It's the truth, isn't it?"

I shrugged. "Hollywood's not the kind of place I'd enjoy living in, Mona. I couldn't consider settling here on any kind of permanent basis. Any more than you could consider moving to New York."

"Okay. So marriage wouldn't work, then."

"No. It wouldn't."

"Is there a truce between us again?" she asked.

"I'm willing."

"So am I," she said. "I won't raise the subject again." She hesitated for a long moment, staring at me steadily. Then she said, "Do you want to sleep with me?"

"I wouldn't mind."

"That the most enthusiasm you can muster?"

I shrugged again. "What the hell am I supposed say, Mona? You haven't even been speaking to me since yesterday afternoon. You want me to get sloppy and sentimental now after that kind of treatment?"

"Don't ever get sloppy and sentimental, Joey. Not for anything."

"Then what do you want?" I asked.

"You," she said.

She was an incredible woman. I began to wonder, as I stood there and watched her take off her clothes, whether there hadn't been some other reasons for the suicide and miscellaneous miserable fates of her lovers. Had Teddy Burns shot himself because a gossip columnist threatened to expose him as a homosexual—a fact that was known to three-quarters of Hollywood anyway? Or had he despairingly put a bullet through his brain after a couple of years of trying to adjust to Mona's alternate moods of bitchiness and melting seductiveness?

She could tire a man out pretty fast.

She stood in front of me, and began undressing. She pulled down the zipper of her dress and stepped out of it. Underneath, she wore a low-scooping bra, and panties.

I had seen Mona swimming and sunning herself in the nude so often in this past month that the sight of her naked body was beginning to lose novelty for me. But I rarely saw her in undies, and somehow this had a strangely powerful erotic effect on me. To see the ripe globes of her breasts held in check by that skimpy bra had a blazing effect on me as I watched her.

"Finish the job," she said.

I stepped forward.

I reached around behind, found the hooks of the bra, opened them. The cups fell away. There were her breasts, rising toward me, twin peaks of glorious flesh, the nipples erecting like dark-red sentinels atop the curving hemispheres.

I put my hands on her breasts, and a little shiver went through her body. "The panties," she said.

I rolled the panties down over her full hips. They dropped from her knees to her insteps, and she lifted one foot and then the other, letting me remove them. I was kneeling, and I rose slowly, putting my hands on the cool mounds of her buttocks, and burying my face in the splendor of her magnificent body.

We stayed that way a long moment.

Then I lifted my lips.

She stood before me, eyes slitted, legs slightly apart, breasts rising and falling with growing excitement.

Why not marry her? I thought suddenly, unexpectedly.

The thought dazzled me. Now, as she stood nude before me, she seemed irresistible. Mona the bitch, Mona the nympho, Mona the sadistic vengeful female—all these flaws were eclipsed by the sheer blazing beauty of her naked body before me.

Marry her.

Live like a king, like a sultan.

My hands trembled. I touched her breasts, felt the stiff little nipples.

She was undressing me now.

My body was on fire. I could live in this mansion, I thought. Write for the movies, make a hundred grand a year without half trying. Swim and sunbathe and doze. And every night Mona, Mona, Mona.

My clothes dropped away. I was naked now. She weaved against me, doing a kind of snake dance, hypnotizing me with her body and her eyes. Her love-hardened nipples grazed the skin of my chest as she moved back and forth in front of me in a weird dance of sheer lust.

Her lips were against mine now. Her tongue darted like a fiery lance into my mouth. I could feel the velvet sheen of her belly rubbing sideways against my skin. We moved backward toward the bed.

Why not marry her? I thought again.

Down on the bed now.

Body twisting against body.

Tantalizing moment as I strove to link my body to hers, and she resisted me, her legs locked tight.

Her eyes glistened. Her voice was a lust-filled throbbing whisper. "I love you, Joey! I love you, I love you, I love you!"

I made no answer. I squeezed her breasts hard, and then silently struggled to part her thighs.

"Say you love me, Joey!" she commanded.

My fingers dug deep into the soft tan flesh of her thighs. But her ankles were locked. Would I have to rape her? I was half out of my mind with desire for her. She had artfully led me on, provoking me with all the skill of an Oriental courtesan.

"Mona—Mona, let me—"

"Say you love me!"

"I want you!"

"Say you love me!"

I hesitated. My jaws quivered. I pried at her legs, but no force could have separated them. Her breasts heaved and bobbed in the struggle. She wore an unearthly smile, a vindictive smile, a smile of triumph.

"Mona!"

"Give me what I want, and then I'll give you what you want, Joey!"

Breasts and thighs, hips and buttocks, loins and lips burning against me, unattainable, unapproachable, inaccessible.

"I can't stand it, Mona. Stop this. Don't go on this way."

"Say you love me, Joey!"

"I love you!" I choked.

"Again!"

"I love you, Mona."

"You mean it?"

"I mean it," I said hysterically.

She laughed in triumph.

She had won.

The next moment her body opened to mine, and we throbbed, rose together in an agony of pleasure, a twisting, lurching, wild symphony of lust. Up, up, up toward the brink, over it in no more than a minute's time. I clamped my eyes tight together as the pounding eddy of fulfillment ripped through me. Below me, Mona's silken body heaved and jolted in her own private ecstasy.

We didn't stop there. We went on, on to new heights, until the world melted away and there was nothing left in the universe but Mona's breasts, Mona's tawny thighs, Mona's firm satin-smooth buttocks, Mona, Mona, Mona.

After a long while I realized that I was alone. I lay crosswise on the rumpled bed, utterly depleted, drained, exhausted. Mona was gone. All that remained was the taste of Mona on my lips.

The words echoed in my brain.

I love you, Mona. I love you I love you I love you I love you I love you—

I quivered with anger. She had forced the words out of me, had used her body the way a torturer would use thumb screws, until she had wrung the lying words from my lips. And now she could toss them in my face whenever she pleased. Now she could flaunt her triumph over me. "See?" she could say. "You're just putty. You can be made to say anything when you're heated up. Like all men."

I sat up, flexed my fingers. I fought back the temptation to go into the next room and throttle the life out of the scheming bitch. That would be a headline guaranteed to stir up even this headline-happy town. MOVIE STAR STRANGLED BY GHOST WRITER.

Calmness returned. Calmness and fierce depression. I looked at my watch and saw that it was three in the morning. According to F. Scott Fitzgerald, it was the most terrible time of all, the time of the dark night of the soul. I sat on the edge of my bed, staring bitterly into nothingness, wishing I could recall those words that Mona had twisted out of me, those damnable lying words.

Fitzgerald was right. There are times when it takes all a man's strength to endure the small hours of the morning. I watched the gleaming minute hand slowly crawl around the dial, until it was ten minutes to four, and I put my head to the pillow and dropped off to sleep.

I still felt depressed in the morning. I woke up around ten with a lousy headache, and got dressed and went downstairs. Kitty was bustling around dusting things on the ground floor, and there was no sign of Mona.

"Where's Miss Thorne?" I asked.

"She went over to see her agent, Mr. Baldwin. Said she wouldn't be back till around lunchtime. I'll put up breakfast for you if you want it now."

"Okay," I said. "And start it off with a pot of black coffee, Kitty."

Last night seemed to be a bad dream. I love you, Mona. That's what I had said. But it wasn't true! She had extorted the words from me!

Or was it true?

Did I love her and hate her all at once?

She was a scheming calculating bitch, and I despised her for the many different ways she had chosen to humiliate me since I had come to live with her. But if I hated her all that much, why didn't I just pull out? The money? That couldn't be sufficient motivation to put up with her this way.

Was I falling into Mona's trap, then? Was she casting her spell over me, drawing me down the way she had lured Teddy Burns and Lee Crosswell and Mark Robinson and every other man she had ever taken a fancy to?

I wondered.

I sat there sipping my black coffee and feeling tired and confused, and then Kitty came in with a half grapefruit for me, and an envelope.

"Letter for you," she said.

I took it from her, saw that it was from Lisa, and slit it open with my knife.

I read it. I read it a second time, just to make sure it said what I thought it said.

"Darling, I have the most wonderful news. I spoke to Jerry and we rearranged things a little and I won't have to wait till August to take my vacation after all. They've decided to let me have two weeks starting next Monday instead. I hope you won't be angry with me when I tell you that I've bought myself a round-trip ticket to Los Angeles. I'll be arriving at four in the afternoon, L.A. time, on Monday, and since I don't know where you're staying I'd be very happy if you'd meet me at the airport, or at least have someone from the agency come out to fetch me. I'll leave the accommodations problem in your capable hands, darling. If it's okay with you, I'd prefer to move into your hotel room with you.

"I know that you said when you left, Joey, that you wouldn't have any time for me if I came out to L.A. But that was over a month ago, and maybe you don't feel the same way any more. I know I miss you terribly, especially when the night comes, and I hope you feel the same way about me. I wouldn't want this separation to do anything to what we had going for us before you left.

"Don't worry about my getting in your way. I'll be a good girl and spend every day sightseeing or sunbathing while you're busy interviewing that movie star. I'll keep out of your way when you're at the typewriter, too. But at least we'll be able to have dinner together and spend our evenings together, and also our nights. Especially our nights. Believe me, I've thought hard about making this trip, and I do hope you won't be annoyed to have me come out.

"With all my love,

"Lisa."

I folded the letter up and stuffed it hastily into my shirt pocket, and swallowed a chunk of grapefruit without tasting it at all.

Kitty came back into the room. She must have seen the odd expression on my face, because she looked at me sympathetically and said, "You get some bad news in that letter, Mr. Baldwin?"

"Bad news? Oh—no—no, it's nothing, Kitty. Nothing at all."

But it wasn't nothing at all.

It was plenty.

I finished breakfast and set up my typing table in the open air and tried to get some work done while waiting for Mona to return. I was in the middle of narrating her stormy siege of alcoholism, following Teddy Burns' suicide, and at least till yesterday the words had been flowing pretty easily.

Now I stared at the page in the typewriter without being able to set a single word down.

I looked at the transcript of Mona's remarks on that time of her life, and looked back at my page, and tried to translate Mona's ramblings into narrative.

I couldn't get any work done.

I tried one of my favorite tricks, and went back a couple of pages and began to retype what I had already written, in order to work up some momentum. But this time it didn't work. I painstakingly copied everything I had written in the last two pages, but when I got up to the point where I had stopped yesterday, I was totally unable to go on. I couldn't work.

I was stymied.

My mind was full of Lisa and her letter.

Christ! Just what I needed—Lisa coming to Los Angeles for two weeks!

"I'll leave the accommodations problem in your capable hands, darling.... I'd prefer just to move into your hotel room with you."

What hotel room?

What was I supposed to do, show up at the airport on Monday and meet Lisa and quietly explain to her that I wasn't staying at any hotel, that I had been living with Mona Thorne all this time and sleeping with her? What was I supposed to tell Lisa? To get her pretty ass back to New York?

Tell her to go home and wait for me to finish the job?

Tell her to go find somebody else because I was in love with Mona?

I didn't know what to say. For a while I was tempted to dash off a telegram to Lisa. UNDER NO CIRCUMSTANCES COME TO L.A. STOP TOO BUSY FOR COMPANY STOP KNOW YOU WILL UNDERSTAND, JOEY Something like that. That was probably the smartest way out. It would hurt her, it would wound her—but not anywhere nearly as deeply as the wound she would receive when she stepped off the plane and learned the truth about the state of affairs that had been existing out here all this past month.

I didn't send the telegram, though.

Today was Thursday. There was time to head her off, sure. But she had probably told everyone around her that she was going to Los Angeles. She'd be put in a bad position if the trip were called off. I decided to let her come, and take the consequences.

I tried to shrug Lisa out of my mind and get back to the job at hand. I looked at the blank page, typed a hesitant sentence, looked at it for a couple of moments, then covered it all over with a row of x's. I typed another sentence. It was lousy. I wrote a whole paragraph.

Lisa's coming to L.A., I thought obsessively.

The paragraph stank. I ripped out the page; balled it up, rolled a new one into the typewriter.

I looked at it for a long, long time. Then I started to write again, stopped, started again. By half-past twelve, I had written a grand total of four hundred words, and I was covered with sweat and sick to my stomach.

"Guess who," a familiar voice said behind me. Hands were pressed to my eyes. Two full firm breasts were jabbing into my back.

"Theda Bara," I said.

"Wrong."

"Minnie Mouse," I said.

"Wronger."

"Queen Victoria."

"How'd you ever guess?" Mona squealed. I turned around and looked at her. She was wearing a bright-yellow playsuit that set off her jet-black hair beautifully. My heart ached to look at her.

Lisa's coming to L.A., I thought leadenly.

"How's the work going?" Mona asked.

"A little slow today," I said.

"You did so much yesterday. I guess it's all evening out, or something." She grinned. "I just saw Carl. He says there's a ninety percent chance that the book is going to be bought for filming in November."

"With you playing yourself?" I asked.

"Naturally. It'll be a real *tour de force*, when I play myself weighing fifty pounds more than I weigh now. The film will be a smash. I think it's the first time a movie star ever played her own autobiography in the movies."

"A real first," I said without enthusiasm.

She leaned up against me, nibbling my ear. "Remember what I told you last night?" she whispered. "I love you, Joey. I mean it. I love you."

I was silent.

"Tell me you love me?" she said.

"Look, Mona, I'm trying to get some work done so—"

"Okay," she said, her voice chilling immediately. "Pardon me for living. You get your work done I'm going to go swimming. If you're feeling more sociable later on, maybe we can get together for a while."

I nodded and pretended to be deep in concentration. Mona moved away, but I could feel the hot waves of her anger directed at my back. I tapped out a couple of words.

Lisa's coming, I thought.

Lisa.

Lisa.

Oh, Christ, what am I going to do now?

12

The rest of the day dribbled away, one sticky hour after another. I got practically no work done, and I had no appetite at dinner, and when Mona asked me if I felt like taking a drive into the hills I said no. I used up the evening watching the Dodgers get shellacked by the St. Louis Cardinals on television.

Mona came in a couple of times during the evening to wrinkle up her nose at me.

"You going to watch baseball all night?"

"I haven't seen a game in years. I feel like a kid all over again."

"You look fascinated."

"I am. I used to go to see the Dodgers when they were the Brooklyn Dodgers. Life hasn't been the same in New York since the Dodgers and the Giants pulled out, you know that?"

She didn't answer. She stalked out, and I turned my attention back to the game just in time to see some Cardinal hit a double with the bases loaded and chase three runs across.

The game ended, finally, 12-4, St. Louis. Too bad. It was a nice tranquilizer, sitting there in front of the idiot box watching a bunch of grown men hitting a ball around while other grown men cheered or booed. I turned off the set, went into my bedroom, got undressed.

Mona didn't come to me that night.

The next day was Friday. I was up bright and early, had a swim before breakfast, got to the typewriter by ten o'clock. Mona didn't make her appearance till half-past eleven. She came out on the patio and asked me if I cared to go on with the question-and-answer sessions.

I wasn't making any progress behind the typewriter, so I said okay and switched on the tape recorder.

"Where were we when we quit the other day?" she asked me.

"You were telling me how you used to drive down into Mexico to get heroin," I said.

She nodded. "Oh. Yes. I didn't want to risk buying from a pusher up here, you see. And I enjoyed the long drive. It loosened me up. I'd leave early in the morning, and I'd do the whole thing at around seventy-five miles an hour and I'd get across the border by lunchtime. Then I'd make my connection and buy the stuff in Tijuana. It's pretty cheap down there. Of course, smuggling it back is rough."

"How'd you do it?"

She laughed. "Sometimes I'd turn on down there. That made the drive back a real gas. Other times I'd come back with the H hidden in my bra."

"They ever check you over?"

"Usual customs stuff," she said. "I wasn't a known addict or a pusher, so they never really gave me a thorough checkout. All they'd have to do was stick me in a room and have a matron look me over and I'd have been cooked." She laughed. "Some girls bring the H across the border hidden somewhere else. A woman's got a natural hiding place, you know. But the cops are wise. If they'll look inside a girl's bra, they'll look in other places too."

"You ever hide it there?"

"Once," she said. "One day when I wasn't wearing a bra. But I never got caught. Never even came close. You want to make up a time when I almost got caught?"

I nodded. "Wouldn't be a bad idea."

"Okay. Let's say that one day I was coming back into San Diego with a load of H in my bra, and the customs boy says pull over and wait there. I saw this happen. So I pull over and sit there wetting my pants, figuring that for sure they'll find the horse and get me on a narcotics rap. Maybe fifteen minutes goes by and they come over and they search my car. But they aren't searching for heroin, it turns out. They're searching for tequila. They got a tip that some broad is trying to smuggle a couple of cases of tequila across the border without paying duty. So they look my car over and don't find any tequila and they apologize and send me on my way, and me with two hundred bucks worth of H in my bra."

"Good enough," I said. "I'll work the story in. It's a nice touch."

"It'll go good in the movie, too," she said. "Drama. Tension. Suspense."

"Yeah," I said.

She got bored with talking into the tape machine after a while, and went away to splash around in her pool. I went back to the typewriter and made some progress for a while until Lisa came back into my mind.

I wondered what Mona did to keep herself amused when she was between lovers. Swim all day? Sleep? Drive aimlessly around the city? It seemed like an empty life. There was music playing all the time, there were good books around the house, all the implements of culture. But Mona didn't pay much attention to them. I got the impression they were there for decorative purposes only. Most likely she had inherited everything from her various defunct lovers.

Lisa's coming.

The thought interjected itself into my thoughts every ten or fifteen minutes.

I couldn't escape it. I couldn't escape it at dinner Friday night, when we dined on tournedos Rossini washed down by a great Chambertin. I couldn't escape it after dinner, when we went partying over at some actor's estate in the canyon country. I couldn't escape it at two that morning, when we returned and when Mona lay naked and writhing and panting in my arms. I couldn't escape it at the moment of climax, when Mona's ecstatic face suddenly turned into Lisa's.

Saturday.

I had a million plans for Lisa's arrival. Ways of lying to her, of concealing things. But nothing hung together. Nothing seemed worth trying.

Where was I going to put her?

What was I going to tell her?

What was I going to tell Mona?

I chewed over it all day Saturday. Saturday night, I decided that I'd put Lisa up in a Beverly Hills hotel, get her a single, and explain that I was temporarily staying over at Mona's place. Then I'd try to work free of Mona's clutches and move into the hotel with Lisa. It might work. Or it might all blow up in my face.

Sunday.

A day of sitting behind the typewriter and pounding away furiously. I had close to 200 pages of first-draft stuff done now. I knocked off at noon after a highly productive morning. Mona's book was taking shape. I was over the hump; the hardest part of the story was told, and I just had to guide it downhill toward the grand finale.

I spent the afternoon sunbathing and drinking too many martinis. Twenty-four hours to Lisa's arrival. I was tense, knotted-up.

Sunday night I almost spilled the whole story out to Mona. We watched a movie in her screening room, an old Charlie Chaplin comedy that she'd bought a print of, and then we had a few drinks and I was just about to tell her that my girlfriend was coming to town and I was moving out, when I saw how impossible the whole thing was. Mona was a little tipsy, and very very affectionate. I'd be asking for all the devils in hell if I spoiled her mood now.

So I said nothing, and she made me undress her, and I laid her right there on the couch in the screening room. Body plunged against body, breath mingled with breath, tongue touched tongue. A real communion of souls. She shuddered out an intense orgasm and then lay there on her side, her buttocks bent into a taut double bow. And tomorrow Lisa was coming. I felt like the cheapest bastard who ever lived, but I didn't stop Mona as she artfully worked me over and set me up for a second round half an hour later.

I took her body and tried to blank out the obsessive voice in my mind. But it was no good. I couldn't drink it away, I couldn't screw it away, I couldn't work it away. It was there for good.

I carried a nude Mona down the hall into her bedroom. She blew me a kiss good night.

Her lips shaped the words, I love you.

I slept miserably that night.

Monday.

The fatal day.

In the morning, I pretended that everything was as it should be. I worked, I taped some more of Mona's reminiscences, I got a little swimming in. After lunch, I phoned the Beverly Plaza Hotel on the sly and reserved a room in Lisa's name. Twenty-five bucks a day. Well, Mona was paying me a hundred a week for expenses, but she was also supplying me with room and board, so I'd hardly spent a nickel in the month I'd been here. I could afford it.

About one-thirty I went over to Mona and said, "You mind if I borrow a car for the afternoon?"

"What for?"

"I feel like taking a drive," I told her.

"Alone?"

"Alone."

She looked up at me, her brows knitting together, and I knew she was dying to ask me all about it, where I was going, what I planned to do. But we had been through this all before, and she wasn't supposed to infringe on my privacy. She didn't have to lend me the car, but if she did lend it it had to be without strings attached.

She said, "The keys to the Bentley are on my dresser, Joey."

"I don't want the Bentley. It's too fancy."

"You can't have the Alfa."

"The Buick is plenty good enough."

"Okay," she said. "Kitty's got the keys."

Kitty was tidying up the kitchen. I asked for the keys and she handed them to me.

"How long does it take to drive from here to the airport?" I asked her.

"Oh, maybe an hour, Mr. Baldwin." She looked at me curiously. "You leaving?"

"Just going sightseeing, that's all."

I hung around till half-past two. Then impatience got the better of me. I pulled the Buick out of the garage, studied a road map for a while, and left. Mona waved to me as I went out the driveway.

I drove slowly toward the airport. These were unfamiliar roads to me, and the other drivers on the freeways were largely a bunch of lunatics, and my nerves weren't exactly in tip-top condition. Even so, I got to the airport by twenty minutes to four. I left the station wagon in one of the parking lots and hoofed it over to the arrivals terminal to see what the story was on Lisa's flight.

It was due in right on time, four o'clock.

I sat down to wait.

Can twenty minutes last twenty months? These did. But eventually it was four o'clock, and I looked out through the big window and saw the huge steel bird taxiing to a halt far out on the runway, and rolling ponderously toward the terminal. It was a 747, and it looked big enough to carry a regiment.

I waited. Passengers started to trickle into the terminal. At least fifty came before I saw Lisa.

She was wearing a white blouse open at the throat, and a short green skirt. I could see her breasts straining against the fabric of her blouse. Abruptly I wondered how I had let Mona cast such a spell over me, when I had a girl like Lisa waiting back in New York.

She saw me and ran into my arms. I took her jacket and weekend bag from her, put them down, and grabbed her hard against me.

"Joey, it's been so long! It's seemed like years, hasn't it?"

"Like centuries," I told her.

There were tears in her eyes, and a smile on her lovely lips. "You aren't mad at me, are you? You're glad I came out here?"

"Of course I'm glad," I lied.

"How's the book coming along?"

"Not bad at all. I'm a few days ahead of schedule on the first draft."

"Great, Joey!"

"Another hundred pages or so—shouldn't take me more than two weeks—and then the hardest part is over. The rest is just revisions and polishing. And then sitting back to wait for the checks to come in."

We walked over to the baggage claim counter arm in arm. So far, so good. I was genuinely glad to see Lisa. Five minutes with her and all my old love for her was rekindled, and Mona was only a distant Jezebel with a tiny voice.

I picked her bag up and we went out to the parking lot. Lisa frowned at the Buick.

"Whose car is this?"

"Mona's. Miss Thorne's. I borrowed it for the trip out here."

"You mean a big star like Mona Thorne drives around in a station wagon?"

I chuckled. "This is for getting the groceries in. She's got a big gray Bentley for formal occasions. And an Alfa-Romeo for informal ones."

Lisa looked impressed. We got in. I was uneasy, so uneasy that I had trouble turning on the ignition.

"Where are we staying?" Lisa asked.

"You're going to the Beverly Plaza Hotel."

"We going to share a room?"

I moistened my lips and shook my head. "It isn't working out that way. Not just yet."

"I don't get you."

I nosed out onto the freeway, narrowly missing a collision with a speeding car coming up behind me. I jammed down on the gas, changed to a safer lane, and sped ahead.

I said, "I'm not staying at any hotel just now."

"Where, then?"

I hesitated. "Miss Thorne has me put up at her place," I said. "We decided it was the least complicated way of doing things. The other way, there were a million phone calls a day, and a lot of time wasted going back and forth from the hotel to her place—"

I expected an explosion, but Lisa was calm. "So I stay at a hotel and you stay at her place?"

"For the time being. Just till I get the draft finished. Then I'll switch over to the hotel. Meanwhile I'll be able to see you most evenings—"

"I'll be back in New York by the time you finish that draft," she pointed out. "I only came out here for two weeks, remember? And if I had known I was hardly going to see you during those two weeks—"

"I warned you before I left."

"But I didn't think it would be like this. Can't you arrange for her to put me up at her place too?"

I smiled grimly. "I don't think that would work out too well, Lisa."

"You told me she had an enormous place. Dozens of rooms. There must be a spare bedroom someplace around. I'd pay her for my stay. And I wouldn't interfere with any of the work, Joey. I don't want to be stuck at some hotel miles from where you're going to be."

"I'll see what I can do," I promised her lamely. This was going to be a ticklish two weeks, no doubt about it. A very ticklish two weeks.

I drove along.

"What kind of woman is this Mona Thorne, anyway?" Lisa asked.

"A bitch. A beautiful bitch."

"More beautiful than I am?"

I shook my head. "No. But there's really no way of comparing the two of you. She's a brunette—very dark. You're blonde. You're a lot bigger than she is. She's older, seven years older."

"How do we compare in bed, Joey?"

The quiet sentence took my breath away. Up till this moment Lisa had been playing it cool, no accusations, no innuendoes, no prying questions. Now she had dropped the bombshell all at once.

"What do you mean by that remark?"

"Don't bluff, Joey. You've been living in this woman's house for a month. I know you and I know what she's supposed to be like. And I could tell from your letters that you were leaving out half the story. Or maybe a good deal more than half."

If I hadn't been driving, I would have wearily closed my eyes and hoped for better times. Instead I said, "I wish you hadn't started this, Lisa."

"You wish I hadn't even come out, don't you?"

"If you were suspicious of me," I said, "why'd you come? To start a fight? To confirm your suspicions?"

"I came out here because I love you," she said in a level voice that made me feel worth about two Confederate cents. "I don't give a damn if you're going to bed with her. I didn't expect you to spend two whole months living like a monk, Joey. I came out here so you wouldn't forget about me. Will you have some time for me, Joey? Or are you so wrapped up in her that you can't spare a moment?"

"Lisa—honey—" I groped for words. I had expected blazing jealousy, fierce screeching denunciations. But I had forgotten what Lisa was like. Mona was the screecher, Mona was the one who had all the jealousy. Lisa was sane. Lisa was well-balanced.

I said, "It's been an unusual situation. Will you let me work it out somehow?"

"I won't interfere. Say the word and I'll go back to New York tomorrow. Tonight."

"No—don't—"

"Do you still want to marry me, Joey?"

"Yes," I said.

"I won't hold you to it. I don't want you to think you're a prisoner."

The contrast with Mona was fantastic. I said, "I love you, Lisa."

"You love me but you wish I hadn't come out here. Right?"

"No. Yes. Christ, it would have been simpler if you hadn't. I'm so damned mixed up—"

We were approaching Beverly Hills. I found the Beverly Plaza, and we pulled into the imposing driveway. Lisa hadn't said much the past ten minutes. We were both trying to work the situation out silently.

She checked in, signing the register. A bellhop took her luggage and we went upstairs. She had a good room, tenth floor, excellent view. I tipped the kid a dollar, and he handed me the key, took a wishful look at Lisa's figure, and vanished.

I turned to Lisa. Tears glistened in her eyes.

"Oh, Joey—" she began.

Then she was in my arms, her body against mine, her kisses hungry.

13

I helped her out of her clothes without saying a word. We didn't need words. The pull of the flesh was enough to set up a complete communication between us.

Off came the blouse, the skirt, the bra, all the rest of the garments, until there was a heap of frilly things on the chair near the window, and Lisa stood in front of me naked, the twin hills of her breasts rising and falling rapidly in her excitement, and I touched them and she sighed and started to take off my clothes.

It was more than a month since we had done this, and from the way Lisa responded to a touch here and a pressure there and a kiss somewhere else, I knew that in all that long month she had kept herself chaste for me. I was certain of it. Her body was trembling with long-repressed desires. Lisa is a healthy girl who likes and needs love, and I could see the effects of that self-imposed abstinence. And I felt like more of a heel than ever, because while Lisa had been taking cold showers back in New York and going to a lonely bed every night, I had been balling with Mona Thorne with extraordinary frequency and abandon.

I was naked now, and the two of us were on the bed, toying with fingertips and nails, little careless love-play, and then I saw the surging impatience in Lisa's eyes, as though she were unable to wait through the preliminaries, and she threw herself at me. Her body twisted and writhed against mine, and it was good, with none of Mona's crazy pyrotechnics, but just simple honest loving, no fancy frills, no wild gyrations.

It went on a long time.

She began to quicken the pace of her movements and then it was happening, the moment of release, the little surprised gasp of hers that I hadn't heard for so long, and next thing I knew she was going berserk and I gripped her tight as ecstasy rocked through her, sending her off into some fantastic world of lights and colors whose nature I could only guess at.

Then we came back down to earth. We lay side by side, and I cupped my hands around the fullness of her breasts, and she drew her knee up to flex her buttocks, and her eyes were tear-glistening and smiling.

"Joey, it's been such a long time. Such a long time."

"I know, baby."

"It was good, wasn't it, just now? For you?"

"It was great."

"Better than—with her?"

"Don't talk about her."

"We can't just ignore the situation, Joey. What's going to happen to us?"

"I'm going to finish the book and we're going to go back to New York and get married," I said firmly.

"I'm so worried. All this month—I was certain I was losing you, Joey."

"I went through hell," I said. "That woman's a witch. She wouldn't give me any peace."

"Tell me you love me."

"I love you more than anything in the world, Lisa." I leaned forward, kissed the firm smooth flesh of her belly, then turned her over and planted a kiss on each of the dimples just north of her buttocks. She laughed in pleasure, some of the tension going from her now.

"Do you regret that I came out here, Joey?"

"No. I'm glad you did. Because—because now I have the strength to escape from her," I said.

I elbowed up from the bed and walked to the phone. I gave the switchboard girl Mona's number. Lisa frowned up at me from the bed, but I simply smiled at her without offering any explanations. She looked so gorgeous lying there in all her golden nakedness on the rumpled bed. She looked absolutely edible.

I heard the phone ringing, three, four, five times. I looked at my watch and saw that it was nearly six o'clock. There was another ring. Then Kitty picked up the phone and asked who was speaking.

"Joey Baldwin," I said. "Will you let me talk to Mona?"

"I'll see if she's free," Kitty said.

A long wait. The sound of another extension being picked up. Then Mona's voice coming over the wire, dripping with thick sarcasm.

"Well, well, well. Nice to hear from you again."

"I'm sorry, Mona. I couldn't possibly phone any earlier."

"I thought you were just taking a little drive. You've been gone about four hours."

"Sorry."

"Can we expect you back for dinner?" she asked frostily.

I took a deep breath. "No," I said.

"No?"

"No. I won't be back tonight. I hope you don't mind my using the car. I'll return it tomorrow morning when I come over."

"What the hell is this, Joey?"

The time had come to take the bull by the horns, I figured. There was no longer any point in stalling, in hiding the truth.

I said slowly, "My fiancée flew in from New York this afternoon, and I drove out to the airport to pick her up. She's staying at a hotel in Beverly Hills for the next two weeks, and I'm going to stay here with her. I'll move my stuff out of your place first thing tomorrow morning."

"Your—fiancée?" Mona said leadenly.

"That's right. I tried to tell you a couple of times, but you wouldn't listen."

"I don't like this, Joey."

"I'm afraid there's nothing I can do about it. This is the way it's going to be."

"Joey, you shouldn't have done it this way. You shouldn't have just pulled out like this."

I ignored the ominous tone in her voice. I said, "It won't affect the book any. We'll get it done all the same. We'll handle it. We're past the two-thirds mark anyway. I'll come over to your place every morning around nine-thirty or ten, and we'll spend a couple of hours at the tape recorder. Then I'll come back here and write. A few weeks more and I'll be able to show you the completed first draft, and we'll polish it up and I'll turn it in."

"You aren't going to move back in here after that girl goes back to New York?" she asked hopefully.

"No, Mona."

A long silence at the other end. Then: "I don't like this setup, Joey."

"I'm sorry."

"I wanted you to live with me while the book was being written."

"It can't be done. I shouldn't have let you talk me into it in the first place."

"I wanted you, Joey. I still want you. And you want me. A lot more than you want that girl of yours. I know, Joey. Believe me. She can't compare with me. She can't match me at all."

I looked over toward the bed, at Lisa, naked, at the proud thrusts of her breasts, at the lush sweep of belly and loins and hips and thighs.

"No, Mona," I said quietly. "You're wrong. It isn't true. I'm sorry, but you're wrong."

"That's your last word, is it?"

"I'm afraid so," I said. "Well? You want to call the whole deal off? You want to stop seeing me altogether? I can finish the book without you, I think. We've got everything important down on tape already. There's no need for further consultations if you don't want to see me again."

"No," she said. "Let's do this book the right way. I'll go along with this new deal of yours. You come over here at half-past nine tomorrow morning and we'll go on from where we left off."

Her voice was icy. But obviously getting the book finished meant more to her than continuing to exert her dominance over me. She was willing to put up with my rebellion so long as she needed me to finish her book.

"Right," I said. "I'll be there. And I'll pack all my things after we finish work."

I put down the phone.

"Well?" Lisa said.

I shrugged. "She's mad. She's mad as hell. But she'll put up with the situation."

"She wants you to keep living with her?"

I nodded. "Worse than that. She's been after me to marry her."

"You're joking."

"Wish I was. She's deadly serious. Turned to me one day and said how about it."

"And you said?"

"I reminded her of all the husbands and boyfriends of hers who had come to untimely fates. She didn't take the remark very kindly. In fact, she was mad as hell. She's easily angered."

Lisa looked worried. "The more I hear of this setup, Joey, the more I wish you had never let yourself become involved in it."

"Relax," I told her. "I'm not marrying Mona Thorne and I'm not even living with her any more. I've escaped from her clutches for good. And I'm marrying you. At the earliest possible opportunity."

Lisa still looked troubled. I went back to the bed to console her.

"She tried to steal you," Lisa pouted.

I shrugged. "Well, it didn't work. I got free of her with my skin intact, if not my chastity."

"I'm trying not to be jealous."

"You've got every right to be mad as hell."

"Kiss me and I'll forgive you."

I kissed her. Then she pulled me back down to the bed, and swallowed me up in her body. For a long while there was nothing on my mind but Lisa. Her body was warm and soft and exciting against mine, and her hips throbbed and her breasts heaved and her whole body quivered with delight, again and again and again.

Toward eight o'clock we decided that the reunion had been a success, and we showered and got dressed. I still had the use of Mona's car, so we decided to make a night of it. I thumbed through a restaurant guide that I picked up in the lobby of the hotel, and we drove down to La Cienega Boulevard and went to one of the better steakhouses for a couple of massive sirloins of memorable quality. Then it was up to Sunset Strip for some neon-lit entertainment, dancing and a bottle of champagne to celebrate my deliverance from the sinister wiles of the tempting Mona Thorne.

We cleared out of the niteries around two in the morning and went for a long, long drive out Malibu way, parking the car and going down on the beach, and Lisa took off her shoes and pantyhose and waded into the cool Pacific, holding her skirt up around her waist and showing her delicious legs and thighs and all to the uncaring ocean.

We walked up and down the beach for a while, glorying in the boom of the surf and the salt spray in the air, and then we headed back for the hotel. It was about five when we started back, and the first glimmerings of dawn were in the sky by the time I pulled the station wagon up in front of the Beverly Plaza.

Lisa was sleepy and happy and a little drunk. Her head lolled against mine in the elevator on the way up, and she only giggled when I asked her for the room key. I took it out of her handbag myself and we went in.

"Undress me," she said drowsily.

I undressed her. I liberated the magnificence of her body from its confinement of fabric, and I slipped one hand under her warm taut buttocks and the other around her shoulders and carried her to bed. Big though she was, I had no trouble carrying her. It was like putting a doll in a bed.

"Kiss me," she whispered.

I kissed her. Her eyes were closed, her lips puckered up like a child's.

"What time is it?"

"Morning," I said. "Go to sleep."

"What will you do?"

"I've got work to do," I said. "You sleep. Sleep all day. I'll be back here in the afternoon and I'll work for a while, and then we'll go out and paint the town again tonight. How's that?"

"I'm sleepy," she said in answer.

I patted her rump affectionately and pulled the covers over her.

"Sleep tight," I said.

"Aren't you going to go to bed with me?"

"I can't," I said. I kissed her gently, and she buried her face in the pillow, and moments later her breasts were rising and falling in the rhythms of sleep.

I took a shower and freshened up. It was a little past seven in the morning, and I hadn't had any sleep at all. The idea of taking a nap was a tempting one, but I didn't dare. If I went to sleep, I'd never wake up in time— I'd probably snooze right through to late afternoon. And it wouldn't do at all to miss my appointment with Mona, on this the first day of the new deal. It wouldn't do at all. I would have to get there on time, do my stint, then pack up my things and clear out.

I went down to the coffee shop in the lobby of the hotel. It seemed to have just opened, and I was the only customer. A bleary-eyed blonde in her thirties served me, not without giving me a wink or two that I chose to ignore completely. I had two cups of black coffee and some toast and jam. I figured that was enough to keep me awake for the next five or six hours, at least.

My next stop was the hotel desk. I explained that Lisa was my wife and that I would be staying with her at the hotel, so would they please change the registration of her room from a single to a double. It meant an extra few bucks a day, but I didn't mind that. I hate to skulk in and out of a hotel as an unregistered guest. Hotels don't mind what goes on in their rooms, as long as everybody sleeping up there is duly registered.

So I was duly registered.

My next stop was the rent-a-car booth in the lobby. By now, it had opened up. I checked on the rates, found that they were pretty reasonable, and arranged for a car rental on a weekly basis. It averaged out to about ten bucks a day plus gas. In this spread-out city, it would cost me about half that much just to make the round trip over to Mona's place every day by taxi. For an extra few bucks I could have full-time ownership of a car. I didn't intend to make use of Mona's Buick past this morning.

By now it was nearly nine o'clock. I took a little walk around the block, figuring that some fresh air would perk me up a bit before I headed over to Mona's place. I peered in a couple of jewelry-store windows and saw a couple of attractive and expensive items that Lisa would appreciate. As soon as the money from this damned book started rolling in, I told myself, Lisa would have the best of everything from me. I wouldn't stint. Money isn't any good unless you spend it for things, and there's no finer way to spend it than on things for someone you love.

Finally I got the Buick out of the hotel lot and drove over to Mona's. I drove slowly. The morning sun was in my eyes, and I had a headache and a little bit of a hangover from the night before.

I got to Mona's about half-past nine. I pulled into the driveway.

She was waiting for me.

She was on the patio in back, wearing a bikini and looking radiant. But after my night with Lisa, I couldn't fall for Mona's charms. I could see her too clearly, now. I could see the first hints of aging around the eyes, around the throat—things I hadn't noticed before, even on the closest inspection. Now they stood out like scars. That seven-year difference between Lisa and Mona really showed clearly. Mona only looked youthful. Lisa had the genuine article. And there was a difference, a big difference.

I got out of the car.

"Good morning," she said.

The two words sent the temperature down about twenty degrees inside of a couple of seconds. If there were some way to convert a frosty Mona Thorne greeting into transmittable energy, the air-conditioning people would be out of business in a matter of hours.

"Morning, Mona. Hope I didn't inconvenience you by borrowing the car overnight."

"We managed without it," she said. Her face was grim, set rigidly. I knew she was seething over with anger toward me, and I was half expecting her to lose her temper any moment and spring screeching at my eyes with her fingernails.

I tried to pretend everything was as usual. "Had your breakfast yet?"

"Yes."

"Then we can start to work. I'll go upstairs and get the notebook while you set up the tape recorder."

"Hold it a second or two," she said. "I want to talk to you."

"Sure."

"You know, you hurt me very deeply last night."

I cracked my knuckles impatiently. "Mona, listen, I'm sorry everything turned out this way. You knew from the start that I couldn't get involved with you. I didn't want you to fall in love with me. We had some sex, sure, but it didn't have to go beyond sex. Only it did. Well, it was a mistake to fall in love with me."

"I'm beginning to see that."

"Can we keep the relationship strictly business from now on?"

She shrugged. "How long is that girl staying in Los Angeles?"

"I told you. Two weeks."

"And you won't move back after she goes away?"

"No. It's safer this way." I looked at my watch. "Why don't we get down to work? A couple of hours at the tape recorder, then I pack up and clear out—"

"You're in a hurry, aren't you?" she said bitterly. "You can't stand the sight of me now. All you want out of me is my collaboration on that lousy book.

You want to use me for making money—so you can have a big bankroll when you marry that chick of yours."

"Look, Mona—"

"I'll ask you one more time. Will you stay here with me? I'm not accustomed to crawling to a man, Joey. But you're an unusual man. So I'll make the exception for you. I'll beg you. Is that what you want? Stay here with me. Live with me. Marry me. Are you going to turn me down, Joey?"

"I'm afraid I am."

"That's your last word?"

"Positively," I said. "The answer's no, Mona. It's got to be this way."

She sighed. "Okay, Joey. If that's the way you want it, that's the way it'll be. You can feel pretty proud of yourself, I guess. You turned down Mona Thorne. You lived with her for a month and you laid her and then you turned her down when you got invited to make it permanent. You used me as a shack job."

I started to say something to soothe her, but she turned her back on me and began to walk away.

Abruptly 1 knew someone else was on the patio.

"Okay," Mona said in a clear voice. "I'm through with him. He's all yours, Clint. Get him!"

I stood there gasping for breath as Clint Marshall came marching out of hiding.

14

He looked mean and he looked angry.

He looked about ten feet high, just then.

I could see a couple of gaps in his mouth, where teeth were missing and where he hadn't gotten around to having replacements made. And there was a strip of bandaging across his lower lip, hiding the place where the stitches probably were. His lips still looked puffy, as though they had swollen up when I had hit him a month earlier, and were still bloated.

He said, "I'm going to get you, man. I said I would, and now's my chance. No more lucky punches for you, Charlie. And when I finish with you it'll take more than plastic-surgery to put you back together."

I glanced at Mona, who stood by with folded arms, wearing a grimly vindictive expression.

"What the hell is this, Mona? What's this ape doing here? Get him away from me!"

"I called him over to have some exercise," Mona said evenly. "I asked him if he wanted a second chance to take care of you, Joey. He seemed almost deliriously happy to oblige."

Marshall came rumbling forward. Six feet three or four, two hundred thirty or forty pounds. And I was the guy who had gravely damaged his acting career with a single punch, the guy who had humiliated him in front of Mona Thorne. He wanted revenge now in the worst way, and I knew glumly that if he ever got his fists near me I'd come out of it in a dozen pieces. He wasn't the kind who lost two fights in a row to the same man.

I backed up, away from him, looking for some way to get out. He came after me. His fist lashed out, and even though I sidestepped the full fury of it, I got caught sideways on the shoulder. Numbing pain ran up and down the length of my left arm.

He closed in. He was making little chopping motions with the side of his hand, as though he was aching to let me have a quick one across the Adam's apple. He chopped at me, quickly, derisively. I hopped back and he chopped empty air, but I was still congratulating myself on my agility when he came moving in with his left and exploded a punch in my midsection that I wasn't expecting at all.

It knocked me down. I went over, gagging and choking and he kicked me in the side, and I rolled away, getting up just before he bashed me in the head with his size-fourteen brogues, and now wobbly, I retreated still further. I could see Mona waiting for the kill in the background.

Marshall advanced as inexorably as a tank. In a moment, he would have me cornered, and then he could beat me to a pulp at his leisure. I envisioned myself, sagging and bloody, being propped up by Marshall's left hand while he bashed my teeth out with his right.

I would live through it. That would be the worst part of it. I'd wake up with a mouthful of stumps and six broken ribs and a hernia, but I'd live.

I backpedaled, wondering how long I could hold off the inevitable. Fighting back was inconceivable. I couldn't make a dent in him, I knew.

Then I brushed against a garden rake.

It was propped up next to the garage. I reached out for it the way a drowning man grabs for a life preserver. Marshall saw what I was doing, and his eyes went wide, and he stepped back in a hurry.

The damned fool.

Stepping back gave me just the maneuverability I needed. If he had hemmed me in, I probably wouldn't have been able to use the rake. But he jumped back. I guess he thought I was going to swing it like a bat, and rake it across his precious face.

But I wasn't as vicious as that. Besides, I didn't think it would work. If he got out of reach and grabbed the rake from my hands, I was sunk.

So instead I grabbed the rake's business end, pointed the handle at him, and came forward like a horseman with a lance. The butt of the rake hit him in the belly at fifty miles an hour. I rammed it into him with all my strength, not really caring if it speared right through him and came out the other side.

Not even the toughest set of abdominal muscle could stand up to a poke like that. The wind left his lungs with an audible whoosh, and I felt his whole body give as the rake handle jabbed far into his guts. He let out a yelp and doubled over on the pavement, retching and puking and gasping for air.

I didn't stop to offer first-aid. I tossed the rake in the general direction of Mona and turned and ran. The Buick was still standing in front of the garage, and on the spur of the moment I hopped into it, twisted the key, stomped on the accelerator, and began to move.

I didn't know where I was going. I didn't care. I just wanted to get away from that house, from that woman, from that gorilla of an actor.

I barreled down the street at what was probably the fastest speed ever recorded on it, came to an intersection, shot wildly across it, and kept on going. I expected to have the motorcycles whining after me at any moment.

But what was following me wasn't any cop. I flicked a glance at my rearview mirror and caught sight of Mona's trim little white Alfa-Romeo humming down the center stripe after me. She was about two and a half blocks behind me, but gaining fast. I risked a second look and saw that she had Clint Marshall sitting in the car next to her.

So they were coming after me. What the hell did she have in mind? Was she going to cut me off somehow, maneuver me to a stop, and have Clint finish the job of mangling me? Or was she just chasing after me for the hell of it?

In a way I was glad she was coming after me. For one moment, as I had driven away from the house, I had been afraid that she would go upstairs and destroy my 200 pages of manuscript. That was all I needed. To scrap all this work, to lose it now—worse, to have to do it all over again, to identify with Mona Thorne from the start—no. I didn't want to think about it. But at least the manuscript was safe now, while she was out of the house.

I turned onto Wilshire and went whizzing west, against the flow of eastbound rush-hour morning traffic. I was going about fifty, which was all I dared to do on a city street. Mona was hanging in there behind me. A traffic light caught her once and I opened out my lead, but she was soon right up a block or two in back of me, moving fast.

A freeway sign loomed up at San Vicente Boulevard. I took it. I put my foot on the gas. The station wagon wasn't new, and it wasn't young. I got it up to about seventy, and kept it there. I looked back and saw the white Alfa-Romeo a long way back behind me. The freeway was practically empty. I swerved across into the left-hand-most lane, pushed the accelerator pedal to the floor, and wondered what the hell I was going to do when I reached the freeway's end. Ride right into the Pacific? Turn around and go the other way? Was Mona going to chase me all over this crazy city until we ran out of gas or until she caught me?

She was no more than a quarter of a mile behind me, in the center lane. And she was coming up fast. She could really move in that Alfa of hers—doing ninety was no problem. I switched lanes, got over to the right, hoping to find an exit and get off while she went whizzing past. I could see faces in the mirror, now. Mona looked angry, Marshall positively furious.

Closer.

Right on my tail, now. And no exit in sight. I was doing seventy, and she must have been doing close to eighty the way she was coming up on me.

I wondered what miracle was going to save me now. The first time I had tangled with Clint, I landed a lucky punch. The second time, there had been a rake standing around handily. What now?

They were in the next lane, pulling up alongside me. What was she going to do, force me to the wall?

A crazy idea occurred. If I could somehow stop the car short, without throwing myself through the windshield—bring it to a complete halt in the right-hand lane, get out, make a run for it right off the freeway on foot. If Mona kept whizzing along at her present speed, she'd be almost a mile past me before she could come to a halt. She'd never find me—wouldn't even be able to get off the freeway for a considerable stretch further along.

I took my foot off the gas pedal. Gently, I began to stroke the brake. I slowed to forty. Mona, taken by surprise, overshot me and went barreling along at eighty miles an hour in the next lane. I braked again.

Then it happened.

I heard a squeal of brakes and glanced forward and saw the Alfa-Romeo standing up on end, as though Mona had braked too hard and blown a tire. I watched, fascinated and appalled, as two doll-sized figures went hurtling through the air, flung from the car.

The Alfa settled back to the pavement with a resounding crash. The two doll-sized figures kept on going, high up, into the air, up over the road divider—

Down again, into the eastbound lane.

Into the steady stream of traffic churning toward downtown L.A.

By this time I was almost parallel with the scene of the accident. I braked to a halt, getting an angry honk from someone behind me. The middle lane had the Alfa in it, and I was in the right lane, which clogged up the freeway beautifully. Cars were detouring around us. I looked across, into the eastbound road, and saw that all traffic had halted there. A Continental had stopped and a distinguished-looking man with gray hair was staring in blank horror at the pool of red trickling out from under his wheels.

I was numb with the shock of it. At least a dozen cars must have passed over the two of them. A leg—Mona's leg—protruded from under the Continental. It was pretty badly mashed. People were milling around in the eastbound lane, and even in my lane cars were halting to see what had happened.

White-faced, shaken, I started the Buick again and drove on. I crawled along at forty miles an hour to the next exit, took it, and got off the freeway. I drove a couple of blocks, found a bar, pulled up in front of it.

I went in. At a little past ten in the morning, there was no one there but the barkeep.

"Double Scotch," I said. "Make it fast."

My hands were shaking. The bartender looked at me oddly and then poured out my double in a hurry.

"You sick, mister?" he asked me.

I shook my head. I caught sight of myself in the backbar mirror, looking like my own ghost.

"Accident on the freeway," I managed to say. "Couple miles back. I just saw it. Man and a girl riding in a sports car. Blew a tire, threw them into the opposite lane. A dozen cars ran them over."

"Happens all the time. Those lousy freeways are death-traps, let me tell you."

"Beautiful girl," I said. "A brunette. I saw her go up in the air. All she was wearing was a bikini. Big fellow with her."

I gulped my Scotch greedily.

"Must have been some crazy starlet," the barkeep said. "They're always driving too fast, those kids. One of them killed every week. Maybe an actor with her. Give the kids something to gush about, the way they did with Jimmy Dean."

"Yeah," I said. "Give me another double."

I belted the Scotch back. The sight of those figures flying through the air still burned back of my eyelids. I could see Mona's arms, her legs, waving like matchsticks as she went up, then down....

I hung around the bar for an hour or so. Then I decided I had had enough. I walked outside, got into the car. I turned it on, but it kept stalling.

So I just sat there. Maybe another half-hour passed, or maybe it was an hour. I don't know. I didn't even look at my watch. Finally I realized I was sober again, and I started the car without a hitch.

I returned to the freeway and headed east at a moderate speed. There wasn't any sign of an accident. The wreckage had all been cleared away by this time.

I drove like a robot all the way back to Beverly Hills. I left the car out front of the hotel and walked in. I passed the newsstand and glanced at the papers.

MONA THORNE KILLED ON FREEWAY.

So they had it in the papers. That meant it had really happened, that it wasn't just something I had dreamed while in the throes of indigestion. I headed for the elevator.

The elevator operator said, "You hear about Mona Thorne? She blew a tire on the freeway and got killed."

I nodded. I wanted to say, "Yeah, I was ten feet away when it happened." Instead I said, "She was probably speeding when it happened."

I went to Lisa's room and slipped my key in. My watch told me it was one o'clock in the afternoon.

Lisa was still in bed. She sat up, naked and lovely and half-asleep.

"Hello, Joey."

"Hello," I said.

"Joey! What's the matter—you look terrible!"

"Mona Thorne was killed in an auto accident this morning," I said.

She let out a little gasp. "OH!"

"I saw it happen," I said. "That's why I'm so shaken up. Not that I give a damn whether she's dead or not. But that I saw her go up in the air… saw her come down…." I shuddered.

Lisa got out of the bed, put her arms around me. Her body was soft, lovely, comforting. I held her for a moment, then said, "I've got some phone calls to make, honey."

"Sure, Joey."

I went to the phone and called Fred Koren.

"Koren," came the soft voice. "J. L. Thomas, Literary Agents."

"Koren, this is Joey Baldwin."

"Oh. Hello, Joey."

"Looks like we don't have any book any more," I said in a flat tired voice.

"What makes you think so?"

I frowned. "You haven't heard the news?"

"About Mona? Sure. Martinson called me around eleven o'clock. I know all about it."

"Well, that's it, isn't it?" I said. "She's dead. And so is the book."

"Bullshit," Koren said. "You've got yourself a goldmine, man. The book is ten times as valuable now. The autobiography of Mona Thorne, edited and polished by Joey Baldwin? It's a natural. I've been on the phone all day. There's going to be a movie of Mona's life. Sort of a James Dean story. Tragedy of how she almost made it to her comeback and got killed on the threshold. They've bid a hundred fifty grand for film rights to the book, but Jack says hold them up for at least twice that. And we'll get it. You ought to clear around half a million on this book, Joey."

I gaped at the phone stupidly. "Half a million—"

"Sure. How long will it take you to finish the book? You said the other day you'd done 200 pages."

"That's right."

"Where are they? Where are you calling from, for that matter?"

"The pages are at Mona's. I'm at the Beverly Plaza. Been booked here since yesterday."

"Okay. Get yourself over to Mona's. Martinson's there, taking charge of the situation. Pick up the manuscript and whatever else you need. You've got to knock out the last part of that book inside of the next two weeks. We'll have it on sale by August."

"Sure," I said dazedly. "Sure."

I put down the phone.

It had never occurred to me that the book would still be published after Mona's death. I just wasn't thinking straight this morning. Of course, we had a hot property. Mona would become a legend now. Ten years from now she'd be almost mythical.

I picked up the phone again, got Mona's number. Kitty answered, and I asked to speak to Carl Martinson.

A moment later Mona's agent said, "You hear the news, Baldwin?"

"I heard it, yes." I didn't see any point in letting anybody know that Mona had been speeding to catch me. "I heard. My manuscript's over at her place."

"I know. I've got it locked up in the safe."

"Right. I'll come over and pick it up tomorrow, along with my typewriter and stuff."

"What's the matter with today?" Martinson said. "Look, we want to get that book finished, son."

So the vultures were moving in, the promoters. Mona's mangled body wasn't in the ground yet, and already she was a hot property.

I said wearily, "I didn't get any sleep last night, and I'm too pooped to work today, Martinson. I'm taking the day off. I'll be over first thing in the morning to pick everything up."

"Whatever you say," Martinson conceded. "If you want to reach me, I'll be here. I'm Mona's executor."

"Okay. I've got Mona's Buick, incidentally. I borrowed it yesterday afternoon."

I hung up and turned to Lisa.

"We're going to be rich," I said. "The ghouls are at work already. Mona's going to make us rich."

"I'm glad she's dead," Lisa said. "It's horrible, but I hated her. Without even meeting her."

I thought of Mona, tanned Mona with the luscious breasts and the undulating hips. Mona in bed. Mona gasping. Mona asking for more.

Mona with her eyes full of hate. Mona urging Clint Marshall to fracture me. Mona driving fiercely after me, trying to force me off the road.

Mona flying through the air.

Mona dead, crushed under a dozen tires.

I shook my head. I opened my eyes, and there was Lisa, and I drew her to me. She caressed me and massaged the tense muscles of my neck.

Then she was holding me tight, loving me.

"We'll clear out of L.A. as soon as we can," she whispered. "We'll go home and we'll get married. And if you make a million dollars on this book, okay, and if you don't, that'll be okay too."

Then her lips were against mine, and her body was coming to life again, vibrant and throbbing with energy, and I smiled, and gave myself up to the sweet fullness of her, pillowing myself on her breasts and holding tight to her, and Mona became only a fading memory.

Our bodies strained, merged, became one.

And I knew that everything was going to be okay between Lisa and me. And that, finally, everything was okay for Mona Thorne too.

THE END

Lust Victim

by Don Elliott

1

Midnight. Dave and Moira Lamson had left the party early; Moira had been feeling tired. Now Lamson was sprawled out comfortably in his bed, watching with pleasure as his pretty wife undressed.

He had been watching other peoples' wives all evening, of course. Why not? But he told himself in all objectivity that Moira had it all over them. She was thirty-three and looked no more than twenty-three. The other women were either haggard with the strains of raising children, or grim-jawed with the tensions of status seeking. At thirty-three most of them looked forty-three.

Not Moira.

Of course, Lamson reflected, Moira had it pretty soft. Relatively speaking. He wasn't any millionaire, not by a goodly distance, but he did more than all right. As president of his own small-size electronics distribution firm he was taking home a nice check each month. Enough to keep Moira swathed in the best clothes, enough to pay for maids to watch the kids, enough to provide them with a good home in one of the best sections of the city. Moira had never known strain or tension or worry. No wonder she had kept her shape and her youthful vivacity.

Lamson watched his wife undress and told himself that he was a pretty lucky man.

She was out of her slip, now, and stood with her back to him, fumbling with the catch of her bra. It opened, and the cups tumbled away, revealing the high, full, creamy mounds of her breasts, tipped with the dark little rises of her nipples. Lamson felt the familiar stirring. After ten years of marriage he still found his wife the most desirable woman on earth. That was something to be proud of, he thought.

"Did you chain the back door after you took the trash out, darling?" Moira asked as she rolled the gauzy fabric of her panties down over her hips.

"I think so," Lamson said vaguely. He eyed the full, curving globes of her buttocks as they were bared to his gaze. There was a dryness of desire in his mouth.

"You ought to go down and check."

"Don't be silly."

Moira turned and looked over her shoulder at him. "You know there was a robbery only two weeks ago on Brewster Avenue. Why take chances, Dave?"

He smiled. "I'm pretty sure I locked the door, Moira. And chained it. Besides, a burglar doesn't need to come through the door. If he's really keen on getting into the house, he'll cut out a window and come in that way. Anyhow, no burglar in his right mind breaks into a house that has people sleeping in it. It's too risky. They go after the houses of people on vacation."

"Well, I don't like the idea—"

"Stop being so jumpy and come to bed," he said with a warm grin. "There's this game I want to teach you tonight. It's called sex, and every little girl ought to find out how to play it before she grows up."

"Is it like jumping rope?" Moira asked.

"A little bit. But it's more fun."

"*Nothing* can be more fun than jumping rope!"

"Give me five minutes and I'll change your mind," he told her.

She laughed. The worry over the chained or unchained door seemed to be receding from her mind. She was so jumpy these days, Lamson thought. Ever since that other burglary on Brewster. Of course, there was a rape involved in that one, too, which was probably what was bothering her—

Moira stood naked in front of the mirror, vigorously pulling a brush through the deep auburn of her hair. He watched in delight. Her hair was so silken, so glossy, so lovely. Everything about her was lovely. It was as if she had been created for his own special delight. He had felt a certain awe the day he met her, more than a decade ago—awe that something so beautiful should fall into the clutches of him, a scruffy engineering student. He had felt the same awe when he had clasped her to him on their wedding night and found her still a virgin. And something of that same awe persisted now, after ten years of loving, mutually faithful marriage.

She put down the brush and crossed the room, lithe and slim and red-headed and infinitely young and desirable, into the bathroom. A few moments later she returned. She paused at the light-switch.

"Lights out?"

"Just a second," he said.

"What for?"

"For me to look at you."

"Oh, you silly." But she remained there, as if posing, while his eyes travelled southward from the even-featured loveliness of her face, past the rising red-tipped bowls of her breasts, down the flatness of her rib-cage and the gentle rondure of her belly to the subtle widening of her hips, the rich promise, the firm white columns of her thighs.

Then she snapped off the light.

A moment later she was in bed with him, her body satin-smooth, cool against his.

His hands went to the heavy swells of her breasts. His straining fingers arched out to encompass them, and he felt the beautiful little nipples turning into rigid nodes against his palms. Her lips, soft and sweet tasting, came up to meet his.

They had made love innumerable times, and each time it was something new, something fresh and exciting. He nibbled at her earlobe, and she laughed softly and kissed the nape of his neck, her breath hot against him. One of his hands left her breast and travelled down the cool slope of her body, past her hip, over her flank, around in back to cup the resilient firmness of her buttocks. She started to move her body in the beginning rhythms of ecstasy.

He knew how it would be tonight. It would be good, because it was always good between them. They would toy with one another, coyly teasing with a fingertip or a nibbling tooth, enjoying the relaxed, low-keyed lovemaking of long acquaintance, and then the moment would come, both of them sensing it wordlessly at the same instant, and she would turn to him, offering him herself, and he would take the gift, gliding gently to harbor, and they would move in perfectly tuned rhythms serenely and smoothly to the climax, and then to sleep.

But tonight there was an interruption.

His head was bent low over her, his lips to one full breast, when suddenly she went stiff and tense and said, "Dave, I think there's a prowler in the house."

He was annoyed with her for this uncharacteristic shattering of the mood. He lifted his head and said, a little more curtly than he usually spoke to her, "You're mistaken. It's your imagination."

"I'm sure I heard a window opening downstairs."

"Why are you so jumpy tonight?"

"Dave, go look. I won't be able to rest until you make sure."

"And if I find out?" he asked, trying to be light about it. "What should I do? Offer him some Scotch?"

"Don't joke. Please go see."

"But we're in the middle of—"

"I can't help that. I'm sure there's someone in the house, and I can't think about anything else right now. Please, Dave."

"Oh, all right," he said, a little sourly. He slipped from bed and drew his robe on. He couldn't ever remember Moira doing this to him before—making him stop right in the middle. His body ached with desire. He felt like a youth who has suddenly found out where his date draws the line. It hurt. He throbbed.

Well, there was no help for it. He'd give the house a quick once-over, come back to bed, and they'd take up where they left off.

He went out.

Moira had wanted him to keep a gun in the house. But he had always refused. There were too many newspaper stories about nosy little boys finding Daddy's loaded gun and managing to kill either themselves or Daddy. He preferred to have no such opportunities available for his boys. Besides, he didn't think he could ever use a gun on another human being, not even on a burglar. And simply waving around a gun that he did not intend to use was the surest way of getting killed by a panicky house-breaker.

Unarmed, and feeling a little hesitant, he came out into the second-floor hall and glanced around. All quiet up here. No furtive figures skulking through the darkness.

He listened for sounds.

None.

Of course, Moira had notoriously sharp ears. She could pick up the sound of a gossip whisper across a crowded room, or hear a crying child above the roar of a noisy party. But this time, he was sure, she was imagining things.

He started downstairs.

His first stop was the kitchen. Sure enough, he had chained the back door. So much for Moira's worries. He stood stock still, listening for the sound of a stranger's footfall.

Nothing

A sudden quiver of terror ran through him as he walked into the living room and saw moonlight shining through an open window. He went closer, and terror turned to something close to panic as he realized that a pane of glass had been cut neatly out of the window. Someone standing in the shrubbery outside had done the job, then had reached in, unlocked the window, climbed into the house—

Moira was right! There's someone in here!

He turned away from the window, seeing no one, and headed for the fire-place to get one the pokers. At least he'd have some sort of weapon if he came upon the burglar unexpectedly. Tiptoeing out of the living room, Lamson peered to the left, into the dining room.

A figure came out of the shadows and said coldly, quietly, "Don't move and you'll be okay."

Lamson whirled. He caught a glimpse of a tall man, a man of about his own height, standing a few feet away. Moonlight showed no glimpse of a gun. Automatically, Lamson lashed out with the poker.

He found his arm being caught, bent backward, before he could land a blow.

"Drop it!"

He dropped it—noisily, deliberately, hoping that Moira would hear the crash and would have the good sense to phone the police. A powerful hand closed on his arm. Easily confidently, the burglar looped him into a half-nelson. Lamson winced, gasped.

"You're—breaking—my arm—"

"Let's go upstairs," the burglar said harshly.

"We've got nothing you want."

"Let me worry about that. Come on!"

Lamson found himself being frogmarched up the stairs to the bedroom. There was an ice-cold knot of fear in his stomach. But he was helpless. The burglar was tough and hard and strong, and held all the aces. Lamson knew that he had muffed his one chance to get the upper hand.

"Where's the master bedroom?"

Lamson nodded straight ahead. He had no choice. He didn't want the burglar going near the children.

"Let's go in. Turn on the light."

The burglar pushed him forward. With his free hand, Lamson opened the door, switched on the light. Moira sat up in bed, blinking, her jaws working. She was holding the bedside telephone.

"Put that phone down lady. *Put it down!*"

Moira gaped at him without doing anything.

"Put it down or do I break your husband's arm?"

Moira put the phone down. She had the sheets pulled up to her throat.

The burglar said, drawing a switchblade knife from his coat and flicking it open, "I want you to get out of bed and open the dresser, and get your valuables out. Dump them on the bed. One funny trick and this knife goes right into your husband's belly."

Moira's lips trembled. She was too frightened even to scream.

In the mirror, Lamson caught his first clear view of the burglar. To his astonishment, he saw that the man resembled him enough to be his brother—except that he had never *had* a brother. They were about the same height, six one. They both had dark, curly hair, square jaws, high cheekbones. The burglar hadn't shaved in three or four days and there was an ugly scar running down one cheek; his ears were cauliflowered and his lips swollen as though he had been a professional boxer some time in the past. The resemblance was still amazing, for all that.

"Did you hear me? Get out of bed and get your jewelry, lady. Or your husband gets cut. I'll give you three."

"But I'm—"

"One!"

"—not—wearing anything."

"Two!"

Moira threw a bewildered glance at her husband. Lamson, feeling the edge of the blade against the thin fabric of his dressing gown, shrugged.

"Do as he says, Moira."

"Thr—"

Moira slipped from the bed, her face crimson. The burglar caught his breath sharply as Moira's slim, full-breasted nakedness became visible. The blush spread down Moira's throat as far as her breasts. She crossed the room, went to the jewelry drawer. As she knelt, the burglar's eyes went to the trim curves of her taut buttocks.

Lamson burned with impotent anger. To be robbed was bad enough, but to have the housebreaker staring at Moira's naked body was intolerable.

She took a couple of trinkets out of the drawer and tossed them to the bed. Nothing very valuable—her watch, her small gold bracelet, her gold pin. The really good stuff, the diamond ring, the choker, the necklace, was deeper in the drawer. She added a pearl string to the pile on the bed. It was all insured, Lamson thought. But still, those things had sentimental value; she'd hate to lose them.

With a trembling hand she reached in for one of the more valuable things. But suddenly, unexpectedly, the burglar said, "All right. That's enough."

Lamson was startled. The stuff on the bed was worth maybe five, six hundred dollars. The jewelry still in the drawer was insured for an additional $25,000. Was the burglar getting uneasy about spending so much time in the house?

Moira straightened up, fanning a hand out over her breasts in a futile attempt at modesty. The burglar was staring at her slim nude form hungrily. A new, sudden, terrible suspicion exploded in Lamson's mind.

Then a fist crashed into his chin with stunning force. His head snapped back. He heard Moira scream, and he went flying off his feet, landing in a dazed heap on the floor. For a long moment he was groggy, unable to rise. It had been a real haymaker. He leaned against the wall, shaking his head. Something was buzzing persistently in his brain.

He realized he was being tied—the burglar had ripped the telephone out of the wall and was binding him with the cord. In moments he was trussed efficiently. Some kind of gag was stuffed into his mouth.

"All right, Moira," the burglar said in a different, strange voice.

"No—no—"

She backed up against the wall. He grabbed her and threw her roughly down on the bed, her breasts bouncing and swaying as she landed.

In horror, Lamson strained against his bonds, unable to budge them. He made futile little noises in his gagged throat.

Moira was his. No other man had ever touched her. She had been a virgin when she came to him, and she had been a faithful wife.

And now—

There was the sound of clothing opening.

Lamson felt as though a sword were being turned in his own belly. There was the ache of his own body, from the interrupted act of love that now seemed a million years in the past. There was the dull buzzing of his head, and the strange numb sensation in his jaw. There was the pounding in his eyeballs as he watched the burglar approaching the bed, where Moira cowered.

"No—please, don't—"

"I'm going to enjoy this, Moira."

"I beg you—"

He dropped down on the bed. She fought him, scratching and kicking, but he easily outfought her, catching both her wrists in one big hand. The other hand gently, almost daintily touched her breasts. With his knee, he inexorably forced her crossed legs and locked feet apart.

He pulled her thighs open.

He pressed his weight down on her. He was still fully dressed. Her naked thighs and hips were visible, her legs at either side of his body.

He made a sudden thrusting motion. Moira uttered a single gasp of agony that sent lances of rage and humiliation through her watching husband.

Only once before in his life had Lamson watched two people having relations. That had been in Paris, fifteen years ago, before his marriage. He had gone to one of the Pigalle clubs, and there had been a "special" act for anyone who cared to pay a thousand francs extra, and a fullblown, heavy-breasted wench had been topped by a lean, muscular, hungry-looking young man.

But that had been different. That had been a merry romp done for money. This was rape.

Hardly believing what he saw, Lamson watched the body of this burglar who so closely resembled him moving up and down over his wife's prostrate, sobbing form. There was the sound of the burglar's rasping breath loud in the room, and then a sudden choking gasp, a moan of pleasure, and it was all over and done with.

It had taken only a few minutes but it had seemed like hours.

The burglar rolled free of Moira. His face was flushed, and he wore a curiously satisfied expression. He adjusted his trousers, scooped up the few trinkets Moira had given him, and left the room without a word.

Lamson blinked in shock. He had taken so little in the way of jewelry—and so much in another way.

"Moira?" he asked hoarsely. "Moira, are you all right?"

No answer. Moira lay sprawled flat on her back, her legs apart, her breasts rising and falling rapidly. He could hear a strange, eerie sobbing coming from her.

"Moira!"

He was unable to get to his feet because of the way he had been bound. Pushing off against the wall, he inched across the floor. Moira lay limp, still, as though the violation of her body had been the ultimate horror and she no longer had the strength to move.

He reached the bed. He wanted to reach out to her to touch her, to comfort her. But he was bound hand and foot.

"Moira, answer me! Did he hurt you? Are you all right, Moira?"

Silence.

"Moira, help me out of this cord and I'll phone the police. Don't just lie there. It's all over, darling. He's gone. It's all over."

She sat up, suddenly. Her eyes looked wild—a madwoman's eyes. She drew her legs up against her belly like a raped virgin.

"Help me free, Moira. We'll call the police."

She stared at him. Then she said, in a cold, spitfire voice that he had never heard from her lips before, "Oh, how I hate you! How I despise you."

2

Her bitter, malevolent reply caught him off guard. It was not a reaction he had expected. Why turn on him? What had he done?

"Moira, please, stay calm. Don't get hysterical."

"I am calm," she said stonily. "But why didn't you chain that door when I told you?"

"I did chain it," he said wearily, as though explaining something to a child. "He came in through the living room window."

"You should have had a gun! He wouldn't have done this to me if you had a gun!"

"It's too late for that kind of talk. It happened and now we have to pick up the pieces. We're lucky he didn't kill us while he was at it. Or rob anything really valuable. We got off lightly enoug—"

"I was raped, though!" Her tone was half a shriek.

Lamson felt dismally depressed. Moira was on the thin edge of insanity right now, he saw. She was taking it badly. Well, of course, getting raped in front of her husband's eyes is a serious matter for any woman. Especially a woman who's never been to bed with any man but her husband, ever. But that was no reason for her to crack up this way, to turn on him.

If only she would let him loose, he could take her in his arms, comfort her, soothe her—

"Moira, will you get these damned cords off me?"

"All right," she said.

She slipped out of bed and knelt by his side, trying to undo the knots. After some tugging she got the cord loose enough for him to free his hands, then his feet. He chafed his wrists, restoring the circulation.

Naked, Moira stood motionless in the middle of the room, glaring at him. He went to her, holding out his arms to embrace her.

"You poor kid. Of all the bastardly things to have happen—"

She shrank back from him.

"Don't touch me. Just leave me alone."

"I wanted to comfort you."

"I—don't want anyone touching me right now."

"Did he hurt you?"

"No. Not physically."

"Look, I'll go get us some drinks. Then we can phone the police."

She shook her head. "No, Dave. I don't want you to call the police."

"Huh?"

"Don't get them involved."

"There was a burglary. And—and a rape. Why the hell shouldn't we call the police?"

She looked at him levelly. "Do you want everyone in the neighborhood to know that I was raped? Isn't it bad enough you had to watch it? Do you want them all to know, so that all their talk is about me, and when I go outside their eyes are on me, and they're thinking, *She's the one who got raped?* No. I don't want anybody to know. If it had happened when you weren't home I wouldn't even tell you about it. It's something that has to be forgotten right away."

"Moira, this isn't sensible."

"*Don't call the police*, Dave. You hear me?"

"I could tell them not to give the story to the newspapers."

She laughed scornfully. "Sure, and you can tell the moon not to rise tomorrow night, too. Don't get the police mixed into this!"

"Jewelry was stolen. How can I report it to the insurance company and not to the police?"

"Tell the insurance company you lost the jewelry. They'll pay you for it. You're a good customer, and it isn't very much money."

He stared at her as though not believing what he heard. To be robbed, raped, and then not report it to the police? What kind of idiocy was that?

He said, "I can't do that."

"Don't call the police."

"I'll call them and tell them we were burglarized. We won't say anything about the rape. How's that? Will you be satisfied with that?"

"You mustn't say a word about the rape."

"Not a word." He peered at her curiously. Well, if she wanted to hide the shame of it, he couldn't blame her. But it was a damned peculiar thing, all the same.

He went out of the room, downstairs into the living room, half expecting to find the burglar still prowling around. But there was no one on the ground floor. Careful not to disturb the open window, for fear of smudging the fingerprints, Lamson peered outside, into the shrubbery. It had been an easy matter to climb in.

Kneeling at the sideboard, he poured two stiff shots of Scotch with a trembling hand and carried them into the kitchen to run a little cold water into them. On a quick sudden impulse he gulped his drink down, then returned to the living room, poured a refill for himself, and carried both drinks upstairs.

Moira was sitting on the edge of the bed, wearing a bathrobe now. She seemed to be shaking.

"Here," he said. "This'll do you good."

She belted the highball away in a few eager gulps. Looking up at him, she said, "He looked just like you."

"I noticed that. It was incredible."

"The same height. The same build. Even the same kind of hair."

"His face was all battered up. He must have been a boxer before he turned to burglary." Lamson touched his jaw gingerly. "That was a very professional smack in the face he gave me."

"But take away all the bruises and scars and he could pass for your brother," Moira said.

"I don't have a brother. Or any relative who looks at all like me."

"I know," she said.

Lamson frowned. "He called you Moira."

She glanced up quickly. "What of it?"

"It seems odd. To be on first-name terms with the woman he's raping."

"He heard you mention my name, that's all."

"When?"

"You said, *Do as he says, Moira.* Something like that. And he heard it."

Lamson nodded. "I guess that's it." He finished his drink. "Feeling better now?"

"I'm not exactly cheerful."

"I didn't ask that. You getting a grip on yourself again?"

She shrugged noncommittally. But it seemed to him that she was back in control of herself again, after that one wild-eyed moment when she had spewed out those words of hate. Well, she had been overwrought, had had to cry out in some way. But now she was calming.

The whole episode was taking on an unreal quality. It was only fifteen minutes in the past, but it was beginning to seem as a sort of dream. There they had been, making love—and then the robbery, the rape. In less than half an hour Moira had been changed from his own particular woman to one that now was shared with—who?

He wondered what effect the rape would have on Moira, Moira who had had such an easy, uncomplicated life with never a dissonant moment. Abruptly she had been transformed into something else from what she had been. She had been yanked from the class of women who have never slept with anyone but their husbands and are glad of it and had been thrust into the class of women who have been raped. Would it shatter the even gloss of her life, he wondered? Would the rape cast a long shadow over the days to come? Everything had been so perfect for ten years.

And now this.

"I'll call the police now," he said.

"Remember—only a robbery."

"Suppose they want to examine you?" he asked.

"They can't examine me without permission. Besides, what would they find? Just that I was having sexual intercourse sometime tonight. That's the truth, isn't it?"

He nodded, feeling the ache in his groin and hating the burglar for having cheated him of his satisfaction.

Tiptoeing downstairs again—the children had slept through it all—Lamson put through the call to the police on the kitchen extension.

"I'd like to report a robbery," Lamson said.

The desk man at the other end did not sound particularly interested—at least not until Lamson gave his name and address, which brought an immediate coming to attention. Robberies in the high-bracket residential area where the Lamsons lived were always important matters to the police.

"We'll have a car right over, Mr. Lamson."

It took ten minutes. The house was full of earnest-looking cops, and Lamson told them the story several times over—just gone to bed roused by his wife to search for a prowler, the scuffle in the downstairs foyer, then marched upstairs, gagged and bound while the burglar forced his wife to hand over jewelry.

"And what was actually taken, Mr. Lamson?"

"Three or four small pieces. Worth about six hundred dollars."

"Nothing else?"

"No. Nothing else. He overlooked some rather valuable jewelry."

"Even though you were gagged and bound?"

"He suddenly decided to leave," Lamson said. "I don't know why. We were lucky."

"All right. And if you'll describe him for us, please—"

"About my height and general build. In fact, there was a strong resemblance between him and me."

A policeman grinned mirthlessly. "You're sure this wasn't some cousin of yours who needed a few bucks, Mr. Lamson?"

"I've got no relatives who resemble me," Lamson said in a cold voice.

The investigation went on and on. They powdered around for fingerprints, photographed the cut-out window pane, snooped through the entire house. It was close to four in the morning before they left.

Drained, exhausted, Lamson sank down on the edge of his bed. "Sun's going to be up soon. But we might as well try to get some sleep."

"Do you think they'll catch him, Dave?"

"Who knows? They usually don't."

"Even with the description?"

"They catch maybe one out of ten. I don't think they try too hard on petty theft." He shook his head. "They were looking at me very strangely. I wonder if they believe my story. They seemed to think more had gone on here than I was telling them about."

"They have no way of finding out," Moira said.

"No. No way if we don't tell them."

He slipped out of his bathrobe and hung it up. He was a little startled to see a momentary expression very much like disgust pass across Moira's sensitive features as he exposed his body. She got into the bed.

As he started to get into bed next to her, she said, "Would you do me a favor, Dave?"

"Of course."

"Sleep on the cot tonight."

"Huh?"

"I—I don't want anyone near me tonight. Not after—that. Please?"

"Well—sure, if that's what you want—"

"Please."

Shrugging, he went into the guest room and got the little cot, and set it up alongside the bed. He hadn't expected this, and didn't like it much. Naturally, he hadn't thought Moira would be in the mood for love, after what had taken place. She would need a day or two to rebuild her personal dignity, before she would feel very much like making love. But to banish him entirely from their bed, on account of it—that seemed like going a little too far, even considering everything that had happened.

But he didn't want to argue with her. She had been through a hellish experience. Let her recover from it in her own way, he thought.

He hoped the recovery process wouldn't be a drawn-out one, though. He had heard of cases where women who were raped went off their rockers entirely or had continuing hysterics for months and months. Moira had always struck him as being a sensible, mature girl, but you could never tell what effect a thing like this could have.

"Good night," he said, settling down in the uncomfortable, creaky little cot, which was two inches shorter than he was. He pulled the blanket up over him and tried to relax.

"Good night," Moira said distantly.

"Good night."

Sleep would not come. He was as wide awake as though this were four in the afternoon, not four in the morning. His tortured mind kept re-enacting the rape scene. Moira crouching naked near the dresser, drawing her valuables out and dumping them on the bed. The burglar, with his distorted, battered face still so oddly similar to Lamson's own. And the rape itself. The little sound of pain Moira had made at the moment she was taken. The burglar's animalistic cries of satisfaction.

A bad dream.

A bad dream that happened to be real.

Ten years of serenity shattered in an instant. He lay stiffly on the cot, sensing Moira's nearness. She was only a few feet away from him, and she was naked, and all he had to do was climb into bed and—

No.

She did not want him.

She had told him to sleep somewhere else tonight. In the same room, yes, because she was afraid now to be alone, but not in the same bed.

Lamson could not remember any other time when Moira had refused to let him share his bed. In fact, never once in their marriage had she refused to make love with him. He had never been forced to put up with the lot of so many husbands, the endless string of "I have a headache" or "My stomach hurts" or "I'm just not in the mood tonight, darling, so sorry."

Moira had always been in the mood. Without seeming wanton or sluttish, she had always responded passionately to his lovemaking.

He couldn't blame her much for not being in the mood now, of course. Right now she just wanted to knit up the shattered integrity of her spirit, and it was unthinkable that she could give herself up wholeheartedly and joyfully to sex right now. But that didn't mean she had to banish him to a cot, he thought. He could hold her in his arms, give her warmth, strength.

Or didn't she have any faith in his strength any more? Was that it?

Did she hold a grudge against him because she felt it was his fault the rape had happened?

That wasn't like Moira either, he thought. She wasn't the vindictive kind of wife who always had some way of putting the blame for any mishap on her husband, no matter how far-fetched the rationalization. Plainly it wasn't his fault the rape had happened even though she seemed to be taking it out on him. A live husband was still better than a dead hero, and that bruiser might easily have killed him for a false move. He had done his best, with the fireplace poker, but his best hadn't been good enough. Was it his fault that he was a civilized man who had been pitted against a ruthless, probably murderous rapist?

Well, in the morning she'd see sense, he figured. Things would straighten around. They would return to normal sooner or later. Sooner, hopefully.

An hour passed.

No sleep came.

The first streaks of dawn were entering the sky.

He could hear Moira tossing sleeplessly on the bed. At length she got up. He looked at his watch. It was ten past five.

"Where are you going?" he asked.

"To take a bath. I feel filthy."

"Have you been asleep?"

"No," she said. "I can't sleep."

"Neither can I. Want me to fix another drink for us?"

"Yes," she said.

She went into the bathroom and closed the door. He heard the water begin to run. For what seemed like the hundredth time that endless night, he went downstairs, again into the living room, to pour two more drinks. This time he resisted gulping his on the spot.

He carried them upstairs. Setting his drink down on the nightstand, he pushed open the bathroom door and took Moira's drink inside. She was in the tub, water up to her navel. As he entered she grabbed a washcloth and clapped it over the high-rising hills of her breasts.

"Can't you knock?" she snapped.

He frowned at her. "For Christ's sake. Moira. I'm *your husband*. I've been seeing you naked for the last ten years, haven't I? Since when do I need to knock?"

She let the washcloth slip. Her breasts were bared again. He felt the dull, insistent urge pounding in his loins, hurting more than ever as he looked at her creamy pink nakedness in the water.

"I'm sorry," she said. "Do you blame me for being jumpy?"

"It's over with. It happened and it's part of the past, Moira."

"I can't blot it out so easily. It's just something you watched, Dave. But it was something that happened to me."

"It happened to me, too. Don't ever forget that. It was the worst ten minutes of my life." He shook his head. "Here. I brought you a drink."

"Dave—"

"What?"

"Look, Dave, I'm sorry if I behave a little—oddly—now. I've been through something pretty rough. Bear with me, will you?"

For the moment, a trace of the old Moira showed. He smiled at her tenderly. "Sure," he said. "Sure. I'll bear with you, kid."

She sipped the drink. He turned, went out, the image of her bare breasts blazing in his mind. He took off his robe, and stretched out once again on the cot.

He didn't at all like what was happening. He didn't like it when his own wife shuddered at the sight of his naked body. Nor when she asked him to sleep in a cot instead of their bed. Nor when she scrambled to hide her nakedness from him when he entered the bathroom and found her in the tub.

These were, he hoped, only temporary confusions. At the moment she wanted nothing to do with sex, nothing to do with men—even him. He shrugged. Tomorrow, maybe, she'd be rational again.

A few minutes later she came out of the bathroom. He looked up at her, and she was naked, but she quickly slipped under the covers. The image of her breasts and buttocks disturbed him. He wanted her. He schooled himself to resist the temptation to get into bed with her. She had been through plenty this evening. Let her rest. If he was to have her at all now, it would practically have to be by rape, and it wasn't a good idea to do that.

The rest of the night ticked away. Six, seven in the morning.

Sounds in the house. The boys were up. Davey, who was eight. Charles, who was six. They didn't sleep late on Sunday mornings, and they didn't let anyone else sleep late either.

At eight o'clock he gave up the pretense of trying to sleep. He dressed and went downstairs. The boys were playing in the yard. He waved to them, hoping they wouldn't notice how haggard he looked.

They came up to him. Chuck hugged him warmly. Davey said, "Dad, I had bad dreams last night."

"What kind of dreams?"

"I dreamed there was somebody in the house. Somebody mean. And then the cops came."

He shook his head and looked off into the distance. "It wasn't anything, Davey. Forget it. It was just a dream."

3

Sunday was a long day.

It seemed to last three million years. Moira moved around the house doing her Sunday chores, but she looked pale, haggard, the ghost of herself. A couple of times Lamson suggested that she just skip the little jobs, leave them for the maid on Monday. But Moira refused, shaking her head doggedly. She wanted to work. Housework would get her mind off what had happened.

He taped a square of cardboard over the open pane in the living room window. He told Moira to call a man in on Monday to replace the pane.

They went to bed early, as though glad to pack the day off to oblivion. They had hardly spoken, all day. A shroud of bleakness seemed to hang over the household. Moira was blackly depressed; Lamson had no idea how to get through her moodiness, and finally decided just to let her work her way out of this her own way. She did not mention it as they prepared for bed. Her exaggerated modesty of last night seemed to have faded, too. She undressed in front of him in a quite normal way, and showed no reaction as he took his clothes off.

Lamson's body ached for her. She moved past him, slim and lithe and naked, and when he looked at her it was like looking at a stranger, not at a woman who had been his wife for ten years. The rape had given her an odd aura. She was *different*, now. Changed.

They got into bed. For a moment Lamson lay silent, rigid, on his side of the bed.

Then he turned toward her. She was lying on her back, staring up at the ceiling. The covers were pulled up above her breasts.

"Moira?"

"What is it, Dave?"

"Still thinking about it?"

"It takes more than half an hour to forget something like that," she said.

"You've got to stop brooding about it, Moira."

"That's easy to say. How do I forget—a man on top of me? A stranger? Doing—*that.*"

"I don't know. But you've got to forget it somehow," he said lamely.

They were silent for a while, neither of them moving or going to sleep. He lifted a hand tentatively, wanting to put it down on her breast, to feel again the warm ripe thrust of her bosom in his hand. But he held back, withdrawing the hand when it was still halfway to its destination.

"Moira," he said quietly.

"Yes, Dave?"

"Moira, I'd like to—make love."

There was a long moment of silence. Then she said, in a hollow, sepulchral voice. "Don't you have any consideration for me, Dave?"

"You're my wife. I love you. I want to show that I love you, that's all."

"If you love me, you'll go to sleep."

He moistened his lips. "Listen, Moira," he said grimly, "you can't let yourself go into a decline over this thing. Declines are out of fashion. They went out with Queen Victoria. You've got to come back to life."

"Maybe it takes a couple of days," she said.

"The best way is just to go full speed ahead, living the way you'd normally live. Don't crawl into your coffin, Moira. The quicker you snap out of it, the better everything'll be—for both of us."

"I'm not in the mood for sex," she said.

"But—"

He stopped. It was hopeless, at least for tonight. He knew that he couldn't make love to her now under any circumstances tonight. Once you begin to argue about it, once sex becomes a matter of negotiation instead of a joyful abandon, there's no point bothering.

Propping himself up on one elbow, he stared at her in the darkness. She had rolled over, presenting her back and buttocks to him, and she had closed her eyes. Lamson nibbled his lip. He still wanted her. But her cold, flat refusal had dashed cold water all over him.

Hesitatingly, he stretched out his hand, arced it over her shoulder, thrust it downward until it encountered the steep hill of her right breast. There was a moment of contact, followed by something that seemed to him unpleasantly like a shudder of revulsion. Then she pulled away and shook off his arm. "Please, Dave," she said irritably. "I want to get some sleep. I'm exhausted."

"All right," he said, in a sharp sour voice. "Good night, Moira."

"Don't be angry with me."

"Good night," he said again.

"Good night," she said.

He rolled over, a roiling, jangling mass of tension and bit his lip as the juices of his desires slowly went sour in his belly. He fought back the urge to turn toward her again, to grab her, to take her forcibly. That would be about the worst possible thing he could do.

The situation, he told himself, called for loving kindness in the utmost.

She was going through some kind of internal psychological crisis, it appeared, and he was going to have to be patient and forbearing with her until she won her battle and went back to being her old warm, passionate self.

Because right now she was just another frigid woman.

Could a rape make a passionate woman frigid overnight? Lamson wasn't any psychiatrist, but he figured it was altogether possible. The shock of it, the pain, the humiliation—it might very well make a woman want to have nothing to do with the male sex for a while. Including, unfortunately, her own husband.

Would it wear off?

Probably. He hoped so.

But he knew that his own attitude would be the key factor in Moira's return to normal balance. If he continued to be demanding, insistent, as he had been tonight, it would ruin everything. Their marriage, which had been so good till now, would turn into the sort of tug-of-war where the husband tries to get as much sex as he can and the wife tries to give as little as she can get away with.

He didn't want that. He wanted the old pre-rape Moira back, warm and vital and vibrant and sexually responsive, the Moira who needed no coaxing, no persuasion, when the time came to make love.

To get that Moira back, he was going to have to go without sex for a while, he saw. Until she voluntarily turned to him in loving embrace. He couldn't force the issue. She had been forced once, and the after-effects were still vivid. It was bad enough that he looked like the rapist. If he started acting like him too, he'd never get Moira's trust again.

Lamson wondered if the rape had actually hurt Moira physically—done some internal damage. Maybe that was why she was so cold tonight. He hoped she'd have the good sense to see a doctor, if that was so. But he doubted that anything like that had happened.

He closed his eyes.

He forced himself not think about the dull, pounding waves of desire eddying up from his loins, or about the nude, desirable girl sleeping a foot away from him. He buried his head in his pillow and waited grimly for sleep to take him.

Morning came. Monday morning.

Lamson felt as though his eyeballs had been sandpapered. The night had been endless, a long white night of tossing and turning and groaning. He had dozed, somewhere along the way, but his journey into morning had exhausted him; he was more tired now than when he had gone to bed. It was a three-coffee morning. Black coffee.

Normally he left the house about eight, which got him to the office by just before nine. But he could tell by Moira's edginess that she did not want to be left alone in the house. The school bus arrived at half past eight for the boys. Lamson waved goodbye to them. They looked puzzled to find him still in the house when they left.

At quarter to nine, the maid arrived. Lamson decided it was safe to leave.

"Don't forget to call the man about fixing the window," he said.

Moira nodded. "If I think of it."

He kissed her goodbye. It was like kissing a cadaver. He was in a bleak, depressed mood as he went out to the garage and started his car.

Minutes later, he was on the highway, heading for town. The warehouse was on New York's lower West Side, in a district of lofts, factories, and wholesale shops. It was a dingy part of town, and as soon as he was able to, Lamson planned to open an executive office uptown, so clients who visited him wouldn't need to thread their way through these gray, disheartening streets of rotting buildings.

Not that Lamson's building was one of the rotting ones. It had been put up right after the war by an ambitious, too-ambitious operator who was going to make a killing in TV tubes just as soon as the new industry got moving. It was a shiny six-story yellow-brick job that stood out like a beacon amid the 19th-century jobs all around it, and it was equipped with the 1946 best in wiring, lighting, and heating.

But the video boom had come and gone, leaving the wily operator high, dry and bankrupt. Lamson, who had been an engineer for one of the super-giant electronics firms, decided to try the business for himself, on the distribution end. He lined up eight backers, assembled a precarious bankroll of $250,000, and went into business. One of his first steps was to pick up the empty but still serviceable warehouse at a distress auction.

He had been in the business for eight years, now. He had bought out five of his original eight partners, and owned a 45% slice of the business outright—enough for control, since the next biggest share was 25%. He had built the business up to a gross of four million a year. He was taking a hefty sum out of the business in salary. An issue of stock was planned that would, if the public responded, leave him a wealthy man for life.

Everything was swell, everything was bright and glorious and exciting. A booming business, sweet children, a happy, pretty wife.

But suddenly the wife was not so happy any more.

He hoped she'd snap out of it. Fast. Right now she was enjoying the luxury of self-pity, and after all it was only a day and a half since the rape. But if she went into a permanent tailspin over this thing, it could get to be a brutal situation.

Lamson entered the building.

"Morning Mr. Lamson." The chorus came from all sides. He was a popular boss, a regular guy. They liked him because he was young, because he was energetic, and because he wasn't ashamed to get down and haul with the rest when he had to. Besides, pay was high, bonuses good.

He knew they envied him. Plenty of his bench men were engineers just as good as he had been, who had simply lacked the guts to go out and found their own companies. So he was on his way to becoming a millionaire by the time he was forty, and they were still pulling down $12,000 a year tops, and would spend the rest of their lives wondering how to finance that new car or that vacation trip.

The phone was ringing in his office. He slid behind his desk. His secretary had already piled up the morning mail to the left of his blotter and a list of the morning's phone calls thus far to the right of the blotter.

He thumbed his eyeballs. Right now he was hardly in a mood to worry about transistors and rectifiers. But business was business and this was Monday and the wheels of industry had to keep turning no matter how hung up he happened to be on his own private problems.

He buzzed for his secretary. "Miss Donovan, would you step in here for a minute?"

Miss Donovan stepped in.

Miss Donovan was a blonde named Ruthie, with long legs and full, heavy breasts. She had been with Lamson Electronics as the boss's private secretary for a year and a half, and during that time Lamson had schooled himself diligently to ignore both the long legs and the full, heavy breasts, to say nothing of the glowing nimbus of blonde hair. He even persisted in calling her "Miss Donovan," though she was Ruthie to everyone else in the place.

Miss Donovan had evidently expected, when given the job of being private secretary to a young, virile, handsome boss, to become the boss's mistress in the natural order of things. But—probably a little to her surprise and disappointment—Lamson had never made even the ghost of a pass at her. There was no reason to.

He was happily married, got all the sex he wanted at home and had no complaints, either qualitative or quantitative, about Moira's bedroom performance. Adulterous ideas hadn't crossed his mind.

But now, suddenly, she entered the room and he was abruptly conscious of round, peaked breasts thrusting out against her white blouse, conscious of the broad sweep of hip and thigh, conscious of the firm buttocks tautly outlined by her plaid skirt, conscious of the golden hair like a silken halo in the morning sunlight.

"You buzzed, Mr. Lamson?"

Lust stabbed at him. Two nights of frustration had done their work. He felt a stirring in his loins and was glad that the desk concealed his physical embarrassment from the secretary's eyes. He felt flustered. His cheeks burned as though he thought she could read his mind.

He said, off balance, "Ah—are there any important appointments for today?"

"The man from Philco will be here for lunch," she said. "Then there's a sales rep from Texas Instruments at three, and you have to call Los Angeles at four-thirty to talk to Owens."

"Right. Thanks, Ruthie."

She blinked at him as the impact of his use of her first name went home. He bit his lip, conscious that he had given himself away.

She seemed to preen. Standing in the sunlight she took a deep breath thrusting the formidable hillocks of her breasts outward.

"Is there anything else, Mr. Lamson?"

"Not—right now," he said.

She turned, went out of his office into hers, switching her buttocks provocatively from side to side. Lamson's throat went dry. An automatic trick of his imagination peeled the plaid skirt away from Miss Donovan's shapely rear, peeled the slip away, peeled away the panties as well, so that in his mind's eyes he found himself staring hungrily at the firm, full pink cheeks of her bare buttocks as she left the room. He gazed with magnetic intensity, nibbling his lower lip and clasping his thighs together as he visualized those two superb masses of flesh, and then the door closed and the vision blinked out of existence.

No, he thought. *No, I will not let myself get hot pants for my secretary.*

It was too hopelessly stereotyped a thing to do he told himself. Everybody laid his secretary—everybody but Dave Lamson, who was happily married and therefore didn't need to fool around with stuff on the side.

If I'm so happily married, why am I sweating like this? he asked himself. *Why do I feel this way?*

He gave way to a moment of blind resentment against Moira for having denied him last night. So what if she had been raped? Was it his fault? Was she going to make a nun out of herself now? For ten years they had been making love five or six times a week most of the time. She couldn't just shut down while waiting to forget about Saturday night's unpleasant experience.

He wondered how long he could stay faithful to Moira while her sex strike continued. Not very long at all, he thought, if a mere two nights of enforced abstinence could leave him letching for his secretary's pretty pink backside this way. Another few days and he'd be grubbing around inside Ruthie's well-filled blouse, the way every secretary expects a normal boss to behave and another day more and he'd be in her panties as well.

Grimly, he set about to catch up with the morning's accumulation of work.

But Ruthie was on his mind. With a woman's diabolical self-understanding she had caught on instantly to the change in Lamson's attitude. She had discovered in one blinding flash that she was no longer an animated piece of office equipment to him but an object of sexual lust. And so she lost no opportunity to wander in and out of his office, display the splendors of breasts and buttocks to him in their tight confinements, and even to lean over his desk with her blouse unbuttoned a bit, to show him the tops of her creamy white breasts.

He tried to ignore her. Even though he broke into a cold sweat every time she passed through, he sternly told himself to get all thoughts of her out of his mind.

But then he would imagine her naked in front of his desk with those big boobs of hers expanding in the sunlight, and the lush flesh of her hips drawing him hypnotically toward her. And he would tell himself that the best thing would be to transfer her to some other department and get himself a nice, gray-haired, 60 year-old secretary until this present domestic tempest blew over.

By eleven o'clock that morning, his nerves were shot, and his blood pressure mounting.

I need a drink, he thought.

Any more normal corporation president kept a couple of glasses and a fifth of Scotch somewhere in his office for times like these. But Lamson—happy well-adjusted Dave Lamson—had never felt the need for such crutches as worktime highballs.

He knew where a drink could be had. Down at the opposite end of the hall was the office of Marty Rich, the company's public relations man, and Marty, though he tried to hide the fact from Lamson, was a compulsive lush who couldn't get a bit of work done without an ounce or two of fuel every couple of hours. Lamson knew about it, but casually ignored the situation, because even a not very sober Rich was worth three or four abstemious but incompetent P-R men.

Lamson went down the hall and into Rich's office. Rich's secretary, a dark-haired exotic-looking girl named Lois Goldstein, looked up at him and gave him the warmest smile in her repertoire, and Lamson quivered a little in response. He had never doubted that Marty was sampling his secretary's charms whenever the mood took him. But now Lamson looked at Lois with new interest. She was a pretty girl. A very pretty girl with her small high breasts and her dark mysterious sparkling eyes.

What the hell's happening to me? Lamson asked.

Lois ushered him into Marty Rich's office. The P-R man, a short, stocky, cigar-smoking dynamo with curly hair, was sitting behind a stack of press releases and yammering into three phones at once, like a movie caricature of himself. But the moment Lamson entered, Rich cut off all three conversations, looked up, and said, "How's it going, Dave."

"It goes. You have that conference set up on the new line of connectors?"

"Tomorrow at noon."

The phone rang. Rich excused himself and answered. Lamson prowled around, going finally to the cabinet where he knew—although Rich did not know he knew—Rich kept his liquor.

A fifth of Jack Daniels stood on the shelf. Lamson took it out, studied it with interest for a moment. Glancing over his shoulder, Lamson saw Rich red-faced with embarrassment.

The P-R man got off the phone and said, "Somebody left that there last night. A funny idea of a joke, huh?"

"Yeah. Very funny. Mind if I have a slug?"

Rich looked startled. He had expected a scolding, not a request for a share. "Sure. Go ahead, help yourself, Dave. Kind of early in the day, or I'd join you, but—"

"Sure," Lamson said.

Lamson poured himself three ounces, ran some water in at the washroom sink, and gulped it down. He thanked Rich, who looked baffled and amazed by his employer's sudden craving for alcohol.

On the way out Lamson found himself peering over Lois Goldstein's shoulder and down the front of her dress, where the beginning slopes of her small breasts could be seen. He averted his eyes quickly.

The drink helped him to relax, but it was not very much help at all. At lunch, two hours later, he had two more drinks.

This was no way to solve the problem, though, and he knew it. Tension gripped him all day.

It was a very long day.

4

He was home by six. The first thing he noticed, as he came in, was the coolness of Moira's greeting. Normally she welcomed him back like Hector come home from the battlefield. Today she gave him a pecking kiss with all the warmth of a spinster's smile.

The second thing he noticed was that the living room window hadn't been fixed. The piece of cardboard that he had taped there yesterday was still in place.

"Didn't I ask you to call the man in to fix the window, Moira?"

She shrugged evasively. "I guess I forgot," she said.

He accepted her answer at face value. But a few minutes later, when he wandered into the kitchen to say hello to the maid, he got a different story.

The maid was a towering Negress who had been with them for eight years, a huge black amazon with enormous strength and gusto. She turned a look of deep concern in Lamson's direction and said, in her booming baritone version of a whisper, "Is the Missus feeling all right, Mr. Lamson?"

"What do you mean?"

"She been acting queer all day. Won't go out of the house. Doorbell rings and she runs upstairs to her bedroom. She scared of something, I tell you. Dunno of what, but she scared."

Lamson moistened his lips. "We had a robbery over the weekend. Didn't she tell you?"

"A robbery? Oh, no, she not say a word!" Bertha rolled her eyes in terror. "What they take?"

"Just a few little trinkets," he said offhandedly. "It wasn't anything serious. But it gave us both quite a scare. I guess she's still jumpy."

"Don't blame her. That how the window got busted?"

Lamson nodded. "He broke in through the living room."

"Uh-huh. She wouldn't tell me what happened. I was going to call a man come fix the window, but she said no, don't call anybody."

"Why?"

"Who knows? But I left the window just like you see it now, Mr. Lamson."

He scowled. "Well, tomorrow you call the glazier, have him get over here and fix that pane. Don't ask her permission. Just do it."

"Yes, sir!"

Lamson walked away. Why was Moira so reluctant to get the window fixed, he wondered? Out of fear of letting a handyman into the house? That was crazy. Nobody was going to hurt her. And with Bertha in the house, only a madman would try to start trouble. Bertha could handle anything under two tons.

Maybe there was some obscure psychological or symbolic reason for leaving the window unrepaired. He didn't know. In Moira's current state of mind, Lamson couldn't figure her out at all.

Bertha had outdone herself on dinner that night. But Moira ate hardly anything, and Lamson, keyed up by the day's tensions, toyed with his food and left most of it. The maid clucked over their full plates as though they were children, and ordered them to eat more—even though that meant less for her afterward.

Bertha cleaned up and left, around eight. Lamson and Moira were alone.

Moira made a grim, self-conscious attempt to start a conversation. "Tell me about work today, Dave."

"There's nothing much to tell. It was just an ordinary Monday."

"Nothing unusual?"

"Nothing," he said. *Except that I went around looking lecherously at every girl in the place. I'm probably the chief topic of conversation everywhere tonight, after that performance.*

They watched television for a while, without interest. At length the program ended; Moira got up and snapped the set off without asking him if he wanted to see anything else. There was silence.

She said, "I can't stand this, Dave."

"What?"

"Living the way I've been living since Saturday. I'm going out of my mind. I feel his touch on me everywhere. I take five baths a day and it doesn't do any good. I—I'm defiled."

"You mustn't take it so seriously," he said, feeling the hollowness of his words.

"But I can't laugh it off. I close my eyes and see him. A tree rustles outside and I imagine it's him. The doorbell rings and I imagine he's coming back."

"They never come back, Moira. There are always more homes to loot. They don't take the chance that a place they've broken into may be boobytrapped the next time."

"But he took so little. He's sure to regret not having looked around more."

"He took plenty," Lamson said in a bitter voice.

Moira put her head in her hands. "I wish it had never happened! I feel so dirty—so changed—"

"Maybe you ought to see a psychiatrist," he suggested. "A few sessions of professional advice—"

"And lie there spilling out all the secrets of my soul to some overpaid phony?"

"They aren't phonies. They help people."

"No, thanks," she said. "I'll pull out of this by myself, or not at all."

He looked at her. "It's pretty rough on me, too," he said. "Just in case you don't realize it. I'm still shaken up, too."

"Why did it have to happen? Everything was so good here!"

"It can be good again!"

"No. I feel him—like a shadow between us, Dave. A stain that won't rub out. I'm not the same woman I was on Saturday. I've been had."

"That shouldn't matter."

"It does to me. Till Saturday I was just yours. Now I've got the memories of being with another man—having a stranger inside me—" She shuddered and looked away from him. He watched her steadily a moment, wondering if he ought to offer her a drink.

Then she looked up at him, eyes reddened and watery. In a low voice she said, "Let's go to bed, Dave."

"It's only quarter to ten."

"Let's go to bed anyway."

Suddenly he understood, and a wave of gratitude washed over him. She was planning to take the bull by the horns, to use direct action. The rape had left her sex life in confusion; very well, the time had come for her to set things straight.

He began to love her again.

They went upstairs together, arm in arm, and he had the warm, relaxed feeling that the worst was over, that by tomorrow she would be well on her way back to recovery and that come the weekend it would all seem like nothing more than an exceptionally vivid bad dream to her. The tensions drained out of him as they entered the bedroom.

"Help me undress, Dave," she whispered.

He hadn't done that in a long time. But now he came around behind her, and reached over her shoulders to undo the buttons of her blouse. She stepped forward, and the blouse shucked off in his hands. He put it down and opened the hooks of her bra. As the cups fell away from her breasts, he slipped his hands over the warm, ripe mounds of flesh.

Moira liked to have him touch her breasts. He could always depend on the quickening of her breath, the indrawn hiss of pleasure, as his fingers touched her nipples and cupped the fullness of her breasts.

But not now.

Her only reaction was a kind of involuntary pulling away, quickly suppressed but not so quickly that he could not detect it. She didn't want him. She was forcing herself to go through with it, but she was just as cold toward him as she had been last night.

Pretending he hadn't noticed, he helped her off with her skirt, her panties, all the rest. She stood nude before him, but the glow of vitality that she usually projected was dimmed, now, by the strange tension that gripped her.

He undressed quickly.

They got into bed. He reached across to snap off the light.

He put his lips to hers. It was a long kiss, a deep one. But it seemed to him that she was not there at all, that he was holding a waxen dummy in his hands. He began to stroke her body, to touch all the little secret places that he had learned, with the years, gave her pleasure to have touched.

No real response. Only a pale counterfeit of passion resulted.

He drew his fingertips along the soft flesh inside her thighs. He gripped her buttocks tight, he nibbled her earlobes, he caressed the small of her back. She clung tight to him, trying hard, trying gamely to want him, but it was as though there were a pane of glass between them.

Desire throbbed hotly in him. He began to realize he was never going to arouse her at all this evening. In the past, there had never been this sort of problem. They would turn to one another, and their bodies would merge, as swiftly and as surely and as perfectly as though they had been born as one two-bodied organism, unaccountably separated in childhood, and reunited by the sacrament of marriage.

But not now.

Now she was cold and remote and distant, putting up with this because it was her wifely duty, not because she desired him or wanted to make love.

It was the most depressing thing in the world. He had slept with loveless women in the past—a long time ago—and he had hated it, hated the phoniness of it, hated the ultimate bitterness of getting to the climax all alone, taking the empty moment of pleasure and then trying to explain to yourself that it wasn't really your fault she didn't make it up there with you.

He didn't want that. He didn't want his marriage to become one of those.

So he worked Moira over. He handled her expertly, doing everything that he knew was sure to arouse her, and the more he did the more artificial the entire act became, the wider grew the gulf that separated them. She lost existence as a flesh-and-blood human being, and became an abstract, mechanized object that he was trying to galvanize into life through a series of intricate and complex maneuvers. No words passed between them. They scrimmaged in silence. He waited hopefully for a sign from her—a gasp, a moan, a catch in her breath—and nothing was forthcoming.

Nothing.

At length he could wait no longer for her. The accumulated load of tension was too great for him. The rape, the burglary, the Sunday of black gloom, the Monday of desire and bouncy bosomed secretaries—it all descended upon him and the spear of his passion thrummed with the intensity of his desires and he had to have some relief.

He turned to her.

"I'm sorry," she whispered sadly.

The weight of his body descended on her. Her thighs parted to admit him, but he could sense her obvious reluctance. She was doing this the way a child takes castor oil, not because she wanted to but because she felt it would make her healthier.

Their bodies joined joylessly. He worked his hands under her buttocks, raising her, and he forced his tongue into her mouth, rolling it over hers and sliding it around, and a tremor went through to the root of his body and he began to move more urgently.

He thrust deep into her. He waited for her answering sigh of pleasure but no sigh came.

Making love this way was almost as bad as not making it at all, he thought. He could remember ten years of happy lovemaking, ten years of thrust and counterthrust of sigh and gasp and moan, of fingers digging into the muscles of his back, of hips pistoning beneath him, of soft lips kissing him, a soft voice whispering wild-eyed words of delight into his ear and breathing hotly against him, of full ripe breasts, warm and almost quivering in his hands.

That was how it had always been between them.

Always.

Never like this. Never this deep-freeze routine.

Moira was trying. He knew that. She wanted with all her heart for it to be the way it had been But something blocked her, something held her back. No doubt every thrust of his impassioned body brought alive in her the memories of another man's thrusting body, and that turned her off beyond all redemption.

He held her tight. He felt the tingling that told him he was near the finish, even though she was still hopelessly stranded at the starting gate. He tried to hold back, but it was no use. When he clamped his eyes shut, he saw the naked, beckoning form of Ruthie Donovan. It was not hard to go on to the next imaginary step and picture himself actually embracing the blonde in place of his own suddenly uncooperative wife.

He began to gasp for breath.

Beneath him, Moira started to move her hips rapidly, intensely. For a moment hope grew in him that she was coming to life after all. Then he realized that she was merely trying to spur him on to his climax so that it would get itself over.

His fingers dug into the warm, resilient flesh of her body. He panted, bit his lip, fought to hold back the climax, failed.

The pulsing moment of fulfillment came.

He climbed for a brief moment toward the summit of ecstasy—and finding it a strange bleak place to reach alone, he instantly plummeted downward.

It was all over.

He lay clasped against the cold form of his wife, listening to the thumping of his own heart; and savoring the melancholy feel of a total fiasco.

Normally, after they had made love, they would remain close to one another, often falling asleep with their bodies still joined. Not tonight. Tonight it seemed Moira couldn't get free of him fast enough. She gave him only a moment or two to catch his breath.

Then she disengaged herself and rolled over once again presenting her back to him.

He stared dolefully at her.

"Moira, I'm sorry—"

"Let's not discuss it."

"I feel like hell. Baby, I tried. I tried my damndest. You know that."

There was a muffled sound very much like a sob. "I know you tried," she said bitterly. "That's what makes it worse. You tried," she said.

"What was the matter? What held you back?"

"Don't talk about it. Let's go to sleep."

"I want to help you."

"I hate post rnortems," she said. "Just chalk it off as a good try and better luck next time."

"We aren't honeymooners," he persisted. "We've been married ten years. This is no time to hope for better luck next time."

"Everything's different, now. Everything's changed. Can't you understand that."

"But why should it be?"

"Go to sleep."

She lay still, but he was certain that she was still awake. Tension rankled in him. There had been relief, yes, but only the lowest kind of physical relief. He could have done as well for himself in the bathroom, he thought.

Moira had tried, and she had failed.

She did not want sex. The rape had done something to her personality. She had been transformed from the sort of woman who enjoyed, who needed sex, into the sort of woman who would *tolerate* sex from time to time but who at no time participated or enjoyed, or did anything but lie back and wait for the messy business to end.

For years, Lamson had listened to other men complain about their cold wives, and he had quietly congratulated himself on having married a live one. But all that was altered now.

He lay awake for a long while. He wondered how they were ever going to untangle themselves from this fix. Sleep in separate beds for a while, maybe? Give Moira a chance to get her bearings again?

But how was he going to manage? What would be his defense against the tempting breasts of Ruthie Donovan, against the available bodies of all the girls a man his position could choose from?

No answer.

He made up his mind to grin and bear it. Sooner or later, he'd break down the barriers of Moira's coldness, and they could start forgetting this whole unsavory episode. Until then, he'd have to be circumspect.

Finally he drifted off to sleep.

In the morning, neither of them made any reference to the abortive, unsatisfying lovemaking of the night before. He could tell that Moira had slept badly. So had he. But they kept their problem well hidden.

He waited till the maid had arrived, then left for the office. Somehow, he got through the day.

Somehow.

That night he made no attempt to approach Moira. They had company, some friends from the neighborhood, and they went through the evening as though all were a hundred percent as it should be, and when the friends left they went to bed and promptly to sleep.

The next night, he wanted her. He had had a brutal day at the office, and in the past there had always been Moira, soft and warm and willing and passionate, to comfort him after the brutal days. Not this one, though. He turned to her in the bed, put his hands on her breasts, felt her shudder and draw away from him.

"Moira—"

"Not tonight, Dave. Please."

He held himself in check. "I want you, Moira."

"Let me go to sleep."

"How long is this going to go on, Moira?"

"I don't know. Do you think I like being this way? I hate it. I hate myself. But I have to say no."

He compelled himself not to force the issue. Give her time, he told himself. All the time she needed. It was only four or five days since it had happened.

But he wondered dismally how much time she would need. Four or five weeks? Four or five months?

Four or five years?

A sex-hungry robber had forced his way into their house and in a few brief minutes had altered Moira completely. Lamson asked himself what was going to become of their marriage now, if she went on sulking for the loss of her honor.

He couldn't understand her. They weren't communicating. He couldn't get through to her at all. These days she seemed to live behind an invisible wall of silent suffering, lost in brooding sorrow over what had happened.

His patience was running thin. The old Moira had been able to snap back from any calamity. This woman in his house was burdened down under the memory as though she would never recover, and that was not like her at all.

On Thursday, his nerves were popping like bowstrings. He hadn't had any sex that meant anything in a week, and he was taking it out on all and sundry in the office, firing nasty memos in all directions, harrying people for the most trivial of matters.

Around four in the afternoon he decided finally to take the medicine that he had been prescribing for himself all week. He buzzed for his secretary.

She entered, smiling, inflating her lungs to show off her astonishing bosom.

"Yes, Mr. Lamson?"

He looked at her for a long, tense moment. Then, in a dry voice that sounded strange and harsh in his own ears, he said, "Ruthie what are you doing tonight?"

5

She looked at him blankly, without understanding, for a moment. Then the message got through. A glint of speculative greed glistened in her eyes.

"This evening?" she said coyly. "Well, if you had in mind my doing some extra work—"

"No. Not work." His voice was clipped, irritable. "I just want some company. For dinner. I've got to stay in town and I don't want to eat alone."

Her expression grew even more animated. She was looking at him strangely, as though wondering why the hell he was suddenly making a pass after having kept their relationship so chaste for a year and a half.

"Well now," she said archly, "if you're sure Mrs. Lamson wouldn't mind—"

"Keep Mrs. Lamson out of this," he snapped. "Is it okay for tonight or isn't it?"

"What time?"

"Say, I'll pick you up around six-thirty," he said. "For dinner."

"You want me to dress up?"

"We aren't eating at the Automat, honey. Wear something fancy."

She whickered. "Sure, Mr. Lamson. It'll be an honor. A privilege. Delighted!"

She left the office, giving him a double ration of hip wiggle. Lamson stared at the wall, feeling sick, disgusted with himself.

Ruthie.

Ruthie was nothing but a gumchewing moron, he thought. A big blonde with spreadable legs. Sure, she was an ace at secretarial work. That didn't take much brains. But he couldn't see her as his dinner companion for an evening.

Then why did you invite her out? he asked himself.

The answer to that one was simple: *Because you want to sleep with her afterward, of course.*

He told himself that he was being a damned fool. Ruthie would probably blab the story to every typist and clerical worker in the building: the big news that after a year and a half of waving her boobs at the boss, she had finally landed a date. The story would work its way up through the echelons, until finally even the top executives knew that Dave Lamson had turned into a nookie-chaser like all the rest.

And then it might get back to Moira—

No. He doubted that. The story wouldn't ever leave the building, he was pretty sure. But even that was bad enough. They would all wonder why he was suddenly going after quail, what was happening to his perfect marriage.

He didn't want anyone to suspect that all was not well in his household.

But he sweated with desire for Ruthie. And he had worked out a complicated and not very convincing rationalization to the effect that if he had an affair with Ruthie, he would feel less sex desire for Moira, and so could give Moira time to come back to normal without his having to press the issue. He didn't really believe it, but it was a comforting thing to tell himself.

He picked up his phone and punched for an outside line. He dialed his home number with none-too-steady fingers.

"Bertha, this is Mr. Lamson. Can I talk to my wife, please?"

A moment passed, and then Moira said, "Dave?"

"Hi. Just calling to let you know I won't be home for dinner tonight. Won't be home till late."

"How come?"

"Big pow-wow just blew up. Couple of boys from the Air Force are coming in on a procurement mission. I've got to wine and dine them tonight. Sorry."

"Dave, I don't want to be left in the house all alone," Moira said tensely.

"Ask Bertha to stay over," he said. "Okay?"

"And if she doesn't want to?"

"Spend the evening with the Jenningses, I'm sure they'd be glad to come over and keep you company."

"Do you have to stay in the city late?"

"Yes," he said stonily. He ran his tongue around his dry, chapped lips and said, "How has it been today? Everything all right?"

"More or less."

"Good. Don't worry about a thing."

"What time will you be home?"

"Midnight, thereabouts. Unless the Air Force lads get into their cups and hold me up. I can't help it, honey. There's a million-dollar contract at stake."

"Don't stay out too late," she said tonelessly. "Goodbye."

"So long," he said. The phone went dead before he hung it up.

The conversation depressed him. It was the first time in his memory that he had consciously, glibly, and calculatedly concocted a deliberate lie to Moira. He didn't like the idea. But he had no choice. He wondered if she had seen through him. Always, when he had a dinner with some big procurement people, she would wish him good luck. Not a word of that, now.

As though she didn't give a damn whether he made the sale or not—or as though she didn't believe there was actually a sale involved.

He shrugged her out of his mind. He had his own welfare to think of, he told himself.

He plunged deep into a batch of memos. At five, the place started to empty out. Ruthie Donovan came into his office and said, "Do you want me to stay around, Mr. Lamson, or can I go home and get dressed?"

"Go home. I'll be at your place at half past six."

"You know the address?"

"Somewhere in the West Nineties. I'll find it."

"See you later," she said with a seductive throb of her eyelids, and slithered out of the office.

He phoned a restaurant a short while later to make reservations for two. He thought of calling the Latour, his favorite French restaurant, but decided against it. The Latour was probably too fancy for the likes of Ruthie. Moreover, they were too slow. With their old-world ideas about cooking everything to order, dinner there was good for at least three hours. Which wouldn't leave enough time for the main event. He vetoed Latour and called Marino's, instead. Ruthie would probably prefer Italian cuisine, and Marino's didn't dawdle over the service.

At quarter to six, with the building all but empty, he freshened up for his date. He kept an electric razor and a clean shirt in one of his desk drawers, for use on evenings when he had legitimate dinner dates, and he shaved now and changed his shirt. He felt a strange excitement, a giddy sense of anticipation that he had not experienced for more than a decade.

He had never been unfaithful to Moira. He had hardly ever even flirted with another woman in the ten years of their marriage. So close had their union been—until last Saturday—that he had felt no adulterous urges at all.

It was a long time since he had last been to bed with anyone but Moira. He thought back. The last time was eleven and a half years ago. He had been in his early twenties, an engineering student at City College, and he had dated a girl named—what was it? Joanna? Joanne? Johanna?—with a turned-up nose and rosy cheeks, and they had gone to a concert in Lewisohn Stadium and afterward to her dingy apartment on Broadway somewhere around 150th Street, and to the accompaniment of a bottle of cheap Italian wine he had seduced her. Two months later he had met Moira and that was the end of his roving bachelor life. And not since then—

—till tonight.

He checked through the personnel cards for Ruthie's exact address, memorized it, and closed up his office. The night watchman waved to him as he left. "Burning that midnight oil, huh, Mr. Lamson?"

"You know how it is, Mike. The top man always works harder than anyone else."

He got into his car. For a moment, reflex had him turning toward the highway and home. But he checked himself at the corner, reversed, and headed uptown to Ruthie's place. He got there a few minutes early and parked down front. It was an oldish, seedy apartment house just west of Broadway, in what had been the most fashionable neighborhood of New York City around the time William Howard Taft had been in the White House.

He went in. There was a directory in the lobby. He found her apartment number and buzzed. She buzzed back almost at once. A tiny voice out of a loudspeaker said, "I'll be right down, Dave."

Dave. The use of his first name hit him as hard as if a small, solid fist had come out of the loudspeaker grid and smacked him in the nose. The thought that Ruth would dare to call him Dave after hours had never occurred to him. But then he had to grin at his own pompous self-importance. *Do you want her to call you Mr. Lamson even while you're laying her?* he asked himself sardonically.

A moment later the elevator door rolled back and there was Ruthie in all her magnificence. He had to admit she was a stunning sight. She wore a dark green sheath that clung to her body as though it had been sprayed on. From the movements of the deep, heavy bowls of her breasts beneath the tight fabric, he was sure she wasn't wearing a bra. She had brushed her blonde hair into an improvised beehive that glittered with reflected splendor. Even in her makeup, she had managed to look impressive without seeming coarse.

Lamson felt a sensation of relief. He hadn't quite known what Ruthie's idea of dressing up for a date with the boss would be, but he had feared the worst. To his relief she seemed to have pretty good taste. She was eye-catching without looking showy, brassy, or vulgar.

"Hi," she said. "Boy, you're right on time!"

He nodded. The dramatic, thrust of her breasts left him speechless. He watched the two heavy globes of flesh rippling under the dress as she came toward him. How, he wondered, had he been able to remain immune to her charms for so long.

They went outside to his car. He held the door for her. "Hey, that's a swell auto you got here, Dave," she said enthusiastically. "What is it, Jaguar?"

"A Porsche," he said.

"One of those little sports cars, anyway. I can't remember the names." She settled into the bucket seat next to him and he put the car in gear. As they began to move, she said, "Tell me something?"

"What?"

"What made you ask me out tonight?"

"I felt lonely."

"Your wife not treating you right?"

"I told you to leave my wife out of this," he said. "I wanted some company."

"Okay, okay. Don't bite! I was just wondering."

He was half amused, half annoyed by the straight person-to-person bluntness of her tone of voice. In the office, it was Mr. Lamson this and Mr. Lamson that, but after hours they were equals in her eyes. Right now she saw him as just another rich man who wanted to go to bed with her.

The car pulled up in front of the restaurant, and they went in. The maitre-de quietly led them to a table in the back. Lamson could tell, from Ruthie's awed silence, that she had probably never been in a restaurant even as elegant as Marino's, with its mirror-and-red-velvet walls and its hanging chandeliers. The plush majesty of the Latour would have given her a stroke, he figured.

Ruthie had no inhibitions about ordering. When she ran across something on the menu that mystified her, she asked, and was told. Lamson watched with awe as she put away two cocktails, a five-course meal, and plenty of wine. Of course she had a big body to feed. In those high heels of hers, she stood nearly five feet ten. Junoesque was the word for her. But not sloppy. He had brushed against her long enough to find out that she didn't have any kind of foundation on. She was big, but not jiggly, not gross.

At half past eight, they were on coffee and cognac. Ruthie leaned back expansively and said, as Lamson signalled for the check, "Well, the evening's young. What do we do now, Dave?"

"Oh, anything you'd like," he said tensely. He realized he was out of practice as a seducer. He couldn't just say, "I'd like to go to your apartment and go to bed with you."

She saved him the trouble of hemming and hawing. With splendid simplicity she said, "Well, we could go dancing or something. Why don't we go up to my place instead, though? We can dance there. Pick up a bottle of something on the way, maybe."

"Swell idea," he said gratefully.

He signed the check—twenty-eight bucks, including tip—and they cleared out. The cool night air was refreshing after the enormous meal.

Lamson drove up Fifth Avenue, headed west across Central Park at 72nd Street, and they stopped off outside a liquor store on Broadway. He bought a fifth of bourbon and they continued on to Ruthie's apartment.

She had three rooms—bedroom, sitting-room, and a tiny kitchen—on the fifth floor of the old house. The furniture was clean but ancient, as though she had inherited it from her parents or maybe her grandparents, Nothing he saw in the apartment betrayed any culture or intelligence. There were no books, only frayed magazines. There was a cheap record-player and a dozen LPs of dance music. No pictures on the walls, just a re-ligious image or two.

Ruthie kicked off her shoes. "Make yourself comfortable. Take your jacket off. Tie and shoes. Might as well relax. Fix a couple drinks, I'll put some music on."

She turned on the phonograph and started some dance music. He fixed up bourbon on the rocks for both of them. They sipped for a moment, and then she moved up close against him and they began to dance.

Her body was warm and ripe and lush against him. He thought of Moira somewhere very far away now. Moira was built well, but not to this abun-dant scale. He could feel the full firm mounds of Ruthie's breasts against him, flattening out against his chest. They were dancing cheek to cheek now, and she was grinding her loins slowly, sensuously against his in time to the music.

Then she said, "You know how to do the Twist, Dave?"

"I've seen it done. Never did it myself."

"I'll give you lessons," she said.

She took the record off and put another one on. Insistent, pounding mu-sic filled the room. She beckoned to him and he came out on the floor again.

"Like this," she said. "Like you're stubbing out a cigarette with your foot."

She showed him. She began to gyrate wildly in front of him, rotating her pelvis, shoving it lustfully out it him, swinging her shoulders, waving her arms. Her great breasts bounced up and down in a wild dance of their own. Her hair flew in golden disarray. The floor seemed to creak under the erotic frenzy of her emotions.

"Come on," she yelled over the din of the music. "You too!"

"I don't know how."

"Nothing to it."

The rhythm captivated him, and he started to move. His hips and knees protested at the unaccustomed exertion, but in a moment or two he was caught up in the swing of it. They faced each other, a yard or more of open space between them, and twisted for all they were worth.

Sweat started to roll down his cheeks. He was pounding hard for breath. He was just about to suggest that they take a breather when Ruthie introduced a new twist to the Twist.

She started to strip.

He watched in astonishment as, without missing a beat, she reached around behind and pulled on the zipper of her tight sheath. It fell away from her shoulders, dropping to bare the upper hemispheres of her breasts. She worked the sheath still lower as she moved in the violent rhythms of the Twist, and in a moment more it was down to her waist. As he had guessed, she wore no bra. The great heavy bowls of her breasts leaped and bounded with every motion. They were very pale, with faint blue veins streaking them. Her nipples were big, set in dark aureoles the size of half dollars. Despite the size of her breasts, they stood out firm and high, close together, without a trace of a droop. They were like two big grapefruit that someone had stitched to her chest.

She worked the sheath still lower, past the rounded voluptuous splendor of her hips, past her navel. Hypnotized by the sight, Lamson kept Twisting, kept jogging along in the knee-punishing gesticulations of the dance, watching in glassy-eyed fascination as her sheath slipped lower and lower, baring her white firm columnar thighs—she had no panties on, either—and then down to her knees, her calves, and with one triumphant shout of glee she kicked and the sheath went flying across the room, and she was stark naked in front of him.

She was incredible.

Lust stabbed at him fiercely as he saw the taut-packed globular rounds of her buttocks, more sensual than he had ever dreamed, as he eyed the leaping mounds of her breasts, the full span of her hips, the pale welcoming beauty of her firm thighs. Not an inch of clothing on her, not anywhere. She was completely exposed to his gaze. His eyes glistened as he stared at her.

Naked, she continued to dance as though possessed by a demon, and her body began to gleam with sweat, beadlets of perspiration forming on her breasts, running out to the nipples and dropping to the gentle curve of her belly. The luxurious mounds of her breasts swayed massively. The wide reddish-pink nipples grew hard and stuck out at him. Everything was visible: the white abundance of her thighs, the fleshy smooth boulders of her buttocks, the swollen, ripe suppleness of her belly, her enormous pointed breasts.

Her pelvis rocked in and out in wild bumps and grinds. He was inflamed, maddened by her.

Suddenly he began to undress.

He was not able to keep the rhythm of the dance as he pulled his clothes off. He simply peeled them away, moving but not Twisting. In a moment or two he was naked. She hardly seemed to notice. She was lost in some private world of her own, as though self-hypnotized by the rhythmic movements of the dance.

He came close to her. He touched her warm, sweat-shiny breasts. He dug his fingers into the heavy mounds of them. He slid one hand down her back until it encountered the outsweeping fullness of her buttocks.

Abruptly she stopped dancing.

She pressed up tight against him, body against naked body.

Together, they slipped to the floor, she beneath him, her buttocks against the dim, faded Persian rug. He felt her hands reaching for him, guiding him to her.

There was no time to waste on preliminaries. They were both eager, both at the peak of passion.

She braced herself, feet flat on the floor, knees high, and thrust upward. He let out his breath in a long ecstatic sigh as they joined. His heart thundered frighteningly. There was something madly orgiastic about this, something primitive, something terrifying in its intensity.

They began to move.

She arched her back, up away from the floor, higher and higher, driving him deeper and deeper. Body thrust against body. She was gasping, making great deep animal-like noises. He opened his eyes for a moment, saw her massive, magnificent breasts heaving and throbbing. He got his hands underneath her, digging the fingers into the resilient flesh of her buttocks.

Like two souls possessed they writhed and wrestled and interwove on the floor. Lamson felt the first quivering sensations of a climax beginning in her, and at the same moment he sensed the early signs of his own. Neither of them held back. He raced madly ahead, giving her all his energy, and she took, giving back her own, and it was up and down and in and out, a hundred sixty pounds of vigorous firm female flesh sighing and gasping beneath him, and then the climax like a roll of thunder, and he closed his eyes and buried his face in the hollow of her throat, and held on tight to her while it happened to him, and in the same moment it happened to her too, and he felt the ecstasy go ripping through her body like an earthquake, and time and space dissolved and the two of them gave themselves up totally, completely, to the roaring rampaging culmination of their passions.

6

And then it was over.

It was over, and he was surprised how fast his mood changed from one of passion-crazed abandon to one of weariness, discouragement; disillusion, guilt. He was still lying on top of her, cradled between her firm thighs. But with the passing of his lusts came a new, cold-blooded way of looking at what they had just done.

What the hell am I doing here? he asked himself.

It seemed strange to be lying here naked atop this hefty blonde, head pillowed in her high rising breasts, his maleness still embedded in the soft moist warm core of her. A quiver of revulsion went involuntarily through him, an awareness of the purely animal thing he had done.

He started to pull free of her.

"Don't go away," she purred drowsily.

"I've got to. It's getting late."

"Stay. Let's have another round."

"I can't," he told her. He drew his body away from hers and got to his feet. She didn't budge. She lay there on the floor, arms sprawling, hair fanning out over the carpet, legs parted sluttishly, knees slightly lifted. He looked down at her and wondered how he could have been so carried away by her. The breasts that had fascinated him so much were just two big bags of meat. What was so interesting about meat? And he saw the sweat all over her, the great heavy fleshiness of her.

He shook his head. He knew that his mood was only the backlash of sexual fulfillment. He had been excited, aroused; he had taken his satisfaction; now came the letdown. Because there had been no love in it, only lust. With Moira, there had always been the special pleasure of their warm love to sustain him after the physical part was over. But now there was nothing but guilt and shame and self-contempt, and even fear. What if she had given him a disease?

He went into the bathroom and washed himself. Her eyes looked at him lazily.

"That was okay," she said. "I wondered about you a long time, you know that, Dave?"

"Wondered how?"

"Wondered why you never made a pass at me. For a while I thought you were a little queer. Then asked and somebody said it was because you were queer for your wife. You had never gone for secretaries, they said."

"Well, I changed my mind. I was in the mood."

"Sure, I get you. A little stuff on the side just to remind you what it's like." She propped herself up on one elbow. He began to feel a renewed interest in her as he eyed the heavy swells of her breasts. She went on, "Was I good? Did you like it?"

"Sure, Ruthie. It was great."

"Why do you have to go so soon? It's only around half past ten."

"I've got to get home. You understand that."

She nodded. "I suppose." After a pause she said, "Is this a one-shot? Or you gonna see me again?"

"We'll see, Ruthie."

"I hope it isn't just a one-shot."

He frowned at her. "We'll see. Remember, not a word about this to anybody."

"My lips are sealed."

"And in the office, no funny stuff. I'm Mr. Lamson in the office, and don't you forget it."

"Don't worry, Dave," she said with calculated familiarity. "I know what's right and what isn't." She clambered to her feet. "Here. I'll put your bourbon away. It's for the next time."

"Okay," he said.

He finished dressing. She padded around the apartment in the nude, tidying the place up. Every time she walked past him, he felt desire mounting again. That first moment of guilt and emptiness was passing, and her lush nakedness was working its magic on him. His throat felt dry. He wanted her again, and he was pleased to be virile enough to be able to want her, but he knew he had to go home.

Home. Home to Moira.

Home to his raped wife, who was now also his deceived wife.

Lamson checked himself out in the mirror. He looked a little flushed, but that could be accounted for just by a night of hard drinking and hard bargaining. Otherwise there was no way for Moira to know what he had been up to. He walked to the door.

"Good night, Ruthie."

She paused and turned to him, arms akimbo, legs slightly parted, loins thrust forward a little, heavy breasts rising and falling gently. Her supple, bursting nakedness was like a hot flare going off in his eyes.

"See you," she whispered huskily.

He turned and walked out.

He felt strangely drained, depleted. So he had finally taken the journey into adultery, he thought. Well, he had enjoyed getting there, but he couldn't much say he liked his destination. He felt that he had done something mean and cheap and low.

He shook his head. It had been a purely physical act, he told himself. He needed some relief from the new tensions at home, and so he had turned to Ruthie, who was more than willing to oblige. That was all there was to it. He still loved Moira. He hadn't been emotionally unfaithful to her, just physically. That wasn't so bad a thing to do, was it, he asked himself?

Was it?

Driving nervously and badly, he headed uptown to the bridge, then swung round onto the highway. A light rain was starting to fall. It was almost eleven o'clock. He felt tired, and the road's surface was slick. But he wanted to get home. He kicked down hard on the accelerator, watching the speedometer needle climb past fifty. The limit on this road was only forty-five, but he couldn't worry about that now. If he got a ticket, he knew where he could have it taken care of so it wouldn't appear on his license, and he wanted to get home.

The rain came down harder. The windshield wipers worked hard. He went sloshing through a floorboard-deep puddle, and then a hundred fifty yards further on he abruptly had to hit the brakes to avoid smashing into a lumbering Imperial that had just come on the highway from the approach to his left. The wet brakes didn't respond uniformly, and the little car skidded a good three and a half feet to the right when he came down on the brakes.

He grabbed the wheel and swung it back in line.

Easy, boy. His little swerve had taken him over into the adjoining lane. If anybody had been riding there he'd have flipped right end over end, and Moira would be applying for his life insurance benefits. Chastened, he got back where he belonged and cut his speed to 45. The next time he had to use the brake, he cut the wheel compensatingly to the right before braking. The Porsche held true this time.

He got home at half past eleven. The lights were on downstairs. Peering through the living room window—it had been fixed finally, the day before—he saw Moira talking to another woman whose back was to him. He put his key in the door and walked in.

The other woman turned out to be Laney Clyde, from three houses up the block—a slim, bedroom-eyed brunette of about twenty-six or so. Lamson was a little surprised to find her here. Laney was a shallow, flashy kind of girl, and not the type Moira picked as a friend. He and Moira saw the Clydes only out of neighborly courtesy, every now and then. But the families weren't friends.

He stood in the living room doorway. Laney swung around to greet him with a big, "Hi there, Dave!"

"Evening, Laney. Moira. I didn't come home too late, did I?"

Moira shook her head. "It isn't midnight yet. How was your dinner conference?"

"So-so. I have a hunch they're not going to give us the contract," he said. He glanced at the Clyde girl. She was wearing a startling getup, bright chartreuse Capri pants and an open-fronted basque shirt that dramatically displayed her small but adequate breasts. She had risen and was standing in a provocative position by the window, hands on her hips, the tight pants lining the contours of her buttocks enticingly.

"Guess I'd better be running along home," Laney said. "Thanks for inviting me, Moira. Goodnight, Dave. We all ought to see more of each other."

When Laney was gone Lamson peered at his wife in surprise and said, "What the hell was she doing here?"

Moira's expression was a sullen one. "Bertha couldn't sleep over. The Jenningses had theater tickets. I didn't want to stay alone, so I invited Laney. I had to have someone in the house."

"You never used to be so timid," he said.

"You aren't very sympathetic, are you?" Moira asked thinly.

"I've told you that you ought to get psychiatric aid instead of huddling here afraid of your shadow. That man isn't coming back."

She looked at him edgily. "Let's not argue, shall we?"

"All right," he said. He was disturbed by the ease with which friction arose between them these days. The least difference of opinion was enough to send them both into a querulous, belligerent mood. "Did you enjoy your chat with Laney?"

"Oh! She's disgusting!" Moira exclaimed.

"How so?"

"You know what we talked about all evening?"

"Can't guess. The stock market?"

"Her love affairs. That was all she could talk about. Adultery is her hobby, it seems."

Adultery was not precisely the subject Lamson was most eager to discuss at this moment. But he felt that he had to pursue the conversation. "Does she make a regular routine of it?"

"Incredible. She's had dozens of affairs. Milkmen, neighbors, anyone she can inveigle."

"What does her husband say?"

"Oh, he doesn't seem to mind. She started it when she found out about an affair *he* was having. But then she discovered it was fun, and she's been doing it ever since. I don't think I'd like to have those people for my friends. But I needed company." Moira yawned delicately. "I'm so tired. Shall we go to bed?"

They turned the lights out and went upstairs. Lamson pondered what Moira had told him. So Laney slept with the neighbors—what of it? Odd that Moira hadn't jokingly asked him if *he* had sampled her favors.

Did Moira hope to unsettle him with this kind of talk? Was she needling him in a subtle way, telling him that she knew all about what he had been up to tonight, and that if he didn't watch his step she'd start carrying on like Laney Clyde?

He didn't try to figure it out.

He undressed, washed up, got into bed. He watched Moira as she crossed the room, nude, to hang up her skirt and blouse. He felt the old yearning for her even after his session with Ruthie.

But then Moira got into bed, turning out the light.

"Good night," she said coolly.

He was silent for a moment. "Good night," he said finally.

He rolled over on his side, biting his lip in anguish. It was practically a whole week, now. Moira cool as an icicle. What the hell was going on. Why did she seem to resent him so much? It was obvious now that she was taking the rape out on him.

Things were getting out of hand, he realized. What had been a perfect marriage was all screwed up, suddenly. He had gone to bed with his secretary. Moira wouldn't have anything to do with him sexually, and when he finally had made love to her the other night she hadn't responded.

She needed help. But she was resisting the idea. She was sitting here all day nursing her neuroses. She hardly seemed to listen when he spoke to her. All right, being raped was no laughing matter. But she was taking an ungodly long time to bounce back from it. And he knew he didn't begin to understand what was going on inside her mind these days.

What was going on?

Was she hiding something?

He didn't know. He decided he'd give it another few days, and then he'd bluntly spell out his worries to her. He couldn't let her go on sulking like this forever. He had to know why she was reacting in this unexpected way to the violent act that had been perpetrated on her.

He saw with a sense of dull foreboding that they might never restore their marriage to what it had been. Already, he had taken an irrevocable step—he had slept with another woman. That was a scar in their relationship that would never heal. No longer could he rejoice in the perfection of their marriage—not after another man had known Moira's body by force, not after he himself had sampled the juicy delights of Ruthie Donovan's fleshy form.

After a long while sleep crept up on him, and he descended into a shadowy realm of uncertain miseries.

The next day was Friday. Lamson left the house at his old regular time— Moira was at least willing to tolerate being alone for the forty-five minutes between his departure and the maid's arrival—and got to the office just around nine. He was a little apprehensive of the sort of reception he would get from Ruthie.

She was there already, patiently going through the morning mail and slitting open the envelopes. No sexy sheaths for her today; she wore sexlessly efficient office clothes, even a pair of harlequin glasses that interfered with the smooth flow of her features. But as he looked at her the chaste white blouse and dark skirt vanished like pricked bubbles, and he saw in her chair the nude Ruthie of the night before, big breasts shiny with sweat, legs parted in expectant anticipation of his lustful thrust. She swung around to face him and the erotic image gave way again to her workaday appearance.

"Morning," he said.

She grinned cheerfully. "Morning—Mr. Lamson." She tacked the last two words on in a casual way. "I was just going through the mail. The important stuff's over here in this stack."

Gathering it up, she handed it to him. For a moment their hands touched. He took the mail brusquely from her, pulling back. He could feel her eyes boring into his. He felt utterly transparent.

He said, "When you're finished with the mail come inside. I've got some dictation."

"Be right with you—Mr. Lamson."

Lamson went into his office. He realized that from now on there was going to be a streak of insolence in Ruthie's attitude toward him. She knew she had power over him, sexual power. Once she had gotten on a first-name basis with him, she had him where she wanted him. In the office she'd be outwardly obedient to him but there'd always be that playful, mocking smile, as an acknowledgment of the after-hours relationship between them.

Perhaps he thought, he would be wise to transfer Ruthie to some other post before things got too complicated for him.

Perhaps. But not just yet.

She came in with her pad. Crossing her legs, she gave him a good view of her thigh, and his imagination automatically supplied the rest. Once again the searing naked image of Ruthie burned in his mind's eye.

He walked to the window and turned his back on her. "Mr. Charles Portnoy," he began. "Continental Semiconductors, Inc., something-or-other Barclay Street, Alameda, California. Dear Chuck: This is by way of official confirmation of our merchandising agreement as reached on the twelfth of this month. The legal department is hard at work on the usual documents and they'll be along in due time but meanwhile I want to provide you with a written binder of the understanding by which—"

He droned on. The sound of Ruthie's pencil rasped into his ears. Ten minutes later, he concluded with a "Best wishes from David Lamson," and, turning away from the window, said, "Have that typed and ready for signature by eleven will you? I want it to go out by the noon pickup."

Ruthie was smiling strangely at him.

"What's the matter?" he said.

"Nothing."

"Why were you looking at me like that?" he asked.

"I was just thinking about last night."

He scowled at her. "*Don't* think about last night. That's an order! For Christ's sake, Ruthie, I told you that everything had to be strictly business down here at the office. Whatever may have happened last night, it shouldn't be in your mind while you're taking dictation."

"Yes, sir."

"And skip the sarcasm too."

"Yes, sir."

He flicked his hand impatiently at her. "Oh, go on. Get that thing typed."

She eyed him seductively and ambled out of the office, with so much hip-and-buttock action as to be almost comical. Lamson sank wearily into his chair.

Women!

How could life get so complicated all at once, he asked himself?

Last Friday at this time he was a happily married man without a care in the world. In one week's time his marriage had gone to hell, his sex life was standing on its head, and his efficient, crisp secretary was now his mistress, with the self-assumed privilege of laughing at him whenever she felt like it.

It had been a mistake to get entangled with Ruthie. So long as he had ignored her sex appeal he was the boss. But now she had had the chance she wanted to show off what she could do. And now, she knew, he'd come back for more and more, like an addict.

Damn women! he thought.

He tried to get some work done. Letters to sign, checks to okay, mail to read. Somehow he got through the morning, developing a blinding headache by noon.

He had a lunch date with a purchasing representative from a big British manufacturing concern. Usually Lamson was a one martini man at lunch dates.

Today he had three.

The Britisher limited himself to one mild sherry before the meal. Lamson sensed the fact that he was being disapproved of. He couldn't help it. He needed the drinks. He wanted to say, I'm not really a heavy drinker, it's just that I'm under some peculiar pressures this week.

The lunch date ended without a commitment. Worriedly, Lamson asked himself if he had done anything wrong, said anything gauche. Or was it just those three martinis that had queered things? Did the British firm prefer to deal with someone a little more stable? What the hell did his personal drinking habits have to do with the contract, if his firm could deliver the goods, anyway?

He didn't know.

He was in a black mood as he returned to the office to finish out the day and the week.

7

The showdown with Moira came late Saturday night. It was inevitable. They had been at swords' points for two days. They had bickered Friday night, about silly, unimportant matters, and Saturday started off the same way. By Saturday afternoon the usually even-tempered Lamson was approaching his boiling point. He had never known Moira to be so bitchy before.

And he knew something had to be done fast to heal the widening breach. In the past in the rapidly receding era of good feeling on the far side of the rape night—they had never had any serious quarrels and any disagreements had been settled almost immediately in the bedroom.

But that means of settlement seemed to be gone from their marriage. Or so it seemed. Lamson was determined to find out at bedtime.

Saturday dragged to its weary finish. They had two couples from the neighborhood over in the evening, and Lamson was none too sociable, waiting tensely for the time for good-byes to come. At half past twelve the party broke up since Lamson's coolness had put a damper on everyone's spirits.

Lamson locked up and followed Moira upstairs. *One week ago tonight*, he thought, *my world ended. One lousy week. It seemed like a couple of years.*

Moira was half undressed. She turned to him as he entered and said, "You weren't very friendly tonight, I must say."

"I guess I wasn't really in the mood for company," he said. His eyes came to rest on the high peak of her creamy red-tipped breasts, bare to his gaze. She saw where he was looking and reddened faintly. Turning from him she pulled off her panties and unhooked her garter belt. He felt a new surge of desire at the sight of her smooth firm buttocks, with their tender rises and dimples. He began to take off his clothing.

Tonight, he decided, was the night when he found out what was what. He had been coddling Moira all week. But it was seven days since the rape. He couldn't let things slide along any longer.

Moira was taking a shower. As he washed up for bed he glanced over his shoulder, saw her slim pink form behind the frosted glass of the shower cubicle. Ordinarily she was at her most loving right after she had had a shower, when she emerged fresh and clean and pink and scrubbed, her skin still moist, her body sweet-smelling, pure. It was one of her favorite times for lovemaking.

It had been, anyway.

But tonight?

Lamson finished brushing his teeth and returned to the bedroom. A few minutes after he had climbed into bed, Moira emerged from the bathroom, nude, glowing with the radiance of new cleanliness. He felt an automatic twinge of desire for her as she stood there, poised by the light-switch, her breasts pink, glowing.

Then she switched off the light and joined him in the bed.

For a long moment neither of them moved. Lamson scowled into the darkness. He knew what this motionlessness meant. It meant that their marriage had degenerated into the kind of mock-marriage so many others had. The kind where the husband lies there thinking, *If I reach out for her, will she put up a fuss?* and the wife lies there thinking, *Maybe if I don't move he'll forget about it and just go to sleep.*

That was the tug-of-war kind of marriage, the contest-of-wills kind of marriage, where on some nights the wife decided it was too much bother to refuse, and submitted, while on other nights the husband decided it was too much bother to attempt it, and just went to sleep. The hateful, sexless, joyless kind of marriage.

He lay there, waiting, hoping, praying for her to make the first move.

She didn't. There was silence in the darkness.

He knew that he would have to do it. Bitter, tense, he reached out for her. His hand closed on the warm, tender firmness of her right breast. He held it for a moment, cupping it, caressing it. The nipple was soft. She felt no desire.

After a moment she said, "Good night, Dave."

Oh, no! he thought. *You aren't getting rid of me that easily.*

Softly, without letting go of her breast, he said, "Don't say good night just yet, Moira."

"Please, Dave. I'm just not in the mood."

He hesitated, knowing that a false word now would ruin everything. And then he plunged ahead anyway, his anger getting the better of him.

"Not in the mood? Christ, Moira, are you ever in the mood these days?"

"Dave, let's not fight. We fight about every little thing under the sun."

"This isn't little, Moira. It's big. It's the biggest thing we've had to face since our marriage."

"Let me go to sleep."

"I want to talk this thing out."

"I just want to go to sleep." She put her hand on his, half affectionately, half to remove his hand from her breast. He pulled back from her. He could hear her sobbing in the darkness. "I don't know what's wrong, Dave, I can't help being this way. I—I just don't want to have any sex these days."

"It's a week since it happened, Moira. It shouldn't take a normal healthy person this long to recover her balance, should it?"

"Let me go to sleep," she pleaded.

But letting her go to sleep would just be to shove the problem under the carpet and try to forget about it—until it inevitably came crawling out again, bigger and uglier than ever before.

He got out of bed and switched the light on.

"Let's talk this thing out, Moira."

She looked up at him, blinking, frightened, a hand across her face to shield her from the sudden light. In a halting voice she said, "I don't know what there is to talk about."

"The reason why you've gone frigid on me."

"I—I don't know."

"You know how many times we've made love since the night you were raped?" he demanded. "Once. Once. And it was no good. It didn't work right at all. Can you remember the last time we had such a total failure in bed? No. Neither can I."

"It's temporary, Dave. I'm trying to work my way out of it."

"It's starting to look awfully permanent," he shot back at her. "And the longer we let it continue, the worse it'll get. We're tense because we aren't getting any fulfillment, and we're snapping at each other right and left. And at the kids. Pretty soon we'll reach a point of no return, where we've said or done things that leave a permanent mark. And then what'll become of us?"

"Have we only made love once this week?" she said, in an all too blatantly obvious attempt to sidestep and sidetrack the main issue of their widening estrangement.

"Just once," he said. "Monday night. Not since then, Moira."

"I hadn't realized it was so long ago."

"Five days. You want me to repeat all the little excuses you've had since then?"

"No—please. Let's not fight about this, Dave." A look of sudden craftiness came into her eyes. She threw back the covers, showed him her nakedness, her parted legs. "Come to bed, Dave. I'll make it up to you right now. For the whole week. I swear I will."

He shook his head. This, too, was no solution of the problem. Giving in to him when he raised the roof—that was just another peace-restoring gimmick of a frigid wife. It solved nothing. I kept him happy till the next time, that was all.

"No," he said. "Don't confuse things. I want to discuss this with you."

"And I'm offering to sleep with you."

"You sound so goddamn cold-blooded about it," he muttered. "Doing me a favor to shut me up."

"That isn't true!" she said. Tears ran down her cheeks—weapon number two, he thought angrily. Having failed to change the subject through sex, she was trying to change it through tears.

He sat down next to her on the edge of the bed. "Will you listen to me?" he said quietly. "Will you keep calm and stop turning this into an emotional bloodletting session, Moira?"

"What do you want from me?" she wailed.

"I want you to be my wife again. The same warm passionate wife you were—before."

"I can't help it! I'm different now! I've been changed!"

"We can change you back. But you've got to get control of yourself."

She looked up at him through the tears. "Get me a tissue," she said in an abrupt change of mood.

He got her one. She dabbed at her eyes. He stood above her, looking down, feeling dull throbbing pangs of desire as he eyed her slim naked form. She finished dabbing, crumpled the tissue, threw it into the nightstand ash tray, and pulled the covers up.

She said, "Turn out the light and get into bed and we'll talk."

"I'd rather talk with the lights on."

"Please. Do it my way."

He shrugged. She seemed to be in control of her emotions again, and there was no sense thwarting her on a small matter like this. Once again the room was dark. He slipped into bed alongside her.

She said in a hollow voice, "I've stopped enjoying sex with you since it happened. That's no secret. We both know it."

"Yes."

"And you want to know why?"

"Yes, Moira."

She was silent for a moment. Then she said, "You're the only man I ever slept with, you know that. Up till last weekend. The only one."

"I know that."

"It hit me hard when that situation was changed. I can't really explain. It was all down deep—on levels that don't work the way a logical, sensible human being works on the surface." She looked at him in the darkness. "Whenever you touch me now, I'm reminded of the rape. Of the pain, the fear, the humiliation. That's why I can't respond to you, Dave."

"But what do I have to do with him?" Lamson asked.

Moira was silent again, as though fighting within herself to get the words out. Finally she said, in a blurting burst of words, "Because he looked just like you, that's why I'm reminded!"

"What?"

"It was like your twin brother raping me, if you had a twin brother."

"I don't. The resemblance was just a coincidence. One of those things. His face was all battered. He didn't really look much like me."

"Under the battering he did. Under the surface. You can't realize how much he looked like you. I saw the two of you side by side. You looked like brothers."

"What of it?"

"Don't you see?" she asked. "When you touch me—I feel *him*. I've got the two of you all tangled up in my mind and I can't get them untangled. That's the reason I'm frigid to you. You're my husband and I want to love you, and he was a rapist and I hate him—but in bed the two of you blur and mix and get meshed. I *know* it's you—but what I know and what I feel are two different things."

"And you feel—?"

"Hatred. Fear. Disgust. The same things I felt while—while he was raping me. Now do you see it? Now do you understand what's happened to me? When you try to make love to me, it's the rape all over again. I can't help it, Dave. I'm all confused. I don't know if I'm coming or going these days."

He stared off into nowhere for an endless moment, dismayed beyond all words by her statement. What kind of business was this, anyway? Mixing him up with the rapist? Just because of an accidental resemblance?

He said, "I don't want to sound repetitious, Moira. But this is the sort of thing that psychiatrists are supposed to handle."

"I know."

"We'll find one. We'll start you right away. Get you untangled."

"No," she said in a choked little voice.

"No?"

"I can't, Dave. I'm afraid."

"Of what?"

"Having a psychiatrist picking around inside my mind. I told you that before. I can't bear the thought of it. I just can't."

"Moira, it's our only hope. You want us to stay in this mess forever?"

"Of course not."

"Then you've got to get help. It's too much for you to handle by yourself. Christ knows I can't fix things. You've got to go to someone who can. If you had cancer, you'd go to someone to cut it out, wouldn't you? If you broke a leg, you'd have it set?"

"Yes, but—"

"This is an ailment too. It doesn't happen to be one you can see and touch, but it's a disease all the same, and you've got to get cured. Before we both go out of our minds. Will you see a psychiatrist?"

"I don't want to, Dave."

"This isn't like you. You're acting like a scared little baby."

"I'm not me any more. Not the me you know. *I am* a scared little baby."

"Please, Moira—"

She didn't answer. He heard her catch her breath in a sob of misery. The next moment, she had turned to him, was pressing her body up against his in an access of panicky need, in a sudden blaze of desire.

"Hold me," she whispered. "Put your arms around me, Dave. I'm so afraid, so mixed up."

He held her. He knew that once again she was sidestepping the problem, but there was no helping it now. Her need seemed genuine at this moment. And his own desires rose to an uncontrollable peak as he felt the hard points of her breasts pressing into him. Her arms went round his body. Her lips sought his, her tongue darting into his mouth, meeting his, sliding sensuously over it.

Hope rose in him. Maybe in this joining of their bodies all her confusion would be burned away, and the old Moira would step shining, Phoenixlike, out of the ashes after the week-long nightmare.

His hands went to her breasts. He cupped the soft warm flesh of them. He gasped as her small cold hands encountered the root of his body. She flattened herself against him, thighs against thighs, breasts against his chest, lips to his lips, tongue to tongue. He could hear her rough, uneven breathing, and he silently begged that this time they could make it all the way and end the torment.

She drew him down to her, and with the ease of long familiarity he joined his body to hers. The moment she had imprisoned him within her, she began to move, a slow, undulating motion at first, then more eager, more excited, more fiery.

A soft, indistinct murmur escaped her lips. He held tight to her, and a new, driving action of her haunches began, a rhythmic action, faster and faster, harder, wilder, faster, faster, and he heard her gasping hoarsely, in excited pleasure, and despite the roughness of his own breathing he managed to smile triumphantly at the thought that they were about to break through the wall that had held them apart for an entire week.

Her body was moving with urgency now. His fingers dug deep into the smooth, satiny flesh of her buttocks, lifting her toward him. The bedsprings protested the violence of their lovemaking. He soared up high, plunging again and again into the deep, clinging channel of love.

And then came a moment when he realized she was faking it all.

He didn't know why he thought it. It wandered unbidden across his mind, and he looked down at her, and there she was with her eyes closed, her lips distorted by the strenuous effort she was making, and he knew intuitively that she wasn't feeling any of this, that she was just putting on a good show to make him happy and let him think everything was going to be all right.

He was furious with her for the deception.

He clung to her, ramming higher and harder, trying by the sheer force of his exertions to awaken the real passions in her, but it was no use. Now he was convinced that all her gyrations and gaspings were phony. She was acting a part, not experiencing anything real.

Faster. Higher. Harder. Faster.

The climax was almost on him now. He gripped the soft flesh of her shoulders, the signal that he was about to reach the top, and sure enough, she went into her final spin also, but he knew beyond any doubt that it was just a ham routine she was pulling.

The hammerblows of fulfillment hit him hard. He shuddered out the moments of ecstasy while Moira bucked and thrust beneath him.

Then all was quiet in the bedroom except for the sound of ragged breathing.

There was the taste of ashes in his mouth.

He lay there quietly in the darkness, Moira's slim naked body still enfolded in his embrace, thinking bitter thoughts. Neither of them spoke. He did not know how to say what he wanted to say, to accuse her of deceiving him this way. After all, there was always the chance he was wrong. And then he would shatter the new, fragile crust of restored love that had formed.

A long while passed. He thought she was asleep. But then she stirred.

"Good night, Dave," she murmured.

"No. Wait."

"What is it, Dave?"

"Was it—really—good for you, Moira?"

"It was wonderful."

"I mean really."

"Of course, really." There was a querulous edge on her voice that told him at once that she was lying. "What are you getting at, Dave?"

"Nothing. Except—"

"Go on."

"Except that I think you were pretending, Moira."

"That's a terrible thing to say."

"I know. I wouldn't have said it if I didn't think it was true."

"Don't you have any faith in me?"

"I've known you long enough to know what's honest and what's faked. Were you faking, Moira?"

"N-no."

"Come on. Don't make it worse."

She looked up at him, her eyes streaming with tears. "All right! All right! So I *was* faking! I admit it! Does it make you any happier to hear it?"

"What did you think you'd gain by it, Moira—"

"I wanted you to love me again."

"You know I love you."

"You think I'm frigid."

"Pretending you aren't won't solve anything, Moira. You know that. You're a mother. If a child of yours is sick, do you like him to hide the fact from you until he's so far gone he needs an oxygen tent? Do you want him to pretend he's well when he isn't?"

"This is different."

"It's the same, Moira," he said inexorably. "You've got a sickness. You can't just pretend it isn't there, and hope that it'll go away."

"Why do I need to be happy in bed?" she asked. "Why won't you let me just pretend?"

"Because that isn't what I got married for, Moira. I can buy pretended orgasms at ten bucks a throw whenever I'm in the mood. That isn't love."

"All right. What do you want me to do?"

"I told you. See a psychiatrist. Get some professional help."

"And I told you. I'm afraid to."

"You've got to, Moira," he said patiently. "You're a grown up girl. You've got to face the music. Psychiatrists don't bite. They help people. They cure people's troubles. Do it for me, Moira. Will you?"

Silence.

"Will you, Moira?"

"I—don't want to."

"Do you want to keep our marriage alive, Moira?"

"Has it come down to that?"

"It may," he said. "It's dying fast, now. You're the only one who can keep it alive."

Silence.

"Well, Moira?"

"All right. All right. I'll go! I'll have my head shrunk, if you think it'll help, I'll go! I'll go!"

He stroked her arm lovingly. She pulled away from him. He listened to her sob herself to sleep. A long time later, he fell asleep himself.

8

Lamson found her an analyst on Monday. It wasn't a very difficult process. One of his college classmates, he knew, was an analyst in mid-Manhattan, with a thriving practice. Lamson had heard that it wasn't a smart idea to get involved in analysis with a friend of the family, but he called his friend for a recommendation anyway. He wanted the name of an analyst not far from his home, one that Moira could visit without too much travelling.

Lamson's classmate's name was Joe Heinsohn. He said, "I know this fellow name of Michalis out your way, Dave. Got his address right here—ah. Here it is. You want to take it down?"

"What sort of guy is this?" Lamson said.

"Youngish, about our age. Very good. A crackerjack, in fact. I'd say he's about the most respected man under forty in the state, for his particular branch of analysis."

"And he'll do a good job with Moira?"

"Depends on what her problem is. And no, I don't want you to tell me about it. Take it up with him. Knowing her, I doubt that it's anything really serious. Even if it is, Michalis is the man to take care of it."

"Sold," Lamson said. "Thanks a million."

He phoned Dr. Michalis next. "Joe Heinsohn gave me your name, doctor. I'd like to have you see my wife, if you can squeeze her in."

"Well, there's a little free time opening up, Mr. Lamson. Of course I won't accept her case until I've spoken to her. Do you think she could drop around for an interview Wednesday morning, say, ten o'clock?"

"I'll arrange it."

"Good. I'll be looking forward to seeing her."

That night. Lamson told Moira that an appointment was all set up. She took the news badly, getting tense and jittery at the thought of analysis.

"You know how you're acting?" he asked her. "Like a ten-year-old with a toothache, that's how. You know you need to go to the dentist, but you're afraid he'll hurt you. So you try to pretend it doesn't hurt. And you're in agony."

"I don't want to go, Dave."

"Wise up, will you? This man will *help* you. I talked to him. He sounds like an ace. Joe Heinsohn tells me he's one of the best in the business. What's the matter? Don't you want to get better?"

"Of course I do."

"But what? You want it go away by itself?"

"I don't want some stranger grubbing around in my mind," she said.

He scowled at her. "Seeing him will do you a world of good. Tell him exactly what happened—tell him about the rape, and everything that's happened since. Don't hide anything from him. Get it all off your chest. It's the only way he can help you."

Moira reluctantly agreed to keep her appointment. But she wore a tense, martyred expression all that night and the next day. Wednesday morning, just before he left for the office, Lamson wished her good luck at the appointment.

"I'll phone you around eleven-thirty," he said. "You ought to be home by then. Let me know how it went. And for God's sake cheer up. This is for your own good, can't you understand that?"

He was edgy all morning. He had to admit privately that he didn't much care for the idea of Moira's spilling the intimate facts of her life out to some stranger. But that couldn't be helped. A man doesn't object when a doctor looks at the nakedness of his wife in an examination. He had no right to object when a different kind of a doctor examined the inmost secrets of his wife's mind.

He phoned home at half past eleven. Moira picked up the phone on the sixth ring.

"Well?" Lamson asked eagerly.

"So I saw him," Moira said. She sounded tired, almost exhausted.

"What's he like?"

"Young. Very tall. Solemn-looking. Smokes a pipe. Anxious to help."

"And what did he say?"

"Well, I told him about some of the things that are bothering me. And he said yes, he figured he could do me some good. I'm going to see him three times a week. Monday, Wednesday, Friday, $25 a session. That sounds like an awful lot. $75 a week just to sit on a couch and talk for three hours a week, Dave."

"It's what they all charge," he said. "Don't worry about it. We can afford it. The important thing is to get you better, Moira."

For a few days he allowed himself the luxury of hope. He told himself that this man Michalis was going to work some sort of a miracle, that he would wave a Freudian magic wand and presto jingo, the harmful effects of the rape would be wiped out and Moira would be restored to him, warm and loving and passionate as before.

On Friday, when he asked her about how her second session had gone,

Moira was evasive. "All we did was talk," she told him.

"About what?"

"Oh—things. All sorts of things. I don't feel like going into it all."

Lamson didn't press her. He didn't press her sexually, either. These were difficult days for her, he thought. All right. He'd give her all the leeway he could. Let her work things out with the analyst. *I'll be patient*, he thought. *I won't force her to sleep with me.*

Of course, there were certain tensions that he was under, and those tensions had to be coped with. It was Friday, and he hadn't had any sex since last Saturday, and his healthy, virile body wasn't used to that sort of sex starvation.

He tried to cope by drinking, figuring that would relax him and take the edge off his desires. It didn't work. On Monday, when he got to the office, he was wound up tight as a drumhead, and in desperate need of relief.

He buzzed for Ruthie Donovan.

She had been keeping her distance, the last week, as though worried that by being over-familiar with the boss she might be putting her job in jeopardy. On his part, he had been trying hard not to look at her, so as to keep temptation behind him. But now he could fight temptation away no longer.

He said in a low voice, "Ruthie, are you free to see me tonight?"

"I was wondering when I'd get my second chance."

"That bourbon doesn't spoil. Unless you've been drinking it on the sly."

"Uh-uh. I've been saving it for the next time."

"Are you free, then?"

"Sure."

"We can go out to dinner, and then—"

"I got a better idea," she said. "It'll save you some dough, and save me the trouble of dressing up. You can come straight to my place for dinner. I'm not such a bad cook. You'll like it."

The idea startled him at first, but the more he thought about it, the more he liked it. And so it was agreed. He trembled with anticipation, and counted the hours until the end of the day. Eight days in a row without sex. He felt ready to explode.

In early afternoon, he called home and told Moira about the unexpected evening conference that was going to keep him in the city jail till midnight again. She accepted the news languidly and suspiciously, as though either she did not care whether or not he might be lying, or she actually preferred him to have a mistress and so not to be making sexual demands on his cold wife.

He asked her about her analysis session. As usual, she was vague and uncommunicative. He got off the phone as quickly as he decently could.

The afternoon ticked away. Ruthie left the office at five sharp, telling him to come over around six-thirty. That would give her time to prepare dinner.

He got to her place at half past six on the dot, went upstairs, rang the bell. Ruthie answered wearing a loose gown that hung open in front, casually revealing the heavy round swells of her breasts, the sensual softness of her belly, the firm columns of her thighs.

"Hi," she said. "We're almost ready to eat. Give us a kiss, big man."

He reached out for her, kissing her not out of affection but out of sheer animal hunger. He had told himself he would never come here again, but that resolution had gone the way of all virtue earlier in the day. He wanted her. The insistent rise of his passion was evident to both of them as her body pressed tight against his. He slipped his hands under the robe, seeking the tips of her heavy, tender breasts, then going down below and behind to the double tautnesses of her buttocks. Eight days of famine were having their effect. He began to breathe hard, practically to snort. He started to edge her toward the couch with the vague idea of having her right on the spot.

She disengaged herself deftly from him. "Easy there, buster," she said lightly. "Let's eat first. Save the fun for later. I've got a special surprise planned for you afterward anyway."

"What kind of surprise?"

"You'll see later. Come eat."

She beckoned him to the table that she had set in the alcove of her little kitchen. The meal was a good one, if on the simple side—meatballs and spaghetti, tons of it, accompanied by a heaping salad, a huge loaf of fresh, tangy Italian bread, and a straw-covered flask of moderately decent Chianti. Ruthie ate ravenously, shovelling the food into her mouth with obvious delight. Lamson found himself hungrier than he thought he was. In hardly any time at all, both their plates were clean, the bread was gone, the wine bottle nearly empty.

"There's more spaghetti," she said.

"I'm stuffed."

"I think I'll have a little more, anyway."

He watched in amazement as she barrelled into a second mountainous plateful. He had never seen any girl with such an appetite. But Ruthie was a big girl, and she had big appetites—for food, for liquor, for sex.

After dinner they sat at the table for a while, just recuperating from the bout of gorging. Then Lamson helped her with the dishes, feeling grotesquely domestic. About half past seven, they retired to the living room. Ruthie put on one of her records and they settled down on the couch. At once his hand dove into her gown, seeking the warm rounded mass of her breasts.

She let him caress her for a while. But when his other hand roved lower, she brushed him away.

"Don't rush things," she said. "I've still got that surprise coming."

"What is it?"

"You'll see," she said. "Another few minutes."

He tried to relax and be patient. Suddenly, the doorbell rang.

"What the hell," Lamson said.

"Don't worry. It's all right." Gathering her robe together, Ruthie swept serenely to the door, leaving Lamson gasping. He didn't even have time to hide. She threw the door open and another girl stepped in.

Lois Goldstein. The petite, dark-haired secretary of Marty Rich.

Lamson's face flamed. He tried to shrink back out of sight, but it was too late. Lois had seen him. She put her hand over her mouth and said, "Oh! You didn't tell me it was going to be Mr. Lamson!"

"I like a surprise all around, honey." Ruthie chuckled ponderously.

"What the deuce is going on?" Lamson demanded.

Ruthie said, "I figured you'd like some fun. Two girls is more fun than one. So I invited Lois over. She sometimes doubles up with me. Don't worry. She won't tell a soul. You can trust her."

Lamson was aghast. Did Ruthie expect him to make love to both of them? And of all the damn fool things, she had to get another girl from the office as her partner in this—this perverted orgy. He was tempted to go stalking out in rage.

But a moment later he was calmer. The damage was done. Lois already knew, now, that he was having an affair with Ruthie. Might as well be hanged for a goat as for a sheep, he thought. Might as well enjoy whatever weird pleasures Ruthie had thoughtfully concocted for him tonight.

"You ever do this before?" Ruthie asked him.

"No. No, never. I—haven't gone in for that sort of stuff."

"It's the greatest," Ruthie said. She shucked off her robe and stood magnificently nude before them, her giant breasts standing away from her body, firm and taut and big as a couple of melons. "Come on. Let's get undressed and get some drinks in us."

The liquor helped. Both he and Lois had inhibitions—Lois because she had been unexpectedly thrust into a compromising situation with her own employer, and he because his sex life had always been a normal, conventional one. It's a big jump from ten years of faithful marriage into bed with two girls at the same time.

They had a drink apiece, and then he and Lois got out of their clothes at Ruthie's prodding. Naked, Lois and Ruthie were an amazing contrast—Ruthie big and overblown and blonde, with her skin so pale and her breasts so huge, glorying in her unashamed Rubensesque abundance. And Lois slim, shy, her breasts small though beautifully fashioned, her expression a reserved one, her eyes soft, her hips narrow, her legs thin, graceful. She was like a gazelle, he thought, timid and fragile. As unlike Ruthie as it was possible for a girl to be. Yet both of them, in their own way, were beautiful and sexually attractive.

The bourbon went round and round until the bottle was nearly empty and the last shreds of their inhibitions nearly gone.

Then the three of them came together in one tangled heap of flesh on Ruthie's wide bed.

Lamson could tell that Ruthie and Lois had pulled this kind of tandem routine before—maybe many times, with many other men. There was a kind of slick precision to their movements that was too good to be improvised. He moved from one to the other, his hands now grasping Ruthie's big jiggling breasts, now Lois's pear-shaped small ones. Blonde hair and brunette alternated in cascading down over him. Lois's sharp breasts poked their naked tips into his chest, and he turned, thrusting upward to link his body with Ruthie, and both girls gripped him tight, and then they shifted, and he held Ruthie's buttocks cupped in his hands while Lois did things to him that no woman, not even Moira, had ever done before, and they played switch again, and again, and again.

On and on Lamson drifted, through the long orgiastic evening. He was flabbergasted by his own powers. The presence of two girls in the same bed seemed to work some weird chemical change over him, so that he was at least three times the man he normally was. He gave Ruthie satisfaction, leaving her limp and sweaty and purring, and turned to Lois, who lay on her back with the pale moonlight creeping across her thighs, and he eased himself to her and she writhed about, impaled on his unquenchable lance.

The bed was a churning mass of gasping, moist, eager mouths, of roaming fingers and heaving bodies. They would rest for a while, then return to the orgy, and at one point when Lamson found himself temporarily too tired to go on, he lay back and watched an incredible performance between the two girls.

As Lamson watched, goggle-eyed, Ruthie began to bring the flat of her hand down on Lois' pink buttocks until they glowed an angry red. Each slap of the hand brought an answering thrust of pleasure from the girl above. They rolled over and over, biting and kissing, thrusting against one another, going down into darkness to give unimaginable thrills, and suddenly Lamson found himself once again evilly aroused, and he waded into the thick of it, pulling the two girls apart and taking the first one who happened to beckon to him, finding that she was Lois.

Then at last the earthquake of passion was ending for all three of them. They had rung all the changes, exhausted all the variations.

It had been an unbelievable evening.

The bourbon was gone. They sprawled out limply on the bed together, and Lamson looked at his watch.

Quarter past eleven. Time to get home. Home to Moira, poor psycho-analyzed Moira, who never in her wildest dreams could picture her husband doing the things he had done in the course of this mad evening.

"Got to be going," Lamson muttered.

He got himself off the bed and lurched into the bathroom to clean himself up as best he could. Some cold water helped to restore his sobriety. He felt completely plugged out after the three hours and a half of orgy.

He washed up and came out. Ruthie and Lois were entangled on the bed, Lois's hand in Ruthie's crotch, Ruthie's hands on Lois's breasts. But there was nothing very passionate about the embrace. They were as tired as he was.

"I'm leaving," he told them. "Remember—not a word about this to anyone."

"You can trust us," they chorused.

Lamson took a last look at them—Ruthie abundant, voluptuous, Lois slim, fawnlike. The two of them nude on the bed, showing everything they had. It was a stunning sight. It had been a stunning evening.

He put his clothes on. They watched him in sleepy contentment. When he looked presentable, he bade them good night as though he'd simply been visiting a couple of old friends, and stepped outside.

The fresh night air helped to revive him. He got into his car, sat for a moment behind the wheel without turning the engine on.

God, what a night! he thought.

He had never imagined that anything like that was in store for him. He had just wanted his ashes hauled a little, to make up for the coldness at home. He hadn't expected a full-fledged orgy. He had to hand it to Ruthie, though when she cooked up a surprise, it was a beaut.

He wondered how many other men she and Lois had entertained in this startling way.

Plenty, he figured.

He wondered how far and wide they would spread the story of tonight's engagement.

Maybe not at all. It wasn't the sort of thing you told other people about. You kept it to yourself, usually. But he didn't know. He hardly knew Lois. Could she be trusted? He hoped so.

Wearily, he turned the car on, and headed for the highway. He was, he knew, considerably pickled, so he drove with more than usual care. The combination of liquor and those two girls had left him lightheaded, and he had to compensate for that as he drove. Getting killed in his present condition wouldn't be any trick at all.

It was well past midnight when he got home. Moira was in bed. But she sat up, vigilant, when he came in.

"That you, Dave?"

"It's me."

"Oh. I was worried about you-know-what."

"I'm no prowler," he said.

She nestled down in bed again. He undressed quickly, but she was asleep or pretending sleep—by the time he could join her in bed. Just as well, he thought. God knows what I'd do if she had been in the mood for love when I came in!

But a week of analysis hadn't made any noticeable change in her, he thought. He wondered blearily how her session with Michalis had gone today, whether she was making any progress toward a cure. Then a tidal wave of sleep came roaring up and engulfed him.

9

The next morning, at the office, there was a call for him—from Moira's psychoanalyst.

"This is Dr. Michalis, Mr. Lamson." His voice was deep, resonant, earnest. "Do you have a minute to spare? I'd like to talk to you about your wife."

Lamson stiffened. He said tensely, "Yes, go ahead, doctor."

"Do you know that she didn't show up for her session yesterday?"

Frowning, Lamson said, "She didn't say a word about it to me. I assumed she had gone."

"No. She skipped it entirely. Called up later in the day to apologize and say she'd send me the money."

"Well, I'm sure she must have had some good reason for not—"

"No," Michalis said. "Last week she was late every time. On Friday she was more than twenty minutes late. She's fighting me every step of the way, Mr. Lamson. I understand she went into analysis at your urging."

"That's right."

"Well, she thinks it'll make you happy if she sees me now and then. But obviously she's damned if she'll let me do any work on her. I doubt that I'll be able to get anywhere with her. I'll keep her on as a patient if you insist, Mr. Lamson, but I warn you now that without her cooperation I can't get to first base, and so far she hasn't been cooperating at all."

"What do you suggest?" Lamson asked tightly.

"That's up to you. You could have her withdraw and try another analyst—though frankly I don't see how that'll alter the situation. Or you could have her keep coming to me, in the hopes that I'll be able to break through her resistance sooner or later. Or you could just drop the whole analysis project and hope for the best."

Lamson moistened his lips. "I don't like any of those alternatives. I want her to be cured, doctor. I don't care how it's done or by whom, but I want her to be the way she was before—before she was raped—"

"That may take some doing."

"You don't have any hope we can cure her?"

"I'm not sure. Listen. Mr. Lamson, I've got a professional meeting this evening in Manhattan. Why don't we meet for a drink around six o'clock and we can discuss the situation more fully?"

"Okay," Lamson said. "That sounds fine. I'll phone Moira and let her know I'll be home late."

"One more thing," Michalis said. "Don't let her know you spoke to me this afternoon, or that you're seeing me tonight. Don't ask her about the skipped session yesterday, either. I wouldn't want her to get the idea we two were in cahoots behind her back. That would kill any chance I might have of winning her trust."

"I understand," Lamson said.

He left the office at quarter of six and drove uptown leaving his car in the lot of the Hotel Mayhew in the mid-Thirties. Michalis was waiting for him in the hotel's cocktail lounge. It was impossible to miss him. The analyst was a tall man with the build of a fullback, about Lamson's age, who was standing at the bar sipping a martini. Lamson looked at him uncertainly and the big man nodded.

They took a booth. Lamson was impressed with the analyst's physical presence, with the bigness of him, with the intense penetrating expression of his eyes, with the deep, hypnotically persuasive cadences of his voice. Puffing on a pipe, he peered across the table at Lamson and said easily, "Your wife's case is a tricky one. Ordinarily I wouldn't violate a patient's confidences, but I think we've got some exceptional problems on our hands."

"Such as?"

"Let's review the facts as I know them. A little over two weeks ago, a burglar broke into your house late at night. Right?"

"Right."

"You went downstairs to investigate. He overpowered you and brought you upstairs to the bedroom, where he tied you up and then raped Moira before your eyes. He then took a small amount of jewelry and fled. Is that correct?"

"Yes," Lamson said.

"The burglar, I gather, had an extraordinary physical resemblance to you. He was seedy and battered, but there was still the likeness."

"A very strong likeness."

"And since that night, your formerly satisfactory sex relationship with Moira has become highly *unsatisfactory*. She refuses to have intercourse with you most nights, and on those rare occasions when she's willing, she turns out to be frigid and doesn't reach an orgasm, which I gather was not the situation before the burglary."

"We were perfectly compatible before the night it happened," Lamson said.

"The final bit of information is that last week you confronted her with her frigidity and asked her why she was taking so long to recover from the effects of the rape. What did she give as the reason, Mr. Lamson?"

Lamson stared doggedly into the analyst's burning, brooding eyes. In a low voice he said, "She told me that the trouble was my resemblance to the rapist. I looked so much like him that every time she went to bed with me, it reminded her of him, and so she was frightened all over again."

Michalis nodded. "So that's what she told you, is it? Nothing else?"

"Nothing else. Why?"

The analyst hunched his heavy shoulders forward and surrounded his drink with a huge fist. He said, "In Friday's session, something slipped out accidentally that I don't think Moira meant to tell me. She covered up immediately for it, and perhaps stayed away yesterday because she didn't want me to press her on the subject. It's this: Moira *knew* the rapist. I mean, knew him personally."

"That's impossible!"

"It sounded pretty fishy to me," Michalis admitted. "But a lot of fishy things come swimming up out of the unconscious and turn out to have meaning when we can interpret them. As soon as Moira saw what I suspected, she clammed up tight. But there's something there."

"I can't believe it," Lamson said. "How would Moira know some housebreaking ex-pug—"

"Maybe she knew him before he turned housebreaker," Michalis suggested. "Maybe she even knew him before she knew *you*."

Lamson blinked. "What are you getting at?"

"How much do you know of your wife's past, before she met you?"

"I know she was a virgin the day we got married," Lamson said with some irritation.

"I don't mean that. Do you know the men she dated before her marriage? I'm not saying she had to sleep with them. I just am interested in men she might have been emotionally entangled with."

Lamson shrugged and said, "I don't know. I never probed into her past. I couldn't care less."

Michalis signalled for another drink. He said, "Let's talk speculatively for a moment. Suppose—just suppose that not long before she met you, Moira was deeply in love with someone I'll call X. That love affair broke up—perhaps left emotional scars on her. A few months went by and she met you, and, lo and behold, you looked enough like X to be his brother— except that you didn't have whatever character fault had caused the breakup of the earlier affair It's very common for women who are disappointed in love to transfer their emotions to someone new who closely resembles the lost loved one. It happens all the time."

"Are you saying that Moira married me because some other guy who looked like me jilted her?"

"There were other reasons, of course. I'm just suggesting that the *original attraction* that drew Moira to you was your resemblance to X. After she knew you, of course, she found reasons for loving you in your own right."

"What does all this have to do with—"

"Okay. Ten, eleven years pass. She's a contented suburban housewife. Suddenly there's a burglar in the house. Lo and behold, it's the long-lost X! The years haven't been good to him. He's in bad shape. But when she gets a close look at him, she realized who it is—the man she loved before you. X recognizes her, too, of course. For them it's a reunion after a decade. And he rapes her because it satisfies an old yearning of his, and then he leaves. He doesn't even bother to take much jewelry, because merely raping Moira was enough of a pleasure."

"This is all pretty far-fetched," Lamson said. "You're spinning it out of whole cloth."

"Let me keep spinning. Let's say that Moira and X broke up, years ago, because he wanted to sleep with her and she refused. Okay? He gave her a take-it-or-leave-it ultimatum and she left it. They broke up. Then she meets you, and you look just like him, but you're willing to respect her virginity until the wedding night. So she sees that you're an improvement over X. Okay. Now X comes popping out of the misty past, and he finally takes forcibly what she wouldn't give him a long time ago. And it awakens all kinds of guilt reactions in Moira. She remembers her old love for him. She feels that maybe if she hadn't been so cold to him back then, he wouldn't have been led into a life of crime and suffering. I don't know. The fact is that seeing him again touches off a whole rag-bag of confused ideas inside Moira. It gets to the point where she can't tell you from X. The two of you blur and fuse into one individual. She's hopelessly snarled up. The place where it hits her is her sex life. She becomes frigid."

"Okay," Lamson said. "It's a nice story. But what proof is there?"

"Did the burglar seem to recognize Moira?"

"How should I know. I was too scared out of my wits to notice—well, he did call her by her first name. But only after he had heard me say it. And when he got on the bed with her, he said something like, 'I'm going to enjoy this, Moira.' Which still doesn't mean he knew her. I don't see where all this is leading."

Michalis said, "It may lead nowhere. It may be pure fabrication. But on the other hand, if there's substance to it, it may lead us to a solution of Moira's problems."

"How?"

"Finding the man. Putting him behind bars. Once she knows he's out of the way, her neurotic fears may calm down. She'll begin to think rationally again."

Lamson shook his head slowly. "I've got to admire you analysts. First you conjure up a guy who has about one chance in a hundred of ever having existed, and then you tell me that if we can arrest him, it'll cure Moira."

"I think I know what I'm doing," Michalis said. "Will you bear with me?"

"What do you want me to do?"

"For one, keep Moira coming to see me. Do it subtly, but make her come to me. I can get some more information out of her. Then, you might do some detective work on your own. Look through her old snapshot collection, if she has one. Maybe there's a photo of this guy. Check with her old friends subtly. If we can get his name, we can make a start on finding him."

"If he exists."

"Let's assume that," Michalis said. "Otherwise we don't have even a place to begin."

"All right," Lamson said. "I'll do my best. I think it's crazy, but I'll do my best. Anything, if it'll help Moira."

It was a wacky idea, he decided as he drove home. Completely wacky and far-fetched. The same kind of analytical guesswork that Freud had used to prove that Moses was an Egyptian, was being used here to conjure up some old flame of Moira's as the reason for her current frigidity.

But Michalis was right in at least one point: this was the only opening they had. If they ignored it, there was no other place to work. So he would at least give it a try. The immediate problem, as he saw it, was two-pronged: he had to get Moira to see Michalis regularly, and he had to hunt through Moira's memorabilia for some clue to the mysterious, improbable Mr. X.

He tackled the first part of the problem that evening, after dinner. On the pretense of wanting to balance the checkbook, he went through the records and then said, "Moira, you forgot to enter the check for yesterday's visit to your analyst."

"I—ah—paid him in cash," she stammered.

"Oh? I guess you must be short of money, then. On Sunday you had only about thirty dollars in cash."

She grinned nervously. "I *am* running pretty low. Maybe if you gave me some—say, twenty to see me through—"

He frowned. "But you also went marketing yesterday. You must have spent at least fifteen dollars. Twenty-five for Michalis, fifteen for groceries—that's forty bucks out of thirty. How'd you work it?"

Color came to her cheeks. "I—I charged the grocery bill."

"They stopped their credit system last month." He eyed her sternly. "Moira, you didn't go to Michalis yesterday, did you?"

"Of course I did!"

"Don't make things any worse by lying," he said softly. "I *know* you didn't go. I—I spoke to someone who said you were home all morning. Why didn't you go, Moira?"

"I had a headache. I didn't feel like going."

"That isn't fair to Michalis. He must have kept an hour open for you."

"I'll pay him for the session."

"Throw away twenty-five bucks because you had a headache?" He walked over to her, took her hands in his. "Moira, please go tomorrow. You promised you'd see him until you got better."

"I've been seeing him. It hasn't done any good, has it?"

"You've only seen him three or four times. It takes longer than that. Give it a chance. Will you go tomorrow like you're supposed to?"

"I don't want to."

"Why?"

"He's—too nosy."

"That's what we're paying him for. To be nosy. To nose around until he finds out what's wrong with you."

In the end, he got her to promise to go. He was fairly sure she'd keep the promise. She seemed ashamed of herself for having chickened out of Monday's appointment with the psychoanalyst, and even more ashamed of the clumsy series of lies she had been trapped in.

The next step was more difficult. He had to wait for the weekend. Saturday morning, Moira and one of the neighbors disappeared in the station wagon on a shopping expedition. Lamson knew that he had three or four hours to himself in the house, before she returned.

He hustled up to the attic. Moira had three or four boxes of memorabilia up there—old theater programs, corsages from high school and college proms, photos, pennants, all the whatnot accumulation of souvenirs that a girl tends to collect. It was years since she had last looked at any of it. A thick coating of dust covered the pile of cartons. If Moira came up here, she'd see that the dust had been disturbed, but that was a risk he had to run.

He opened the uppermost carton.

There was something ghoulish about digging through his wife's past like this. Nearly all of the contents of the cartons had been put away in her teens, and so referred to a time before he had had any existence in her life. It was something like peering through a telescope that extended back into time—and there she was, a dim, half-seen figure, moving among strangers in a world that excluded him.

A dust-covered book was labelled PERSONAL DIARY OF MOIRA ANNE CARPENTER FOR THE YEAR 1946. LET HE WHO SNOOPS IN HERE DIE THE DEATH OF DEATHS.

He knew he had no business looking in it. But a strange curiosity impelled him on. Maybe there were photos inside, he thought. A snapshot of Michalis's "X."

There were no photos. Just entry after entry of youthful pleasures, written in Moira's simple, open handwriting. He felt like a peeping-tom as he turned the pages of the teenage Moira's diary.

"Sheldon took me to see the new Henry Fonda movie today. Sheldon is much too fast for me. We sat in the balcony and he kept trying to put his hands inside my blouse. Remind me not to go out with him any more. Who does he think he is, Casanova...?"

"Beach party today. Very hot weather. I went with Elliott. Wore my green bathing suit. Mother doesn't like it. Says it's too loose in front. When I bend over too much of my bosom shows. But that's all right. On the beach today all the boys kept looking at me. I don't mind that. When I changed in the locker room I was with Gloria and I saw her naked. She hardly has any breasts at all. I could tell how envious she was of my breasts. Mother is all wrong. If I have nice breasts, why shouldn't I show them off? As long as I don't let anybody handle the merchandise...."

"Pajama party at Marcia's. We discussed sex, mostly. Some of the girls said they would go all the way with a guy they really loved even if they weren't engaged. Jane said she would do it only with a guy who had given her a ring. Marcia told us she had done it three or four times already. I wonder whether to believe her. I said I was waiting for my wedding night no matter what. Am I old fashioned? I don't think so...."

Reddening, Lamson put the dairy aside, telling himself he had no right to go prying here. Moira's personal diaries were closed books. All that concerned him now was the existence or non-existence of "X."

If Michalis's theory was right, "X" was somebody Moira had known fairly shortly before meeting him. Which eliminated her teenage years, since Lamson had not met her until she was twenty-two. If nothing turned up among the recent material, he would go back to the older stuff. But first the college-years material, he thought.

He turned through endless reams of essays and school papers, of yellowing clippings about the engagements of friends, of sprigs of dead flowers, of souvenir programs. He turned up snapshots galore, mostly of thin, uncertain-looking teenagers squinting nervously at the camera.

But no "Mr. X."

He kept going. He found the bundle of stuff from their own engagement. Pictures of him, programs of the shows he had taken her to, wedding invitations and announcements. He skipped hurriedly through it. This was no time for sentimental journeys into the past.

Then he dipped into the carton of stuff from Moira's senior year at college. He had met her after her graduation, so possibly there was something significant in this pile. He leafed through it.

Plenty of photos. Hundreds of them.

The hours rolled by. All he needed, he thought, was to get caught up here going through her stuff. That would really put the kibosh on everything.

He moved faster. Sweat rolled down his sides in the stuffy attic. He was just about to give up, to shovel everything into the cartons and put it all back where he had found it, when, at the bottom of one stack of souvenirs, he came upon a cache of photos of—

Himself?

No. Impossible. He hadn't known Moira then. But his flesh crawled as he looked at these photos of a clean-cut, wide-eyed, grinning kid who looked so much like his own twenty-two-year-old self that it was hard to believe. His hand trembled. He wanted to rush downstairs, phone Michalis, tell him that his theory had checked out.

There was an X!

There were dozens of pictures of him. There he was in a swimsuit, with his arm around a lithe, youthful Moira who wore a scanty, provocative bikini. Lamson felt a surge of retrospective jealousy. And there they were again, grinning into each others' eyes. And sipping a soda with two straws. And at a prom, Moira resplendent in her glittering evening gown. And pictures of him alone, against backgrounds of summer, winter, fall.

He turned each of the photos over, hoping to find some identification. But there was none. Obviously Moira had found it unnecessary to label pictures of anyone she knew so well.

Who was he?

No name. He rummaged through the carton for a diary, but there was none. Moira had probably been too busy to keep one in college—or maybe she thought she had outgrown the practice.

Lamson shrugged. He stared again at the incredible array of pictures. The resemblance was fantastic. Michalis had hit the nail right on the head.

But now to find out who X really was.

How?

Ask Moira outright? Impossible.

No, Lamson thought. He'd have to use some more subtle method of identifying the man. This would call for a little Sherlock Holmsing.

Carefully he selected a dozen of the best photos of the mysterious X. He put them aside, and loaded up the cartons again, restoring them to their original place. He opened the attic window a bit so that the dust would enter faster. If Moira didn't come up here for another month or two, she would never notice that her cartons had been opened. And by that time, he hoped, it wouldn't matter.

He went downstairs, his heart racing with excitement.

10

On Monday, he called the analyst at his office shortly after eleven in the morning.

"Did Moira show up?"

"Yes," Michalis said. "She just left, about five minutes ago."

"Glad to hear it. You accomplish anything with her this morning?"

"Not much. I'm still probing around the edges. But at least she came back. That's a sign we're moving in the right direction."

"I've got an even better sign," Lamson said, barely able to keep from spilling the words out in an untidy heap. "I've found your X."

"What do you mean?"

"I looked through Moira's junk in the attic, and there was a flock of photos of some fellow she knew the year before she met me. He looks so much like me that I'd almost swear they were pictures of me, except that they can't possibly be."

"What's this fellow's name?"

"I don't know. There's nothing on any of the snapshots to indicate it. But I'm going to try to find out. I'll see if I can't contact one of Moira's college friends and find out that way."

"Be careful. We wouldn't want word getting back to Moira about your investigations."

"I'll watch out," Lamson said. "But I thought you'd like to know."

"I'm delighted," Michalis said. "I won't deny it's a great thrill to find out that you've taken a stab in the dark and struck it lucky. You've brightened my day, Mr. Lamson."

"I've brightened my own," Lamson said.

That night, at dinner, Lamson brought up the subject of Moira's old school friends—handling the topic in a round-about, casual way. It turned out that Moira had drifted away from most of them, hardly remembered their married names. But she was in a nostalgic mood, luckily, and mentioned two of the girls she had remained friendly with longest—Gloria Hazen and Marcia Keeler.

Lamson remembered them vaguely from the early years of his marriage. Gloria a slim, almost skinny blonde, Marcia a full-blown redhead. He wondered privately if this was the same Gloria, the same Marcia who had been mentioned in Moira's diary—Gloria who had "hardly any breasts at all" and Marcia who "told us she had done it three or four times already."

He let the subject drop as casually as he had begun it. But the next day, at the office, he called the Alumnae Department of Moira's school.

"I'd like to trace the whereabouts of two of my wife's classmates," he said. "I'm organizing a little surprise party and I'd like to track some of her old college friends down."

"Certainly, Mr. Lamson. What are the names?"

"All I can give you is their maiden names—Gloria Hazen, Marcia Keeler. They graduated eleven years ago June, I imagine."

"Just one moment. I'll check the records."

The records were duly checked, and Lamson was told that Gloria was now Mrs. Gloria Redman, of Riverside Drive, and Marcia was Mrs. Marcia Holfield of East 66th Street. Lamson scribbled the address down, feeling very much like a detective on the trail of his quarry.

He called Gloria first.

A maid answered. "Mrs. Redman, please," Lamson said, and identified himself.

A moment later, a sharp, high-pitched voice said, "Yes? Who is this, please?"

"Gloria? Maybe you don't remember me. I'm Dave Lamson. I married Moira Carpenter."

A pause. Then: "Oh, yes! My God, it's been years since I've heard from either of you. What's on your mind, Dave? How've you been? How's Moira? We just drifted out of touch, didn't we?"

"We're all fine," Lamson said. "I was wondering if—if I could drop around to see you some time later today. There's a favor you can do me. I've got a photo of someone Moira used to know, and I'm trying to get in touch with him, as a kind of a surprise for her birthday. But I don't know his name, and I wonder if perhaps you could identify him from the photo."

"Well, I could try," Gloria said. "Suppose you drop over—around four, would that be all right?"

He arranged it so that it was. Ducking out of the office, he drove quickly over to her place—a large, sprawling apartment on the eleventh floor of a Riverside Drive apartment house that had been the height of elegance at one time and still retained much of its old grandeur.

The sixteen or seventeen years since Moira had made her diary entry about Gloria's flat chest hadn't done much for Gloria's figure. She turned out to be a matchstick of a woman, so thin he was sure he could shatter her with a single backhand slap. She had aged, too. Although she was no older than Moira, she could pass for almost any age between thirty-five and fifty. Her once-blonde hair had been died with henna, and there were frown-lines on her face and puckered flesh at her throat. Her thinness gave her nose an exaggerated sharpness, drawing it out into a beak. Her eyes were fast-moving, beady. The touch of middle age was on her already, Lamson thought, and it depressed him to think so, because she was a couple of years younger than he was, but seemed so terribly much older.

Part of the effect was the way the apartment was furnished—funereally in lavish but out-of-style taste, with heavy hangings, ornately carved furniture. Gloria went to a massive Victorian sideboard to get him a glass of sherry.

Yet the apartment reeked of money. The stuff might be old-fashioned but it was expensive. The paintings on the wall, though all nineteenth-century and dull, were originals. The thick carpet was no dime-a-yard stuff.

Lamson said, "What sort of work is your husband in?"

"He's an importer," Gloria said. "Right now he's off in Afghanistan or someplace, lining up a deal. He's in and out of the country five times a month."

"You don't go with him?"

"I hate to fly, and he's too impatient to take a boat. That's his picture over there. It's a very good likeness of him."

She pointed to a framed eight-by-ten color photo. It was a portrait of a man in his late fifties or early sixties—bald, fleshy-faced, Germanic-looking, with a solid, dogmatic expression.

"You have children?" Lamson asked.

"No. No children."

Suddenly he wanted to get out of here—out of this musty, fusty, over-furnished apartment, with its echoes of a dead generation. Away from this shrivelled, emaciated old woman of thirty-three, this old friend of Moira's turned prematurely into a withered hag.

He said, "I really can't stay long. But this is the photo. I hope you can identify him."

He took one of Moira's photos of X from his wallet and handed it across to Gloria. She studied it. A frown added new furrows to her furrowed forehead.

He said, "I'm trying to round up a few of her old flames for a kind of birthday joke. There were a bunch of photos of this fellow in the attic, so he must have been important. But I don't know his name."

"I—I can't remember," she said. "It's been so many years, so much has happened. But I recall him. It was in our senior year. He looked a lot like you. After Moira stopped seeing him and started seeing you, we were all confused for a while. We didn't know whether she had really changed beaux or not."

"Can't you remember the name?"

"It began with a J. Jeff? Jack? Jim?" She shook her head tiredly. "Jerry?"

"No idea of the last name?"

"Sorry," she said. She handed the picture back. "I just can't place it. I suppose it'll come to me in a couple of days. Have to jog the memory a little. I'll call you when I think of it. You're still at the same number you were the last time we were in touch?"

"Still at the same number," he said. He drained his sherry, thanked her for her trouble, edged toward the door.

"Oh, it was no trouble at all," she said. "No trouble at all. We must get together some time. When Richard is back from his travels. We'd love to see you. You'd like Richard. He's such a successful man. So forceful. And it would be so nice to see Moira again. So nice. Give her my best, will you?"

"I'll do that," he promised, as he made his escape.

It was good to breathe fresh air again downstairs. He pitied her, sitting there alone in that huge, dark apartment, waiting for the return of her 60-year-old husband from Afghanistan or wherever.

Well, that was her life, and presumably she'd wanted it when she went into it. She hadn't been much help, except to confirm the fact that Moira had dated someone else who looked just like him, and that it had caused a lot of confusion eleven years ago.

But he needed the name.

Well, there was still Marcia.

He telephoned her from a booth on the corner in front of Gloria's building. The moment she heard his name, she knew who he was, asked after Moira, exclaimed on how long it had been since their last get-together.

"It's at least five years," she said.

"More than that. I'm sure we haven't seen you since Chuck was born, and he's six."

"Well, for God's sake. Why don't we ever get together?"

"Swell idea," he said. "What about right now?" And he told Marcia the same story he had given Gloria, about his reasons for wanting to find out the identity of the man in the picture.

"You come right on over here," Marcia said. "I'll get some martinis ready."

He threaded his way across town to the East Sixties, and after some difficulty managed to find a parking spot not too far from Marcia's place.

It was a glossy new multi-story co-op, with terraces and air-conditioner grills going up and up toward the stratosphere. Marcia hadn't married a poor man, obviously. He rode to the nineteenth floor in a smoothly purring elevator, got out, turned to the left, pushed a button, heard a chime bong discreetly inside.

The door opened.

"Hi," Marcia said.

He was taken a little by surprise. After the gloom of Gloria's place, he had expected almost anything. But Marcia answered the door wearing a pair of silk lounging pajamas and high-heeled pumps, nothing else. The sheer, high-sheen pajamas molded every contour of her body in a startling way, and he could see not only the outlines of her full, heavy breasts but also even the smaller rounds of her nipples surmounting the large fleshy globes. Her hair was redder than ever, too, a great blazing beacon of shining hair done in a sweeping bouffant mass.

He stepped in.

The apartment was large and well furnished, in the best modern taste, meaning expensive. An enormous picture window provided a view of half of Manhattan. Thick carpeting covered the floors from wall to wall.

"Make yourself comfortable," Marcia said. She crossed in front of him, buttocks twitching visibly against the taut, straining fabric of the pajama bottoms, and settled herself in a Danish-style couch, beckoning him to sit in a facing couch. A mosaic coffee table between them held a pitcher of martinis and two frosted glasses.

She poured drinks. "Olive?" she asked.

"No, thanks."

"I don't like vegetables in mine either," she said. "Here."

They clinked glasses gravely, sipped the cold, excellent martinis. He had difficulty keeping his eyes off her. She had gained some weight since he had last seen her, but, even though she was on the short side, the extra poundage didn't seem to do her any harm. His gaze rested almost hungrily on the steep, swelling rises of her breasts. That wild night with Ruthie and Lois was far in the past now, and he hadn't gone near Moira at home.

He was hungry for it.

He tried not to let it show.

They sipped martinis and chatted innocuously. She asked about the kids, about Moira, about his company. He answered concisely, not bothering to go into any details.

"And what's been happening to you?" he said, as they began the second martini.

"Well, I'm separated, for one thing."

He lifted an eyebrow. "Last I heard, you were married to a real estate investor. That right?"

"Right. Bruce T. Holfield. His corporation owns this very building. Well, we split up around two months ago. We aren't divorced, just separated. I'm living here, and he's got a penthouse on Fifth Avenue, and so far everything's still friendly. He pays my bills, and we phone each other. All buddy-buddy. Till the lawyers move in."

"You had children, didn't you?"

"Two girls, yes. They're staying with Bruce's mother in Connecticut. We figured it was best that way. Have them out of the way till all the nasty stuff is over. I think there'll be a custody suit."

"And you think it's safe to leave the kids with your mother-in-law? They won't be turned against you?"

"Not a chance," Marcia laughed. "She hates her son. It was my idea to send the kids there. You want another drink?" Without waiting for an answer, she poured a refill. "So here I sit. Little me. All alone in a nine-room apartment. You know what this place costs? Let me tell you. $55,000 down, and monthly maintenance charges of $700 a month. That's because it's a co-op. Apartments like this, they rent for $2000 a month and up, some places. I take long walks here. There are some rooms I haven't even seen yet."

"The apartment's furnished very nicely."

"The decorator did it all. Bruce spent about half a million. You know how they say, money's no object? That's how it is with him." She gulped down half a martini. "But you wanted me to see a picture. You better show it to me now, before I'm too crocked to help you."

Nodding, he took the snapshot from his wallet and slid it across the table to her. She picked it up, looked at it, and immediately said, "Oh, him. You mean Moira never told you about your twin?

"Jerry Foster. It was the most amazing damn thing. Moira was really serious about this guy. They were going to get engaged and all. Then next thing I hear they've busted up. It was a real scene. Month or so later, I walk into the coffee-shop, there's Moira sitting there with Jerry. I say hello, and later I see her, I ask her, 'What goes? I thought you busted up with the guy.' And she said, 'That isn't Jerry, that's somebody new. His name is Dave.' And then the two of you got married."

"She never said a word about him," Lamson murmured. "But now a lot of things are starting to make sense about our early dating days. I seem to remember a lot of people being surprised to see me with Moira. I didn't pay any attention, but now I get it."

"Sure. You looked enough like this guy to be his twin."

"Jerry Foster. Mm. What sort of guy was he like?"

"Oh—flashy. Big man on campus. I didn't like him much. He was always looking for the easy way out of things. Not Moira's type at all."

"You have any idea what happened to him after graduation?" Lamson asked.

Marcia shrugged. The shrug did exciting things to her breasts and sent a quiver of lust through Lamson's loins. "No idea," she said. "He could be in Alcatraz, for all I know."

She was closer than she thought, he mused. But he kept that to himself. He took the photo back from her. "Jerry Foster," he repeated. "Well, maybe I'll be able to get in touch with him. I hope so."

He stood up. It was half past five. A brilliant sunset was just getting under way in the picture window. Time to head for home.

"Going?" Marcia asked.

"I have to. It's late."

"No—please," she said. She stood up, facing him, coming close to him. He could see the raw yearning in her eyes, and he was startled by its intensity. In a low, hungry voice she said, "You're an old friend of mine—a friend of Moira's is a friend of mine. I ask you as a friend. Don't go. Please don't go. Not just yet. Stay a little while. Have another martini with me, I don't want to be left alone here."

There was a pitiful note in her voice that he could hardly resist. He eased down on the couch again. She poured a third martini for him.

"Nine rooms," she said. "All alone in nine rooms. You can't imagine what I've been going through, Dave. It's been hell. I try to be a decent woman, but I've got needs, desires like everybody else. Always have. You ask Moira. She'll tell you I always used to shock the girls with the things I did. Lost my cherry when I wasn't even sixteen. I didn't believe in making a guy crawl for it."

She was very drunk, he realized. She had matched him martini for martini, and had probably had a head start before he arrived.

She said, "You can stay a little while, can't you? As a favor to an old friend?"

"I suppose."

"You aren't disgusted by me?"

"Why should I be?"

"Women aren't supposed to do the propositioning. But I know you. You're too much of a decent guy to make a pass at me. So I had to make the pass. Moira will forgive you. She won't have to know. It's for my sake.

I need it so bad, Dave. Do you think I'm good looking?"

"Plenty good looking."

"I know I've been putting on weight. But not much. And mostly in my chest. Nobody minds that, huh? I'm still pretty. I've kept my looks. And I'm plenty hot, too. You know what they say about divorced women? Well, it's true, at least with me. And I'm not even divorced. Not yet. But you'd feel sick if you knew the things I've had to do to keep from going batty. Guys are afraid to make passes at me. They think they'll get in trouble. But I've got the goods. I can deliver. Here. Take a look."

She stood up again. She began unbuttoning the silk jacket of her pajamas, began struggling out of them. In a moment her breasts were bare—two heavy swells of pale creamy flesh, tipped with large dark nipples that were standing up stiffly in what must have been painful desire.

Lamson felt dryness in his throat. She was built like Ruthie, he thought. Only shorter. But the same kind of breasts. Big and hard, no droop to them.

She was getting out of her pants, now. Her face was flushed, her eyes wild. She pulled the pants down, and he saw the soft flesh of her belly now, and the soft inviting fullness of her thighs. She kicked the garment away and was naked but for the high-heeled pumps.

He drained his drink.

She stood in front of him, hands outstretched, pleading silently with him to come and take her. Her breasts rose and fell rapidly. Beads of sweat rolled down her bare sides.

He went to her. Her lips rose to his in a searing kiss, and his hands ran down her bare, satin-smooth body, down to her flanks, to her haunches. He buried his fingers in the soft, yielding generosity of her buttocks. Their kiss was a long, burning one, her nakedness pressed tight and hard against him, her lips grinding, her thighs rubbing together in eager anticipation.

"Come on," she said hoarsely. "Inside! Into the bedroom. Hurry, Dave! Hurry! I can't stand it any longer… I can't wait."

11

She practically dragged him inside. Lamson hadn't expected this little dividend on his request for Mr. X, but he was in no condition to refuse. Marcia seemed to need it so badly—and he was pretty horny himself at the moment.

The bed was rumpled, unmade. She tugged him over to it and began to pull his clothes off. He edged away from her and did the job himself; in her hurry, she was going to pop all his buttons, it seemed.

When he was naked, as naked as she was, she stretched out full length on the bed, eyes shining, and beckoned to him to join her.

"Come on," she husked. "Do it to me, Dave. Hurry! Do it."

He tumbled down next to her on the bed. He put his hands on one of her bare breasts and she began to pant. Her nipple was like a rock against his palm. Her wild inquisitive hands sparked the torment in him. She clung to him. Her mouth was on his ear and her caressing tongue sent writhing tendrils of ecstasy through him.

Blood thundering in his veins, he slowly kissed one heavy breast, and lightly caressed her stomach with tender fingers. She made little whispering sounds, the whispers turning to tiny cries.

His lips moved across the smooth, luscious skin to the other breast, and his hands became more demanding. His mouth savored the sweet taste of her, his tongue driving deep within, meeting hers coiled like a serpent at the back of her throat. He continued to play with her nipples, and then she pulled him down, and her body ground into him. Her entire body was dewed with sweat. Her eyes were cat-like slits of smoky lust.

Their bodies joined. She made a little soft whimpering moaning sound, and dug her fingers into his back. He could feel her nails raking his flesh, and wondered vaguely if Moira would notice the marks tonight. She began to piston her hips in frantic convulsive motions, and he stopped wondering about anything at all, just hung on tight and went along for the ride.

It was fabulous all the way.

It was also a little frightening.

He had never known anyone with such a hunger for love. Not Moira, not Ruthie, not Lois, none of them had this furious burning craving for it. Marcia moved with almost panicky urgency, trying to engulf him completely, to swallow him up with her questing body, and he bit down hard on his lip, trying to hold himself back as she swung and spun and circled and twisted against him, and he felt the inner grasping quiver of her body, heard the hoarse endless ah-*huh* ah-*huh* ah-*huh* sounds of her ecstasy, and right at the top of her passion he met her and matched her with hard driving thrusts and the sudden spurting fervor of fulfillment, and the two of them gasped their way to pleasure.

But she wasn't through with him.

Not by a long shot.

He was tired, he just wanted to rest, to cool off, to let his heart go back to normal. Not Marcia, though. She kept moving. Faster and faster. He stayed in there with her, all his desires exhausted but willing to cooperate anyway, and she pivoted and thrust and bucked and then all of a sudden it was happening again to her, a groundswell of pleasure that came rippling up out of her toes, it seemed, and eddied upward through her body until it passed her loins, passed her breasts, reached her lungs and throat, and emerged as choking sighing gasps of unimaginable delight.

The second climax came and went. Still no rest for him. That voracious pelvis kept thrusting. He looked down at her and saw her face weirdly distorted with lust, the eyes tight shut, the cheeks swollen, the lips clamped together hard and twisted lopsidedly, then opening as new gasps emerged from her.

She pounded savagely at him. It was starting to hurt, now. His exhausted nerves cried out for release. Every node of sensation in his body was rubbed raw with overstimulation. But she could not stop, would not stop. Onward and onward, while a third and then a fourth tide of satisfaction swept up over her.

And then, finally, she was finished.

She sank back limply on the pillow. Her breasts were still moving fast, but they slowed, the gasping stopped, her eyes opened part way.

"Oh, Christ," she said in a husky voice. "Christ, I needed that! You don't know what a good Samaritan you were, Dave."

He nodded. He was too drained, too depleted to answer. He rolled free of her and got up shakily. The martinis were rolling around in his belly and his head felt light, and he knew he was drunk, drunk on an overdose of sex. Dizzily he walked to the window, looked out at the fancy sunset, then looked back at her. She lay flat on her back, her arms dangling over the sides of the bed, her legs spread. Even now, even after all that he had just been through, the sight of her brazenly exposed nakedness sent the barest little quiver of returning desire through him.

I'd better get out of here, he thought. *Before she gets into the mood for another round.*

She sat up. "Get me a martini," she said. "Get one for you, too."

He went into the living room and poured one martini. When he brought it in, she said, "Where's yours?"

"I'm not having any."

"But—"

"I've got to leave. And I'm driving home. I want to get there alive."

"Stay, Dave. Phone Moira, tell her you've got a business engagement. Stay another couple of hours. Will you? I'd give anything if you'd stay the night."

"No," he said. He looked at the lush, heavy contours of her breasts and thighs and buttocks and hips and belly, and he felt a sadness stealing over him, the let-down that follows love. "I've got to go home, Marcia."

"Yeah. Yeah, I suppose you do." She looked up at him, and he saw tears brimming in her eyes. "Christ, I hate this. It's like I'm on fire all the time. Nobody can put me out. You know why I'm getting divorced? Because Bruce thought I was too passionate. He couldn't keep up with the pace. Nobody can, I've got to get it all the time. A regular nympho, you know? Delivery boys, salesmen, doormen—so we split up." She gulped half her martini in one swallow. "I'm sorry. I didn't mean to do this to you. You're a married man. My friend's husband. I didn't have any right to make you."

He hunted for his scattered clothes. She kept on talking, a long, drunken, self-pitying monolog about her sex needs, her dreams, her love affairs. He barely listened. He had stayed here a long time, much too long.

When he was dressed, she followed him to the door, naked, rubbing her breasts against him, her loins, her thighs. He could see the excitement starting all over again in her. It didn't take much.

"You'll come back?" she asked. "A couple of afternoons a month? It isn't much. I'm a good lay, anyhow. And you're good, too. Moira's lucky to be going to bed with somebody like you. Give me another chance. Come around again. You're always welcome here. Don't be disgusted with me, Dave. Just remember I've got needs like everybody else. I'm a human being. I feel desires."

"Of course, Marcia." He gave her one last kiss, ran his hands down her back to the smooth swells of her buttocks, held her tight for a moment. Then he released her and slipped away, out the door, before she could inveigle him into staying any longer.

It was almost seven o'clock. Moira was going to be furious with him. He hadn't meant to get so entangled. He just wanted the name of Mr. X—and he had that. Jerry Foster. All the rest of his visit had been trimming.

He drove a block, stopped in front of a phone booth, called Moira. To his surprise, she didn't sound upset when he explained that he would be late. "I'm on my way now," he said. "Things got kind of hectic here."

"All right," she said. "I've given the boys their supper. I'll wait for you."

He moved fast on the highway, got home before eight. It was a peaceful evening. They went to bed early. If Moira noticed any scratches on her husband's back, she said nothing about them. When they went to bed, there was no attempt at sex. Moira seemed to have forgotten that married people usually had sex at bedtime. Tonight, Lamson hardly minded. After the session with Marcia, he was scarcely in the mood for more.

In the morning, he started to think over the situation as it stood, from top to bottom.

He had the name of the rapist, now. But there was a question of what to do with it. He couldn't simply go to the police and tell them the man's name, without explaining how he had suddenly come into possession of it. And if he did explain, it would lead to all kinds of other embarrassing and unanswerable questions. "Why," they would ask him, "if this man was someone your wife knew, didn't she tell us this the night of the burglary? Is she trying to conceal something? Is this an attempt to defraud the insurance company? And why come forward with the information now? What's this all about, Mr. Lamson?"

They would ask a lot of questions, too many questions. They might uncover the fact of the rape, and then they would want to know why he and Moira had suppressed that part of the story in the first place.

Round and round.

The conclusion was obvious. He couldn't go to the police. At least, not just yet.

He wondered if he could somehow track this Foster character down on his own.

A phone call to the alumni bureau of Foster's college turned up nothing much. They told him that the last recorded address for Jerry Foster dated from some time in 1952—a Greenwich village address. Just on the off chance that he might still be living there, Lamson checked, only to discover that the building had been demolished in a slum clearance project four years ago. No lead there. Someone like Foster probably drifted around from place to place, anyway.

The next step was to check on his boxing background. Judging from the looks of his ears and lips, and from the haymaker he had tossed, Foster had put in some time as a professional boxer. Lamson phoned the state athletic commission first, but they had no record of any boxer by that name in the last ten years. Undaunted, Lamson tried the office of a boxing magazine that was supposed to keep the most complete records in the world on the sport.

They had it. It took some digging, but they had it.

"Here we are. Yes. Jerry Foster. Boxed under the name of Tom Heenan in 1955 and 1956. Eighteen bouts in local clubs. Heavyweight division. Ten wins, seven loses and a draw. Scored six knockouts and a TKO, knocked out seven times. Is there anything else you'd like to know about him?"

"His present address, if you've got it."

"Sorry. We don't. If you'd like to send a letter to him care of this magazine, we could try to track him down and forward it. But no guarantees."

"Never mind," Lamson said. "Thanks all the same."

Now he had an important confirmation. The man named Foster *had* been a boxer—which proved as conclusively as possible that the ring-scarred bruiser who had raped Moira was one and the same with the clean-cut youngster in the attic photos.

And he had an alias for Foster. If he couldn't be found as Foster, maybe he would turn up as Heenan. Unless, fearing that Moira would report his identity, he had skipped out of town and was somewhere in Canada or California right now.

A couple of days went by. Lamson was stymied, for the time being. He kept in touch with the psychoanalyst, but Michalis had no suggestions for finding Foster either. He reported on Moira's progress, said she was coming along slowly—very slowly—but still reticent about the rape. "I'm trying to get her to tell me the story of the rape," he said. "But she's afraid to lie to me and she doesn't want to tell me an edited version of the incident. So she keeps changing the subject."

"Does she seem cooperative otherwise?" Lamson asked.

"More or less," Michalis said. "At least she shows up on time. That's a step in the right direction. And she talks freely enough—except about what's really bothering her."

"You have any new theories about her?"

"I'm still sticking to the old one," the analyst said. "She's definitely got a fixation on this Foster character. She's afraid he's going to come back and make love to her again. And I think I know what's really bothering her, too. She's afraid that if he *does* show up, she'll run away with him."

"You aren't serious!"

"I think that's down there deep. Moira doesn't *want* to run away, mind you. She finds you completely adequate as a husband and as a lover. But there's this kind of suicidal urge in her somewhere that is pushing her to do something crazy—like running away with Foster if he ever comes back. She's resisting the idea like mad, but it exists."

"I've got to find this guy," Lamson said. "Put him behind bars. That's the only way we'll ever have any peace again."

But finding Foster somewhere in the fifty million people of the New York metropolitan area wasn't so easy. It had been deceptively simple to guess at his existence and to discover his identity. Finding the man himself was a far more challenging job.

He needed a lucky break.

He got it.

It came in the form of a newspaper article—a tabloid squib about a bunch of gamblers taken into custody by the police. Someone had left the paper on Lamson's desk, and he was riffling through it idly to kill a dull moment at the office, and for no particular reason his eye came to rest on the story headed, RAID, CRAP GAME, ARREST 8.

There had been a police raid in Greenwich Village, the story said. Eight gamblers had been arrested. Their names were given. Lamson casually scanned the list. And then one name rose up and blazed out of the page.

"Also arrested was Jerry Foster, 33. A former heavyweight boxer under the name of Tom Heenan, Foster lives at—"

It was an address in the Village—the West Village, the sleepy near-slum far from all the bohemian gaiety. Lamson's heart pounded wildly as he read and re-read the article. The unlikely had happened—Foster had been handed to him on a silver platter!

He phoned the police, asked about the raided gamblers, learned that they were all out on bail pending trial. The case wouldn't come before the court for a month or more, he learned.

He took the afternoon off and drove down to Greenwich Village to do some preliminary scouting. Leaving his car a couple of blocks from Foster's address, he wandered over on foot. It was a seedy, run-down street, lined with old brownstones on one side and old brick buildings on the other. There was a saloon on the corner opposite Foster's place, and a grocery store with fly-specked windows, and two other stores of vague sorts.

Lamson entered the saloon. He took a seat near the window and looked out across the street at Foster's house. It was a three-story brick building, probably a hundred years old, with cracked windows and a general tumbledown look to it. He wondered which apartment was Foster's.

The bartender came over. "Help you?"

"Beer," Lamson said. "A tall one."

The saloon was practically empty. Two weather-beaten old men sat in one corner, staring with methodical fixity at the television set. Since it was mid-afternoon, there was nothing much on but soap opera and kiddie programs, but that didn't seem to bother them. They were watching one of the soap operas as intently as though it were *Hamlet.*

There were only two other people in the bar—the bartender, a beefy, red-faced man of about sixty, and a slim, moderately attractive girl in her middle twenties, who Lamson imagined was the bartender's daughter.

A moment later he began to get the idea that she wasn't. Because she crossed the room with a slow undulating motion of her hips, thrusting her breasts saucily at him, and came over.

"Hi," she said. "Mind if I sit here and talk a while?"

"Not at all."

She slipped in opposite him. He frowned. Since when did B-girls go on duty in the middle of the afternoon? Or was she just an amateur who paid the bartender to let her hang around and kill time here? She was possibly pretty, but nothing sensational. There were a few old acne pits on her cheeks, and her long brown hair had a greasy, unkempt look to it. But her breasts filled out her sweater well, and he got the idea that in the dark she was very, very nice indeed to be with.

"Can I buy you a drink?" he asked.

"I wouldn't mind," she said. "Beer'll do."

He signalled to the bartender, who drew a beer and brought it. Lamson paid him for both beers.

The girl was eyeing him with blunt curiosity, as though puzzled by his expensive suit and unbohemian appearance. She said after a moment, "You a tourist or something?"

"Just passing through and looking for a beer."

"Uh-huh. What's your name?"

"Dave."

"I'm Laurie."

"Hello, Laurie." He sipped his beer. It was thin and acrid and nasty. But he forced it down all the same. He kept one eye looking out the window just in case Foster should come sauntering by.

The girl said, "People don't come over to this part of the Village much."

"I was out strolling."

"Nice day for a stroll."

"Yeah. Very nice."

Her eyes narrowed. "You look like somebody I know, you know that?"

He hid his tension as best he could. "Yeah?" he said. "Who?"

"Guy name of Foster. Jerry Foster. Looks a hell of a lot like you."

"Never heard of him."

"Used to be a boxer, name of Heenan then. Heavyweight. Five-six years ago, maybe more."

"I don't follow boxing much. You say this guy looks like me?"

"Well, sort of. He's all banged up from boxing you understand. But the build's the same, and the face. Except where he's banged up."

"Maybe he's a long-lost cousin of mine that I don't know anything about. What did you say his name was?"

"Foster. Jerry Foster."

"He live near here?"

"Right across the street," the girl said. "That brick building over there."

"Maybe I ought to meet him," Lamson said. "They say everybody has a double walking around somewhere on the earth. It's supposed to be good luck to meet him."

"You'll have trouble meeting Jerry. He got arrested yesterday. Crap game was raided."

"Oh? He in for long?"

"I don't know. Hey, Mike," she called. The barkeep looked around. "Mike, what happened to Jerry?"

"Out on bail. They let him go this morning."

"You seen him back?"

"Not yet. But Larry was in and said they all got let out," the bartender said.

The girl smiled at Lamson. "You see? Maybe you can get to meet him after all. You want we should go across and see if he's home?"

"Not yet," Lamson said quickly. "I—ah—I'm still thirsty. A couple more beers before I go calling on anybody. Join me?"

"Sure," she said. "Maybe he'll come in here first, anyway."

"Is he in here much?"

"A lot of the time. Especially when he's got dough."

"And he's got dough now, huh?"

"Well, I guess he put it up on bail. But he had dough last week." Her eyes narrowed. "Hey, you aren't a cop, are you?"

"Not a chance."

"Why you asking all these questions?"

"Just to pass the time," he said. "Honest." The new beers arrived. He put change on the tray. "I'm a guy with some time to kill."

In a low voice she said, "I know a better way to kill it than sitting around in a bar, pal."

"Like how?" he grinned.

"You and me, maybe, go up to my place a little while? I'll show you some games you maybe haven't played lately."

He looked at her steadily. She wasn't bad-looking. But he hadn't come here for sex. On the other hand, he could use a go-between, a contact with Foster. This girl knew him. She could be useful. But he had to win her trust first, prove that he wasn't a cop. What better way was there than—

"Will it cost me?" he asked.

"What do you think?"

"How much?"

She hesitated a moment. "For you, ten bucks. Okay?"

He didn't know whether she was raising her price because he looked well-heeled, or lowering it because he looked friendly. One way or the other, it didn't make much difference, he thought.

"Okay," he said.

12

She lived in the same building as Foster. On their way up the dark, musty-smelling stairs, he asked her, "Which is his apartment?"

"That one." She pointed to a door just off the second-floor landing. "Want me to knock and see if he's home?"

"Not now," Lamson said.

They continued on up to the top floor. She pushed open a frayed-looking door, and they went in.

The apartment was not exactly luxurious. There were two small rooms, some ancient furniture, dirty cracked windows. Lamson reflected that just a couple of days ago he had been in Marcia Holfield's Beekman Place eyrie, and now this little flea-trap. The contrast was startling.

Laurie pointed to the bedroom. "Let's go in. You mind paying me now?"

"Here," he said, handing her a ten-spot.

They went into the bedroom. "I'll get undressed," she said. "You look like the type who likes a girl to take her clothes off. Some of these guys, they just want me to haul up my dress, spread my legs. But college types like you want to see what I've got."

He didn't argue with her. She peeled off her sweater and unhooked her cheap pink bra. Her breasts were big, but they had a discouraged kind of droop to them. In another few years they'd be hanging down, he thought sadly. She shimmied out of her skirt and panties. She looked pretty good naked, but he could see that she was starting to thicken up around the buttocks as well as at the breasts. She was a little older than he had guessed, too—maybe as much as thirty. There were faint marks of childbirth on her belly.

"Okay," she said.

She lay down on the narrow bed. There was something pitiful and joyless about the whole procedure. But he was committed to go through with it. He walked over to the bed and dropped his trousers, and got down next to her. She saw that he wasn't quite ready to make love, and with a few deft motions of her fingers she remedied that.

Then she drew him to her.

After the tempestuous furies of Marcia, this was practically like sleepwalking. He felt her warm yielding body beneath his, and she opened for him, guiding him into the harbor of her womanhood, and her knees went up in the air and she twined her legs around him. He tried to kiss her, but she turned her head to one side, getting her cheek, as though she didn't object to selling her crotch but regarded a kiss as something too serious to throw in.

His hands stole upward to cup her large breasts. She moved her hips faster, faster. He could feel the immediacy of his culmination. There was no finesse about what they were doing, no excitement, no real pleasure. Her heart, he saw, wasn't in it. There was none of the joyful abandon of Ruthie, none of the passionate fervor of Marcia. There was just a mechanical bucking of the hips, a steady rhythmic thrusting of the pelvis. He enjoyed the sensations, but there was no real thrill to it. And she didn't seem to be feeling a thing. Like most whores he had known, she seemed to be frigid. For all he knew she was a lesbian, like many of her profession were reputed to be.

She stepped up the pace of her movements, arching her back to press him deep, and he let go of her breasts and grabbed the edges of the mattress and held tight while the moment of ecstasy hit him. She was breathing hard and gasping in an imitation of excitement, but he knew it had to be phony, just done for effect, because it had begun too suddenly to be real. There had been no rising arc of excitement in her, just an abrupt shift from coolness to seeming passion.

Then it was over. A few gasping moments of pleasure for him, and it had ended.

He felt tired and a little cheated. The glowing promises of pleasures untold had turned out to be just an average lay, done without enthusiasm or joy. He slipped away from her and stood up.

"There's a clean towel on the dresser that you can use," she told him.

He tidied up, adjusted his pants. She got off the bed and walked naked into the bathroom. When she came out a few moments later he was standing by the window, looking off at nothing in particular.

"I'm sorry," she said.

He turned. "For what?"

"For being such a lousy lay. You probably think you've been swindled."

"No—not at all."

"Don't think you need to be kind. I know when I'm good and when I'm not. I wasn't good now. It isn't your fault. I'm just tired, I guess. I couldn't work up any interest. You might as well have your ten bucks back."

"Don't be silly, Laurie."

"You didn't get your money's worth," she insisted.

He shook the bill away. He took a long look at her as she stood there, pale and discouraged and naked, with her heavy breasts starting to sag, and he said, "What the hell are you doing in this business, Laurie?"

"I've got to make a buck."

"There are other ways."

"Not me. I've got no talents except sex. And I'm not even very talented there. But at least I can make some money this way. A good week, two or three hundred bucks sometimes, when there are lots of sailors around."

He glanced at the furniture. "This doesn't look like the apartment of a girl who makes two or three hundred bucks a week."

"I send the money to New Jersey," she said. "My kid lives there. Girl. Six years old. Lives with my brother. She thinks she's my brother's daughter. Wouldn't know me if she fell over me. But I send money. I sent four thousand bucks last year. They keep it in a bank account, to send her to college." Her lips curled bitterly. "You know how many guys I got to lay to earn four thousand bucks? You wonder why sometimes I get tired with sex?"

"Where do you find all the customers?"

"I scout around. Jerry helps some. Maybe I shouldn't have said that. He doesn't like people to know he pimps. Him being a college man and all that."

"You pay him for that?"

"Some. Not much. I pay him off in sex, mostly. It's a bitching life, mister."

Lamson moistened his lips uneasily. The girl had turned away from him now, and was picking up her clothes. He looked at the heavy globes of her buttocks and wondered how many men's weight those buttocks had borne. Thousands, maybe. And Foster her pimp. The bleakness of this whole house, and of the lives of the people in it, left him feeling gray and forlorn. He watched her dress.

He said, "Would you do me a favor for twenty-five bucks, Laurie?"

"I'll do it for you for free. Just because I'm a whore don't mean—"

"No. I'll pay you. It's important to me, and I want to pay you for it."

"What is it?"

"I'm going to write a note to your friend Jerry. I want you to give it to him for me. And I want you to promise me you won't tell him who gave you the note, or how you came by it."

She frowned. "Suppose he asks?"

"Just say that you found the note in the lobby downstairs, and you brought it up and gave it to him. I don't want him to know anything about how you got it. Just give it to him."

"What's the pitch?"

"I can't tell you. But this is important to me, Laurie. Very important. And if you don't do things the way I want you to, you'll be doing me a great harm."

"I wish I understood."

"I'll explain it to you next week, okay? I'll come around and tell you all about it. For now you've just got to trust me. Okay?"

"You aren't a cop, are you?"

"I told you I'm not a cop."

"I don't want to get into any kind of trouble on account of this."

"I give you my solemn oath, Laurie. For whatever the solemn oath of a stranger is worth. You won't suffer for this. Just hand him the note. And don't let him know who you got it from. Will you do that?"

"Okay," she said. "I'll do it. I think I can trust you."

He looked at her steadily, wondering if he could trust *her*. A couple of words from her to Foster and the whole thing would blow up in his face, he knew. All she had to say was, "A guy who looks a lot like you came snooping around today. He asked a lot of questions. He left this note for you." Then Foster would open the note and read it and see the trap that was laid for him, and he'd take the next banana boat to Venezuela.

I'll have to risk it, he thought.

He took two tens and a five from his wallet and handed them to her.

"Here's your payment," he said. "Buy your little girl a new dress or something. Do you have some notepaper I could use?"

She brought him a sheet of pink paper and an envelope.

"Would Foster recognize this as yours?" he asked.

"No. I doubt it."

"Let's hope so," he said.

He took out his pen and sat down to compose the letter. Mystified, Laurie watched him from the other side of the room, making no attempt to read what he was writing.

After some thought, Lamson began:

"Jerry darling—

"Yes, I know it was you who broke into our house that night. I didn't recognize you at first; but then I did, and it awakened old memories. Many old memories, most of them painful.

"I've been wondering all these years what became of you. I guess, to look at you, that you haven't had much luck out of life. I'm sorry about that, I really am. I hope our breakup way back then didn't have a bad effect on you.

"But I am sorry to see that you have to rob and rape. There must be a bet-

ter way. Why don't you come to see me again? I am terribly bored with my suburban life. My husband treats me well but he is very dull, and I often regret having tied myself up for life with him after having known someone as interesting as you. I often feel like scrapping it all and just running away.

"Why don't you come visit me next Tuesday morning around ten o'clock? My husband will be at work and the children at school. In case you need more money I can help you out. My husband is a wealthy, successful businessman as you may know. And we have much other jewelry that you did not notice in your hurry to escape that night. Also when you come we can talk about the old days and maybe make up for some of the things that went wrong then. There won't be any need for you to rape me this time. I will be more than willing. Your embrace is the most exciting thing I ever imagined, and I have been on fire ever since, a fire my husband cannot put out. Naturally when you were here I had to pretend not to recognize you, to be afraid, etc. But when we are alone all will be different.

"Yours affectionately,
"Moira."

He read the letter over a couple of times, hoping that it sounded at least reasonably convincing. He had written it in as close an imitation of Moira's handwriting as he could manage—wide, open, feminine but not fussy—and unless Foster had an extraordinary memory for handwritings he'd probably accept it as Moira's. Lamson wondered if perhaps he had put too much bait in the trap. Too much might make Foster suspicious.

Finally he folded the letter, slipped it into the envelope, sealed it. He handed it to the frowning girl. "Here. Give this to him tonight."

"I wish I understood this."

"I wish I could tell you, but I can't. I'm just asking you to trust me. I'll explain it all next week, Laurie. Just don't fail me."

"Okay," she said. She took the envelope from him and put it in a dresser drawer. "I'll give it to him, if he's around."

He wondered if she would. He realized that he was actually playing a dirty trick on her, by making her the instrument that would betray her own pimp. For all he knew, she loved Foster—and she would be helping to send him to prison this way.

Lamson shrugged the thought off. He couldn't stop to be gentle. He was dealing with a man who had brutally raped his wife, and there was no such thing as a foul way to capture him.

"I'll be going now," he said. He moved a few steps toward the door.

"Wait," she cried.

She ran up to him. For a moment they stared at each other silently, uncertainly. Then she said, "If—if you'd like to kiss me—you can—"

He smiled. He reached out for her, and she came into his arms, and he could feel the heavy swells of her breasts flattening out against him, and he put his mouth to hers. There was something urgent, violent about her kiss; it had as much smouldering passion in it as her lovemaking before had lacked. For a long moment they clung to one another, her loins grinding against his, her tongue probing deep into him. He held her tight, feeling her body quiver and throb with desire. She pulled her lips away.

"Stay with me," she whispered. "Stay with me once more. For free this time. Please?"

There were tears shining in her eyes. Lamson looked doubtfully at her, but when he saw the tears, the fear, he knew that all she wanted was a simple thing from him, the chance to give herself once of her own free will, in passion, not in fee simple.

They moved back into the bedroom.

Her hands went to the hem of her sweater and in a moment she was naked before him for the second time in an hour. This time his desires rose automatically, without the need of any help from her.

She reached out for him, gathered him in.

This time it was entirely different. It was as though he were sleeping with some other girl altogether. Her hips churned, her whole body rocked, as she took him into her. She made a little soft sound of pleasure, and he gripped her buttocks tight, and suddenly lifted her from the bed, holding her aloft, and she looked at him in surprise and pleasure, and tightened her legs about him. Then they dropped to the bed again. Her body twisted wildly under his.

"Oh," she whimpered. "Oh, yes!"

He doubled his efforts.

"Ooooh!"

There was a churning, a burning, a twisting, a lunging. He felt her quietly going wild inside. All her liberated passions were exploding at once. There was a tremendous throbbing within her, a great upwelling outpouring of emotion, and he remained calm in the eye of the hurricane, bringing her along, making this one for her to remember.

"Ahh," she moaned. "That's good... so good... so very good...."

She went into a final frantic dance of ecstasy beneath him. He felt the easing of his own lusts, but the sensation was almost lost within the savage fury of her fulfillment. Sounds of almost bestial ferocity ripped from her throat, and she heaved her body violently, and then abruptly subsided as though someone had switched the current off.

For a long while they lay still.

Then she said, "You don't know how much good you've done me. I was beginning to think I'd never make it again, you know how it is. I was so stale on sex. It was just a lot of sweaty nuisance that I did for money. But now doing it for free—"

"What about with Foster?"

"That's not free. That's so he'll get customers for me. Not the same thing at all. Christ, I feel great now. I feel like floating through the air."

She kissed him. She looked transfigured with joy—flushed, radiant, exciting. Even her breasts had come alive, losing that discouraged droop, standing up firm and full and high.

He stayed with her a few minutes more, so that she would not be left alone while still in the afterglow of her happiness. Then he withdrew from her and for the second time adjusted his clothing.

"I've really got to go now," he said.

"Sure. But thanks for coming around. Thanks for everything."

"Thank *you*."

"And I'll take care of that note for you, just like you want me to. Don't worry about it."

She kissed him lightly on the lips, and he left, hurrying down the dark stairs and scurrying out of the building. He wanted to avoid any accidental meeting with Jerry Foster now.

He felt relaxed, free and easy. Now he was sure that she trusted him and would turn over the note. She couldn't have made love that way, the second time, if she didn't trust him. And she would feel some sort of debt to him for having given her so much pleasure.

It was a good feeling to give a woman pleasure—especially one who was worried about turning frigid. It was a hopeful sign. Perhaps someday soon he would be able to re-awaken Moira the same way.

Perhaps.

He made up his mind to send the girl Laurie a fat check if she cooperated. Five hundred bucks, maybe. For that kid in New Jersey who didn't know who her real mother was.

He walked back to his car, got in, drove away.

Tuesday would tell the tale, he thought. If Foster fell into the trap, fine. With luck, Moira would be on the road to recovery after that.

If not—

He preferred not to think about that.

He hit the accelerator hard and headed for home. In his mind's eyes there was the image of a naked girl with a sad face and full breasts and the marks of childbirth on her belly. He wished her well. She had been a great help to him. He hoped things started breaking for her a little better in the future. But it was a futile wish, he knew. Some people are fated to get nothing but misery out of life, and Laurie was one of them.

At least he had given her a moment of brightness, he thought. Not to mention thirty-five bucks.

He got the speedometer needle up as high as he dared, and moved along toward home and Moira.

13

Lamson spent most of Monday afternoon making plans for the big event, conferring in detail with the police, reporting his progress to Michalis. He was nagged by the hollow feeling that it would not work out, that either Foster would see through the shallow trap that had been set for him or that Laurie would betray the truth. But he had to go ahead with things as though everything was going to be perfect, and hope that he was right.

He kept the truth from Moira. So far as she was concerned, Monday night was just like any other night at home in the past few weeks. He did not even attempt to make love to her that night, as though he had written off in advance all chance of success in that department.

Lamson slept badly that night. Very badly. He lay awake, twisting and turning restlessly for hours, his active mind trying to probe into tomorrow, working out a hundred different possible ways in which tomorrow's events might unroll. At long last sleep came, but it was thin, insubstantial, frequently punctured by moments of dreary wakefulness.

And then it was morning.

He tried to pretend that it was just an ordinary morning. He rose at the usual time, managed to shave without cutting himself, had a light breakfast of juice, rolls, coffee. He left the house about quarter after eight, waving goodbye to Moira in a sleepy, mechanical way and watching her close the door behind her.

He got into his car. He drove eight blocks, turned left, drove five blocks more, and pulled up in front of the police station. The precinct house had a placid, pastoral look at eight thirty in the morning. Lamson had never seen the inside of it before. He looked around with curiosity while he waited to see the detectives he had spoken to yesterday.

They came out in a few minutes, two of them—O'Connell, tall and lean and slab-jawed and grim, with a blue stubble sprouting on his face only an hour after he had shaved, and Baccholi, short and round and pleasant-looking, like someone who packed bundles in a supermarket.

"You're sure you want to go through with it this way?" they asked him.

"Positive."

"You understand that we can't be held responsible if anything—"

"I understand."

O'Connell shook his head mournfully. "I still don't like it. Citizens shouldn't get themselves mixed up in the job of the police."

Lamson drew a deep breath. "I keep telling you it has to be done this way. For personal reasons. If I had known you'd make this much trouble about it, I wouldn't have told you in the first place until it was all over."

"Okay," O'Connell said.

"We'll do it your way," said Baccholi.

Lamson left the precinct house at ten minutes to nine and drove slowly back the way he came, parking his car three blocks from his house and going the rest of the way on foot. The note had asked Foster to come around ten in the morning. More likely he'd be late than early, but there was no sense taking chances.

He crept up cautiously to his own house, making sure Moira was not standing by any of the windows. He came up the back way and saw a light on upstairs. Moira was cleaning in the bedrooms. Good.

He had left one of the living room windows open that morning. Now, he circled the house, moving step by step through the shrubbery. There was something grimly ironic, he thought, about having to break into his own house like this. He approached the window he had left open, wondering coldly whether or not Moira might have noticed it and closed it.

No. He pushed it open, swung himself up onto the sill, lowered himself easily inside, and noiselessly shut and locked the window.

Vacuum-cleaner sounds came from upstairs. So far so good. In five quick steps Lamson crossed the living room and darted into the guest's coat-closet in the downstairs foyer. He nudged the door seven-eighths shut and sat down on the bench, hiding himself behind his own dangling overcoat.

It was twelve minutes after nine.

He put his head in his hands and tried to relax.

He had never known that an hour could last so long. He was sweating ferociously in the stuffy closet, and was fearful of a giveway sneeze, and now and then the nightmare thought occurred to him that Moira might come downstairs and pop her head in the closet and—after she was through having hysterics—want to know what the hell he was doing hiding in there. He wouldn't have any quick explanations handy to offer, either.

There was one strange thing about the hour. He began to daydream, without even wanting to. Weird, erotic daydreams of startlingly vivid intensity stole unbidden into his mind.

He imagined himself with Marcia, in her plush apartment. Her lush body lay fully revealed to him, the white, heavy breasts filling his hands, and as he stretched out on the bed she settled above him, straddling him, impaling herself on him, moving with passionate fervor, while from somewhere Ruthie descended over his face, locking her thighs around his neck, and even as he gasped for breath he drank the sweet liquor of her womanhood. Then there was Lois, stretched out on her belly in the sunlight somewhere, lean and tanned and sylph-like, and he approached her, looked down at her small taut buttocks, and lowered himself suddenly on top of her, warming her, then sinking deep into her, feeling the satin cushions of her buttocks against his groin, listening to her first groans of surprise and pain, which gave way in a moment to soft purrs of pleasure.

And then there was a strange tangle, Lois and Ruthie and Marcia and Laurie, all four women naked and he in the middle, a jumbled intertwined tangle of arms and legs and breasts and thighs, and while he buried his maleness in Ruthie's warm, inviting body he gripped Marcia's breasts in one of his hands, and sank his face deep into Lois's belly, bringing gasping murmurs of delight from her with each exploration of his tongue, and with the other hand he stirred and probed the depths of Laurie's body. And then with boundless virility he withdrew from Ruthie and in the same moment plunged into the ready, panting Laurie while Lois and Marcia embraced each other in a loins-rubbing fury of lesbian desires.

The daydream went on until he was in a sweat of desire himself. He shook his head, trying to clear his brain from this fog of lustful visions. He wondered if the tensions he had been under were causing him to lose his mind. He had never experienced anything like this before—this welter of perverse and grotesque images running wildly through his consciousness.

It went on and on. New positions of sex that he had never dreamed were possible and that probably weren't. Combinations of women and men that approached the preposterous. New sensations, new gratifications—

And then he heard the doorbell ring.

He snapped out of his fog in an instant. Looking at his watch, he saw that it was just a few minutes past ten. Foster—if it were Foster—was right on time!

He heard footsteps. Moira, running past the closet on her way to the front door.

"Who is it?" she called.

From his hiding place, Lamson strained his hearing to the utmost to pick up the reply. But all he heard was a muffled sound from without.

"*Who?*" Moira repeated.

This time Lamson heard it clearly. "Jerry. It's me, Moira. Jerry!"

"Oh, no!"

"Let me in, Moira."

"Go away! Please go away!"

"No—don't say that. Christ, will you let me in? It isn't safe for me to stand around out here. Suppose a cop comes along?"

"I don't want to see you."

"You said you did."

"No I didn't. Go away, Jerry. Please."

"Let me in!"

"I can't. I'm—afraid."

"Jesus, girl, don't pull that now! Open the door and let me in. I'm not going to hurt you. I swear it. Are you home alone?"

"Yes."

"Okay. Come on, open that door."

Crouching against the closet door to listen, Lamson bit his lip in tense anguish. He heard the sound of Moira lifting the lid of the door-viewer to peer outside. Then he picked up the sound of the door-chain being unlatched.

She was opening the door now.

Someone was coming in.

Lamson's flesh crawled with unbearable tension. He wanted to leap out of hiding, to throw himself on this man who was his double, this man who had done his marriage such great harm, and choke the life out of him.

He forced himself to stay out of sight.

This had to be done just right, he thought.

"Moira!" he heard Foster say. It was the hoarse voice of the rapist, all right.

"Jerry—why did you come back?"

"I had to see you."

"You shouldn't have come here."

"Maybe. But I had to. Christ, it's been so long, so goddamn long."

"Eleven years," Moira said. "I never thought I'd want to see you again."

"Do you want to see me now?"

"I'm not sure. That night—when you raped me—you did a terrible thing, Jerry—"

"I couldn't help it. There you were naked. I recognized you, and I remembered what you had said to me the night we broke up, about how you wouldn't ever sleep with me before you got married. And I had to have you. With your husband tied up like that. And so—so I took you—"

"It was the wrong thing to do, Jerry."

"I couldn't help myself. But at least now we'll do it the right way," Foster said. "After eleven years we'll finally go to bed with each other and enjoy it. It'll be a kind of wedding night for us."

"What are you talking about, Jerry?"

"You know. Come on upstairs with me."

Lamson's heart pounded. This was the crucial moment. If she gave in to him—

But she said, "No. Keep away from me, Jerry. Keep away or I'll scream. I was crazy to let you in. Get out of here!"

"No, Moira."

"Don't touch me."

"You promised me, Moira."

"I *what?*"

"In your note. The note that you sent me. You said you'd sleep with me."

"You're out of your mind. You must be. I never sent you any notes."

"Huh? But—"

"Get out of here, Jerry! And don't ever come back! You musn't ever come here again."

"You sent me a note," Foster said in a dogged, confused voice. "I don't know how you found out how to get it to me, but you did. You said to come to you on Tuesday, that you'd sleep with me, give me money—"

"Someone's been kidding you. I wouldn't send you a note like that. I didn't ever want to see you again, and I meant it."

"Huh? Well, if you didn't, who did?"

"How should I know?" Moira asked.

Lamson tensed. This was the moment for action, he thought. Foster would realize that he had been suckered into a trap, and he would turn and flee. And Lamson would sound a police whistle that would be a signal to the squad cars waiting just out of sight around the corner. They would grab him before he got half a block.

But then he realized that Foster's punch-drunk mind wasn't reacting logically. The man hadn't stopped to figure out the dangers that he was in now. He was only interested in Moira

"Keep away from me, Jerry," Moira warned him. "Don't take another step or I'll scream."

"I've got to have you, Moira. Right now. That's what I came for. That's what I'm going to get."

"No—"

There was no scream. Instead, there was the sound of a scuffle just outside the closet. Lamson heard Moira uttering muffled cries of fear.

He burst from hiding.

Foster had pinned Moira up against the hallway wall. He had clawed at the front of her housecoat, and it hung down in shreds, baring her breasts. With animal-like frenzy, he was trying to force her to the floor and rape her again. His big, gnarled hands tightened on the bare pink nipples of her bosom.

"Foster!" Lamson yelled in a harsh, fierce voice that he hardly recognized as his own.

For one peculiar moment neither of the struggling duo seemed to react, so intent was Foster on raping Moira, so intent was she on defending herself. Then they both froze and Foster looked up over his shoulder, an expression of bewilderment and terror on his face.

"Dave!" Moira cried in astonishment.

Foster rumbled at him in an incoherent roar. Lamson started to go for the police whistle the detectives had given him, then changed his mind.

This was something he had to handle without any outside help.

Foster started to whirl.

"Lock the door!" Lamson called to Moira. "Chain it! Keep him in!"

She didn't move. But Foster turned away from the door though it were locked and charged headlong at Lamson instead.

Lamson took the charge in stride. He was as big as Foster and as heavy, if not as professionally trained to handle himself. The other man cracked into him hard, but Lamson stood his ground. He lashed out with his fists, driving one punch into Foster's solar plexus, the other into his chest just above the heart. He realized that he still had the advantage of surprise. Foster was panicky and confused. His attempt at a counterpunch went wild past Lamson's nose.

Lamson hit him again, three quick solid punches in the breadbasket. Foster turned pale, started to stagger, then collected himself and came back with a solid smash to the shoulder that stunned Lamson a moment, spinning him half around and numbing his arm.

For a long instant Lamson stood still, expecting to be demolished by the next few punches. But Foster did not hit again. He turned and scrambled past Lamson into the living room.

Lamson followed.

Foster was heading for the window, the window through which he had broken into the house the first time, on the night of the rape. But now the window was closed. Lamson had locked it when he entered the house.

As Foster reached the window, Lamson grabbed up the fireplace poker. He lunged toward the fleeing Foster, waving the heavy poker menacingly.

There was the sound of breaking glass.

Four panes gave way at once as Foster hurtled headlong through the window and out into the garden. Lamson stared dazedly at the shattered window. Then, hefting the poker, he leaped to the windowsill and followed Foster through, feeling a jagged fragment of window glass slash through his trousers and slice his thigh as he jumped. He heard Moira's faint hysterical screaming somewhere far behind him.

He landed in the soft dirt of the rhododendron bed and looked around, trying to get his bearings. He caught sight of Foster weaving raggedly across the front lawn toward the street. Poker in hand, Lamson followed.

And then he saw the trail of blood.

It was a bright purple-red trail running from the rhododendrons across the lawn behind Lamson. Dashing forward, Lamson caught up with the rapist. Poker high, he whirled Foster around, ready to smash him into unconsciousness.

He stared aghast at Foster.

The other man's face was a ruin. He had been cut in fifty places. Thin slivers of glass were sticking from his cheeks. One ear was so much hamburger meat. A deep slash in the corner if his mouth grotesquely seemed to extend his lips an inch and a half up his left cheek.

But those were just minor scratches.

A dagger of glass a foot long was sticking out of Foster's throat. He clawed at it ineffectually with his hands, making horrifying gurgling sounds. Lamson watched him from a distance of a couple of yards, making no attempt to go closer as Foster struggled with the shard of windowpane protruding from his throat.

He got it free.

Blood from a severed artery spurted high in the air like the spray from a rebellious garden hose. Foster staggered, took a couple of dizzy steps back toward the house.

He said something that might have been the word "Moira" or that might have been simply an incoherent gurgle of meaningless noise.

The dagger of glass fell at Lamson's feet. He saw the spurting blood from the rapist's throat bathe his clothes from head to foot. Then Foster toppled, landing face down on the lawn. He scrabbled desperately in the grass, uprooting great tufts of it. Terrible convulsive motions rippled his body into bizarre angles. A slowly spreading pool of red widened beneath him, staining the ground.

Lamson let the poker drop from his nerveless hands. There was no need for it now. Watching Foster's body jerk like the corpse of a decapitated chicken, Lamson reached with trembling fingers into his pocket for the police whistle. But when he put it to his lips, he was unable to produce a sound. He let the whistle tumble to the ground.

Not that it was necessary. The squad cars had arrived, and police were running up from all directions. Lamson saw O'Connell and Baccholi approach, and threw them each a wild, glassy-eyed smile.

"What the hell happened?" Baccholi asked, staring in horror at the twitching body on the lawn.

"He tried to rape my wife again. I caught him and he jumped through the window. Cut his throat on a broken piece of glass."

O'Connell turned to one of the uniformed policemen near him and said, "Get an ambulance in a hurry."

"Don't think we're going to need it." Baccholi said, kneeling near Foster. "We got a D.O.A. on our hands here, something tells me."

He straightened up. "You okay?" he asked Lamson.

"I suppose."

"You got blood all over you."

"Mostly his," Lamson said. Then he remembered the slash in his thigh. He looked down. A river of blood was cascading down his trouser leg. His blood. There was a burning sensation in his upper leg. His foot was starting to grow numb.

Suddenly it all swept in on him at once. He looked at the body face down on the lawn, looked back at his doorway, where Moira stood with an expression of pure mindless terror on her face.

Then his legs buckled.

Baccholi caught him easily. They carried him into the house. Somewhere along the way to the bedroom, he blanked out.

14

The doctor had just finished removing the stitches from Lamson's thigh. Lamson looked down at the bare, pink, puckered flesh, with the fledging scar running an inch and a half down his flank.

"It's going to itch like the devil," the doctor said. "Don't scratch. It'll be okay in a couple of days or so if you leave it alone."

"Will there be much of a scar?" Moira asked anxiously.

The doctor chuckled and pointed to Lamson's other, unshaven thigh, which was thick with dark, matted hair. He said, "There'll be a scar, all right. But I don't think you'll have to worry much about seeing it once that hair grows back. You won't even know it's there." He started to pack up his bag. He said to Lamson, "Remember, no bowling, no fencing for two or three days. The cut's healing nicely, but I wouldn't want to see it open again."

"I'll take it easy," Lamson promised.

The doctor left. Lamson got out of bed and walked to the window, moving slowly, trying not to flex his thigh. He could feel the itching already.

Moira sat on the bed looking through the newspaper. After a moment she shoved it away from her. She was calmer, now, three days after it had happened. Last night she had been able to sleep right through the night for the first time. The pain of Lamson's stitches had kept him awake most of the night, but he had been careful not to disturb Moira, since this was her first good sleep.

Moira said, "Suppose he hadn't died. What kind of jail sentence would they have given him?"

"Life, I imagine. A second rape attempt, and while he was out on bail on another charge—they'd have put him away for keeps."

She shuddered. "To spend the next thirty or forty years in jail—what a horrible thing! He's luckier where he is now. To get it over with quickly."

"Quickly but not painlessly," Lamson said.

"It must have been horrible. I couldn't even watch it. I saw the glass sticking out of his throat, and then I couldn't watch any more."

"It wasn't pretty," Lamson said. He slipped his robe on and belted it. "Let's go downstairs. It's time for lunch. I've got to call the office and see how things are going, besides."

"Are you going to go to work on Monday?"

"I'd better," he said. "Things are going to hell without me, I'll bet. That's the trouble with these goddamn one-man corporations. Take away the man at the top and everybody marks time till he gets back."

Moira laughed. "Don't think you're so important. I'm sure they've gotten along quite well without you."

They went downstairs. Lamson moved gingerly on the stairs, afraid of popping open his newly healed cut. He was annoyed by the wound. He and Moira hadn't been able to make love since the day of Foster's death, because of his inconvenient cut. And she wanted to. He knew that. She was eager for it—to start their marriage over again, now that the threat from outside was ended. But until his thigh healed, they would just have to wait.

They waited through the weekend. The itching was fierce, but Lamson manfully kept away from the rapidly forming scab. The cut had been a deep one, but it had missed the muscle, simply slicing through fat, so there would be no lasting effects once the short-term annoyance was ended.

On Monday he went to the office, driving his car for the first time. He was queasily afraid of splitting the healing wound the first time he stepped on the brake, but he felt nothing but a faint twinge.

As Moira had insisted, the place had not gone to hell in his four-day absence. It had moved along quite efficiently. There were new contracts to sign, important people to speak to.

They looked at him with new eyes at the office. They all knew the story—it had made the papers next day, all about how the brave husband had routed the would-be rapist, complete with gory news photos in the tabloids of the dead Foster weltering in his own blood on the Lamson lawn. Lamson didn't much like the idea of being a hero or a nine-days wonder, but it was better than living under the shadow of Jerry Foster's continued existence. He felt purged, now.

But there was one final purgation he had to undergo before he could call the thing done with.

Despite the press of piled-up work, he left the office at half past three that afternoon, telling Ruthie that he'd be in tomorrow but not again today. She looked at him perplexedly, sputtering something about all the letters to answer, but he only smiled.

He drove over to Greenwich Village, going so far west that the river was almost in sight, and parked in front of a drab saloon on a dreary street.

He went in.

There were three people in the bar, all of them men, two stubble-faced oldsters fascinatedly watching a soap opera on television, and the bartender. Lamson went up to the bar.

"Laurie in?" he asked.

"Nope."

"You expect her?"

A shrug. "Hasn't been in for a couple days. Friend of hers got killed in a fight and she's been in her room ever since."

"I see," Lamson said leadenly. "Thanks." He took a quarter from his pocket, laid it on the counter. "Let's have a beer."

Putting down the beer in three quick gulps, he crossed the street to the dingy brick building and went in, and up three flights of stairs, and knocked on Laurie's door. He felt tense and apprehensive, and almost was tempted to turn and leave. But he knew he had to see this through.

"Who is it?" Laurie asked, in a faint, almost inaudible voice from behind the closed door.

"Dave. Dave Lamson."

She opened the door, frowning. "Who? Oh—oh, it's you!"

The door slammed in his face.

He knocked again. "Laurie! Laurie, please, let me in. I've got to talk to you."

"Go away," came the wail from within.

"Laurie, please," he begged. "Give me five minutes. That's all I ask. Five minutes."

She asked him again to leave. But he was insistent, and after a moment she opened the door.

"Come on in if you won't go away," she muttered.

She looked terrible. She was wearing nothing but a pink nightgown through whose gauzy fabric the lines of her body were plainly visible, the heavy rounds of her breasts, the full masses of her buttocks, the dark shaded triangle at her loins. Her hair was stringy and unkempt. Her eyes were red-rimmed, dark-circled. She wore no makeup.

The small apartment had a musty smell. Ash trays overflowed everywhere. There were two empty fifths of cheap rye on the dresser. The room was a tangle of dirty linens, soiled glasses, crumpled clothes.

"Well?" she asked. "Are you proud of yourself? You made me sell him out. And now he's dead. You made me his murderer, you know that? If you hadn't given me that note to give to him, he'd be alive today."

"He tried to rape my wife, Laurie."

"What's that to me? He was good to me. That's all that mattered. And you made me sell him out. For twenty-five lousy bucks. I wish I still had your money. I'd tear it up and fling it in your face."

He eyed her sadly. Her thinly veiled nakedness aroused no desire in him now. He remembered how—on that same unmade bed—he had buried his manhood in her soft yielding body and felt her come alive with a tremendous rush. But now she was just a tired, lonely, drab girl past the first bloom of her youth, living in a room overflowing with gray cigarette ash.

He said, "Let me tell you what he did. And then ask yourself if I didn't have a right to trap him."

"I don't give a damn about it."

"Listen, please, Laurie."

"I'm not interested."

"I'll tell you anyway. He broke into my house one Saturday night. He tied me up and raped my wife while I watched. He was an old boy friend of hers, from years back. But they broke up because she wouldn't let him make her. And then he came creeping back, eleven years later—he raped her in front of me, robbed us. You know what my wife's been like since that night? Maybe you don't know what it's like to be raped in front of your husband's eyes. But she suffered. It damn near broke her. Broke me, too. And I had to catch this Jerry of yours. Had to get him out of the way so he couldn't harm us any more. I didn't want him to die. Just to go to prison. But he tried to get away. He jumped through that window."

He let his voice trail off. Laurie said hollowly, "He was the only person in the world who gave a damn about me, and now he's dead."

"He gave a damn, did he? That's why he pimped for you? And lived off you? And laid you when he felt like it? Look at me, Laurie. Was he really such a saint, or are you making things up about him that you know aren't true?"

"I—you—" she lifted tear-glistening eyes. For a moment she was silent, struggling with words. Then she said softly, "You know something, mister? You're right. He was a bastard. He treated me like dirt."

"I knew it."

"But even treating me like dirt was better than the way most people treat me. So I'm sorry he's dead. I'll miss him. I—oh, Christ, I don't know what I'm saying! I'm sorry he raped your wife. I can imagine how you feel. I—I'm not angry any more—I—"

Suddenly she turned from him and ran wildly across the room, throwing herself down on the bed. Her nightgown ran up above her waist as she landed, baring her buttocks. There was a lump in Lamson's throat as he walked over to her and sat down. He let his hands rest on her shoulders, then moved them lower for a moment to touch the soft flesh of her backside.

"Do you forgive me, Laurie?"

"I—forgive you. Yeah."

"I had to use you. I had to trap him."

"Yeah. Okay."

She turned, looked up at him. She tried to smile.

She said, "You want to stay with me? You want one on the house? It's yours. I can use some cheering up. I remember the ball we had when you were here." She reached for him, opening the nightgown to show him her breasts, her softly rounded belly, the whiteness of her thighs.

He shook his head. "No. Laurie. I can't. I've got to go home—home to my wife."

"You didn't care about her when you were balling me that other day."

"I *did* care about her," he said, thinking about Ruthie and Lois and Marcia, thinking about the breasts and buttocks and spread legs of the women he had slept with during the three weeks of hell, the three weeks of not having Moira. "But I needed someone else for awhile. I can't explain it. Maybe you can figure out why. But now I've got to go. Home to my wife."

"All right," she said. She buried her face in her pillow.

He looked down at her nakedness, and a tremor of desire passed through him, and he wanted to have her. But he forced himself to blot the thought from his mind.

He walked to the door. He opened his wallet, took out three crisp hundred-dollar bills, and slipped them under a vase on her table. After a moment he added two more bills. She did not look up.

He glanced at her, his eyes taking in the trim lines of buttocks and back and thighs.

He said, "I'm leaving something on the table, Laurie. For your little girl in New Jersey. Thanks for what you did for me. I'm sorry it had to work out this way—but it had to be. So long."

"So long," she said. "See you some day."

"I hope so," he said.

He turned and walked out.

He was home before five. It was a beautiful spring day, cascades of green unfolding in every tree. He let himself into the house and Moira came out of the living room in surprise.

"What are you doing home so early?" she asked. "Is something wrong?"

"Nothing's wrong. I just left the office a little early today."

"How's your cut?"

"Haven't thought about it at all today. I guess it's okay. Where are the boys?"

"Over at the Marshal's," Moira said. "I told them to come back here at half past five."

"Then we have the house to ourselves," he said. "For the next half hour."

"That's right."

"Let's go upstairs," he said.

She looked at him, and she frowned, and then understanding glimmered in her eyes, and she took his hand and they went up the stairs together, moving fast, almost in a little race to the top. His leg failed to twinge. He forgot all about it as they entered the bedroom.

And then she was in his arms, apron and all, her body pressed hard against his, her mouth tight to his lips, her tongue seeking his.

After a long moment they came up for air. He held her away from him, looking at her. He felt that she was his again. The night of Foster's death, they had had a long talk, going over all that had happened, and she had confessed that she had foolishly not wanted him to know about her old romance with Foster, for fear he'd be jealous of a relationship that had never been consummated. So much could have been avoided if she had spoken up, right on the spot, and told him everything, instead of forcing him to collaborate with Michalis to worm the truth out.

But all that was over with now. They were together again, and that was what counted.

Their clothes seemed to melt away like dream-garments. They were naked together, in each other's arms, and for the first time in what seemed like a hundred years they were in bed together welcoming each other's embrace joyfully and openly.

Her fingers ran down his body, touched the puckered scar on his thigh a moment, then moved higher. He sucked in his breath in a sharp indrawn hiss of pleasure as she reached the root of his body and lingered there.

Then he was cupping her breasts, toying with the stiff little nipples, tonguing them, savoring the sweet smell of her body. He clasped her to him.

"It's been so long, Dave!"

"So goddamn long."

"But now we can start all over."

He nodded.

He got his hands underneath her, catching her buttocks, heaving her haunches and thighs up. Her legs parted. In one eager thrust he drove home the sword of his passion, and she gasped, and he felt her teeth nipping his shoulder, and her body moved with urgent little rocking motions, embracing more and more of him with each shivering thrust. He closed his eyes, let himself slip down, down into a warm, bright sea of pleasure.

Then he heard her catch her breath. He felt the first tremors of fulfillment coming up from her, with the slow inexorability of the returning tide. He opened his eyes, looked into hers. She was smiling.

"I love you," she whispered.

He nodded, kissed the stiffened tip of each breast, kissed her lips, kissed the tip of her nose.

"I love you, Moira."

She clung to him. Her legs wrapped themselves about his body, and he felt her heels digging hard into the backs of his legs. Their intertwined bodies convulsed with one shared pulse of excitement, and they began to move now, faster, ever faster, and he put his lips to hers, drove his tongue deep within her mouth, and listened to the harsh irregular sounds of her breathing, and then he had to pull his mouth away, to gasp for breath as the jackhammer blows of the climax hit him, and he soared higher, toward the stratosphere, taking her with him.

She uttered a long, low, sighing sound of pleasure. Her entire body trembled and quivered. He could feel the inward convulsion of her ecstasy, and that was the sign he was waiting for, the sign that all was well again, that she had broken through the icy bonds that had held her the prisoner of fear for so long. Together, now, they rushed on to the final frenzied moments of their lovemaking.

It was finished. For now.

They lay back, side by side. The fullness of her breasts weighed down on his cupping fingers. She was smiling, the warm, content smile of a satisfied woman.

"Love me?" he asked.

"Love you."

"Always?"

"Always and a day," she whispered.

He relaxed against his wife's soft, yielding nakedness. The war of nerves was ended. Once again, he and Moira would know peace.

He thought of a twitching, hulking figure spouting blood on his lawn. Then he drove the image from his mind. That was the dead past and the past no longer held power over either of them.

There was just tomorrow, from now on.

THE END

Bibliography

Don Elliott (all published by
Greenleaf under various imprints)
Love Addict (1959)
Gang Girl (1959)
Naked Holiday (1960)
The Flesh Peddlers (1960;
  reprinted as The Flesh
  Merchants, 1973)
The Lecher (1960)
Mistress of Sin (1960; reprinted as
  Depravity Town, 1973)
Party Girl (1960)
  Sin on Wheels (1960; reprinted
  as The Instructor, 1973)
Passion Trap (1960; reprinted as
  Carnal Cage, 1973)
Sex Jungle (1960; reprinted as
  Jungle Street, 1973)
Convention Girl (1960; reprinted
  as The Man Collector, 1973)
Summertime Affair (1960)
Woman Chaser (1960)
Backstreet Sinner (1961; reprinted
  as The Bed and the Beautiful,
  1973)
Expense Account Sinners (1961;
  reprinted as Keep the Clients
  Happy, 1973)
Lust Goddess (1961; reprinted as
  The Temptress, 1973)
Lust Queen (1961; reprinted as
  The Decadent, 1974)
The Lust Seekers (1961; reprinted
  as Till Love Do Us Part, 1974)
Sin Club (1961; reprinted as The
  Lady from Soho, 1974)
Sin Cruise (1961; reprinted as
  Fifteen Nights of Love, 1973)

The Sinful Ones (1961; reprinted
  as Every Night in Rome, 1974)
Wild Divorcee (1961; reprinted as
  Nowhere Girl, 1973)
Streets of Sin (1961; reprinted as
  The Untamed, 1974)
Hotrod Sinners (1962)
Kept Man (1962)
Lust Captive (1962; reprinted as
  The Game Susan Played, 1974)
Lust Cat (1962)
Lust Cult (1962; reprinted as None
  But the Wicked, 1974)
Lust for Two (1962)
Lust Lord (1962)
Lust Market (1962)
No Lust Tonight (1962)
The Orgy Boys (1962)
Passion Thieves (1962)
Roadhouse Girl (1962; reprinted
  as No Pleasure So Painful, 1974)
Sex Fury (1962)
Sexteen (1962)
Shame House (1962)
Sin Bait (1962)
Sin Kin (1962)
Sin Quest (1962)
Sin Sick (1962)
Three Sinners (1962; reprinted as
  A Change for the Bedder, 1974)
Wild Flesh (1962)
Lust Crew (1963)
Passion Patsy (1963)
Sex Bait (1963)
Sex Bum (1963)
Sin Crazed (1963)
Sin Made (1963)
Sin Servant (1963)

Beatnik Wanton (1964)
Black Market Shame (1964)
Flesh Bride (1964)
Flesh Lesson (1964)
Flesh Melody (1964)
Flesh Pawns (1964)
Flesh Prize (1964)
The Flesh Seekers (1964)
Flesh Taker (1964)
Gutter Road (1964)
Lust Burns (1964)
Lust League (1964)
Lust Set (1964)
Lust Spree (1964)
Orgy Isle (1964)
Orgy Maid (1964)
Passion Pair (1964)
Passion Partners (1964)
Passion Trio (1964)
Pickup (1964)
Shameless (1964)
Sin Bin (1964)
Sin Circuit (1964)
Sin Partners (1964)
Sin Service (1964)
Sin Sold (1964)
Switch Trap (1964)
Wanton Web (1964)
Alternate Wife (1965)
Carnal Carnival (1965)
Escape to Sindom (1965)
Flesh Bigamist (1965)
Flesh Boarder (1965)
Flesh Cry (1965)
Flesh Man (1965)
Good Girl, Bad Girl (1965)
Lust Doomed (1965)
Lust Finale (1965)
Naked She Died (1965)
The Nite Lusters (1965)
Nudie Packet (1965)
Of Shame Reborn (1965)

Only the Depraved (1965)
Orgy Slaves (1965)
Passion Killer (1965)
Passion Peeper (1965)
Passion Pusher (1965; cover listed
   as by Don Holliday)
The Shame Protector (1965)
Shame Scheme (1965)
Sin for Solace (1965)
Sin Kill (1965)
Sin Spin (1965)
The Sin Switch (1965)
Sin Warped (1965)
The Sins of Seena (1965)
Teaser (1965)
Would-Be Sinner (1965)
The Young Wantons (1965)
All on Sunday (1966)
Big Blast (1966)
Campus Traders (1966)
Cousin Lover (1966)
Diary of Desire (1966)
Every Bed Her Own (1966)
The Gay Girls (1966)
Initiates (1966)
Lust Demon (1966)
One Night Stand (1966)
Pain Lusters (1966)
The Passion Barons (1966)
Take My Wife (1966)
The Virtuous Ones (1966)
All the Best Beds (1967)
Carnal Counselor (1967; ghost-
   written, author unknown)
Diary of a Dyke (1967)
Flesh Fever (1967)
Flesh Tryst (1967)
Orgy on Wheels (1967)
Registered Nympho (1967)
Rogue of the Riviera (1967)
Those Who Lust (1967)
The Wanton West (1967)

As by Loren Beauchamp

Love Nest (Midwood, 1958)
Another Night, Another Love (Midwood, 1959)
Connie (Midwood, 1959)
Unwilling Sinner (Midwood, 1959)
Meg (Midwood, 1960; reprinted as All the Best Beds as by Don Elliott, 1967)
Nurse Carolyn (Midwood, 1960; reprinted as Registered Nympho as by Don Elliott, 1967)
And When She Was Bad (Midwood, 1961)
Sin on Wheels (Midwood, 1961; reprinted as Orgy on Wheels as by Don Elliott, 1967)
The Fires Within (Midwood, 1961)
Campus Sex Club (Midwood, 1962)
Sin a la Carte (Midwood, 1962)
Strange Delights (Midwood, 1962)
Wayward Widow (Midwood, 1962; reprinted as Free Sample, 1968)
The Wife Traders (Boudoir, 1963)

As by David Challon

Campus Love Club (Bedside, 1959; reprinted as Campus Sex Club as by Loren Beauchamp, 1962)
French Sin Port (Bedside, 1959; reprinted as Rouge of the Riviera as by Don Elliott, 1967)
Suburban Sin Club (Bedside, 1959; abridged & reprinted as The Wife Traders as by Loren Beauchamp, 1963)

Thirst for Love (Bedside, 1959; reprinted as Wayward Widow as by Loren Beauchamp, 1962)
Man Mad (Chariot, 1960)
Suburban Affair (Bedside, 1960)
Campus Hellcat and Other Stories (Bedside, 1960)

As by John Dexter

Stripper! (Nightstand, 1960; reprinted as One Bed Too Many by Jeremy Dunn)
Sex Thieves (Nightstand, 1961; reprinted as Wife in Name Only by Jeremy Dunn, 1974)
Sin Festival (Nightstand, 1961; reprinted as The Goddess Makers by Jeremy Dunn, 1974)
The Bra Peddlers (Nightstand, 1961; reprinted as The Venus Affair by Jeremy Dunn, 1974)
The Lust Plotters (Nightstand, 1962)
Passion Bum (Nightstand, 1962)

As by Dan Eliot

Dial O-R-G-Y (Ember, 1963)
Flesh Flames (Ember, 1963)
Lust Lover (Pillar, 1963)
Nympho (Ember, 1963)
Sin Doll (Ember, 1963)
Sin Hellion (Ember, 1963)
Sin Mates (Pillar, 1963)

As by Marlene Longman

Sin Girls (Nightstand, 1960; reprinted as The Tormented, 1973)

As by Ray McKenzie

The Wild Party (Chariot, 1960)

As by Gordon Mitchell
Immoral Wife (Midwood, 1959;
  reprinted as Henry's Wife, 1961)

As by Mark Ryan
Company Girl (Bedside, 1959)
Streets of Sin (Bedside, 1959;
  reprinted as The Passion Barons
  as by Don Elliott, 1966)
Twisted Love, (Bedside, 1959;
  reprinted as Strange Delights as
  by Loren Beauchamp, 1962)
Savage Love (Bedside, 1960)
Illicit Affair and Other Stories
  (Bedside, 1961)

As by Stan Vincent
The Hot Beat (Magnet, 1960)